Detective Müller
Imperial Austrian Police

Detective Müller
Imperial Austrian Police

VOLUME 1

The Man With the Black Cord
•
The Pocket Diary Found in the Snow
•
The Case of the Pool of Blood
in the Pastor's Study
•
The Case of the Registered Letter

Augusta Groner

LEONAUR

Detective Müller: Imperial Austrian Police—Volume 1
The Man With the Black Cord, The Pocket Diary Found in the Snow
The Case of the Pool of Blood in the Pastor's Study,
The Case of the Registered Letter
by Augusta Groner

Leonaur is an imprint of Oakpast Ltd

Material original to this edition, this editorial selection and
presentation of text in this form copyright © 2010 Oakpast Ltd

ISBN: 978-0-85706-284-0 (hardcover)
ISBN: 978-0-85706-283-3 (softcover)

http://www.leonaur.com

Publisher's Notes

The views expressed in this book are not necessarily
those of the publisher.

Contents

About Joe Müller

Joseph Müller, Secret Service detective of the Imperial Austrian police, is one of the great experts in his profession. In personality he differs greatly from other famous detectives. He has neither the impressive authority of Sherlock Holmes, nor the keen brilliancy of Monsieur Lecoq. Müller is a small, slight, plain-looking man, of indefinite age, and of much humbleness of mien. A naturally retiring, modest disposition, and two external causes are the reasons for Müller's humbleness of manner, which is his chief characteristic. One cause is the fact that in early youth a miscarriage of justice gave him several years in prison, an experience which cast a stigma on his name and which made it impossible for him, for many years after, to obtain honest employment. But the world is richer, and safer, by Müller's early misfortune. For it was this experience which threw him back on his own peculiar talents for a livelihood, and drove him into the police force. Had he been able to enter any other profession, his genius might have been stunted to a mere pastime, instead of being, as now, utilised for the public good.

Then, the red tape and bureaucratic etiquette which attaches to every governmental department, puts the secret service men of the Imperial police on a par with the lower ranks of the subordinates. Müller's official rank is scarcely much higher than that of a policeman, although kings and councillors consult him and the police department realises to the full what a treasure it has in him. But official red tape, and his early misfortune... prevent the giving of any higher official standing to even such a genius. Born and bred to such conditions, Müller understands them, and his natural modesty of disposition asks for no outward honours, asks for nothing but an income sufficient for his simple needs, and for aid and opportunity to occupy himself in the way he most enjoys.

Joseph Müller's character is a strange mixture. The kindest-hearted man in the world, he is a human bloodhound when once the lure of the trail has caught him. He scarcely eats or sleeps when the chase is on, he does not seem to know human weakness nor fatigue, in spite of his frail body. Once put on a case his mind delves and delves until it finds a clue, then something awakes within him, a spirit akin to that which holds the bloodhound nose to trail, and he will accomplish the apparently impossible, he will track down his victim when the entire machinery of a great police department seems helpless to discover anything. The high chiefs and commissioners grant a condescending permission when Müller asks, "May I do this? ... or may I handle this case this way?" both parties knowing all the while that it is a farce, and that the department waits helpless until this humble little man saves its honour by solving some problem before which its intricate machinery has stood dazed and puzzled.

This call of the trail is something that is stronger than anything else in Müller's mentality, and now and then it brings him into conflict with the department,... or with his own better nature. Sometimes his unerring instinct discovers secrets in high places, secrets which the police department is bidden to hush up and leave untouched. Müller is then taken off the case, and left idle for a while if he persists in his opinion as to the true facts. And at other times, Müller's own warm heart gets him into trouble. He will track down his victim, driven by the power in his soul which is stronger than all volition; but when he has this victim in the net, he will sometimes discover him to be a much finer, better man than the other individual, whose wrong at this particular criminal's hand set in motion the machinery of justice. Several times that has happened to Müller, and each time his heart got the better of his professional instincts, of his practical common-sense, too, perhaps,... at least as far as his own advancement was concerned, and he warned the victim, defeating his own work. This peculiarity of Müller's character caused his undoing at last, his official undoing that is, and compelled his retirement from the force. But his advice is often sought unofficially by the department, and to those who know, Müller's hand can be seen in the unravelling of many a famous case.

The following stories are but a few of the many interesting cases that have come within the experience of this great detective. But they give a fair portrayal of Müller's peculiar method of working, his looking on himself as merely an humble member of the department, and the comedy of his acting under "official orders" when the department is in reality following out his directions.

The Man With the
Black Cord

CHAPTER 1

Leopold Erlach Disappears

The little hamlet of Inzersdorf, near Vienna, enjoyed the melancholy distinction of being one of the very few spots in the vicinity of the Austrian capital which could not lay claim to natural beauty. The dusty straggling little village existed mainly for the sake of the great brick-works which were its chief industry. There were few people in Inzersdorf living there from choice. Almost everybody had something to do with the brick-works or with the official administration of the village.

But here and there on the dreary expanse of open fields and moors lay the oasis of a private garden or small park, surrounding its dwelling house, and in its turn hidden from the passersby on the high-roads by tall brick walls.

Among these homes of greater ease, the Erlach mansion was one of the oldest and best known. The house itself, imposing in structure in spite of its one and a half stories only in height, was of the solid build of a former century, and had its every door and window guarded by heavy iron bars. The slow growth of many years had enwrapped the severity of its exterior in a mass of rich-toned green, half a dozen different clinging plants striving for a place there. This rather unusual completeness of nature's encroachment gave the building the popular name of the "Green House."

Mr. Leopold Erlach, the owner of this attractive property, was neither popular nor gregarious. Few visitors passed the heavy gates in the high brick wall that enclosed the pleasant well-kept garden with its wealth of flower-beds under spreading trees.

On a bright September morning, warm even for the season although following a night of storm the Green House dozed in its customary quiet. The gardener moved silently about the grounds at his task of gathering up the leaves and twigs torn down by the night wind. Within the kitchen, Mrs. Teresa Tonner, Mr. Erlach's cook and housekeeper, stood at the table preparing her master's breakfast tray. Her movements were slow and heavy, and the expression of her worn and haggard face, which yet gave evidences of refinement beyond her station, was more than usually distraught and uneasy. She caught herself two or three times in little forgetfulnesses of the daily routine, even in such a simple matter as preparing the breakfast, and it took a visible effort for her to pull herself together.

She was well aware of the fact that any carelessness coming to Mr. Erlach's notice might cost her her place. For this elderly bachelor was a very particular and exacting employer and there were many changes in his household force. The few people who had occasion to observe it were rather surprised that a woman of so sensitive a nature as Mrs. Tonner should have endured his eccentricities for nearly two years.

When the tray was finally ready and carried into the dining-room, Mrs. Tonner was relieved to find that Mr. Erlach was not already seated there, as was his usual custom. It gave her time to cast a last glance around and to see whether everything was in order. Then she returned to her own room, which lay between the kitchen and the dining-room and through which she had to pass when going to and fro between these rooms. She left the door into the dining-room open that she might hear Mr. Erlach when he came out from his own bed-chamber.

Mrs. Tonner sank down into a chair, and her eyes, full of a dreary despair, glanced abstractedly about the neat little apartment. Suddenly she started, a quick flush mounted to her faded cheeks and she sprang from her seat. She had caught sight of a bright-coloured piece of silk, a man's neck muffler, which lay thrown over the arm of the sofa. She snatched it up and threw it into a cupboard drawer, looking about uneasily.

Then she relaxed into troubled thought again, until suddenly the realization that Mr. Erlach had not yet entered the dining-room penetrated her consciousness. She glanced at the clock and saw that the tray had been standing on the table for fifteen minutes. She rose, took the hot milk and the coffee back to the kitchen and put them on the stove. Then she went to her own room again, but a feeling of growing unease would not let her rest. Such a change in her employer's methodical habits was unprecedented.

Mrs. Tonner walked slowly into the dining-room and stood there waiting and listening for some noise from her master's apartment. In the utter stillness of the heavy-walled house her own breath seemed to stop, as she stood there with her hands pressed to her heart. Then, as if driven by some impulse she could not understand, the woman moved forward slowly until she found herself in the hall in front of the bedroom door. Here she knelt with her ear to the keyhole and listened again. Not a sound, no moving about, not even a breath, came from within.

The kneeling woman rose suddenly to her feet and fell back against the doorjamb, her face ghastly pale, her lips parted in a gasping sob. Her heart stood still before the sudden horror that had seized it. She controlled herself with an effort and turned the doorknob resolutely. The door was locked on the inside, another most unusual thing. But in spite of its unusualness this fact seemed to bring relief to Mrs. Tonner's mind. She moved quickly to the next door down the hall, which led into Mr. Erlach's study. This door also was locked on the inside and again Mrs. Tonner felt a surge of relief roll over her troubled mind.

But it was only momentary. The dread came back again and she beat at the door, rattling the knob and calling her employer's name loudly.

No sound came from within the closed rooms.

"Oh, what is it?—what is the matter?—what has happened?" exclaimed the woman.

She ran to the front door and found it locked as usual. The outer iron gate was also locked and the keys of both doors were presumably in their usual place on the little table near Mr. Erlach's bed.

The now thoroughly frightened woman hurried back to the dining-room and through it and her own room to the kitchen. The straight broad hall that ran the length of the house was divided two-thirds of its length by a cross-wall, so that it was necessary to go through the dining-room to reach the kitchen and the back door. As she passed through her own room, and also in the kitchen, Mrs. Tonner cast a glance of anxious scrutiny in every corner. Some hideous unspoken fear lay in her eyes, crushed down by a conscious effort of the will. She paused in the kitchen for a moment and then went to the back door of the house and called to the gardener.

Andreas Till, bending over a flower-bed, looked up with a start as he heard the woman's voice. For in spite of Mrs. Tanner's effort to control herself, the words came in a tone of agony.

"What's the matter?" cried Till, running up to the door.

"Mr. Erlach—he hasn't come out of his room—I don't hear him moving about—"

"Well what is there to be so frightened about in that?"

"Come—come to his room."

"Did you knock?"

"Of course."

"Well, come on, let's see what the matter is." In spite of his bluster the gardener felt the contagion of Mrs. Tonner's anxiety and he followed her into the house with a grave face.

They knocked and beat at the doors, shook the knobs and called loudly, but still there was no sound from within.

"Maybe—maybe he's gone out," murmured Mrs. Tonner between pale lips.

"I've been up since dawn," answered Till. "He's not gone out since then. Anyway, I opened the little gate myself an hour ago and it was bolted then. He couldn't have bolted it behind him."

"But—the great gate—"

"The iron bar was in its place—the bar that locks it from the inside, you know." As the gardener spoke he bent to look through the keyhole. He saw a pale glimmer of light within the darkened bedroom and the stale odour of heated oil came to his nostrils. The little nightlight by the bedside was still burning.

"The key is inside," said Till. "He hasn't left his room."

The two looked at each other with an anxious question in their eyes.

"I'm going to the factory to get a locksmith to open these doors. I'll ask them to telephone for the doctor too." With these words the gardener started on a quick pace back into the kitchen. Mrs. Tonner followed, panting.

"You needn't be so frightened," said Till when he saw her face in the bright light. "Old people like that can have a stroke easy or go off into a fainting fit."

"Oh—oh, let us pray that it's only a fainting fit," gasped Mrs. Tonner.

The gardener shook his head, surprised at the agony in her voice. "Why, you're all shook up—you'd better go over to my house—or I'll send my wife here to you. Hello, who's that?" he exclaimed as the bell of the back door jangled over their heads.

When the gardener had left the room, Mrs. Tonner sank into a chair, and dropping her arms on the table she buried her face in them, sobbing convulsively.

"Oh—thank God—thank God," she gasped between her sobs. "Both doors are locked from the inside—no one could get into his room—*no one*—it must be only that he is ill."

When Till and his wife came in a few moments later they were surprised at this evidence of emotion on the part of the usually silent, reserved woman.

"Don't take on so," said the gardener. "We'll have the doctor here soon. Volkner dropped in to see if there was any work for him after the storm, so I sent him over to the brick factory; he's younger and quicker than I am. He ought to find somebody there by this time, and we'll have those doors open in a jiffy."

Then the three sat down to wait in a silence broken only by Mrs. Tanner's gasping breath and an occasional murmur of sympathy from little Mrs. Till.

The brick factory was less than half a mile distant from the Erlach property and in a short time the assistant gardener, Volkner, came running up the garden path, followed by a locksmith.

The group of frightened servants watched the operation of opening the door and then peered anxiously into the dimly lighted room. The shutters were tight closed on both windows, and the light that fell through the half opened door into the study beyond made a twilight in which the dying flame of the little night-lamp flickered pale.

The bed was empty.

The housekeeper hurried to the windows and threw open the shutters. Then she looked around her. Leopold Erlach was not in his bedroom.

Till went through into the sitting-room and in a moment his voice came to the listeners in a note of surprise and fear. "He's not here either."

"Not there either?" repeated Mrs. Tonner bewildered.

The locksmith, a young man with an intelligent face, held back Mrs. Till and Volkner in the corridor. "You stay where you are," he said. "There's something wrong here and you'd better keep out of it."

"It's enough to drive one crazy," said Till, mopping his brow.

Mrs. Tonner stood as if dazed and the gardener had to fairly push her back into the corridor. "You go in and look," he said to the locksmith. "I can't find him. He's gone."

"Then I don't see what good my looking can do.

I've done all I can. I'm willing to give my testimony about the doors to the constable when he comes."

"Oh, yes, we must send for the constable—I don't know what I'm doing—it's all so queer," stammered Till. "Volkner, you run to the police station. I'd better stay here."

Mrs. Till went to the door with Volkner, while Mrs. Tonner, Till, and the locksmith remained in the room. The gardener brought a chair for Mrs. Tonner, who could hardly hold herself upright. Then they waited in silence while the shadow of suspense and fear sank down over the vine-wrapped house.

Chief Constable Kern came himself and heard the story from the three witnesses. Each had only the same simple facts to tell—all doors locked from the inside, iron bars at all the windows, and yet Mr. Erlach missing.

"It's a queer go," said Kern, "some of those bars at the windows must be looser than they look."

The constable entered the bedroom, taking the locksmith with him, while the others, at his command, remained in the corridor.

The bed had evidently been occupied but looked as if it had been vacated in haste. This was the only sign of disorder, however, and the two bunches of keys as well as Mr. Erlach's watch lay undisturbed on the little table by the bed. But there were no clothes to be seen anywhere, the suit and the underwear which he had had on the day before, even his shoes and socks, were missing, as well as the night-shirt which was usually laid ready for him on the bed.

In the sitting room, Everything showed in its usual neatness—for Mr. Erlach was a most orderly old gentleman and exceedingly tidy about all his belongings. One-half of one of the high windows stood open, but the iron bars in front of it did not yield even to the pressure of two pairs of strong arms. Nothing larger than a cat could slip between these bars, so closely were they set into the window frames.

The two men examined every cupboard, closet and corner in either room, every place in which a living man, or a dead body might be hidden. There were no signs of Leopold Erlach anywhere, nor any clue to the manner in which he might have escaped, or been carried from his room.

"I don't see how it was done," said Kern—"he must have gotten out somehow—he wasn't a wizard."

"What's the matter here?" exclaimed a cheerful voice at the door.

"Oh, Doctor," said the constable, "we don't know what the matter is—unless it's a miracle that's happened."

"What did you send for me for then?" asked Doctor Bergmann. "Is Mr. Erlach ill?"

"No, sir, he's gone—nobody knows where or how." Then the constable detailed the case to the physician, his eyes the while following the movements of the locksmith who was carefully examining the fixtures and bars of all four windows.

The room was a corner one and had two windows each on two of its sides. In the other walls, one large door led into the bedroom, while another, a smaller one placed near the corner, opened out into the main corridor. Between this door and the nearest window stood a little table. Something on the table attracted the constable's attention and he walked over to it, followed by the other two men.

On the table stood a candlestick holding a half burned light, the wick of which was pressed down deep into the wax. Spattered drops of grease lay on the table top and on the leaves of an open book beside the candlestick. It was a large old-fashioned volume, a work of ancient history. It was held open by a letter weight, and three words, on different parts of the page, were underscored in ink. They were scattered words but they formed a complete sentence, the sentence: *He was here.*

****

A few hours later, the official police commission from Liesing, the County seat to which Inzersdorf belonged, had taken possession of the Erlach mansion, and was in official charge of the case.

Mrs. Tonner, and the gardener and his wife were examined again, but could tell nothing more than what they had told to Constable Kern and the physician,

Till was the last member of the household force to have seen Mr. Erlach. As he was passing the study window about 8 o'clock the evening before, his employer called to him and they had a short conversation about some work to be undertaken in the garden the following day. Mr. Erlach, Till said, looked extremely well and seemed very contented and happy.

Then the gardener and the housekeeper were questioned as to any relatives who should be informed of the occurrence. They both asserted that Mr. Erlach had had few intimate friends and only one relative to their knowledge. This was his nephew, Lieutenant Paul Erlach, who lived in Vienna and occasionally visited his uncle.

A telegram was sent to the address given, and about three o'clock that afternoon a good-looking and extremely bewildered young officer arrived in Inzersdorf. As he was the next of kin and only representative of the missing man, the police did not dare to undertake the opening of the safe without his presence.

Lieutenant Paul Erlach had nothing to say that could throw any light on the mystery. If there was any secret passageway from the room, a passageway which might have been known to the owner of the house, or to whoever it was that had carried him off, his nephew knew nothing about it. He also had very little to say, likewise from a lack of knowledge, about the missing man's financial standing. Paul Erlach was a frank, sincere nature, and had little in common with his crabbed and eccentric relative. The fact that he was his uncle's sole heir made their association doubly difficult to both. The elder man was of a petty and suspicious nature, and had his nephew given evidence of any affection or interest Leopold Erlach would doubtless have thought it an intentional flattery. Paul felt this and never came to see his uncle unless by special invitation. He considered himself as of no more importance than any other passing stranger in the house that would one day be his. Therefore he was not in a position to give any information as to what might or might not be missing from his uncle's safe.

The police commissioner opened the heavily barred door, and he and Lieutenant Erlach drew out the various drawers of the safe and examined their contents. The key to the safe had been found in its usual place on Mr. Erlach's key-ring by his bedside. And within the safe there was no sign of disturbance or robbery. Four or five of its deep drawers were filled to the brim with fresh new gold pieces of high value. In another compartment were several leather cases containing old-fashioned but costly jewellery. A bitter smile curved the young officer's lips as he saw all this wealth which his uncle had so carefully kept from his knowledge.

Still another compartment of the safe was filled with documents, securities, bonds and shares, and family papers. Among these last, quite at the bottom of the pile, was one labelled: "My will."

"I wonder when we'll be able to open that," murmured one of the police officials.

The money, jewellery and documents were placed in a suit case, which was closed and sealed in the presence of the police commissioner and Lieutenant Erlach. Then after another thorough examination, Mr. Erlach's two rooms were also officially closed.

Mrs. Tonner informed the police commissioner that she did not care to remain another night in the house, with its gruesome mystery. The official told her that no objections would be made to her departure but that she must inform him as to her future address. He gave a sharp glance into her troubled eyes, then as she left the room, he motioned one of his men to follow her. He also told Till to delay the woman's departure until evening, by any means that would not arouse her suspicion. The gardener promised this, saying he would inform Mrs. Tonner that it was impossible for him to take her trunk to the station until a late afternoon train.

"I wonder why," thought the gardener to himself. In the two years of their living in the same establishment, neither Till nor his wife had become really acquainted with Mrs. Tonner. The woman's embittered reserve was calculated to arouse suspicion, but Till was a good soul and did not think it necessary to make any remarks to others about what might interest him.

When she had packed her trunk, Mrs. Tonner went over to the gardener's house to wait until he should be ready to accompany her to the railway station. Mrs. Till bustled about hospitably, preparing the supper. Mrs. Tonner had just drawn her chair up to the table, when suddenly her face flushed and she started up, taking a step or two in the direction of the door.

"What's the matter? Have, you forgotten anything? Or is it something you wanted to say to the police?"

Mrs. Tonner shook her head, controlled herself and sat down at the table again. She tried to eat but it was only by a severe effort that she could force herself to swallow anything.

"I wonder what's the matter with her?" thought Till again. "She's not the scary kind, this thing shouldn't upset her so. What makes her so excited?"

But he said nothing to the police, for his good heart refused to let him add to the troubles of this woman whose unhappiness and distress were so evident.

When the time for the evening train approached, they walked to the station in silence, Till pushing the trunk on a wheelbarrow. When Mrs. Tonner entered the train, a man who had been sauntering up and down the platform stepped into the compartment after her. Till recognized him as one of the plainclothes men who had come that afternoon from the police station, while Mrs. Tonner was in the gardener's house. Mrs. Tonner herself did not notice that she was being followed, so engrossed was she in the gloomy cloud of her own thoughts.

Chapter 2

The Mother's Fear

A. week had passed since the disappearance of Leopold Erlach, and still the clouds of mystery hung black over the occurrence in the Green House. The local authorities seemed powerless to unravel the riddle. A thorough and careful search had been made of the premises and the entire vicinity, but Leopold Erlach, living or dead, was not to be found. Nor was there any clue as to how he could have disappeared from the locked room. No arrests were made, as there was no charge upon which to rest suspicion. The occurrence was the talk of Inzersdorf and the neighbouring towns, and the Viennese papers gave considerable prominence to it as the mystery thickened,

One chill wet evening, a week after Mr. Erlach's disappearance, Teresa Tonner came hastily down the stairs and out of the door of a tall tenement house in a poor quarter of Vienna. She glanced furtively about her in the hallway and at the door, and seemed relieved as she saw how empty was the ill-lighted street. Mrs. Tonner's face was gray and the glance of her weary reddened eyes wavered as she drew her shawl closely around her and hurried along in the shadow of the houses. The woman looked old and haggard, crushed by some over-powering grief or anxiety. The distance she had to traverse was short but it seemed long to her troubled mind.

A block or two further on, she paused before the door of a cellar coffee room, one of the gathering places for the market people who came here in the early morning after bringing their wares from the country. At most other times of the day the dingy unattractive little room was empty.

When Mrs. Tonner descended the few steps and opened the door timidly, she found herself alone in the low-ceilinged, long, narrow space. A single gas flame threw a tiny radius of light beyond which was darkness. The room was empty and Mrs. Tonner came in so quietly that the people she could hear and see moving about in the kitchen beyond did not notice her entrance. She took a seat in the darkest corner, a place from which she could watch the door. She sat there waiting. Waiting in impatient anxiety, her eyes fastened, as if hypnotized, on the spot of brightness made by the metal doorknob. Finally, fifteen or twenty minutes later, the shining knob turned, and the door flew open. A young man entered hastily slamming the door roughly behind him. He was tall, and broad-shouldered although thin in figure, and his smooth-shaven face, even in the dim light, showed signs of dissipation. The furtive glance of his keen eyes was lacking in the candour and brightness which should belong to his years.

"Karl!"

The voice came out of the darkness and he peered through the gloom until he caught sight of the woman sitting there.

"Oh, you're there, are you?" he answered angrily. "Why didn't you creep into a rat-hole and be done with it?"

"That is what I would like to do," said Mrs. Tonner bitterly. "Come over here to me."

The young man laughed and replied in a lower tone, "Not much. I'm not over anxious to sit right under the gaslight either. And if we stay in that corner they'll light the lamp right over your head. If we go nearer the other light, it will be still dark enough, and they are not likely to burn extra gas for us two."

He moved over to another place and Mrs. Tonner followed him. She sat so that she had the light at her back and could see his face clearly. It was a face of good lines, which would have been noticeably attractive had it not showed all too plainly the marks of a life of dissipation. The woman's eyes seemed to drink in its every feature with a look of love that was like physical agony. In spite of the hollows drawn by years of sorrow and toil in her own face, there was enough resemblance between the two to mark them as mother and son.

"Did you just come too?" he asked.

"No, I've been here some time."

"And no one saw you yet?" he continued.

When she shook her head in reply he drummed on the table with a knife, and the door at the end of the room opened.

"Why, there's someone here," exclaimed an astonished voice as a young woman peered out from the kitchen.

Karl Tonner ordered two coffees and when the woman had returned to the kitchen he addressed his mother again, in a low but impatient tone. "Did you bring the money?"

Mrs. Tonner straightened up suddenly, the sadness in her face giving away to a look of determination mingled with burning anxiety.

"Why are you going away now? Why do you have to go so suddenly? What is it that is driving you away? Just now—now that—" She stopped and looked at him, her whole troubled soul in her eyes.

Karl stared at her at first in astonishment, then his eyes dropped, and he moved his hand mechanically over the tablecloth.

"Answer me," commanded Mrs. Tonner.

The boy raised his head again with a look of defiance. "I'm going away because I happen to want to—because I can't find anything to do here—because I *have* to go away, if you must know. Anything more you'd like to ask?"

"Karl!—"

"Yes, that's my name."

"Then you have sunk—as low as that?"

"Pretty low—and it's your fault."

"Mine?—my fault?"

"Whose else? Who's going to help me if not my own mother?"

"Haven't I helped you many times?"

"But your affection appears to have a limit. You said just now—" Karl Tonner broke off his speech as the woman came out from the kitchen with the tray. After serving them she started towards the next gaslight but Karl motioned to her that it would not be necessary. The woman, who was quite pretty, smiled in answer to his impudent glance and left them alone again. Karl put his spoon in his cup, and began to pick off the skin formed by the hot milk, as carefully as if he hadn't another thought in the world. His mother clenched her fists and almost hissed through her closed teeth.

"What's the matter?" said Karl lazily.

"Everything," she began, in a tone that was low but pitilessly hard. "Yes, you are right There *is* a limit to my affection. I seem now to be able to see clearer than a mother usually does. I have always been able to see your faults, and I see them all the more clearly now. Try as I may, I can find no excuse for them. You have not inherited them and I have done all I could to bring you up properly—to make an honest man of you. You have never heard me utter an untruth, you have never seen me idle or exacting—and yet you are a liar, you are lazy, seeking only your own pleasure—no matter at what price. No—don't interrupt me! If you don't want to drive me to despair, let me talk now. I sit here like a beggar woman—with my son who is no better than a tramp and a vagabond."

"Mother!" he hissed.

"It is the truth, my son," she exclaimed bitterly. *"You,* the grandson of a general, the son of a noble father, you are nothing but a tramp today—perhaps even worse, much worse."

"Mother! What do you mean?—what is it that you think me capable of then?" Karl's voice shook with anger in which there was a note of fear.

"I believe you—now—to be capable of—*anything!*'

The word was like a knife thrust. And the young man shuddered as he sat there, his face drawn, his hands clenched. Suddenly the blood that had rushed up to the roots of his hair went back again, leaving his face white. He leaned back in his chair, his hands dropped helplessly in his lap. The terror in his face was reflected in that of his mother.

"Capable of anything," she murmured with pale lips.

They sat for some few minutes in silence, a silence that was heavy with an unspoken horror. Finally the woman regained control of herself.

"I believe you capable of anything," she said again. "Of course you know why I am no longer in the Green House, why I am now living with my former cook.—" Again she paused. "Now you might speak and yet you will not," she continued, her lips trembling. "I can imagine why you sent that suspicious looking messenger to ask me to meet you here. You didn't dare to write me. You supposed that I would be under suspicion—that I would be watched—because I am your mother. Someone may have seen you the various times that you have visited me. It was five times in all and the last time—in that dreadful night—you came without letting me know beforehand—you climbed over the wall—and you went out that way too, because I could not get the key to the gate." Her voice dropped more and more towards the end of her sentence and her strength would have failed her, but for the firmness of her will.

Her son did not answer, did not attempt to defend himself.

"It is only *now* that I am forced to believe you capable of—*anything,"* she began again, her voice growing harder. "Now that you tried to make me the instrument of your greed—of your criminal desires—now that you dared to demand of me that I should ask Erlach for money—and said that if he would not give it to me—*you* would get it from him. I do not know what it was you intended to do, to obtain money from a miser like Erlach. I did not ask you, I turned you from the door. When you had left me I fainted. I do not know how long I remained in that condition—and I do not know what happened during that time. I realize only now that you are the sort of a man who would force his way into a strange house to get what he wanted." She stopped and sat still, scarcely breathing. Still there was no answer from her son.

"I must get out into the air—I am ill," she murmured. She put her hand into the pocket of her dress and laid a purse on the table. "Here are five hundred crowns—you can get away with this. I have no more—I have helped you too often. In the purse is a slip with the address of Katie's sister.

"Write to this address when you have found some place where you are safe. Karl—I am going now—haven't you a word for me?"

Karl Tonner did not raise his head. He had neither a look nor a word for the mother who had sacrificed everything for him—for the mother who, brought up in a home of luxury, had worked for years in menial positions to support him in idleness.

She crept slowly to the door and turned back with a last look at her son, a look of unutterable love and unutterable sorrow. Then she went out into the wind and the rain, glad of the unfriendly elements that gave her strength again. Outside, she lingered for a few moments hoping Karl would follow her. When he did not come, she feared to attract attention by standing there and walked on slowly until she came to the open door of a church. Here, in a dark corner, she sank to her knees and breathed out the anguish of her soul in a sobbing passionate prayer.

****

Karl Tonner sat for some time where she had left him, motionless. Finally he realized that he could not stay there forever. When he raised his head, his eyes looked dull and lifeless. He stretched out his hand to draw the purse to him, and saw through its red silk meshes that it contained a white slip of paper as well as the money. He opened the purse hastily and took out the paper with hands that trembled. He could not read the few words that were written there, for his eyes were dim with tears. Finally he managed to make out the writing.

My Son,
My love, my prayers and my forgiveness will follow you wherever you may go. I am not strong enough to do what I *should*

do perhaps and to accuse you openly. Save yourself and let me know when you are in security. But try to save your soul too, that I may not repent of my great love for you.

Your Mother

Karl Tonner sat looking down at the slip for some time. Finally he put it back in the purse, laid a piece of money on the table and went out into the street. He wandered aimlessly about in the rain and the wind, heedless of the discomfort. His face was pale and his eyes dimmed with sadness.

Suddenly he realized what he was doing and looking about, found himself outside of the city, on the edge of an empty lot— "Ridiculous!—how foolish of me," he murmured and turned brusquely. But in spite of himself his step dragged again and the same sentence that circled through his brain and had driven him out into the night, stood clear as if in letters of fire before his inward vision again. He dropped down on a stone by the wayside and buried his face in his hands, groaning aloud, "She believes me capable of *anything*—and Oh, God! it is true—it is true!"

CHAPTER 3

Joseph Müller Takes Up
the Erlach Case

Ten days after Leopold Erlach's mysterious disappearance, Dr. Franz Lehr, commissioner of the criminal police in Vienna, sat in his office in earnest conversation with his good friend Lieutenant Paul Erlach. The young lieutenant's attractive face looked worn and strained. After the usual first phrases Dr. Lehr asked the question that had been on his mind since his friend entered the room.

"You're not looking a bit well, Paul. Has your uncle's disappearance anything to do with k?"

"I don't mind *your* asking that," replied Lieutenant Erlach with a bitter smile. "But I'm afraid there are a number of people *thinking* that same question without asking it. Here, read this letter—the second of the kind that I have received. This is what brings me to see you this morning, not only a desire to chat with you."

"Well, I wondered," laughed Lehr. "But you really look as if this affair meant a lot to you. Now don't get angry—I mean it looks as if you were really greatly interested—and yet I understood that there was no particular love lost between yourself and your uncle."

"Quite right."

"Then what's the matter now?"

"These letters?"

"Anonymous letters?"

"Naturally. Letters like this are not usually signed."

Lehr opened the envelope that was handed him.

"A man's hand disguised. What is it he has to say?"

Debts—card debts—other debts—difficult father-in-law—and a missing uncle—that's a rather good combination. The uncle will be found sooner or later—dead of course and no traces left by which anything could be discovered. Then the heir can come into possession of his fortune.

Prost Mahlseit: One who knows.

"A rascal—and a cowardly one at that," said Lehr when he had read the letter. "When did you get this?"

"This morning."

"Will you leave it here with me?" the commissioner asked. "And you haven't an idea who wrote it?"

"Not an idea. Not the faintest suspicion."

"But the clause about the father-in-law is news to me. I didn't know you were engaged. My heartiest congratulations."

"Can't accept them, I'm sorry to say. I am not engaged yet I haven't even spoken to her.—Why should I? I don't want to bind her when I can't marry her—she shall be free."

"But you love each other—and there's someone who knows it—and who isn't pleased at the fact."

"Yes, I have thought of that already," said Paul.

"It was a natural conclusion. It will be more difficult—but not too much so possibly, to find out just who he is."

"How am I to do that?"

"With the help of the lady you wish to marry."

"Nellie?"

"Nellie's her name, is it? It's a pretty name. I suppose the lady herself is equally attractive."

Paul Erlach smiled up at his friend, a smile of happiness that was tinged with melancholy. "I shan't try to describe her. What's the good? What's the good even of *thinking* of her, it only saddens me."

"What's the trouble?"

"We can't either of us raise the money demanded by the law—her father—he's retired now, was my superior officer—went bond for a friend and got caught—what's the use of talking about it. But to this matter? How can I drag Nellie into this? How can she help us?"

"She can help us very much. I am taking for granted that this letter was written by a rival in love. What were the contents of the other letter you speak of?"

"Just about the same as this."

"*Umph!* the writer has very little imagination, and few ideas."

"It's postmarked Linz," said Erlach.

The commissioner laughed. "That shows how little you know

about those things. A letter can be sent from anywhere through a third party. Under the circumstances—the fact that you are not yet engaged I mean, the writer's knowledge of your interest in Miss Nellie—and hers in you, shows that he must be someone who is also interested in the young lady. She must know who her various admirers are—a woman always does. You ask her about it, it is the only way. Mercy, what's the matter! Why that deep sigh! Are you really so badly in debt?" The commissioner bent over to look his friend in the eyes, a sincere sympathy in his own glance.

The lieutenant shook his head. "That's a lie about the card debts," he said sadly. "I got out of that by going more deeply in debt to a money-lender. It's a burden of course, but at least it's not a debt of honour. But how am I going to face Nellie and her father with a letter like this casting doubt on my honour?"

"Now that's ridiculous," said Lehr calmly. "An anonymous letter hurts nobody, throws no slur on anybody but the writer. Your prospective father-in-law, if he's a man of sense, will tell you that also."

"But there's another thing," said Paul. "How do I know that the suggestions in this letter are not being circulated as gossip among my acquaintances? How do I know that malicious hints are not being thrown out—even going so far as to accuse me of having a hand in the disappearance of my uncle?"

"Yes, that's a more important side of it," said the commissioner, holding out his hand to his friend. "Call on me if there is anything I can do for you in the matter. In fact I was about to ask you to put the case into our hands—although from another reason."

"What other reason?"

"This anonymous writer appears to know so much about your uncle's disappearance that it might be he had a hand in it himself."

"Oh—!"

"It is possible I say—I'm not yet ready to assert that it is probable—"

"Then you think we had better not ignore these letters?"

"We must not ignore anything that might in any way have to do with your uncle."

"That's true. I'll be very glad if you will give me your advice in this matter. You see here what the man says—' The uncle will be found sooner or later—dead of course, and no traces left by which anything could be discovered. Then the heir can come into posses-sion of his fortune.'"

Lehr interrupted hastily. "That is very important. Don't you see that this man is in possession of the fact that you are your uncle's only heir—a knowledge which lessens still more the number of those upon whom suspicion could fall. And here, here's another thing. You see this '*Prost Mahlseit*'? We use that very little in Austria. It's a north German expression altogether. Do you remember any of your friends in the habit of using it?"

Paul Erlach pondered a moment. "No," he said then, "I don't know of anyone. But there was something else I wanted to say to you. It concerns my uncle's disappearance."

"About which you probably know less than we do here. The local authorities haven't asked for any assistance in the matter as yet, but the case interests me and I have been following the developments closely. But I don't see just how I am going to help you there."

"You can help me by recommending a capable detective. I want a man—if there are such—who would take up the case not merely as a matter of professional duty but because it interests him. I've heard that there are such people."

"Yes, there are," said the commissioner.

"But I suppose their services are very expensive!"

"Everything that's really good costs money. The men such as you describe are the rare talents that are sought for everywhere. Hold on, I know the man you want!"

"A capable man?"

"Capable? He's the best detective I ever knew or heard of."

"What's his name?"

"His name is very unimportant. He has a hundred names and a hundred different disguises, and in every one of them he has done marvellous things. But the name he was born to is Joseph Müller."

"A very ordinary sounding name."

"It suits the man's ordinarily quiet appearance.

He left the official force some time ago, but he is still busy as a private detective."

"I don't suppose I could afford it," said Erlach, sadly. "Anyway I should have to suggest to him a rather peculiar method of payment."

"What do you mean?" asked Lehr.

Erlach flushed hotly and looked embarrassed. "I —you never thought of me as avaricious, did you?" Lehr laughed. "The last person in the world—what's the trouble?"

"And yet I can't seem to think of anything else these days except uncle's money, and the fact that I am his heir and that he has never had any reason to disinherit me and that he has never hinted at any other disposal of his fortune. Now if he were *dead*—if we knew he were dead—but you see we don't know, we only know that he's disappeared—and that we haven't found him—and we may never find him—and if we don't, then thirty years have to pass before the state will hand the money out to me. Thirty years!—I'll be sixty-four then if I'm alive at all. I keep thinking of this all the time and—and I despise myself for doing so."

"There's no reason why you should," said the commissioner. "It's perfectly natural of you to feel that way—anyone would in your position. I quite understand that it is a matter of the greatest importance for you to discover proofs of your uncle's death—if he *is* dead. And I think I know now what you mean by the peculiar method of payment. You mean you want a detective who will undertake the case on his own risk, because if he discovers proofs of Leopold Erlach's death you will then be in a position to pay him well. Am I not right?"

"Perfectly," said the Lieutenant with a faint smile. "And I'd much rather you'd say it than I."

"You're ridiculously sensitive," continued the commissioner, pressing a button on his desk. When the attendant entered Lehr said: "Call up No. 1234 and ask the gentleman if he can come here to my office."

"You must telephone Müller pretty often if you know his number so well," said Paul Erlach.

The commissioner laughed and wrote out the numbers 1 2 3 4 on a slip of paper. "It's easy you see," he said, then turned to the attendant who re-entered.

"Mr. Müller will be here in twenty minutes," said the man.

Lehr nodded and turned to Erlach. "Can you wait?"

"I'll run across to the cafe to say a word to a friend who is waiting for me there, and I'll come right back."

"You'll find Müller a most original person. But you mustn't judge of other detectives from him. He's what you might call a white crow, a very remarkable man in every way. He is one of the really wise people in this world, those who understand everything and can forgive everything. He is almost a rich man now and has a very comfortable little home. I visit him occasionally and it is always a most enjoyable evening. The woman who has kept house for him for many years is a former thief who has served a term in prison. His coachman and his gardener are also released convicts. They'd go through fire for him."

"He certainly must be an unusual man."

"He is indeed, a man of remarkable capability. We'll not find another like him on the official force. We hated to have him go. But he has one serious fault."

"That's interesting, what is it?"

"His heart runs away with him."

"Why, what do you mean?"

"I mean that when he has discovered the criminal—-solved the problem that no one else could solve, then he's so sorry for this criminal that he helps him to escape."

"Why that's delicious—really it's great!"

"It does sound attractive. And after all it's practical too, for there are several times when he has saved the innocent family of a criminal from shame and disgrace. Because some of those he warned have taken the matter into their own hands and played the executioner themselves, thereby saving time and money for the state as well."

"I certainly am curious to meet such a man," said Erlach. "I'll run down now and be right back."

As he stormed up the stairs on his return Lieutenant Erlach almost ran down a man slowly and quietly going the same way. "I beg your pardon," he exclaimed hastily without turning and disappeared into the commissioner's room.

"Isn't he here yet?" he asked.

"He's too punctual to be here yet. There is still fifteen seconds' time. There he is at the door. As I told you, he is very punctual."

The door opened and on the threshold stood the middle-aged gentleman whom the lieutenant had collided with on the stairs.

"Good morning, commissioner," he said in a gentle pleasant voice.

Dr. Lehr greeted Müller cordially and introduced the two men. The detective placed his hat carefully on the table and settled himself comfortably in the chair which Lehr had placed for him. Then he said: "Well, gentlemen, I am ready. What can I do for you?"

The impressionable lieutenant felt a wave of sympathy and confidence fill his heart at the calm steady glance of the older man's quiet gray eyes. In spite of the simplicity of Müller's bearing, there was an authority about it that seemed to invite reliance on his capabilities. The young officer began at once: "First of all, Mr. Müller, I must explain to you that I am a poor man, and not in a position—"

"To pay for detective work?" Müller finished the sentence calmly. "Suppose we talk about the case, sir, and leave the unimportant details until later."

"But it isn't unimportant for me—this matter of putting myself under obligation to anyone," continued the young officer gravely. "Before I dare take advantage of your valuable services I wish to have it clearly stated that it is only possible for me to pay for them when, and *if*, my uncle's death is proven. If he is not dead it will be only possible for me to pay you slowly in instalments, after I have worked off other debts, previously contracted. I feel that I must explain this first before taking up any more of your time." Erlach leaned back in his chair with a deep breath.

Müller smiled pleasantly. "Well, now you have explained it, Lieutenant, and I understand perfectly. Now let's talk about the important matters. What opinion have you formed about your uncle's disappearance?"

"Then you've been following the case in the papers? And haven't come to any conclusion yourself yet?" The detective shrugged his shoulders. "Neither have I," continued Erlach eagerly. "Although of course it is easier for me to overlook this case than it would be for you, as you know neither the person or the neighbourhood in question."

A scarcely perceptible smile hovered on Müller's lips, a smile noticed only by the police commissioner whose eyes gleamed in response. Doctor Lehr took out his cigar case. "This looks to me as if it were going to be a lengthy conference," he said, "suppose we have a cigar."

"My uncle was a bachelor," continued Erlach.

"The newspapers mentioned this point also. But what they did not mention was the fact that no woman has ever been concerned in his life at all. I am telling you this now, that you may not waste time in the usual search for the 'woman in the case.'" Müller bowed lightly and the young officer kept on with his report. "My uncle had no vices and very few secrets in his life. He was sixty-five years old when his mysterious disappearance occurred, and his life had been so absolutely commonplace that this happening is quite incomprehensible. As to his servants—the gardener Till and his wife, and his housekeeper, Mrs. Tonner, were the only ones there at the moment. The Tills had been with him for fourteen years. Mrs. Tonner had been in uncle's service only two years but she had proved herself faithful and willing, and had given many evidences of the fact that she was not in the least greedy for money."

"May I ask how you know all this about the servants?" put in Müller. "I understand that you were not on any terms of intimacy with your uncle."

Erlach sighed deeply.

"It wasn't easy to get on with him," he answered. "He was distrustful and believed no good of anybody. If I showed friendliness or affection for him he would have taken it for toadyism, and yet he was continually accusing me of ingratitude and coldness of heart because I did not bother myself more about him. I don't see exactly how I could have done it. I've had very little time to myself since I have been here in Vienna, and I was stationed in Linz before that. My visits to Inzersdorf were necessarily few and far between. I can't say that I was anxious to make them any more frequent for they gave me no particular pleasure. But, when I *did* go there uncle's servants were his main topic of conversation. He was no great reader, cared little for art in any form and knew nothing of politics.

"All that occupied his mind were the petty affairs of his garden and his household. There was very little he could talk about, but he could talk about his servants rather interestingly. His mental horizon was narrow but within these limits he was a keen observer. He could talk well about his garden and his experiments with his flowers and he knew the composition and the quality of almost any dish he had eaten which had particularly pleased him. As these things were about all he talked about when I did visit him, I couldn't help remembering someone or other of his remarks. This is how I came to know that my uncle was perfectly satisfied with the Tills and with his housekeeper."

"With his housekeeper too?" inquired Müller.

Erlach was surprised at what appeared to be a particular interest on Müller's part in this woman. Like the gardener Till, the young officer had noticed Mrs. Tonner's look of anxiety and trouble. He had always respected her quiet reserve and faithfulness to duty, and like Till also, he did not wish, through anything he might say, to bring more worry and trouble to this woman. He cut in hastily now:

"Yes, my uncle was particularly pleased with Mrs. Tonner. She was quite alone in the world, which was a quality that uncle liked in a servant, and she was an excellent worker although she was very evidently a woman of refinement and intelligence above her station. She was the most economical housekeeper uncle had ever had and when he was sick she took the best of care of him. He told me several times that he had never been so comfortable. It does not seem to me in the least possible or necessary to connect this woman in any way with my uncle's disappearance—although I know that the local authorities have considered it a possibility."

"One must not neglect any possibility in a case like this,"

"Perhaps even the possibility that I might have something to do with it?" exclaimed the lieutenant in a tone of irritation.

"Even that possibility must be taken into consideration."

"Sir!"

"We are merely talking of all the possibilities which might be concerned in this still unexplained case," replied Müller quietly. "You have told me much of importance, Lieutenant. But even you have not been able to shed any light upon the most incomprehensible part of this mystery."

"You mean the locking of the doors on the inside?"

"Yes. And then when one considers the way the house is built—"

"What do you know about the way the house is built?" interrupted Erlach, in surprise which was increased by the detective's answer.

"I obtained a plan of the house a few days ago. For when four or five days had passed and nothing had been discovered in this case, the matter began to interest me."

The lieutenant gave an exclamation of astonishment, and the police commissioner smiled as he said to himself "that was a real Müller-trick."

The detective turned to him now. "You'll be interested to see the scene of the mystery, Dr. Lehr," he said. "I have the plan in my pocket here. Let's have a look at it."

The commissioner laid down his cigar and bent over the paper. The young officer sat still in surprise at this man who had already taken up an investigation of the case, even before he was engaged for it.

"It's exceedingly interesting," said the commissioner. "The walls are nine or ten feet high, both garden gates bolted on the inside, both the old gentleman's rooms locked on the inside and yet he has disappeared. Really, it is quite incomprehensible."

Müller pointed to a particular spot on the plan: "Right here, at that spot of the brick wall which lies opposite the gardener's house and the stable, somebody has climbed either in or out recently."

"How do you know that?" exclaimed Erlach.

"I have been examining that spot."

"You were there?"

The detective smiled at this unnecessary question: "It must have been a young man, or if not young, still very active."

"Who told you that?"

Müller smiled again, this time quite broadly. "I told it to myself," he answered calmly. "I'm no longer young but I'm still quite active and I climbed over the same place myself."

"You were in the garden too?"

"Yes, I was there for four hours. Quite time enough to get wet to my skin, for it was raining hard. But I was rather glad of the rain, because it gave me the assurance that there would be nobody else prowling around in the deserted estate. No one saw me go out either, for I did not leave until it was quite dark."

"Did you go into the house too?"

Müller shook his head.

"No, I couldn't get into the house. The keys were at the county station,—and the locks were complicated ones." The detective halted with a laugh, and the commissioner, laughing also, completed the sentence. "So you couldn't open the doors with your own instruments."

"Exactly. But I didn't even try to get into the house nor into any of the other buildings, which would have been easier. For it was really no affair of mine."

"But you did climb over the wall," said Erlach.

"Exactly. I thought I might take that much interest in the matter. And I didn't even do that until I was quite convinced that someone else had done the same thing a short time before."

"You are quite sure of that? And did you discover anything more?"

"No, nothing more, there was no one anywhere about the place."

A clock in the next room struck eleven. Müller rose. "Have you anything else to say to me, sir? I must be in my own home again by five o'clock."

"No," said Erlach, "only please leave me your address. I am supposing that you have already undertaken the case. And we really must talk about the payment—"

"Some other time," interrupted Müller. "Really and truly that is only a side issue. Or if you insist, it's easy enough settled. If it's not possible to discover your uncle's whereabouts or the fact of his death, then I'll look upon the whole thing as simply an interesting experiment. If you do come in possession of his fortune, you can pay me whatever you like. The commissioner is witness to this agreement."

"But I can't accept any such arrangement," persisted Erlach.

"Oh, yes you can," said Dr. Lehr. "You see, you don't happen to know that our friend Müller has a perfect passion for interesting cases. Also that he is very well off."

"And also that I do not accept *this* interesting case under any other conditions," said Müller firmly.

Erlach struggled with himself for a moment, then took Müller's outstretched hand.

"Very well then. But you must give me your address."

The detective shook his head. "No, you shan't have it."

"Why not?"

"Because you must not come to see me nor must you write me. No, I cannot explain it now."

"But I have your telephone number."

Müller gave a start. "Please do not make use of it. This is a very important matter, Lieutenant, please do as I ask. You may spoil an important line of investigation if you will not. You can send me news through the commissioner, or meet me here or at any other place— any place *except* my house, at any time you wish. Also you can leave *your* address with me."

When he had taken the officer's card Müller turned to Dr. Lehr. "And now I have to thank you, sir, for helping me to get the official charge of this most interesting case."

The commissioner smiled. "I suppose you'll never lose this passion for your work, will you?" he said.

"When will you begin your investigations?" asked Erlach.

"At once. I must make an examination of the Green House between now and four o'clock. For I have an important appointment in my own house at five and the journey will take about an hour." Müller's eyes shone and his cheeks were flushed His whole frame seemed more tense in the excitement of his task. His enthusiasm was contagious.

"Then I must get you the keys at once," exclaimed Erlach.

"Yes, please, my carriage is waiting."

As the little brougham drove rapidly through the streets the two men inside sat in silence. Müller was no great talker, particularly not in the beginning of a case, and the young officer had not yet recovered from his bewilderment at finding the investigations, which he had thought to start, already in full swing. It lacked still some minutes of one o'clock when the carriage stopped at the Court House in Liesing, but it was nearly half an hour before Müller could come into possession of the keys. Then he drove the lieutenant to the railway station and returned to his carriage.

"Now, Heberlein," he said to his coachman, "drive me to the place where you waited for me three days ago." Again the carriage rolled along the highroads to Inzersdorf, past meadow land and ploughed fields, then again along a stretch of dreary waste land which was known as the Black Moor. They turned off at a little dip in the road, down a grass grown lane to a spot that was hidden from the main street by a heavy high willow thicket. Müller dismounted here and set out across the open land, above which floated a heavy mist. Several paths, some of them almost roads, led across this dreary stretch of country. Müller already knew the various directions of these roads, he knew also that two stately gardens, protected by their high walls, broke the monotony of this damp expanse of moorland. There were a few little streamlets flowing across it, hardly worthy the name and yet wide enough to need a bridge. Müller crossed one of these bridges now,—it was scarcely more than a plank,—and took the path to the left, About a hundred paces further he found himself in an avenue framed on either side by tall old beech trees. The avenue was not long and ended at a high green-painted iron gate in a brick wall. This was one of the entrances to the Erlach property.

During his walk over the moor Müller had been looking around him cautiously and was satisfied that there was no one within sight. Nothing broke the silence of the dreary spot as he stood listening at the gate. He opened it and went in, remaining inside for two hours. When he came out he knew little more than he did before, but he had made one discovery.

In the drawer of a cupboard in Mrs. Tonner's room, a drawer which was filled with old newspapers, he had found a man's silk muffler. It was a piece of cheap brightly-coloured silk of the sort affected by young dandies of the lower class. He had found it thrust in hastily under the papers. This attracted his attention. For everything else in the room showed him that Mrs. Tonner was an extremely neat and tidy person.

She must have put the muffler in its place at a moment when she was in haste or greatly flustered about something. For otherwise she would not have been likely to keep the piece of silk in a drawer with newspapers. The last paper which had been put in the drawer bore the date of the 8th of September. The issue of September 9th lay in Erlach's room, and Erlach had disappeared on the night of September 9th. If nothing had happened in the house, Mrs. Tonner would probably have read the issue of the 9th on the 10th of September and would have placed it in the drawer. But on the morning of September 10th all was in confusion in the Green House. Mrs Tonner's own room was in order, but the dining-room and Erlach's apartments were in the same condition that they had been from the moment of the discovery. Müller knew that Mrs. Tonner had not been alone in the house after the discovery until the time when she had left it in the afternoon. He knew also that she had returned to her own room only to pack her trunk and that this had been done in the presence of a constable. She had therefore not had time to take the muffler from the drawer in which she had thrust it. Nor had she had time to put the muffler in the drawer, for she had taken only a few most necessary things with her.

Now this muffler must have been put into the drawer on the morning of the 10th of September before the arrival of the police commissioner, and there must have been some reason for the woman's desire to hide it.

It had very likely been left in her room during the night of the 9th to the 10th of September. For Müller had discovered another proof that at some time during that night Mrs. Tonner had had a visitor in the kitchen. A tea service for two people, with remains of a light repast, was thrust in a heap on a corner of the kitchen table. The dishes used were the heavier kitchenware, quite different from the fine porcelain kept for Mr. Erlach. It was clear that Mrs. Tonner had had a visitor at some time in the evening after the hour when she had served her master's supper, for all the dishes used for this meal were clean and in their accustomed places.

Müller was almost certain that he knew who it was that had visited Mrs. Tonner on that critical evening. And yet as he walked back over the Black Moor he felt that he knew little more about the mystery than he did before. But Müller had learned to be patient.

He reached his own home a few minutes before five o'clock. It was a comfortable little old-fashioned house set in a garden, with hedge and wall protecting it from passers on the main street of the suburb.

"Has the new cook arrived?" asked Müller of the young man who opened the door for him. "And has Mrs. Grützner left?"

"Yes, sir," said the young man, taking Müller's hat.

"Send the woman up to me at once," said the detective, mounting the half flight to his sitting room. He stood at the window looking aimlessly out into the garden. The gleam in his eyes showed satisfaction with just a hint of curiosity. There was a knock on the door and as he answered it the old detective turned slowly round.

A tall gaunt woman stood on the threshold, a woman whose face might at one time have been beautiful. But the lines of it were faded and worn now and the great dark eyes were full of sorrow. Müller came a few steps to meet her.

"Welcome to my house, Mrs. Tonner," he said cordially. "I hope that we will get along well together. Two such quiet elderly people as we are, certainly ought to be able to make life easier for each other."

He held out his hand to her, and as she took it two great tears rolled down her cheeks.

CHAPTER 4

Müller's New Housekeeper

It was on September 20th that Mrs. Tonner entered Joseph Müller's service, ten days after the disappearance of Leopold Erlach and the third day after her painful meeting with her son.

No mere chance, but Müller's own determination had brought the woman to his house. From the moment that the Erlach case began to interest him, he had been making inquiries about the servants in the establishment. There was nothing whatever to be found out about the Tills. They were ordinary commonplace faithful people. But Mrs. Tonner proved more interesting. Müller's experience had taught him that widows who are serving in a menial position, although noticeably above their station, were apt to have a past that might prove worth investigating. He looked up Mrs. Tonner's record in the Inzersdorf police station, found the date of her arrival there and also the statement that she had been born in Innsbruck in the Tyrol and was now forty-eight years old. He traced up her former terms of service without difficulty until about fifteen or sixteen years back. In his search Müller found that there were several other people in Vienna who bore the name of Tonner. Only one of these people interested him. This was a man by the name of Karl Tonner, who was twenty-seven years old and who was also recorded as having been born in Innsbruck. This young man had wandered about the country a good deal, according to the record, and had had various professions. He had been assistant to a photographer, he had been a chorus singer in one of the smaller theatres, and he had also been in vaudeville. As he followed up the official records of the life of this versatile youth, Müller became more and more convinced that Karl Tonner was Teresa Tonner's son.

Müller knew also the address to which Mrs. Tonner had gone

when she left the Green House, furthermore he knew that she had advertised for a position. He let his own faithful housekeeper answer the advertisement and engage Mrs. Tonner for her master. Mrs. Tonner saw no reason to doubt the other woman's story that she was obliged to leave her position, possibly for several months, to take care of an invalid sister.

All this Müller had done on his own responsibility. Therefore he was greatly pleased when he was officially engaged for the Erlach case. He had also learned several things of importance from the young lieutenant. When the latter asserted what his uncle must have told him, that Mrs. Tonner was quite alone in the world, Müller who knew better, wondered why the woman had lied.

When she entered his household he apparently troubled himself very little about her after the first greeting. But in reality he himself, as well as his servant Conrad, and his coachman, both of whom were in his confidence, were watching the woman's every movement. Everything that was needed for the household had been bought for the next two or three days, and it was Conrad's duty to post all letters, and to receive those left at the door. Therefore, there was no way in which Mrs. Tonner could communicate with the outside world unnoticed. But the woman herself was quite satisfied with this arrangement. The less she had to go out the better she liked it, and she knew her son to be in safety. For before she had left Mrs. Menger, the woman in whose home she had been living, the latter's sister had already received a letter from Karl to be forwarded to his mother.

Mrs. Tonner could not bear to destroy the few lines written by her only child. She put them in her trunk. She thought that now, in the house of this pleasant old man, about whom she knew nothing further than that he was living quietly on his income, she would be safe from all intrusion. On her first entrance into the house some of the strain of her nerves seemed to relax and she felt that if it were possible for her ever to be happy again she might be happy here.

The day following her arrival Müller sent for Mrs. Tonner and asked her if she would mind going out. He had to send Conrad on an errand and he discovered that Mrs. Grützner had forgotten to order some articles from the delicatessen store, of which he was particularly fond. He would give her a list and Conrad would drive her in Müller's own carriage. As he handed her the list and the money, he looked at her sharply, and asked:

"Are you ill, Mrs. Tonner? You don't look a bit well today. Perhaps

I had better not send you out, it's so raw and cold. If you don't want to go don't be afraid to say so."

"Oh, no, sir, indeed I am not ill. And I'm not afraid of the weather. But it's no wonder I look sick after what I've been through with."

"Indeed! what was it?"

"Haven't you heard of the occurrence in Inzersdorf, sir?"

"No, I don't seem to remember. What was it?"

"A rich old man disappeared mysteriously."

"Oh, yes, yes, I remember now. It was in the papers. But how does that concern you?"

"Concern me? Why, I was his housekeeper, and I was alone with him in the house at the time of his disappearance."

"Indeed! that is most interesting. You must tell me all about it. You will probably be able to give many more details than the newspapers did."

"Oh, no, sir. I know nothing whatever about it. Nothing more than anyone else—nothing more than what was in the papers."

These last words were spoken in a quiet monotonous tone. Müller wondered whether the woman had uttered them so often that they became like a speech she had learned. He also wondered at her deliberately calling up the subject herself. Was it intentional? Was it from a desire on her part to avoid an unexpected mention of it?

These questions filled Müller's brain as he pushed a chair forward for her and said, in the tone of a child pleased at the thought of hearing a gruesome story: "Oh, do sit down here and tell me all about it. I read only a short notice, just mentioning the occurrence, and it's so much more interesting to hear about it from someone who was there. You must tell me all about it."

Mrs. Tonner smiled slightly at his childlike eagerness. She told her story with the same bare fidelity to facts that she had shown all along. She did not mention her son nor did she say anything about the spectre of horrible doubt that had clouded her mind since the morning of the 10th of September. Müller threw in a question now and then, a question cleverly devised to lead her on to say more. He knew enough of the case to see that the woman, in what she did say, was telling him absolutely the truth. But with the keen unexplainable other sense that made him the man he was, he felt that Mrs. Tonner was hiding something from him. Something that might not have been actual knowledge but was at least a supposition.

When she had finished her story she rose from her chair with the words: "So you can imagine, sir, that I did not want to stay in that house another night."

"I can indeed. It is quite natural that you should have preferred to go back to your own family."

"Mrs. Menger is no relation of mine."

"Are you alone in the world then?"

The question came quite naturally from Müller's lips. The woman hesitated a second or two too long, then she said: "I have a son."

"Indeed, and he is not with you here?"

"No, I do not know where he is. I have had no news from him for some time. He is at sea—he is a sailor."

The words came very slowly, heavily. Müller could see how hard it was for this woman to lie. He felt sorry for her.

"That was very interesting. The carriage will be ready at three o'clock."

Mrs. Tonner bowed, took up the coffee cups and left the room. The detective looked after her, his face very grave."

"Why did she lie to me? Anybody could see she was lying."

Müller's face was very sad, for the woman had already aroused his full sympathy.

****

Conrad and the new housekeeper drove off at three o'clock, and Müller went down stairs into Mrs. Tonner's room. He was now entirely alone in the house and the little room looked out only on the garden. He drew the curtains and lit his tiny lantern, for it was a gloomy day and already almost dark. Then the detective started in on the examination of the belongings of his new housekeeper.

There was little to be found in the cupboard and closet of the room. A few pieces of clothing only, neat and clean but much mended, lay packed away in the drawers. Müller wondered why this woman, who had been through many years of service in well-paid positions, should be so poor, should have so little money to spend on herself. She must have had some use for her salary which deprived her of any advantage from it.

Then Müller turned to the trunk. The lock was simple and he could open it easily. It was only half full. A large package done up in white paper lay on top. Müller opened the package and found himself looking down at a handsome white satin gown cut in a style of several decades back, the costly stuff already yellowing from disuse. A white veil lay with the gown in the package, and a faded myrtle wreath.

Müller's eyes grew dim with sympathy as he carefully rewrapped the package. Below it in the trunk, were three smaller boxes. In the first he found a pair of baby shoes, worn and faded. Also a folded school composition book of the primary grade, on which stood in a stiff childish hand the name, "Karl Tonner." In the second box was the uniform cap of a general of infantry, and a death certificate written by an Innsbruck priest to the effect that General Anton Mautner, Chevalier von Rauch, had died on the 26th of July, 1879. In the third box, which Müller opened after carefully closing the other two, were photographs, bundles of letters and family papers. He sat down to the examination of this box and it took him more than an hour. When he got through he knew the history of Mrs. Tonner's life. He knew that she had been brought up in luxury, in a high social position, that she was the daughter of a General, and wife of a man of means, but that death and reverses had left her alone in the world to bring up her son by her own efforts. There were several photographs of this boy at various stages of his childhood and youth. The latest one, taken possibly a year or two ago, interested Müller most It was a costume portrait of a very good-looking young man in Greek dress, with the exaggerated hair and jewellery of a comic opera part. Written on the back of this picture were Karl Tonner's own remarks as to his success in the part. Also there was a letter written somewhat later, in which he said that he was tired of the photographic business and wanted to return to the stage, for which he felt he was well fitted. In the few letters that were there Müller could see what Mrs. Tonner must have suffered from the vagaries of her son, whose idle, pleasure-loving, and unscrupulous character lay clear before the reader. The last letter that the detective found was hastily written with pencil on a torn slip and thrust into an envelope which was not addressed. The word "Tonner" was written on it in pencil. The letter read as follows:

I was a fool to suggest what I did to you on that dreadful night. If you could only have helped me in time I would not now be in hiding. I thank you from my heart for what you have now done for me. The money will help me to get away. I thank you deeply for your letter. You can be easy about me. I will tell you more when I feel that it will be safe for me to see you again. K.

Müller read these lines carefully several times, his face very grave.

Then he copied them in his notebook, murmuring half aloud: "On that dreadful night."

He closed the trunk and left the room. His heart was full of pity at the thought of what this woman must have suffered in the varied experiences of her life. Then his mind came back to the business of the moment, to this woman's possible connection with the mysterious occurrence in Inzersdorf. Was the "dreadful night" of which Karl Tonner wrote, the night of the 9th of September? This much stood clear: Karl Tonner was in hiding, had fled from the city; his mother had not been able to help him in time but later she had given him considerable money. And mixed up in this somehow was what the careless lad himself spoke of as "the dreadful night."

Chapter 5

The Return of the Prodigal

Conrad and Mrs. Tonner returned to the house about five o'clock. The housekeeper set about preparing the afternoon coffee and as she did so her thoughts went back to her son's last letter.

"You can be easy about me," she repeated half aloud, while a sad smile flitted across her pale face.

These words gave her renewed hope and comfort, although there was nothing to tell her whether they indicated his innocence in regard to the occurrences in the Green House, or had reference merely to his present safety. She did not know where he had posted the letter to Katie's sister, for she had not seen the envelope. Karl had not told her where he was, so she could not write to him. But she was not anxious to do so. She realized that she was probably being watched by the police, and any move on her part to communicate with Karl might be dangerous to the latter. For even if her worst suspicions were not justified he must have done something wrong, that was certain.

And this wrong thing, whatever it was, had been done on the night of the 9th of September or shortly afterwards. For it was several days after that that he had sent a messenger to her, asking her to meet him in the coffee cellar and to bring money for him, as he was obliged to leave Vienna at once.

She could only hope and pray that whatever might be the reason for his flight, it would not be the one terrible thing she feared.

Shortly after she had carried up the coffee tray to

Müller's sitting room he sent down word for her to come up again, as he had something to say to her. She ascended the stairs mechanically and found Müller seated at his desk in the cosy room. He held a newspaper in his hand and there were several more heaped up on the side of the desk. The lamp was already lit, although there was still some daylight outside.

"You sent for me, sir?" said Mrs. Tonner, walking slowly over to the desk. Müller raised his head to greet her and his left hand fell carelessly on an open newspaper that lay near the edge of the desk. The paper fell to the ground.

Mrs. Tonner moved to bend down for it, her hand outstretched. Then she stopped as if suddenly turned to stone and her left hand slowly extended itself with a gesture of hiding something from her own gaze. Her eyes widened as they rested on the top of the desk and her face was ghastly pale. She gave one deep gasping breath, then fell forward unconscious in the arms of the man who sprang up to catch her.

"I didn't expect it would have that effect," murmured Müller, as he rubbed her temples with water and then started for the next room in search of something stronger. But before he reached the threshold he heard a deep sigh behind him.

He turned back to the sofa. Mrs. Tonner was conscious again but she lay there motionless, her wide-open eyes full of the same horror as before.

"Where am I? Who are you—who are you?" The words came low from between her trembling lips. Her eyes never left the edge of the desk, on which lay a bright-coloured silk muffler.

The master of the house drew a chair up to the sofa and sat down upon it.

"My name is Joseph Müller, as you know," he said. "And it's also the truth that I am living retired, on my income. We did not lie to you in that respect. But if we had told you that I am a detective, you probably would not have entered my service. Is this not so, Mrs. Tonner? No, don't move, and now drink this water," Müller continued in a more friendly tone, as he laid his hand gently on hers. "Don't try to hold back your tears. They may relieve you. Then we can talk about your son Karl."

He rose from his chair and went to the desk to lock the muffler in one of its drawers. Mrs. Tonner leaned her head on the arm of the sofa and wept bitterly. Müller's soft heart was torn with pity for the unhappy woman. He retreated to the depths of the window niche and waited there until the first spasm of her sorrow and fright had passed.

A sudden noise behind him made him turn. Mrs. Tonner had risen from the sofa so hastily that the glass on the silver tray on the little table in front of her jarred loudly.

"Well?" said Müller, turning his serious eyes full on the excited woman. She stood erect, her hands clinched, her eyes flaming, and hissed between her gasping sobs: "Oh, it's cruel—it's horribly cruel to force a mother to betray her own child in this way!"

"Then you *have* something to betray?" The words came quietly and slowly.

The woman staggered and grew even more pale. Her mind seemed frozen, she could not master her thoughts. She grew dizzy and caught at the arm of the sofa to support herself. In the haze in her brain she felt Müller's hand on her arm and heard his calm and gentle voice saying: "I am not your enemy, Mrs. Tonner. I am nobody's enemy—and if I ever can help anyone who is in trouble, I always do it I have such deep sympathy for the fear, the shame, the despair of the captured criminal, that I am often obliged to help him to relieve the pressure of my own feelings. Therefore, you need not be afraid of me. And it will be better for yourself as well as for your son if you tell me the truth."

While speaking he had pressed Mrs. Tonner gently down on to the sofa again. She looked at him, still with the hanging horror in her eyes, and breathed low: "I—I don't know the truth."

"You do not?"

"I do not know what happened in that dreadful night. I know nothing about it."

Müller's voice was cooler as he asked quickly, at a random shot: "You do not even know that your son climbed the wall to come to you that evening?"

Mrs. Tonner pressed her lips tight together and her eyes dropped. Finally she said: "Yes, I know that one thing. But that does not prove anything." She spoke with a pause between each word, as if fighting for strength.

"One thing it proves," replied Müller, "and that is that your Karl came to you secretly on the very night of the mysterious occurrence in the Green House."

"Why shouldn't a son visit his mother?" stammered the terrified woman.

"A son doesn't usually climb walls to get to his mother," replied the detective. "Although this is an unusual case and therefore—"

"Oh, my God! if I could only do something to explain it," cut in Mrs. Tonner.

"You fixed some supper for your son," continued Müller.

"Yes, I did. He was cold and hungry. I gave him an old woollen vest that Mr. Erlach had done with. That was why he forgot his muffler." Mrs. Tonner's voice was firmer now and just a little defiant.

"Those are unimportant details," said Müller with a smile. "The main point is, why did he come to you in such secrecy that night? The cold supper and the old vest you gave him would hardly be the reason for his climbing the wall. He wanted something more, Mrs. Tonner. You surely must know that sooner or later we will find out why your son came to you that evening—it will be much better for you to tell me now, yourself."

"But suppose I will not tell you," murmured the unhappy woman.

Müller bent forward and lowered his voice. "Then you know what my duty demands, if you will not speak?"

"What—what is your duty?" she asked shivering.

"It is my duty to tell the authorities that your son was in the Erlach house that night and that you know of it."

"Well then? What will happen then?"

"You will be arrested at once."

"Why?"

"You ask?"

Mrs. Tonner covered her face with her hands and sat for a few moments in silence. Finally she spoke: "If I tell you all that I know, the only thing I know, must you then go to the authorities?"

"No. For then I could take the responsibility about being silent for a while yet. I will then know by your own confession that your son was in the Green House that night and no one else need know it for a while. And as yet I am the only person who knows it."

"You? You alone know it?" murmured Mrs. Tonner, slipping to her knees and holding out her hands, clasped in pleading: "And you will not say anything?—oh, I know you will not—and you won't force me to speak?—your heart is so good. You are too kind, too noble to force a despairing mother to give up her only child this way!"

"Then you will not speak?"

"No, no—I can't—I can't."

"Very well then—I must do without your assistance."

"Assistance? Did you really think—did you really believe—"

"I believed that you would talk to me freely—I believe that you yourself really do not know what happened that night, and therefore I cannot think that you, his mother, would believe the *worst* of your son."

"But I do not!"

"You must, or else you would talk freely with me. You would do everything you can to clear him from this suspicion."

"But I have cast no suspicion on him."

"Yes, you have. You are doing it through your silence. You surely ought to know better than anyone else what might be expected of your son. You need not talk if you do not want to. I will follow up your son and I will find him. For I usually find those I seek. You can go now if you want to, you can even leave my house if you desire it, you are not a prisoner here. But I warn you that as soon as you do go, it is my duty to tell the authorities, to let them know that you believe the worst of your son, that you know where he is, and that you will probably find some means to help him to a further flight, as you have already helped him to leave Vienna."

"You—know—that too?" breathed Mrs. Tonner.

"Yes, I know it. He thanks you for it himself."

"You know that too?" she repeated dazed. "Then you have—?"

"I opened your trunk. Yes, I did it. It was my duty, for I have been officially engaged to investigate the matter of Mr. Erlach's disappearance."

"And what did you find out from my trunk?" the woman queried again, in a tone of bitter contempt.

"Only that you are a woman whose life has seen terrible reverses and great struggle and sorrow," replied Müller gravely. "Also that you have the misfortune to be the mother of a good-for-nothing son who has already caused you great trouble and anxiety. But I—and that is the difference between us—I cannot yet believe the very worst of your son."

"You can't—you can't? You don't believe then that he—" her eyes softened, the tension in her face relaxed.

"I did not find any evidence in his letters that he has passed beyond the stage of mere recklessness and selfish carelessness to a state of mind that would lead to—to murder. That does not come easily, even to a man who has sunk quite low. And I think that your son can still be saved."

Mrs. Tonner sobbed aloud. She caught Müller's hand and pressed a passionate kiss on it.

"Why, what are you doing?" he exclaimed, drawing away his hand.

"Only what any mother would do—any mother whom a stranger must teach to trust her own son. Oh, how could I—how could I have ever thought it?"

"I can understand," said the old detective, gently. "You are a serious-minded woman and your son's life thus far has been a terrible cross to you. When he came to you in 'that dreadful night,' as he calls it, he may have come in great need and you could not help him. He had to help himself somehow, in what way we do not know, but we know it must have been a wrong way. Into what it may have led him, what may have happened with or without his own will and intention, I do not know. You do not seem to know it either, but we both know that whatever it was, it drove him to flight. All that I ask of you now is to tell me what it was that he had wanted of you—according to his own letter. Your love for him is so strong that it leads you to exaggerate his faults, just as a great love leads some mothers to underestimate the lack in their children. I stand outside of the question altogether and I think that I see more clearly than you do."

"Oh, I thank you—I thank you for those words," sobbed the woman. "Yes, I can talk to you now. But only to you. For what I have to say may mean great danger for my boy. Karl came to me that evening to tell me that he had been in Vienna for several weeks and that he had been trying in vain to find work. He told me that he had scarcely eaten anything for two days and that he would have had to sleep in the parks had not a friend taken him in."

Mrs. Tonner stopped and sank back again on the sofa, shivering. Müller went into the next room and returned with a glass of wine which he offered her. She drank it and then continued her story in a hopeless monotonous voice.

"He asked me to help him, to give him money. All I had in the house was four crowns which I had saved from my last salary, the rest, as usual, I had sent on the first of the month to Mrs. Menger, my former cook. She put it in the savings bank for me. Karl was not satisfied with the little I could give him. He was greatly excited, and told me that a good position had been offered him, which he would lose if he couldn't raise a bond of one hundred crowns at once. I had never seen him quite so upset before. It seemed to drive him nearly crazy when I told him that I couldn't possibly get the money under three or four days. You see Mrs. Menger would have to give notice at the savings bank and then call for the money a day or two later."

"How could Mrs. Menger get *your* money?" asked Müller.

"She's taking care of it for me," replied Mrs. Tonner with a sad smile. "Four years ago, at the insistence of this good faithful soul, I began to lay aside something for my old age. I had given Karl all my wages before that But Katie Menger gave me no peace until I had started a savings bank account in her name, and promised to send her all I did not absolutely need just as soon as I received it So now, if Karl came to ask for money a day or two after the first of the month, I never had any to give him. That night he was so angry that he lost his head completely. He made a demand of me which I dismissed indignantly at once—it was so dreadful—."

"'What was it?"

"He demanded that I should ask Mr. Erlach for the money."

"Well, that was nervy! Did he want you to drag the poor old man out of bed and force the money from him? Rather inconsiderate of him."

"That was Karl's way," sighed Mrs. Tonner. "He never considered any one else when he wanted anything. Even as a baby he expected to have his own will always, at any cost"

"This time too?"

Mrs. Tonner grew still paler at the question. "I don't know," she answered slowly. "For when Karl insisted and finally at my refusal declared that he would go in to see Mr. Erlach himself if I was too much of a coward to do it, I lost my patience too and sprang between him and the door, locking it. It was a terrible moment for me, for I almost hated my son then. But I was not yet—*afraid* of him. I pushed him away and I pointed to the other door, the door into the garden, and told him to go, ordered him to leave the house at once. He did so without another word for me. His face was pale and his step unsteady. When he had gone I rushed to the door to call him back—that is, I wanted to rush to the door, but instead I fell in a faint. I do not know how long I lay there. I awoke to find myself on the kitchen floor and it was some little while before I could remember what had happened. I ran to the back door and called his name out into the night, but the howling of the wind drowned my voice. I dragged myself back into the hall, locked the door and went to bed. It was long before I could get to sleep, as you might well imagine. I awoke again at five o'clock. At eight o'clock I discovered that Mr. Erlach was missing, and since then I have not known a quiet moment. Now I have told you all." The unfortunate woman fell back again into the sofa corner, her hands clasped in her lap.

"Take some more of this wine," said Müller. "And now tell me something more. You say you do not know how long your faint lasted? Was there nothing to give you an idea of the time?"

"No, nothing. I did not even look at the clock before I crept into bed."

"And now tell me something of your last interview with your son."

When she had obeyed his behest and somewhat controlled the stress of her emotion, Müller ordered his carriage and they drove together to Mrs. Menger's flat. All they could find out here was that the letter received by Katie's sister from Karl Tonner had borne a Hungarian stamp. This seemed to suggest something to Mrs. Tonner and Müller asked her what it was.

"I think he must be in Pressburg," she said, apparently greatly relieved.

Müller was much surprised. He stood for a moment motionless, then a faint smile curled his lips and shone in his keen eyes. He told Mrs. Menger to come to his house whenever she had any news that would interest Mrs. Tonner. Then he led the latter down stairs again to the waiting carriage. As they drove through the streets Müller saw that his companion was much easier in her mind. The tension in her face relaxed and the ghost of a smile appeared now and then on her pale lips. It was a long drive and neither spoke until they were nearly home. Then Müller said gently:

"What were you thinking of all this time, Mrs. Tonner?"

She turned to him, her smile grown brighter, a look of hope in her eyes: "I am thinking of the crisis that this will mean for Karl, the crisis he must pass through if he is ever to be saved."

"Then you will be satisfied with whatever I undertake—even if I find it necessary to arrest him?"

"Yes, I am willing that you should do even that. It will be good for him. I no longer believe the *worst* of him and if he has committed some minor fault, it is right and just that he should atone for it. It may be what he needs to make a decent man of him."

"I think he can be saved," said Müller. "I begin to *believe* it, now that you think he is in Pressburg."

"What has that to do with it?"

"It has a good deal to do with it. Do you believe that a man who has the *worst* to fear, would go only as far as Pressburg?"

"Oh—"

"What made you think of this city at once?"

"Because his best friend lives there—a young man who is not much better than Karl," sighed the mother. "Bela von Lankowitz considers himself an artist and therefore justified in living a reckless life. Karl mentioned recently that he is now engaged at the Pressburg Theatre. His mother lives there. She too has been a widow for many years."

"I'll go there myself today."

"But if you don't find him there," said Mrs. Tonner hastily, "please don't think that it is my fault. The Hungarian stamp reminded me of Lankowitz. I know of no other friends of my son's there, nothing else that would take him into Hungary."

"I understand that," said Müller. "I'll take the responsibility."

They drove the rest of the way in silence.

****

Müller reached Pressburg that evening after midnight and went to a hotel at once. He was up again at seven and walked over to the theatre. The bills for the performance of the day before were still hanging on the boards, and an attendant came out to change them as the detective stood there. *"This* is the bill for today, sir," said the man. "That's what we gave yesterday."

Müller inquired about Mr. von Lankowitz and the attendant shrugged his shoulders with a smile. "Oh, he never gets his name on the bill," he said. "He sings along with the rest of them in the chorus."

A silver piece pressed into the man's hand brought forth the necessary information regarding the address of the young chorus singer. As it was at a considerable distance from the theatre Müller set out in spite of the early hour. The number he sought was in a new street of cheap tenements, where the outer wall of the houses, newly erected as they were, was already cracking and peeling off. The interior, the halls and the many stairways, were equally unattractive.

Finally, after many inquiries, Müller found the apartment he sought.

As he stopped in front of the door he could look through its little glass peep-hole into an untidy kitchen, about the walls of which women's garments were hanging. The whole look of the place, as far as he could see it, told him that even if the two young men were alike in character, this mother was very different from Mrs. Tonner. On the door were two visiting cards decorated with a crest of arms and a crown. On the one card stood the name *Henriette Amelie Lankowitz de Zobor et Erdofalva.* Underneath was written in ink *Lessons in Dancing and Deportment.* The other card showed the name of young Lankowitz.

The writing on the first card gave Müller the excuse that he needed to enter the apartment, and he pressed the button at once. He had to wait some time. Finally he heard steps coming to the door from another direction and it was opened on a tiny crack. "What do you want?" asked a small plump woman, whose untidy gray head showed in the opening.

"I would like to speak to Mrs. von Lankowitz."

"I am Mrs. von Lankowitz."

Müller excused his early coming by saying that he was busy the rest of the day, but that he wanted to speak about dancing lessons for his nieces. This won the confidence of the woman on the other side of the door and she asked him to come in. Inside, in an untidy room, he saw that she was at least sixty, short and fat. Her face, swollen and puffy, was already thickly powdered, although her hair had not yet been combed. She wore a torn and faded dressing gown, and the whole look of the woman was unattractive in the extreme. But Müller controlled his first feeling of repulsion and soon discovered that the poor old I creature was half crazy and quite harmless in her foolish vanity. His kindness and gentle flattery won her heart and she told him all he wanted to know. Her son had a friend staying with him, she said, a nervous young man who seemed to be uneasy all the time, who only came Sunday evening and was now going away again that very day. At the present moment the young gentlemen were out on an excursion, just where the old lady did not know. She did know, however, that the friend, who had been introduced to her as Karl Tonner, intended to leave Pressburg by the six o'clock train.

When Müller had learned all this, he took his farewell, promising that Mrs. von Lankowitz should hear from him the very next day regarding the lessons. The detective was glad to escape into the pure air outside and as he had nothing to do, he spent the rest of the day in the charming surroundings of the city.

An hour before train time he went to the station, took his ticket, ordered a compartment reserved for him and then strolled about, apparently careless but in reality watching every young man who passed him. He was quite calm and collected, there was not a sign of excitement about him.

The experienced detective had by this time made up his mind that Leopold Erlach had been murdered and his body hidden somewhere. But since the last evening he no longer considered Karl Tonner as the possible criminal. For in his mind a crime such as he now believed to have been committed, needed careful cold-blooded preparation and a nerve and self-control of which this young vagabond would hardly be in possession. It would have been quite impossible for him to have carried out the crime unless his mother were in league with him. And this, Müller now knew, was not the case. With his knowledge of human nature he realized the honesty and uprightness of the woman's character. The boy was a good-for-nothing, he was lazy, he might be a thief possibly, but he could not be a murderer, not yet at least.

Müller was honest with himself also and he indulged in a quiet laugh at his own expense just now. Before he took the train for Pressburg the evening of the day previous, he had known perfectly well that Karl Tonner had nothing to do with the murder and yet he devoted twenty-four hours to finding the young scapegrace and bringing him home to his mother. And he did it for no other reason than the fact that he felt sorry for this mother and that she at least seemed worth a little time and money spent in the rescue of her boy. It was one of the little digressions that he could not help and he excused it to himself by saying that from the next morning on he would devote all his energy to the Erlach case.

The time passed finally and about ten minutes before the departure of the train two young men came in hastily, in earnest conversation. They parted just inside the door and the taller of the two hurried to the ticket office. Müller, who followed close behind, heard him ask for a third-class ticket to Vienna. There was no third-class on the express so the young man was obliged to go second. When he had his ticket, he hurried out to the platform, Müller still following. The detective motioned to the waiting conductor and the official helped the young man into the compartment that Müller had reserved. The latter got in himself and a moment later the train started.

"Good afternoon, Mr. Tonner," began Müller, when they were well on their way.

Karl Tonner sprang from his seat, then sank back again, stammering inarticulately.

"You want to know who I am?" asked Müller with a smile. "I am a man who has come to find you and take you home—I am a detective."

"Did that fool Stillinger give me away—when there was no need for it?—or—have they arrested him again?"

Müller was surprised, but now he knew why Karl Tonner left Vienna. "Don't be angry," he said, "you ought to have known that you couldn't depend on Stillinger."

"But it was he who told me to stand watch."

"Even then you didn't have to do it."

"Did *you* ever go a whole week without anything to eat?"

"No, I'm not afraid of work."

Karl Tonner's eyes dropped. "I was coming home," he said after a pause. "I wanted to come back and be a decent man again—I was coming back to see my mother. But I won't be able to do it now! I won't be able to ask her to forgive me. I never thought that I'd be arrested now—oh, my poor mother will never outlive it!"

"But you will, all right"

"Oh, don't make fun of me. Haven't you got a heart?"

"About as much as you have, to judge by your conduct towards your mother."

"Oh, I'm a good-for-nothing.—I know it. But how do you know so much about me? Have the police been watching me?"

"They've naturally been looking up your record."

"On account of that little fool thing? Stillinger sent me word that the man wasn't really hurt. Why did they arrest him again then? And why did you follow me here?"

"See here, young friend, you'd better not be asking so many questions. Leave that to me."

"Very well then. But I don't have to answer you, do I?"

"Oh ho, we're defiant, are we? That will only make things worse for you. The best thing for you to do is to stick severely to the truth. Then you won't mix yourself up in what you say and set the Judge against you."

"The Judge? Are they going to bring me to trial?"

"Why, of course. They want to find out about the other matter, the more important one."

"What other matter? What do you mean?"

"I mean what happened in the Erlach house."

"What happened there?" Tonner's voice was full of defiance. "I told my mother she ought to ask Mr. Erlach for money, if you want to know. I don't know why that should interest the police? She didn't do it anyway. She turned me out of the house and—"

"And then she fainted and lay there unconscious ever so long—and next morning Mr. Erlach had disappeared and has not been found since."

Karl Tonner stared at the man opposite him as if dazed. It was clear that he did not understand the matter at all at first. But as the comprehension came to him, he screamed aloud and sprang up. He stood before Müller, his face white, his big blue eyes full of horror, trembling in every fibre, and stretched out his hand as if pleading for mercy. "Then *that* was what she meant," he groaned. *"That*—she even believes me capable of murder—*that* was what she meant and I didn't dare tell her that it wasn't true—because just a few days before I'd helped to knock a man senseless and rob him!"

The poor boy sank back in his seat, trembling all over. Müller looked at him pityingly, although his mind was busy with the question: "Who then, is the unknown murderer, and where must I seek him?"

It was some time before Karl Tonner could control himself. Finally he began to speak again: "You say that Mr. Erlach disappeared that night?"

"Yes, that was what I said."

"And in my excitement I imagined of course that he must have been murdered and buried somewhere."

"You may possibly be right about that."

"Possibly? Don't they know?"

"No, nothing has been discovered."

"Why did they think of me? I hadn't anything against the old man. I never even saw him."

"Robbery may have been the motive for the murder. It is known that you were with your mother that evening, after Erlach had gone to bed." Young Tonner clenched his teeth and groaned aloud as Müller continued calmly: "We know your past career, we know that you are idle and disinclined to work; we know that you are pleasure-loving and unscrupulous with but a very poor idea of duty or consideration for others. It's easy enough to be led into murder when one is determined to get money at any cost. You confessed to the other matter, might it not have been the same with Erlach? He was an old man, not strong; it would have taken little to finish him—especially when he had been awakened from sleep—"

"Who says he was asleep while I was in the house?" interrupted Karl.

"What do you know about it?"

"I know there was a light in his room. Not a night-light, a regular lamp."

"Did your mother know that?"

"No, I didn't tell her. She thought he was asleep."

"It would be difficult for you to convince people that you could climb that wall without help."

"So they know I came in over the wall, do they?" said Karl bitterly, "and they think I must have brought an accomplice with me. Do they—do they believe that my mother—"

"No, they do not," said Müller quickly. "Your mother's life would give the lie to any suspicions."

Karl's head sank on his breast. After a while he spoke slowly and grimly: "Yes, Stillinger was with me, but he stayed outside the wall. It was he who drove me to do it—to go to my mother that evening,—and he waited outside for me."

"Why did you want a hundred crowns? Of course I don't believe the story of the position and the bond. But I certainly don't think you're bad enough to frighten your mother to that extent, just because that rascal Stillinger demanded it of you."

Again Karl paused a moment before he spoke. "Well, I suppose you'll have to know that too. I had a position as errand boy with a tailor and he gave me an overcoat to take to the furrier. I pawned the coat and Stillinger and I used up the fifty crowns it brought me. Of course it was found out, on the 8th of September it was. The tailor found the pawn ticket and told me he'd give me two days to return the money. I was living with Stillinger then and of course I told him the story. He said to go to my mother about it."

"And you asked her for a *hundred* crowns? Man alive! Isn't there any limit to your heartlessness and your impudence?"

Karl Tonner's head sank again. In spite of his show of bravado he was only half-heartedly a rascal.. Meekly he endured all this scolding at the hands of a man who, although Karl did not know it, had no authority for the position he took. But it was one of Müller's characteristics that he invariably knew the right time to say a thing. It was this that gave him his power to touch the heart of even the most abandoned criminal,

His present task was an easy one. Karl Tonner had reached the crisis which comes to all at some time or other, the moment when the natural good, hidden down deep in the boy's heart, began to assert itself in a wave of disgust at the life he was leading. For in spite of his selfishness and laziness Karl was not really bad at heart. He had a hidden fund of inherited good qualities to fall back upon, and the crisis of emotion through which he was now passing had served to bring it out. He bared his soul pitilessly to this utter stranger, as a sort of penance for his misdoing.

"And when your mother couldn't give you the money what did you do then?" inquired the detective.

"Stillinger and I spent all day making plans. Finally we decided to try the holdup. Do you want me to tell you about that?"

"No, you needn't. I know about it."

Müller had read the police account of the farmer coming in to market in the early morning hours and being held up by a young man by the name of Stillinger, who was known to be an assistant at the city market. In spite of the victim's intoxication he had managed to call for help, and Stillinger was arrested. His accomplice, who had stood sentry, escaped. Müller was now the first to know that Karl Tonner had been this accomplice. The victim of the holdup had not been in-jured at all and the prisoner protested that it was a misunderstanding, therefore he was released after two or three days. Müller continued his questioning.

"How did you know that your mother had left Inzersdorf?"

"She wrote to me."

"But she told you nothing about Mr. Erlach's disappearance? And you didn't see it in the papers?"

"I don't often get a chance to read a paper—and since I've had so much trouble I haven't taken any interest in anything. I lode over the advertisements in the *Crown Gazette*—that is I've done so since the 12th of September."

"Oh, I see," smiled Müller "That was how you knew it was safe for you to come back. An arrangement with Stillinger, eh?"

"Sure. He let me know it was all right and I wanted to come back to give my mother the rest of the money—to tell her everything—"

"And to promise her you'd turn over a new leaf?" The detective's tone was slightly sarcastic.

Karl looked at him pleadingly and answered: "I really want to do it this time—will I be allowed to see my mother—? Soon—real soon? If she's got to live through this disgrace, at least I want her to know that I'm not a murderer." The young man burst into tears, and Müller let the crisis of his emotion pass without interruption. When Karl had controlled himself again, he said: "And when I serve my term, when they let me out again, will you let me hunt for Erlach's murderer? If they haven't found him till then, *I'll* find him."

A smile and a quick look of interest illumined Müller's face.

"That's not a bad idea," he said after a moment. "How much schooling have you had?"

"Normal school and a business school."

"And yet you've never been able to accomplish anything?"

"I—I—I didn't half try, I'm afraid."

"Do you know any foreign languages?"

"I can talk French. My mother speaks it just as she does German. And we always spoke it at home when I was a child. I kept it up ever since."

"That might come in handy," said Müller thoughtfully.,

After this they both relapsed into silence. Karl did not say another word even when the station was reached. He followed Müller quietly into the cab and sat cowering in the corner as they drove through the lighted streets. Supposing that he was being driven to prison he paid no attention to his surroundings. Mechanically he alighted when the carriage stopped and followed the detective into the house and into a room on the ground floor. It was a comfortable, warm and well-lit room, but the unhappy boy did not notice it. He sank into a chair and covered his face with his hands.

"And I've come down to this!" he thought—"But no one will pity me, for I've deserved it."

He sat there for some time until he heard steps outside and the door opened softly. Even then he didn't dare look up. "Now they're coming after me to take me to the cell," he thought. Finally, as no one spoke, he mustered up courage to raise his head, looking toward the now open door. With a cry he sprang up, ran forward and fell on his knees at the feet of the woman who stood there.

"Mother, oh, mother!" he sobbed.

Chapter 6

What Stillinger Saw
on the Black Moor

That same evening, while Müller and Karl Tonner were making the journey from Pressburg to Vienna, Lieutenant Paul Erlach sat by the side of Miss Nellie von Feldern, in a cosy drawing room, bright with lights and flowers. There had been no definite word spoken between the young people. But they themselves were as little in doubt as to their feelings for one another, as was the rest of the family gathering that filled the adjoining rooms of the Feldern home. Paul was poor and Nellie's father, the retired Colonel von Feldern, had suffered financial reverses owing to his generosity in shouldering a comrade's debt. Neither of the young people could raise the sum of money required by the Austrian military authorities as a first condition for consent to the marriage of an army officer. Paul was a man of sensitive mind and high ideals of honour. He would not consent to bind the girl to him thus hopelessly. But the renunciation cost him many an hour of suffering. It seemed doubly hard this evening. With her grave sweet beauty enhanced by a simple and becoming evening gown, with the pretty flush on her soft cheeks that betrayed her happiness in thus having him at her side, Nellie had never seemed so lovable, so desirable. Apart from the one absorbing topic of his affection for her, there was something else in Paul's mind that night, something he wanted to speak to Nellie about. But he could not find courage to broach the subject.

When they had sat silent for some little time, Nellie said:

"You asked me to leave the others and come in here because you had something to say to me. What is it?"

"It's difficult for me to say it," said Paul. "But the matter is important—very important for me."

"Don't be afraid to talk," said Nellie gently. "You know I'm always glad to hear anything you have to say."

Without answering, Paul handed her the anonymous letter. She read it, then turned to him in surprise. "Is this what was worrying you?" she asked. "I don't understand!—and why—why did you want me to read it?" Nellie's voice trembled, the lids drooped over her eyes and the colour came and went on her soft cheeks.

"It doesn't worry me as much as it did at first," said the young officer. "I can think about it more calmly now. And it is you, just you who *must* read this letter, Miss Nellie. This about the father-in-law, don't you understand? It means your father."

"Oh—"

"At least I am forced to think it does, because yours is the only house to which I have come with any frequency at all. But believe me, Miss Nellie, never with any word or hint, have I suggested that I might be so fortunate—"

Paul stopped, unable to find the words in his eagerness.

The girl looked at him gravely—: "You need not tell me this—I know it—I trust you."

"Thank you—thank you!—and now may I bother you with a few questions?"

"Certainly."

"Does this handwriting remind you of any you might have seen, at any time?"

He handed her the letter again. She looked at it carefully: "It's a disguised hand I suppose. It doesn't seem to remind me of anyone."

"It must have been written by someone who knows you, and who envies me the happiness which he believes—without any justification,—to be mine. It must have been written by someone who hates me because he loves you."

"A nice sort of love that."

"Every man loves as his nature is."

"This man loves like a villain then—if you do not mistake the motive of this letter."

"I cannot understand any other motive for it."

"Well, then," said Nellie, settling back in her sofa corner, "let's go at the matter in a business-like way. Now the number of those who might have written such a letter from such a motive is not as great as you seem to think. In Linz for instance, there were only two suitors, one was Captain von Schlemn and the other was a lawyer, Mr.

Stöger. They're both married happily now, you know, and therefore need not come in for consideration."

"No, indeed. I know both these men, they are not capable of an action of this sort. But can't you remember someone else? Someone who might never have come sufficiently into the horizon of your life to be called an official suitor, but someone who loved you at a distance for instance? I hate to ask all these things, Miss Nellie. But my friend Commissioner Lehr, and the detective who is in charge of the case concerning my uncle, believe that this letter might have something to do with it and they are very anxious to find some clue to the writer."

"Why, certainly. I don't exactly see how this letter could have anything to do with your uncle's disappearance but I'll gladly do all I can to help you. Now for instance at the present moment—I don't have to think very far—I don't know of anybody at all."

"Now Miss Nellie! Why I could name two, besides my own self. One of them is in the other room now. There he stands talking to your father, and probably wishing me in the farthest corner of the earth."

Nellie laughed brightly. "You mean Mr. Kress? Oh, he's such a decent sort, even if he *has* a red beard. You surely don't think that he—"

"Certainly not No more do I think it of my comrade Lorwin, who's now up in the mountains of Hungary. But there must be someone else. A man doesn't need to have said anything to a woman and yet somehow she understands that he is in love with her. Can't you remember any such secret admirer?"

"Oh, yes!—there *is* someone—he sends me flowers anonymously."

"Indeed!"

"And poems too."

"Have you any of them?" asked Paul eagerly.

"No. I'm sorry now."

"What happened to them?"

"I burned them. I didn't like the tone of them—it was too passionate—it wasn't nice. Altogether I received about six or seven of these bunches of flowers, each time with a poem. I sent the flowers to the hospital. I read only two of the poems, the others I burned without reading them."

"That's too bad. Did that happen in Linz too?"

"No, that began in Mauer, you know, the little village outside of Vienna where we lived for nearly a year."

"Two years ago then—and you never heard any more from this admirer?"

"Why, I don't know—I get flowers occasionally; perhaps they're from him. But he doesn't send any more of the poems."

"How did these things come to you?"

"When we were in the country, they came with the parcels post from Vienna. Here they're brought by a messenger."

"Now may I ask where you lived in Mauer? Did you have a house of your own there?"

"No, we rented the larger part of a house from a Mrs. von Probst. She owned the house and also a very unpleasant son. He was one of those conceited individuals, although goodness knows he had no right to be, for the only thing noticeable about him was his ugliness."

"I suppose he tried to attract your attention?"

"No more than he did that of everybody else. But I shouldn't talk so about him. The poor fellow can't help being ugly. In spite of his conceit, he was not very aggressive, and they said that he was honest and very capable too."

"And you can't remember anything else? nothing at all that would give us a clue to the writer of this letter?"

"No, nothing at all. Then you've engaged a detective about your uncle?"

"Yes, a very good one, they tell me."

"And yet nothing's been discovered, no word of your uncle—or—of his death?"

"No, nothing. This detective has only just taken up the case, you know. I am sure no one could wish to have light brought into this mystery more than I do."

Paul sighed deeply and an answering sigh came from the girl beside him. Then they both blushed and did not dare to look at each other for the moment, for the same thought had passed through the mind of each—the thought of what definite news of Leopold Erlach's death would mean to them. Nellie bent her head deeper over the fragrant mass of violets that filled the glass bowl on the table. They were Paul's gift, while the great bunch of glowing roses that stood near had been brought by Mr. Kress, the rich merchant who now stood in the other room talking to the Colonel but glancing impatiently towards the corner where the young couple sat.

There was a heavy silence between the two, full of unspoken emotion. Finally Paul said slowly and gravely: "Miss Nellie, you're working too hard at your studies,—you are so pale. I don't half believe that you have the strength to stand the strain of teaching. If I dare give you any advice at all, it will be to—to prefer—those roses—It is now the thirteenth day since my uncle's disappearance and there has been no sign of him, living or dead. If it cannot be proven that he is alive or dead—we know what that means.—Why Miss Nellie!—Nellie!—what are you doing?"

Nellie had arisen from her seat, taken the vase with the roses and carried it away to set it on a cabinet at the other end of the room. Then she came back to the sofa.

"What are you doing?—what have you done?" he asked again.

"The only thing I *could* do," said the girl gently, her cheeks a soft rose as he bent to kiss her hand. "I prefer violets."

****

The morning after his return from Pressburg, Müller made an early call on Johann Stillinger, Karl's accomplice of the attempted robbery. He had the address from the police and walked into the young man's room without much ceremony.

"You are Johann Stillinger?" the detective said.

"And who are you?" asked the man who sat at the table, a true type of bully of the tenement districts.

"I'm a police agent."

Stillinger said nothing for a moment. He'd had so much to do with the police recently that he judged silence to be his best policy. He continued to drink his morning coffee as if the matter didn't concern him at all. But it did not escape Müller's notice that the spoon shook in his hand.

The detective sat down on the only other chair in the bare little room and began comfortably—: "Don't let your coffee get cold. I just want you to tell me a little more about that holdup last week. Now Karl Tonner—"

Stillinger jumped up, dropping his spoon on the floor. "Has that fool been talking—the damn idiot—" he screamed. "Just wait till I settle him—when I get out again."

"Do be quiet. You'll alarm the whole house, and besides, nobody's locked you up yet."

"What do you mean by that?"

"Merely a hint that I haven't come to arrest you—in fact I haven't any warrant to do it."

Joahnn Stillinger looked at his visitor in surprise.

"Then what'd yer come for?" he asked, sitting down again.

"I'll tell you."

"Hurry up about it!"

"I'll take my own time, please. First of all I have a suggestion: suppose you take a position with the Street Cleaning Department."

Stillinger shook his head and asked ironically: "Now where'd yer get that idea?"

"It's not such a bad idea. They are not likely to take you on again at the market. And I suppose you haven't learned any trade or you wouldn't have been in that work. It won't be easy for you to get work by your own efforts now and I don't suppose you're particularly anxious to come down in the world any more than you have. Am I right about this?"

"Guess yer might be. I ain't hankering after having anything more to do with the police."

"Well, then? You've got to work if you want to avoid the police and you can have a position at street cleaning if you want it."

"But see here, there's somethin' queer about this, that you're so anxious to help me. Where's the hook?"

"I want you to do something for me and I don't want you to do it without payment. I can't get you a position at Court but I can arrange for your employment in the Street Cleaning Department. I'm willing to do that for what I want of you. I don't see any particular good in putting you in prison again—although you did get free a little too easy this time. You might as well have a try at leading a decent life. Therefore I'm not troubling my conscience about keeping silent on what—"

"On what that damned idiot told you?" interrupted Stillinger angrily.

Müller pushed him back in the chair again. "Go easy now. Tonner told me the truth about the matter without any intention to injure you at all. I'll explain to you later how it was. Now I have a question: did you spend a part of the night of the 9th of September in the neighbourhood of Inzersdorf?"

"Yes. Well, 'spose I did?"

"What were you doing out there?"

"I went out with Karl—he was going to his mother."

"What did he want? At that hour of the night?"

"He wanted money. He had to have it next morning. If he didn't get the fifty crowns they'd lock him up."

"But he asked for a hundred."

"Oh, you know that, do yer? Then what do yer ask me about it?"

Müller looked straight at the man and the bully's eyes sank.

"It was you who got him to do that," said the detective calmly, "and you went with him to be sure he wouldn't turn back at the last moment."

"Yes, that's true. Karl's a weak sort of chap; he's sure the kind that turns back at the last minute."

"I shouldn't call a man a coward merely because he hasn't the courage to do an evil thing. Now I want you to tell me exactly what happened that night."

"Well if yer know it all, why should I tell yer about it?"

"You will do as I tell you and do it right now!"

"All right then. Well, we went out to the country and it was pretty late. I heard it strike eleven in Inzersdorf when Karl climbed over the wall. I walked up and down, then I stood by a tree, a poplar tree it was, at the edge of the meadow. That's how we'd arranged it. I waited and waited and it was the longest time before I heard anythin' movin', nothin' but just the wind. Then I hear somethin' moving in the avenue—under the row of trees that goes out from the garden to the highroad. But there was such a mist on the moor that the moon didn't help yer to see much. All I knew was, that what was movin' under the trees wasn't comin' from the same place where Karl climbed over the wall. So I thinks she saved him the trouble and opened the gate for him. Then I calls to him two or three times 'cause I thinks he's forgotten where he was to meet. He was going in the opposite direction from my tree. When I shouted, there wasn't a sound in the avenue. I called again but there was nothin' happened. Then I hears the dry leaves in the avenue making a noise as if somebody was walking very quick and I calls again. Then way off in the fog I see a man's figure only just for a minute and I don't see him very distinctly. Then he's gone again. I yelled after him and suddenly I hears Karl behind me sayin' to me: 'What are yer yelling so for, you fool!' There he was, come over the wall, just where he'd gone in. I asked him for the money and he tells me, very mad, that he couldn't get it. So we comes back here and then I thinks out the holdup."

Stillinger stopped and sat looking at the detective in astonishment. Müller was evidently, greatly interested by the man's story. He sat leaning forward in his chair, his lips firmly set, his eyes sharp as steel, and his face pale in excitement. Finally he breathed deeply and leaned back more comfortably. Then after a pause he asked:

"Then you saw the man only very indistinctly?"

"Yes, just dim like in the fog."

"Was there anything you particularly noticed about him?"

"No, or yes. He seemed pretty big—but perhaps that was only the fog."

"Yes, that's possible. Did he seem to be carrying anything?"

"No."

"Or were there two of them?"

"No, there wasn't but one."

"Do you think that if we stood under the poplar tree you could show me the direction the man took?"

Now Stillinger became interested himself. "Is that so important?" he said.

Müller replied sharply: "Answer my question."

"Sure, I think I could tell yer."

"Very well. Six o'clock this evening you are to meet me in front of the church of St. Roch. I'll have a carriage there and we'll drive out to Inzersdorf."

"I'll be there," said Stillinger. "But why is all that so important?"

Müller stood up and took his hat. "I suppose you never read the papers," he said.

"I get a blink at one occasionally when I have the cash for a glass of beer in the cafe."

"Well, you don't miss much. And the matter concerned here probably wouldn't interest you. So you needn't ask any more about it. Be there on time and now goodbye."

The detective was already at the door when Stillinger called to him: "But you want me to do some-thin' for yen You ain't getting me a position for nothing?"

Müller laughed: "You've done it already or nearly so."

"What?"

"You told me a story which I think will be of great value to me."

"Is that all?" asked the man, astonished.

"And then you'll take a drive with me this evening."

"And yer going to get me a place for that?"

"Yes, a place and a chance to be a decent man. You're in luck, young friend. But I don't know as I'm doing it so much for you, as for all those to whom you might be dangerous if you keep on as you are now."

Another nod and Müller was outside the door. He had gone to

see Stillinger simply so as not to reproach himself for having neglected any possible clue. Since Karl Tonner told him that Stillinger had waited outside the Green House that evening, Müller knew it would be wise to find the man and question him, for he might have seen something during his vigil.

But experienced detective as he was, Müller never imagined he was going to get as much out of this visit as he really did.

Stillinger had undoubtedly seen either Erlach's murderer or Erlach himself, probably the former. For unless the old gentleman had suddenly lost his senses, it was not at all likely that he should have voluntarily gone into hiding and remained absent so long.

But if the figure seen through the fog was Erlach's murderer, where was the old man himself? According to Stillinger's report the man he had seen had not been carrying a burden. And he had been quite certain that there were not two of them. Therefore it could not be a case of kidnapping, as Müller had thought might be possible. The mystery deepened the more he went into it, and Müller's interest grew with the growing difficulty of the case.

His carriage stopped in front of the church exactly at six o'clock and he found Stillinger waiting for him. They drove out into the country at a sharp pace, and reached the poplar tree by the wayside just as twilight was falling. Müller let his wagon wait for him at some little distance.

The poplar tree lay about fifty paces from the garden wall and about an equal distance from the end of the avenue of trees.

"Over there is where I see him disappear," said Stillinger, pointing towards the southwest, where another avenue of very old trees cut off the horizon line.

"Was it lighter then than it is now?" asked Müller. "You said the moon was shining."

Stillinger shook his head. "Yes, but there was a fog. If you want to know how far yer could see that night, you'll have to wait a bit."

"All right, we'll wait a bit"

The Black Moor, on the edge of which the two watchers stood, was a low-lying, almost treeless waste, already veiled in twilight and in the fluttering ragged ends of mist that rose from it in spots. In the direction to which Stillinger pointed there were several roads, leading various ways.

"Did the man change his direction after you called to him?" asked the detective.

70

Stillinger did not think that this was the case. Then they stood in silence for some time till finally the younger man said: "There now. This is about like what it was that night. Yer couldn't scarce see the trees in the avenue one from another. So yer see I couldn't get more than just a squint of him. I'll go over there and then you can see how it was."

He ran out into the gloom. Müller watched him disappearing into the avenue of trees, heard the leaves rustle under his feet and saw him come out again at the other end. Stillinger ran on for some few yards in the direction in which he had pointed, and Müller could see him most of the time. But he knew that on the night in question there had been very much more of a fog and the air was not nearly as clear. This rendered it much more difficult to estimate the distance and size of any object.

Müller returned to Vienna with Stillinger, leaving the latter at the church where he had found him. "Go to the main office of the Street Cleaning Department tomorrow morning at seven o'clock," were the detective's parting words. "They know that you are coming and your position is assured."

And the young man, who now drops out of the story, did really enter the service of the Street Cleaning Department and led a more or less decent life. This was just one of the many good things that Müller did, so quietly and unassumingly that few people heard of them.

CHAPTER 7

Mr. Robert Hartmann Comes
to Inzersdorf

The great brick factory, the chief reason for existence of the little village of Inzersdorf, lay about half an hour distant by foot from the official centre of the town. Near the factory was the large and attractive dwelling house in which Richard Plöhn, General Manager of the works, lived with his family. Tall heavy-foliaged trees and wide stretches of lawn separated the comfortable home from its utilitarian but unattractive surroundings. The main highroad, leading to the south, lay along one side of the garden.

On this road, in front of the main entrance to the Manager's garden, a well-appointed carriage halted one rainy evening. A young man who sat beside the coachman on the box sprang out and rang the bell at the gate. The servant who opened, bowed deeply before the gentleman in the wagon.

"Too bad you should come in such weather, sir," he said. "Shall I take your trunk?"

"Please do. And Karl, you take the handbags. No, leave me the umbrella myself."

Following the two servants up the path through the heavy rain, the stranger entered the main door of the house, greeted most cordially by Manager Plöhn.

"*I* am Manager Plöhn," said the latter. "Welcome to my home!"

"My name is Hartmann, Robert Hartmann," answered the elderly gentleman who had just arrived. "I hope sincerely that my coming will not cause any inconvenience in your household and that you will not be angry with the Baron because he sends me to you."

"No, indeed," answered Plöhn. "You do us a great favour by coming, for I assure you it is dreary enough in Inzersdorf sometimes."

"But you must know I have the reputation of being an original."

"Oh, I'm not afraid of that," laughed the manager. "We have two or three other originals in our family already. But now tell me, would you rather be domiciled down stairs or up one flight? There are two rooms at your service in either story. And we can easily take care of your valet also."

"May I be quite frank?"

"Please do."

"The Baron told me something about a pavilion in your garden."

"Yes, there is such a one. But it's quite a distance from the house. And if you want to have your man with you there, it would give you only one room for yourself."

"I don't mind that. And I am used to living alone."

"Then I will have them put the pavilion in order for you."

"You go and help them, Karl," said Mr. Hartmann to his servant.

"It will be damp and cold in the pavilion,", continued Plöhn. "They will have to air the rooms and heat them thoroughly. Won't you join us in the sitting-room until the place is ready? And you're sure that you will not be afraid to sleep there? The pavilion is in a distant corner of the garden, right by the wall beyond which is the open moor. And our neighbourhood, I am sorry to say, is not a safe one.

"I am not afraid. I am strong and well and am not unarmed. Besides I am not alone if I have my man with me."

Mr. Plöhn gave orders to have the pavilion put in readiness and then asked his guest to follow him into the sitting-room. An hour later the stranger was the centre of attraction in the family circle. Plöhn's little boy rode fearlessly on his knee, while Mimi, a year older, tugged at his coat with perfect confidence and begged for another lovely story. The great St. Bernard dog sat beside Hartmann, looking at him with cordial interest. And the three grown members of the family, Manager Plöhn and his wife, as well as his sister, Miss Suzanne, had already decided that the advent of this stranger into their midst was as pleasant a thing as could have happened to them. For they found Hartmann a highly cultivated, delightful conversationalist who bade fair to be an entertaining addition to the small social circle of the neighbourhood.

The stranger, Robert Hartmann as he called himself, a landed proprietor from Poland, had discovered brick clay on his estate, and determined to start a brick factory. But as he knew nothing whatever about this industry he concluded that it would be well to study it up first His friend Baron von Stein in Vienna had suggested to Hartmann that he might live in Inzersdorf for two or three weeks and study the brick-making there. The Baron wrote to the Manager about this and the latter had at once invited his employer's friend to be his guest for an indefinite length of time. The Baron had hinted that any courtesy offered to Hartmann would be considered as a favour to himself, and Plöhn was only too glad to oblige his chief. The servants had been told to make everything as comfortable as possible for him, and the family were now greatly pleased to find their unknown guest so delightful a person.

About an hour after Hartmann's arrival the pavilion was ready for him and his host accompanied him through the garden. The little house itself was a comfortable structure built of bricks raised up on a foundation of the height of half a story, and containing one large room and one smaller one. The windows were protected by iron bars and the door was a heavy one ornamented with iron.

The rooms were comfortably, even handsomely furnished, for the Plöhns used it for extra guests who came unexpectedly when the main house was full.

"Why, how pretty this is!" exclaimed Hartmann as he opened the door of the main room. The heavy curtains shut out the storm and the bright fire, as well as the shaded electrics, gave an inviting glow of warmth and light. Hartmann looked about him with great pleasure and set about making himself comfortable, after having promised his host to return to the house punctually at seven o'clock for the evening meal. When left alone with his servant the guest opened each of the windows in turn, examining the lay of the land outside. Then he helped the valet dispose of the contents of his trunks and bags, and finally lay down on the sofa and lit himself a pipe.

At the stroke of seven he was again in the main house and found four other guests there beside himself. Two of the three other men were introduced to him as officials of the factory, Gebhart the cashier, and Bauer, the head bookkeeper. The third guest was named by Plöhn as: "Dr. Maximoff, my future brother-in-law." With Maximoff, who was a tall, fine-looking Russian, was a charming little girl of five years old, his daughter. As they sat at table, Hartmann, apparently engaged in doing all justice to the abundant repast, was the while looking carefully around him and taking stock of the others of the party. Instinctively from the first he took a dislike to Bauer, the bookkeeper. He chided himself inwardly for this, saying that the poor man could not help his very unattractive appearance, his coarse irregular features, immense mouth, and ugly yellow teeth. Nor was he probably altogether to blame for his very clumsy and awkward manners. But there was something in the man's expression, a shifty look to the pale eyes which glanced about him nervously from time to time, that particularly antagonized the stranger. Gebhart, the cashier, was merely a commonplace type, whereas Dr. Maximoff was in every way a noticeable personality, a complete contrast to the unfortunate bookkeeper. The Russian, apparently about forty years of age, was a superbly-built man whose strength was combined with a quiet dignity and an easy grace of movement that was most attractive. He was an excellent talker, bright and cheerful, his handsome face lighting up with frank, smiling animation at every subject that interested him. Yet in repose there was a deep melancholy in his great eyes that gave an added charm to the man's personality. Hartmann quite understood the affection with which Miss Suzanne Plöhn, otherwise a calm and self-possessed young lady, glanced up now and then at her betrothed.

The meal progressed comfortably and when it was over the company adjourned to the cosy living-room. The gentlemen had just started out on an animated political discussion when the maid-servant entered the room with an appearance of haste and excitement.

"What's the matter?" asked Plöhn, who saw the girl first.

"There's something happened, sir. There's been a fight and one of the workmen is badly hurt—the constable's there already," replied the maid. Plöhn left the room hastily, followed by his two employees. Maximoff went with them. Hartmann sat quietly with the ladies, although they both looked at him somewhat in surprise. But they were quite satisfied that he made no move to follow the others, as they did not enjoy being left alone.

The sudden disturbance naturally made a break in the conversation. The guest broke an uneasy little pause by asking if these fights were customary among the workmen in the factory.

"Yes, unfortunately they are," sighed Mrs. Plöhn.

"Particularly on Saturdays," put in Suzanne, "when they get their money and gather in the saloon, there's sure to be trouble. But I suppose it's so everywhere in these big establishments."

"Yes, that's true," added Mrs. Plöhn, "only our particular misfortune is that among our men there must be a monster of quite particular and unusual wickedness."

Hartmann looked up with great interest. "Must be, you say?" he asked. "Why so indefinite?"

"Why, I don't know," said the lady. "I suppose I might have spoken quite definitely, for we know that he is here, only no one has ever seen him, at least not to know it. His existence, however, is too unfortunately an evident fact."

"Anna," said her sister-in-law, "I think I'd better take the children up to the nursery." Mrs. Plöhn nodded and Suzanne led the three little ones away.

Hartmann waited for their departure with impatience.

"Do tell me, dear madam, what you mean by this? It is most interesting. What has happened here? and why are any of your workingmen suspected of whatever deed it is you are thinking of."

"It began about three years ago in the autumn," said Mrs. Plöhn. "They found the body of an old pedlar in one of our shallow ponds. He had not been drowned, but had been strangled before being thrown into the water. The cord that had pressed his life out was still around his throat. It was a bit of black cord of an unusual sort."

"And the criminal, or criminals, were not discovered?"

"No, the murderer—we are quite certain there was only one—has not been discovered even yet."

"Was there any motive that one could find out? An act of personal revenge?—or was it robbery? Even the pedlar's little pack can sometimes excite cupidity."

"Oh, no, the man was a poor old soul who hadn't an enemy in the world and his pack was found untouched beside the pond."

"*Hm!* And then what else?"

"Oh, there were other cases."

"Other murders?"

"No, minor crimes."

"For instance?"

"An empty house was broken into. A private house belonging to people who came here for the summer."

"Was there much taken from the house?"

"There was nothing taken at all."

"Then the criminal—or criminals, were frightened away?"

"No, no one saw the man."

"You are quite sure there was only one?"

"Yes, there was only one, that was proved by the tracks in the snow. Our constable happened to pass the house the next morning and saw footprints in the deep snow leading from the street up to the empty house."

"*Hm!* And then?"

"The official followed these tracks up to the house, stepping carefully beside them. The tracks, he said, were of unusual size. The house has only a small garden and is surrounded by a high iron railing. The constable noticed that the house door and all the windows were opened. There was no smoke from the chimneys but the constable thought it possible that someone might have come merely to air the house and to look about inside. So he rang the bell.

"There was no answer even to his repeated ringing. He saw that the footprints led up to the front door, and that other tracks led out again from the door and around to the back of the house. The policeman followed these tracks back to the end of the garden and saw that there were several boards broken out of the fence. From there the tracks led into the grove beyond.

"Our worthy constable went around to the front of the house again and hailing a passerby, sent him to the police station with news of the occurrence. He himself waited in front of the house until the police commission came, then they all entered together. The house was empty and there was no sign of damage done within. In one particular only was there any trace of an outsider's presence there. The lock of the sideboard was broken open and a bottle of expensive wine taken out. This, two-thirds empty, with a used glass, were on top of the sideboard. A cigar box was open and one of the cigars missing. A little heap of ashes on the sideboard showed that the intruder had been smoking there. But where do you think that half of the cigar was found?"

"I haven't an idea."

"No, nobody could imagine it that hadn't heard of it. The rest of the cigar was found in the mouth of a snow-man which was built up in the yard at the back of the house, a remarkably well-modelled figure."

"What a delightful idea!"

"Yes, the owner of the house thought so, too, as he is a man with a sense of humour. Only he did not care to run the danger of more such unexpected visitations, so he sold his house to people who would live in it all the year round. The whole performance was astonishingly impudent, to say the least."

"But that isn't all Mrs. Plöhn. I can see by your face that you are keeping back the most interesting morsel for the last."

"Your guess is correct, Mr. Hartmann."

"And may I not know what it is?"

"I'm waiting for you to ask how it was we knew that this impudent trick was played by the murderer of the poor old pedlar?"

"Please imagine the question asked. I'm very curious as to the answer."

"The originator of this trick had left something else on the snowman besides the cigar."

"And what was that?"

"A black cord."

"Oh—that *is* interesting." Mr. Hartmann straightened up in his chair and looked out into space, his gray eyes brilliantly keen.

"I thought you would be surprised. It certainly is a piece of astonishing cynicism—this leaving the black cord around the neck of the innocent snow-man, in the very same manner that it was found about the neck of the unfortunate pedlar," said Mrs. Plöhn.

Hartmann passed his hand over his forehead. "In this case it took the place of a visiting card." His voice had a peculiarly hard tone as he spoke.

"Yes, of course, there was no other reason for it this time. But it's strange this unknown monster should have been so ready to let us know that he was still in the neighbourhood, after such a murder."

"Yes, it was quite unnecessary, wasn't it?" put in Miss Suzanne, who had just returned. "Did you tell Mr. Hartmann about the attack on the cattle-dealer?"

"No, I left that for you. That happened since you've been here."

"Oh, then Miss Plöhn hasn't lived here always?" asked the guest with polite interest.

"No, I've only been here since my mother's death, which happened about a year ago. And this other incident occurred just after my arrival."

"Then you tell Mr. Hartmann about it," laughed Mrs. Plöhn. "That is, if you're sure you will not feel creepy when you get back to your lonely abode," she added turning to her guest. "For it happened just outside our wall, about opposite the pavilion."

"That makes it all the more interesting," said Hartmann with a smile which cloaked the tense lines of his face. "Now I really must hear the story."

"You may have noticed that a lane goes past our wall at the end of the garden. It goes through a sort of a cut right there, for the ground is higher on the other side and the bushes are thick. It was just such a rainy evening as this one when a cattle-dealer of Inzersdorf walked past here alone, on his way to the more distant of our two railway stations. It was a rather thoughtless thing for the man to do, for he was known to have made a big deal at the market that day and might be supposed therefore to have considerable money with him. As he approached the cut in the lane, the cattle-dealer had the feeling that someone was following him on the other side of the bushes. He stopped and listened, it was already too dark to see anything. He thought he saw a figure behind the bushes, but when he went over to look it was gone. The man took his revolver in his hand and went on his way. Suddenly his hat was torn from his head and something struck his face like a whip-lash, drawing a long cut in his cheek. The dealer shouted and fired his revolver in the air. With the other hand he caught at the thing, whatever it was, that was on his face. He only just caught it lightly, something that seemed to him like a thin cord with sharp edges, then it was torn from his hand and he saw a figure disappear into the woods. He shot again in that direction but had no means of knowing whether the bullet took effect. Everything was quiet after that, but the cattle-dealer returned to the Inzersdorf police station and told what had happened to him. Next morning, the ground around the spot was examined."

"Was anything found?"

"Nothing but a number of footprints in the rain-soaked ground, footprints of unusual size."

"All footprints seem large in rain-soaked earth," remarked Hartman.

Suzanne smiled. "That may be," she said, "but the footprints of this lasso-thrower measured sixteen inches at least, and the space between them was nearly six feet. The man must have fairly jumped from step to step."

"Yes, that's so. That was a wide stride."

"Particularly when you consider the condition of the ground."

"Which shows that the man had very long legs, great physical strength and activity," said the guest, and Suzanne added: "And it shows also, doesn't it, that he must be a man in the prime of life."

"Quite right, Miss Plöhn," replied Hartmann, "your conclusion would do honour to an experienced police official."

"Oh, here they come," said Suzanne rising quickly and going to meet her brother. "Where is Sergius?" she asked. "Is he still with the injured—or dead man?"

"It was only an injury," said the manager. "Maximoff has treated his wounds and will stay with him until the ambulance comes. He will join us again when he has cleaned himself up, he says."

"Who is the victim?"

"He's one of the newer men. I don't think you know him. His wounds are not fatal but they're pretty bad."

"Do they know who did it?"

"There seem to be three of them. It was a drunken brawl of course. Bauer, will you kindly telephone to the police station? This thing has got to stop, if I have to have the inn-keeper's concession taken away."

Bauer left the room and the ladies continued to question Plöhn.

"Who are the three attackers? Have they been arrested yet?" asked Mrs. Plöhn.

"Yes, the constable has taken them off. The chief sinner is Leeb, who is at the bottom of everything of that kind here, and then the two Polish brothers with the unpronounceable name."

"But this is really distressing," said Hartmann. "Will I have all this trouble when I start my brick factory?"

Plöhn laughed. "I couldn't say in advance," he replied. "There is sure to be trouble of this kind everywhere where you "have a lot of workmen together, a number of them unmarried men living in barracks."

"But the brutality in this neighbourhood seems to be worse than anywhere else, even including murders and night attacks."

"Oh, then the ladies have been telling you—"

"Yes," said Mrs. Plöhn, "the occurrence of this evening naturally suggested the subject."

"Well then, as long as we have started that topic, suppose our friend Gebhart here tells us about his adventure. We must all do what we can to entertain our honoured guest." Plöhn spoke with a laugh in his eyes.

"Oh, don't you make fun of us," said Suzanne quickly. "You're just as much excited over all these things as we are. You won't even let us walk to Inzersdorf without protection. Didn't we have to borrow Sergius' carriage the other day, because our own was being fixed, and we had to be out until dark? No indeed, this 'unknown monster,' as Anna calls him, worries you just as much as he does us."

"Who is it that worries you?" asked Maximoff, entering the room just then.

"We're talking about the unknown criminal who must be living here among our workmen," said Mrs. Plöhn.

"But why are you so sure that the man must be one of your workmen?" asked Hartmann, and Maximoff, who took a seat beside Suzanne, added: "Yes, that's true, Anna, I've often intended to ask you why you are so sure that it is one of your men?"

The hostess shrugged her shoulders. "I really don't know why I should be so sure about it," she confessed. "But the whole neighbourhood seems to think so and I fell in with the general opinion. Besides, the police authorities know every one of the permanent inhabitants of our village and there is nobody among them who could come under suspicion. But these workmen come from nobody knows where, stay with u? for a little while, and then pass on. There is no way of controlling them or even of getting to really know them."

"But don't you know," said Dr. Maximoff gravely, "that sometimes the most dangerous criminals can be found in the class of people whom we invite to our dinner table?"

"Here, here," cut in Plöhn "Don't let's start a discussion. We want our guest to hear Gebhart's story."

The cashier told them how he had been attacked one evening as he was leaving the village inn rather late on his way to his own rooms, which were in the office building. The incident happened last spring, and he still carried traces of it.

"You can see here," he said, pushing back his left sleeve, "here is where some heavy, blunt instrument struck my arm. It split the bone and tore a tendon, but my assailant did not get off undamaged. Since our neighbourhood has become so unsafe I carry a leaded cane when I go out at night, and I struck out with this when the man jumped at me suddenly from behind a bush. He screamed and I knew that I must have hurt him, I must have hit his shoulder or breast. He sprang back into the bushes and although I tried to follow him, he had soon disappeared in the darkness. Next morning, all our men were at their posts. But of course it was impossible to have a physical examination made of over two hundred workingmen, so that I could not tell whether anyone of them was suffering from a broken rib or collar-bone. However, since then I agree with Mrs. Plöhn that this unknown criminal must be one of our factory hands. I know that I am not a favourite with them, although I do not know why they should hate me enough to want to kill me. And yet there must be someone who feels that way towards me, someone who belongs to our establishment, for he found his way into my room the day after the attack."

"He came to your room?" exclaimed Hartmann astonished.

"Yes, he came right into my room, in my absence of course."

"Then how did you know he was there?"

"I knew it from something that he left behind him, a noose made of an odd sort of black cord."

"Oh—"

"You can imagine that the discovery did not please me very much. It seemed like a threat and I have not gone out unarmed since then."

"Then you are sure that your assailant was the unknown murderer?"

"It looks that way."

Hartmann turned to the manager. "And you haven't the faintest idea, sir, which one of your men it could be who keeps the entire neighbourhood in such fear and anxiety?"

"No, not the faintest idea," was the answer. "I have had a capable detective living and working among my men for six months now. He found that several of them were under suspicion for crimes committed elsewhere, but he found nothing that would identify the man with the black cord. But now enough of this unpleasant subject for tonight! Do you care to join us at our usual game of cards?"

The game lasted for an hour or so, then Maximoff's carriage was called and he and his little girl left the house. Hartmann bade his hosts good evening and took his way down to his lonely pavilion, accompanied by the manager and a servant. Karl opened the door to receive them and held it open to light the way for the return to the house.

"Have they taken good care of you?" said Hartmann when he was left alone with his valet.

"Oh, yes, very nicely. They even brought my supper out here to me when I asked for it."

"That's good. But from tomorrow on I have arranged with the manager that you are to eat in the factory mess room, or else in the village inn. You are to mix in with the workingmen and pay particular attention to men of unusual size."

"Pay particular attention to big men? All right, sir." Karl's face showed great interest, but he did not dare to ask any further questions.

"And now you can go to bed," said Hartmann, "and remember it is only you who must clean my clothes and shoes. The others must not see them at all."

Karl bowed and left the room. When alone, Hartmann began to undress. When he had taken off his coat and vest and his boots, his figure was much shorter and less ample. And when he had finally laid off a costly diamond ring and a handsome scarf pin, Joseph Müller stood there in all his own unobtrusive humbleness. He slipped on a dressing-gown, turned off the electric light, and parting the curtains of one of the windows he looked out into the darkness. When his eyes had grown accustomed to the gloom, he could see the level outlines of the moor stretching away into the distance beyond the bushes on the other side of the road, and to the right a few groups of trees and some of the out-buildings of the factory completed the skyline.

"What a pity!" he thought. "What a great pity that I didn't hear about this man with the black cord before tonight. My two years in the South lost me several interesting things, but I suppose I needed the rest. No, I don't agree with my charming hostess as to the fact that this black cord man is one of the workingmen. The sense of humour shown in the airing of the villa and the building of the snow figure it not usual among men of that class. And then this unheard-of reckless-ness in so impudently leaving his traces behind him from case to case! I suppose I will be able to see one of these bits of cord. Anyway it's exceedingly interesting. And this last mystery is the most interesting of all. I wonder if there is any connection here? Nobody mentioned the Erlach case tonight—but it probably won't be difficult to get them to talk about it."

At this stage in his meditation, Müller devoted his attention again to the landscape. Then he went to bed.

"The idea of the black cord is really delicious—most romantic," he murmured once more before he went to sleep, "but it's too reckless. This man will hang himself with a bit of his own cord before *long.*"

CHAPTER 8

Midnight in the Green House

Mr. Hartmann began his studies in the factory the very next day. The bookkeeper Bauer had been appointed his guide, and showed him all the rooms in the establishment, describing the various stages of the process with considerable intelligence. The man knew his business thoroughly and Plöhn had already spoken of him to his guest as a faithful and capable employee. But Bauer himself, as a man, was extremely unattractive and the impression of distaste gained by Hartmann the evening before was increased by a further acquaintance with the bookkeeper.

Bauer was tall, and fairly well-built The somewhat too heavy lines of his figure gave an impression of great strength. But his repulsive face, and his bad table manners, were as disagreeable as was his constant inclination to bring up only unpleasant matters in his conversation. Müller wondered that the rest of the company did not seem to notice this. Then he realized that they were accustomed to it from seeing Bauer almost daily for several years. Also that they were willing to overlook the man's disagreeable qualities because of his other good traits. When the detective found a moment to talk it over with the General Manager, he discovered that Bauer was one of the originals of whom Plöhn had spoken the evening before.

"He's the most prosaic man you could imagine, ordinarily," said the manager. "But I happen to have discovered that he writes poems in secret and sends flowers to a lady, whom he loves equally secretly and without any hope whatever. It is the contrast between his ordinarily prosaic nature, his complete lack of attraction, and this secret sentimentality, which seems to be beyond his control, that makes him such an original. It makes him somewhat ridiculous, I must confess. I know he is not an agreeable table companion, but we overlook it because of his other good qualities and because the poor man is so alone in the world."

Müller didn't ask who the other originals were and he was not particularly interested in the matter at the moment. The house and all those within interested him only as headquarters from which to pursue his investigations. Once Lieutenant Erlach had put him in charge of the affair, he had taken the keys of the Green House, and had obtained from the local authorities a promise that nothing should be changed in the entire place until he wished it done. This was not a usual proceeding, but then Müller was not the usual sort of detective. And the police in and around Vienna knew that it was worth while to let him go his own way in any case he had undertaken.

Everything was done that could make the investigation easier for him this time. A high police official introduced him to Baron Stein, the owner of the brick factory, and made it possible for him to enter the manager's house in the role of Robert Hartmann the Polish landed proprietor. The Baron himself suggested his living in the pavilion, because right near it there was a small door in the garden wall through which he could go in and out without being seen. He asked for the key from his host, on the pretext of not disturbing the family in his comings and goings, and he soon made use of it.

The day after his arrival was a Sunday. He spent the morning in the factory and in the afternoon he went out for a solitary walk. His path led him past the Green House. He made a thorough examination of the avenue of trees and followed it up in the direction in which the man seen by Stillinger had gone. The end of this short arboured road led out onto one of the two main highroads which crossed the Black Moor. It was the road known as Laxenburg Avenue, shaded by ancient trees which shed their leaves heavily in the autumn wind. It was a very ancient street, but not altogether a favourite one because of the loneliness of the country through which a greater part of its length led. At either end of this arched avenue were the royal castles Laxenburg and Schönbrunn. Did the man whom Stillinger had seen go down this avenue or did he turn off into one of the side roads which crossed it? One of these led to the factory, another to the second highroad, and a third to a mill on the river. And each of these side roads had presumably several forks. One thing only was certain. That was that the man in the fog had gone first towards the southwest. This direction would lead him, if he continued in it, past a little shallow pond surrounded by bushes, which lay between the Erlach property and Laxenburg

Avenue. Müller stood on the edge of this pond, gazing down into the water. It lay so thickly hidden between its fringe of bushes that the wind scarcely ruffled its surface.

The detective stood looking at the dark, silent stretch of water. "Now in case that man had been carrying Erlach—the murdered Erlach—in his arms when he first heard the shout behind him, he may have left the body by the wayside and gone back for it later;" he pondered. "But he didn't put it in this pond." And again he looked down at the water plants which showed just below the surface over the entire expanse of the little pool. Then he took up a heavy stone and threw it into the water. He could see it quite clearly and was thus certain of the shallowness of the pond.

He turned away from it back to the Avenue, walked down to the bridge and then returned in the direction of the factory. He had almost reached the buildings when he heard his name called and saw Dr. Maximoff behind him, waving his hat and hurrying to catch up.

The Russian was on his way to the Plöhn house and carried an armful of unusually beautiful chrysanthemums. Müller's sincere admiration of the superb flowers pleased the other so that he gave him a cordial invitation to come and see his conservatory.

"It's not very far from here," said the Russian. "When we pass these bushes we can catch a glimpse of my house. There, do you see that red roof behind the trees? That's where I've lived for the last four years. You must certainly come and see me."

"I shall be very glad to. Then you've been in Austria for some time?"

"Oh, I've been here before that even. I studied in Vienna as so many of my countrymen do, and grew very fond of the neighbourhood."

"But this particular spot of it can't have very much attraction for you, apart from Miss Suzanne," said Hartmann smiling.

The doctor answered with a sigh. "I did not know Miss Suzanne when I moved here," he said with a touch of melancholy in his voice. "I came here in the desire to get away from everything that reminded me of the short but very happy years of my first marriage. I didn't care where I went. After my wife's death I left my own country with my little girl, went to Paris for a while and then came to Vienna. I looked about for a country home, for my baby is not strong and I did not want to keep her in the city. My agent found this little place here, Rose Cottage they call it I came and looked at it. The place was pretty and I was so indifferent to everything else that I scarcely noticed how unattractive the country about here is."

"And now I suppose you notice it less than ever," remarked Hartmann good-naturedly.

"Yes, indeed. Now that I have found Suzanne—we have been engaged for nearly two months—now I am happy again. If only nothing happens—to prevent—"

"What do you fear?"

"I fear that something may come between me and my happiness."

"But why should you fear it?" Müller halted and looked up into the other's melancholy eyes with true sympathy. Maximoff smiled sadly. "You may not know how we Russians are constituted psychically," he said. "Either our blood is over-light or else heavy and black as the storm-night. I am not of the first type, I think. I can be merry with others for a time, but I cannot shake off my natural melancholy. But really," he continued in a lighter tone, "this is selfish of me and it can't interest you. And I see Suzanne and the children waving to us from the window. Let us hurry to greet them."

"Where's your little girl?" asked Müller as they walked on more quickly.

Maximoff explained that Sonya had taken a slight cold yesterday and that he was afraid to bring her out. His face softened and his eyes shone in tenderness as he spoke of his little girl, and the soft-hearted detective felt a warm wave of sympathy for this good-looking and attractive man. The Russian seemed to reciprocate it and the men parted at the door apparently the best of friends.

During the conversation that evening, Müller managed cleverly to bring the talk around to the topic which interested him most. And without anyone noticing his management of it, he soon had them all discussing the Erlach case. He pretended to have heard nothing whatever about it and he showed an interest that flattered the ladies into giving him all possible detail. After he had been informed as to the disappearance of old Erlach from within his locked room, the men of the party had something to say as to the character of this eccentric, elderly bachelor. They both agreed on the fact that Leopold Erlach was a totally uninteresting personality. Maximoff, who said that he occasionally went to the Green House to play chess with its owner, had some amusing anecdotes to tell about the pettiness of the other's outlook on life, which was oddly combined with considerable personal arrogance.

"But the authorities have evidently not given up hope of bringing some light into this mystery," continued the Russian. "For our constable, whom I met this afternoon, told me that an experienced detective was expected shortly from the city to take charge of the case."

"That's a good idea," said Mrs. Plöhn. "It struck me they were giving it up very quickly."

"But when no one else has discovered anything after two weeks of research, I don't see how a new detective is going to help," remarked Suzanne.

"No. If there was any clue to be found at first, all traces of it are probably gone by this time."

"And the criminal himself has had quite sufficient time to cover all his tracks," said Hartmann, who was playing with the little boy on his knee. "I wonder," he added casually, "whether the occurrences of which you told me yesterday have any connection with this last mystery?"

"Whether the man with the black cord had a hand in it, you mean?" said Plöhn. "It might be—but he didn't leave the cord this time. And he seems to take a pride in doing so."

"There's an astounding, almost an admirable insolence in that," was Hartmann's next remark. "Then they didn't find it this time? This odd visiting card?"

Maximoff laughed heartily at this designation for the black cord and the talk turned on lighter things. The guest seemed to have very little interest in the subject and did not mention it again. Saying that he was tired, he left the company earlier than usual, reaching his own little habitation before nine o'clock.

At about ten o'clock that night a key was turned carefully in the great gate leading to Erlach's property. Müller entered and closed the door behind him with the same caution. Then he opened the house doors and closed them again by the light of his electric lantern. He went quickly from room to room, crossing through into the kitchen and the back hall. He examined the rear door and found it firmly closed and locked. Then he went through the rooms on the other side of the hall, back into the main corridor, out of which Erlach's bedroom and sitting-room opened. His main object in this nightly visit was to examine the papers and letters in the missing man's desk, in the hope of something that would give a clue to his disappearance.

When he entered the sitting-room he closed the window shutters carefully. Then he examined equally carefully the little table on which the open book and the candlestick stood. But what he saw there gave him no particular ideas, awoke no illuminating train of thought. He turned away from the table with a shake of the head and carefully locked the doors of both rooms on the inside. He smiled at himself as he did it. It seemed such an unnecessary caution in a house that was so carefully closed at its entrances. And besides, as the event that had happened there proved, there was some way of getting in and out of this room otherwise than through the doors and windows.

Then Müller sat down at the desk and began to examine the bundles of letters and papers in all of its drawers. Those papers the age of which were shown in their yellowing edges, he laid carefully back in their place. His time and his interest were given to the more recent correspondence, which was very scanty. There were a few letters from Paul Erlach, written in a formal style. Not a single letter contained a request for money nor a word of thanks for any gift. In spite of his financial difficulties, the young officer, had never asked his uncle for help and the latter had never volunteered assistance. There were a few business letters and some bills and two or three in a woman's hand which were signed "Eva."

"Your grateful Eva."

"Aha! then there *is* someone, and a woman at that, who has reason to be grateful to this old egoist," thought Müller, as he read through Eva's letters. There were just thirteen of them. But they told him little. This Eva was evidently a person of education, but the letters were so very formal, stiff and cold, that they threw no further light on her mentality. The contents of all were exactly alike. She wrote each time to acknowledge the receipt of some gift and to express her thanks for it. But she did not mention clearly in any letter what this gift was, and there was something forced and reluctant about her thanks.

The last drawer that Müller opened contained notebooks carefully ordered, each one of them dated with the beginning and end of the period over which the memoranda extended. Müller began to read the two upper ones of the pile.

There were figures for every day, even for the smallest expenditures. The last book contained memoranda beginning with the first of March and ending with the 9th of September. And on the first of each month below the item noted as "Wages for Mrs. Tonner" came another, "Twenty crowns for E." The old gentleman, for some reason unknown to anyone else, had sent twenty crowns every month to this Eva, whose cool letter of thanks might mean either a cold heart or a very youthful mind unused to expressing its thoughts.

Müller found this matter rather interesting. But he soon came to something that was even more so. In an older book, one which bore the dates of June 1st to the end of December of a year back, Mr. Erlach had made up a summary of his entire fortune which was invested in stocks and bonds. Müller carried in his pocket a copy of the official list of what had been found in the safe. He took it out now and compared Erlach's own list with the one made by the police on the 10th of September. There was something wrong there, something decidedly wrong. Papers to the value of at least twenty thousand crowns were missing from his safe. And in none of the notebooks of a later date was there any memoranda of the change in investment or any other disposal of the sum. And yet Erlach had written down every half pound of butter, every bag of salt that came into his house.

Müller leaned forward, resting his head in his hands, while he pondered deeply on this matter. Suddenly he started. He thought he had heard the closing of a door and yet he realized it might have been only the creaking of a bough outside, or a turn of the rusty weathercock.

The detective rose softly from his seat and listened. Then he put out his left hand to catch the lantern and took his revolver with the right. There was no mistake possible now. Someone was moving in the hall. Müller had left the key in the inside of the sitting-room door, a key on a ring from which hung several others. The detective's eyes watched the flickering of light which these keys threw out in the faint gleam of his lantern. Then he moved forward slowly and listened again. Someone was moving out in the hall. It was so quiet within the heavy-walled old house that even the gentlest sound could be plainly heard.

Müller had reached the study door by this time and again he stood, listening. The corridor was about fifteen yards long, three rooms opening on it from either side. The door to Erlach's bedroom was the centre door on that side of the house. Whoever it was outside there, creeping so softly through the hall, was now standing in front of that bedroom door. A hand turned the knob. Müller took his revolver in his left hand while with his right he quickly turned the key and swung the study door open. But the hanging bunch of keys rattled betrayingly, and he who stood outside had quick ears. As the detective pulled the door open a tall figure glided past him towards the front of the house.

"Stop right there or I'll shoot," called Müller, but the man did not stop. He flung open the front glass door and dashed down the five steps leading to the ground. Müller was equally quick in pursuit and fired as he ran. But the man gave no sign of having been hit, and did not lessen his pace in the slightest. The sharp light of two electric beams threw his quick moving shadow along the ground, for he carried a lantern also. Müller fired a second time, but just as he did so, the man ahead of him made a quick dive around the corner of the house. As Müller followed him in this direction, something hard struck him on the head and dazed him for a moment. But he was not injured and took up his pursuit in a second or two. The slight pause, however, was sufficient to enable the other to dash through the garden door and disappear in the blackness outside.

The detective stood by the gate peering out in all directions, but the night was absolutely dark and the blackness was impenetrable beyond the ray of his lantern. He closed the door with the key which he found on the outside and then put it in his pocket. On his way back to the house, he found the object that had hit him on the head. It was a little lantern of unusually fine and costly workmanship. He took this in too. Both the front doors had been unlocked from the outside. The keys were still in the locks. Müller closed them and put both the keys with the others in his pocket.

Then he let the light of his own lantern move over every foot of the floor in the corridor. He saw several new footprints there, the wet earth still clinging to some of them. He recognized his own footprints and beside them were enormous tracks that he had not seen there before. Müller drew a deep breath; his eyes shone with the gleam that came into them when he was on the trail.

But he did not stay in the hall, he went back into the study, locked it carefully and from there passed on into the bedroom. The first thing he did here was to fasten a tablecloth up over one window and a bedspread over the other. He was not at all anxious that anybody from outside should see him through a possible crack in the shutters. For he knew that his life wasn't worth much after what had happened, and then besides he wished to be left to work undisturbed. He took his seat on a comfortable armchair near the door that led to the corridor, and pulled a little flask from his pocket. After a hearty drink, he rubbed a lump that was growing on his head, and then lit a cigar. Then finally he disposed himself to meditate over this unexpected night visitor.

"Who could it have been?" he said. "Could it have been the same person who underscored those three words in the book in the next room there?"

Those words "He was here" had not seemed to mean anything to the local authorities. And Müller himself had been able to find no fitting explanation for them until he heard the story of the man with the black cord. Even then it meant no clue which led to anything. Who had underscored these words? Erlach himself when he saw his life threatened? Or his murderer? But why should Erlach do such a thing? The incident had no sense to it unless it had been written by the other. For this Other might have intended thus to notify the authorities, who were so unable to cope with him, that he was the terrible Unknown who kept them all in fear and terror for years, that he had been in this room, and had given them another uncanny riddle to solve.

"Who was it who was here a few moments back?" Müller asked himself again and again. It was not Leopold Erlach, of that he was certain. Leopold Erlach was small and slight and this man was of unusual size. A man may increase his height and his breadth by a disguise, but he cannot change the length of his stride. No man under middle height could take the steps left as a clear trail by the fleeing unknown. And no old man could move with such haste. It had not been Leopold Erlach, even if the latter were still alive.

"Of course it may have been an ordinary thief who managed to get the three keys and thought this a good chance to plunder an empty house," said the detective to himself. But this idea didn't seem right to him. He was glad he had forgotten to bar the garden door through which he entered himself. For if this had been done the unknown would have realized that there was someone in the house and would not have come. The man, whoever it was, seemed to know the locality, and went directly to the bedroom. What could he want in this room? He must know that all valuables, as well as the contents of the safe, had been removed to the police courts. Was there some clue, some trace of his presence that he may have remembered leaving, and that he wanted to take away?

The detective asked himself all these questions, while his eyes wandered slowly over every inch of the room. He knew that the bedchamber had been thoroughly examined by the local police several times. Every inch of the wall and floor had been sounded, the larger pictures and the mirror had been taken from the walls in search of a possible secret door. The bed had been dragged out from the wall, but had not otherwise been disturbed. It was impossible that Erlach could be concealed in the bed anywhere. For although the wooden part of the structure was very old, the spring and mattress were new and modern.

On Müller's first visit to the house he also had examined the room very carefully. But he had not seen anything beyond what the others had found. He knew now however that there *was* something more to be seen, something which he must find, something which brought this nightly visitor to the door.

Suddenly the veteran detective rose with a start, while a crimson wave of blood shot up over his face to the very roots of his hair. One of his sudden intuitive flashes had illumined his brain. He had realized that all the colours in this room were *dark*. From the browns of the inlaid floor up to the paler ceiling everything was dark. The furniture was of ebony and the picture frames, heavily carved, of the same wood. The wall paper was of a dark shade which had grown deeper with years. The light ceiling and the white coverings of the bed were all that brought brightness into the room. Müller's eyes now rested on the old-fashioned woodwork of the bed structure, its richly carved high head and foot boards. On top of the head board, two little angels, carved out of the black wood, leaned forward as if to look down on the one who should sleep there. With their little fat fingers they held fast to a *rococo* railing which formed a border for the heavier carving of the solid wood below. It was this railing and its many corners and curves that now attracted Müller's eyes. A faint memory of something seen before but only half noticed, came back to his mind.

It seemed to him that when he first saw this bed he had casually noticed that the lines of the pretty composition at its top were not quite clear. It was this memory that now sent a searchlight flash through his brain. He stood with the light of his lantern thrown full on the carving, and his tightly closed lips parted in a smile. His free hand carefully disengaged the black cord which was twisted about the black carving, the cord left there by an incredibly audacious criminal.

Then Müller examined his latest discovery. The cord was about ten inches long, evidently a bit cut off of a larger piece. The strands were loosening on either end. The cord was made of braided horsehair and was about as heavy as a large steel knitting needle.

"That's what he was after," said Müller aloud. And then he wondered mildly whether the man who escaped was not likely to be waiting outside on the moor until he himself should come out. If he were, there would probably be heard the sound of a shot through the night, or safer still, there would be the quick thrust of a knife, and the man with the black cord would no longer have to fear the only foe who was as brave and as clever as he was himself. But Müller, who though fearless was not reckless, decided that there was no necessity of running into such an avoidable danger when he could easily pass the rest of the night in the Green House. He looked at his watch and found it to be just twelve o'clock.

Having nothing else to do the detective turned to another examination of the bed. The first time he had seen it, on the 20th of September, he was already convinced that that bed had not been slept in on the night of the 9th. But he knew that some one had lain down on it—for a few moments, lain down in his clothes and his shoes. He discovered this through the magnifying glass with which he had thoroughly examined the sheets and the coverings. The glass showed him infinitesimal bits of earth on the white surface. And these soiled spots were very near the front of the bed, at the place where the coverlet had been found thrown back. Müller was sure that somebody had lain on that bed with his knees drawn up, and that the soles of his boots had come into contact with the clean sheet. Whoever it was had been careful to brush away all the stains except the few microscopic bits which no one had noticed. The top pillow still held the pressure of a head and the sheets showed the folds into which they were thrown by the body resting there.

But at the lower end of the bed there was not a single fold to be seen. Whoever had lain there had not stretched himself out comfortably as a man naturally would when sleeping in his accustomed bed. Why had the unknown criminal desired to give the bed the appearance of having been slept in? For no other reason possibly than simply to give an added touch of mystery to the affair.

And all of the clothes which Erlach had worn through the day on the 9th of September were missing. Müller knew by this time that the old man had not yet gone to bed when he was attacked. This corresponded with Karl Tonner's report that he had seen a light in Erlach's room when he had entered the garden. The lamp hung above the desk in the study, and the study shutters were not closed, so that the light could easily be seen from outside.

While pondering all this, Müller made himself comfortable in the corner of a big sofa, settling down for the rest of the night But he had not sat there long before he raised his head again and listened.

Again he heard someone moving, outside the house this time. He stood up, closed his lantern, took his revolver and moved softly out into the corridor. When he reached the front door he looked out through the glass and could dimly see the figure of a man waiting there.

The man moved, pressed the knob of the outer iron gate and shook it. Finding this of no avail, he put his arm through the bars and knocked on the glass pane.

Then Müller knew who it was and turned the light of his lantern full on the face outside, as he opened the door.

"What are you doing here?" he asked in surprise, as Karl Tonner slipped hastily through the opening.

"Thank goodness, you're all right," murmured Karl, wiping his face. "I thought sure he'd shot you."

"Who had?"

"The man I met as I ran up here."

"Where did you meet him?"

"About one hundred paces outside the gate, at the end of the Avenue. He suddenly jumped out from behind a tree and ran off over the moor."

"Did you call after him?"

"Yes! 'Stop, you rascal!' I cried. You see I heard the shots and saw him running away."

"Did you climb over the wall again?" asked Müller when they were back in the bedroom, and he was gathering up the trophies of his evening's work. Karl nodded an affirmative.

"You didn't call my name, did you?"

"Oh, no."

"Well, we can go now. Even if he should have come back, he won't dare to attack two of us."

Müller locked the front doors carefully, thinking that the Unknown would not be able to get into the house again as it was scarcely possible he would have duplicate keys. Then the detective opened his lantern and let it move over the ground in front of the door and up the path. There were a number of tracks to be seen in the soft earth. Müller recognized his own footprints and Karl's, and beside them the traces of an enormous foot, at astonishingly wide intervals. He stooped to examine one of them. It was a very odd track, having none of the usual outlines of a boot sole. It was just one big even oblong, rounded off a little at either end.

"He's wearing overshoes," said the detective. "Not rubber shoes, either, for these have very characteristic soles and can be recognized at once. This man is much too clever for that. He chooses felt slippers or something of that sort. It's a very good idea, an excellent idea, one reason the less to fear discovery."

Müller straightened up and put out his light even before they came to the corner of the house.

"Now watch out well," he said in a whisper to Karl, "and stay close beside me. Take this leaded cane and if we should be attacked and you can get at him, try to hit his legs. But don't make a mistake and hit mine instead."

Then they went forward through the blackness. But the eye grows accustomed even to such darkness, and when Müller had locked the garden gate behind them he could already distinguish the outlines of the tall old trees.

Once outside, the two men set out on a strange wandering about the moor, going now to the right, now to the left, then back again, stopping now to listen, creeping forward again. Finally after numerous twistings and turnings and zigzaggings they came back to the little gate that led them into the garden of their present home. Before Karl opened this gate they both listened and looked in all directions. Then when they were quite certain that there was no one within sight or hearing they slipped quickly through and into the pavilion. They went to bed in the darkness. For if anyone outside on the moors should have been following or watching their wandering, it would not be wise to let him see light at that hour in the little house inhabited by Mr. Hartmann and his valet.

Müller lay awake for some time, going over all the impressions he had received during this eventful night. Of one thing he was certain, a certainty which thrilled him with pleasurable excitement. He knew now that the person concerned in the Erlach mystery was the same clever, cynical, reckless rascal who had kept the entire neighbourhood in terror for the last three years.

And Müller was certain of something else too. The Unknown was not one of the factory workers. The peculiar style and evident costliness of the little lantern that had come into his possession in so unpleasant a manner, was a proof that the man who had thrown it at him did not belong to the working class. And as the Unknown, fleeing before him, had opened the front door of the house, the light of Müller's lantern fell on his hand. All the detective could see was that the hand was covered by a glove of soft, reddish-brown leather. He could get no correct impression as to the size or structure of the hand itself.

"Anyway it's not the custom among factory workingmen to wear kid gloves. In fact, it's not a usual thing for criminals accustomed to such nightly excursions to wear gloves anyway," said Müller to himself. Then he suddenly sat up in bed. Although he was already growing old, the veteran detective was young in heart and spirit, and he never lost the acuteness of the shock when one of his flashing thoughts came to him. This was one:

"Does this super-intelligent, this quite extraordinarily clever villain, always wear gloves when he is doing something whereby the impression of the skin of his fingers might leave a fatal clue? He must be familiar with criminal proceedings and know how important that point is."

But in spite of a sleepless night, Müller was up early the next morning. Karl was awake still earlier, and stood ready with the heavy-wadded vest and coat which gave his slender employer Mr. Hartmann's comfortable embonpoint. When Müller had finished dressing, he said to Karl: "You know what you are to do today?"

Tonner bowed: "Yes, Mr. Müller"

"Mr. Müller?" repeated the detective sharply.

"Mr. Hartmann, sir," the young man answered with a smile.

Müller's glance was still sharp. "My dear young man, it is no laughing matter that we are engaged on here. You may have noticed that last night, when you proved yourself worthy of my confidence. Both you and I must be careful in everything we say and do, for we are here on very serious business. And it would be well for you to look a little more seriously at life if you ever want to make anything worth while of your existence. And now once more: do you know what you are to do?"

"Yes, sir," said Karl, now quite grave. "I am to clean off all traces of the nightly expedition, to lock up the clothes you wore last night and then to look about the neighbourhood and talk with people about the occurrences in the Green House. I am to take dinner at the Inn in Inzersdorf and need not return here, today at least, until about four o'clock."

"Good. And one thing more. I am not so much interested, not as much as I was yesterday, in very large men or in men of the working class."

"I thought so," said Karl lightly.

Müller looked up quickly. "Why do you think that?"

"Because the man who shot at you yesterday—" Müller started to interrupt, then concluded that he wouldn't. Karl needn't know everything—"is not an ordinary workingman."

"And why do you think *that?*"

"From the way he spoke."

"You heard him speak?"

"Yes. As he ran past me I heard him say, not very loud though, 'devilish adventure this!' That was all I heard."

"And you didn't tell me that before now? I thought you were an intelligent man!"

"Should I have told you right away?"

"Yes—yes—of course. That's most important. You are to tell me everything you see or hear at once. You are to tell me if you hear a fly hum and think it could be of any use to me in my work." Müller's sentence ended in a smile in which Karl joined.

"And one thing more," continued the detective. "You are to take an interest in men's gloves of dark reddish-brown leather. And you must still watch men of over middle height, who wear long cloaks with hoods."

Karl repeated every sentence until he was sure that he understood, and then in answer to Müller's question replied that he had quite enough money for the day's expedition.

"Very well, then, you need not be too careful of the money. Only don't go ahead too fast. It may be necessary that you should invite the one or the other to have a glass with you. Most people talk more easily when drinking. And be careful to emphasize the fact that you know nothing more of me than that I am the landed proprietor Hartmann from Poland, that I am here to study brick-making, and that you entered my service in Vienna."

"Thank fortune, *that's* the truth," said Karl warmly. Müller answered with a friendly smile. "That's all right," he said cordially. "Keep straight and that will be enough to show your gratitude for the little I've done for you and for your mother's great love."

Müller left the garden through the little door. And as he walked along his thoughts were still busy with the Unknown. "So he talks High German, does he? I was right then, he is no workingman. A devilish adventure you say, my friend? It may be that it will prove devilish for you! It was a lucky thing he had no idea who it was that was after him. For if he discovers me before I discover him, my life will hang on a thread—or on a black cord rather."

Müller walked along with his eyes on the ground. Suddenly he stopped and bent down to examine the moist earth. He was at the corner of the wall where the lane led into a wider street. The soft ground was covered with tracks of wagon wheels, horses' hoofs and human footprints. Among them was a trail of enormous feet of unusual shape. Müller recognized them as the same footprints he had seen that night in the Erlach garden.

"So he followed us after all," murmured the detective. And the discovery did not contribute to his ease of mind.

CHAPTER 9

Müller Visits Eva Geiringer

Müller's intention was to utilize this day in searching for "Eva." He went to his own house first to ask Mrs. Tonner whether she knew anything that would aid him in this matter, as well as in the mystery of the missing twenty thousand crowns.

It certainly was strange that the miserly old man who, as Dr. Maximoff said, wept in emotion at his own generosity when he gave a beggar a copper piece, should have sent this "Eva "twenty crowns every month. His heart had opened to her it seemed. Müller wanted to see this "Eva" personally to find out whether the larger sum, the twenty thousand crowns, might have found their way to her also. Even the most miserly of elderly bachelors are generous sometimes, or have to be when it is a case of preserving their reputation.

Mrs. Tonner was overjoyed to see her employer. He set her mind at rest at once by a good report as to her son's welfare and present conduct. Then he proceeded to the matter in hand.

"Do you know anything about a woman by the name of Eva, who stood in some relation to Erlach?"

"No."

"And you do not know that he sent money away the first of every month?"

"I didn't know that it happened every month. But once, about a year ago, I had to go to the post office with it myself and make out the money order."

"Do you remember the name?"

"No. I scarcely even looked at it and forgot it immediately. Mr. Erlach was sick, which gave me a great deal more work than usual, and just at that time I was particularly worried about Karl. I hadn't head for anything except my most necessary duties."

"Too bad. Do you remember what month it was?"

"Yes, I remember that. It was in October."

"Well, it will be easy to find the address at the Inzersdorf post office. Don't worry about cooking dinner for me. I am going right out again."

"Oh, I've just thought of something," said Mrs. Tonner.

Müller had already started to leave the room but he turned back and sat down again, looking inquiringly at her.

"Mr. Erlach was quite well again before Christmas and asked me to go to the city with him one day," began the woman. "He said he wanted new underwear and he was afraid to buy it alone for fear he would be cheated. So he took me with him and from something that happened I believe he had a secret errand which was the main reason for his going to the city."

"Tell me. It may be of importance."

"The first thing I noticed was that he didn't take his own carriage to go to the city as usual. We went in the train instead, and took a cab at the station. He left me at the store where I was to buy the underwear and told me that he had some errands in a distant part of the city. He would be back in an hour and I was to wait for him in front of the shop. I finished my errand in about twenty minutes and as the day was pleasant I took a little walk down the street. A block or two beyond I passed a barroom out of which a boy was bringing a glass of beer for a driver whose turnout stood in front of the door. By merest chance I glanced that way and recognized the cab and the driver as the same that had brought us from the station, and with which Mr. Erlach had driven into the city. I was alarmed at this and asked the cabman whether anything had happened to the gentleman. I thought Mr. Erlach might have been taken ill and gone in somewhere. But the cabman, who was already in a jovial mood, laughed at my question and answered: 'Oh, no, he didn't want to go across the city at all. As soon as you'd gone into the shop he told me to drive to 5 Linden Street and sent me up three flights with a package while he stayed down and watched the horse. The package was for a lady up there.' The man remembered the name and told it to me. The first name I think was Eva. The second I know was Geiringer."

"Why are you so sure of that?"

"Because I have relatives of the same name. That was why I remembered."

"Eva Geiringer, No. 5 Linden Street, third floor." Müller wrote it down in his notebook. "Let us hope it's the same Eva. Now tell me more. What happened after that?"

"I waited in front of the shop and Mr. Erlach arrived on time, walking from the direction in which he had driven off before. He said he had just dismissed his cab, as he thought the little walk would do him good. So we went on on foot for a little way and then Mr. Erlach looked at his watch and said we would have to take a cab or we would miss the train. As we drove to the station he was most unusually talkative, telling me all sorts of things he had done in the quarter of the town in which he was supposed to have been. I wondered at all this secrecy, because he was certainly his own master to do whatever he liked."

"Was it a large package?" asked Müller.

Mrs. Tonner did not think it was, because she had not noticed her companion carrying anything. The package must have been in his coat pocket.

An hour later Müller's carriage stood before the house in Linden Street and he himself mounted the stairs to the third floor. On one of the many doors on this landing he saw the name of the woman he sought. He knocked at the door and it was opened by an elderly woman, poorly but neatly clad. Müller inquired whether Miss Geiringer was at home. The woman smiled sadly and answered: "Oh, yes, she's at home."

"May I speak to her?" he asked again.

And again the woman answered, with sadness in her face and voice: "Yes, you can see her today."

"Evidently the young lady is not always in the mood to receive visitors," thought Müller as he entered the small, dark vestibule. The whole look of the place was totally different from what he expected, and when the woman went off to announce him, he looked about carefully. Signs of poverty were everywhere, but poverty combined with exquisite neatness and the ability to make the best of every little thing. The tiny little kitchen into which the vestibule opened was bright and cheery, and, as well as the hall, was spotlessly clean.

"Will you please come in, sir," said the woman, returning and holding the door open.

Müller entered a small, sunny room, furnished with the greatest possible simplicity, but cosy and homelike in spite of it. In front of the window was a large table and beside it a great soft armchair. In the chair sat a thin, faded, little woman whose face seemed shrunken with its many wrinkles. Only the great gray eyes still showed signs of life, and traces of former prettiness.

"You are Miss Geiringer?" asked Müller bowing. "I see you are not feeling well today and I'm afraid I have disturbed you. Shall I not come some other time?"

"I have not been well for thirty years, sir," answered the lady, with a gentle smile in which was a hint of roguishness. "And I hardly think you will care to wait until I am well again. So if there is anything that you have to say to me, Mr.------?"

"My name is Müller."

"Then will you please take a seat, Mr. Müller, and tell me what it is?"

The other woman brought up a second chair to the table, and Müller sat down in it. On the table were heaps of materials and instruments for making artificial flowers. Miss Geiringer laid aside the rose she had just finished and folded her delicately shaped hands wearily in her lap. The other woman left the room.

Müller was still dazed from the unexpected adventure. The Eva he had thought to find was something very different. Without knowing why, he had half expected to see a pretty young woman, possibly of doubtful reputation, and now he found himself sitting opposite an elderly invalid of the utmost respectability. He pulled himself together, readjusted himself to his surroundings and explained the reason for his visit. He introduced himself as a friend of Leopold Erlach and asked permission to put several important questions to the lady.

The mention of Erlach's name threw Miss Geiringer into considerable excitement. "Oh, don't they know anything about him yet?" she exclaimed clasping her hands. "Is he dead? Has he been murdered?"

"You know then?" asked Müller.

She nodded. "I saw it in the papers a kind neighbour brought me," she said. "I know that Leo—that Mr. Erlach has disappeared most inexplicably from his house, or has been taken away from there."

"Leo—that sounds rather intimate," thought Müller, "and quite different from the formality of her letters." But what he said aloud was: "Mr. Erlach has not yet been found. But this conversation is fatiguing you. Is there anything I can do for you?"

"No, thank you," she murmured, straightening up again in her cushions. "I must try and control myself. You think there is anything I can tell you about Mr. Erlach?"

"Yes, I think there is."

"You mean something that has to do with his disappearance?"

"Possibly. From letters that were found in his desk we discovered that he corresponded with you."

"They found my letters? Only my letters of thanks? Or should he have still kept the—others?" A delicate rose flush illumined the faded cheeks and a soft smile curved the pale lips.

Müller saw during this smile that the fragile invalid still had very beautiful teeth. He answered gently: "The only letters that were found were those dated during the past year. There were a number of bundles of older letters there, but they were not examined."

Miss Geiringer's face was pale and still as before.

"He sent me twenty crowns each month since August of the previous year," she said softly. "It was an alms, but it came with a few kind words each time and I was obliged to accept it, for I can do very little work now and we would have gone hungry many a day but for that." Her voice trembled and she put her hand to her eyes. Then she continued in growing excitement: "My sister sews for a large shop and rents the best room in our flat. I, as you see, make these flowers. We manage to get along somehow, but if we have to pay the doctor and the apothecary it goes hard with us. I have been helpless for many years and I know that of course I could find a place in the Home for Incurables. But I shudder at the thought and my sister knows what it would mean to me to have to go there. She is too good to send me to such a place, although people tell her that she is foolish to have to work so hard just to keep me here. Is it not my duty therefore to accept this charity, which makes things a little easier for her?"

"Dear lady, please don't excite yourself, I'm afraid it will be bad for you," said Müller sympathetically. "Why should you not take the help that was offered you? We were only surprised that Erlach should have been so charitable. How did it happen that he opened his heart to you, and you alone?"

The old. lady wiped the tears from her eyes and said in a firmer tone: "Oh, yes, you do not know then in what relation we stood to one another? I was engaged to him—thirty years ago."

"Ah, indeed! And yet they say that there was no woman in his life?"

"I am telling you the truth and have letters to prove it. I am still, as you see, wearing the ring he gave me in an unforgettable hour. Erlach then was a warm-hearted sincere man, although he changed sadly later. I was poor. He found a richer and more beautiful woman who claimed his interest. When I saw that his heart turned to her, I broke our engagement myself."

"But he did not marry the other woman?"

"No," said Miss Geiringer, with a bitter smile. "He was ready to marry her, but she found someone else who had more money than he and whom she liked better. He came back to me then, but I would not have him. We were both sentimental in those days though, and we did not give back our letters nor the rings we had exchanged. And so you see I'm old-fashioned enough to still keep his letters—but they won't do you any good in your investigation. For the Erlach who wrote those letters is long since dead."

"But how do you know that, if you haven't seen him for so long?"

"I heard indirectly through people who live in his neighbourhood that he had become hard and narrow-minded, making no friends and seeking none."

"Yes, that seems to have been the case."

"In the same way, without any desire of mine, news of our situation came to his ears and he has been sending me this money ever since."

She sat staring out into the room, her hands pressed close together and great tears rolling unhindered down her cheeks. Müller understood now why her letters of thanks had been so cold and formal. It must have been very hard for her to take this money from the man whose wife she was to have been. But she had had to take it, for hunger is painful, and still more terrible was her dread of the Home for Incurables with all its surroundings of hopeless misery.

And Erlach's pettiness of heart and mind was shown clearly by this meagre gift, which out of his plenty he had sent to the woman he once had loved. "Probably he wept at his own generosity every time he sent the money," thought Müller, a feeling of utter contempt in his heart for the man in whose interest he was busying himself. He felt nothing but sincerest pity for Miss Geiringer; he could understand what her life had been the last thirty years, in sickness and poverty. His face showed his feelings so clearly that the invalid's great soft eyes grew bright again and she held out her frail little hand to him.

"What will you think of me?" she said, "Here you come to me a total stranger and in less than half an hour I have told you things that very few know."

"We're like steam engines, dear lady," replied Müller with a smile of encouragement. "We have to open the valves sometimes you know. Need I assure you of my sympathy for you?"

"No, I think I can feel it without words. Your visit is an oasis of brightness in the dreary loneliness of my life. I am only sorry for the sad reason of it and I am sorry that I have so little to tell you that would be of any good for the investigation."

"Erlach has never been here?"

"No. It was my wish that he should never come. Even the most unfortunate of us has still a touch of vanity left, and I could not bear the thought that he should see me as I am now."

"Then I have annoyed you quite uselessly?" said Müller rising from his chair.

Fraulein Geiringer straightened up. "Oh, I have thought of something," she said. "He sent me an extra present last Christmas. It was a reminder of old times, and therefore very dear to me. He had remembered that in those days I was particularly fond of miniatures. Also he remembered that in those days I was said to look something like the Empress Josephine—with the exception of my eyes."

"And of your teeth," said Müller smiling. "The Empress is said to have had very bad teeth, you know."

Miss Geiringer flushed again but she continued: "When we were engaged Erlach showed me a charming little miniature of the Empress and one of Napoleon. He had bought them from the collection of a French nobleman. They are pretty pictures and oddly framed. Last Christmas he sent me the picture of the Empress and a silk scarf of antique design. There was a letter with the present, I will show them all to you." She touched a little bell on her desk and when her sister came in Eva caught at her hand and said: "Here, Mr. Müller, is the best sister that ever lived. She has kept me with her and made a home for me in spite of everything. I am afraid now that I will have to go to the asylum after all."

"Dear little stupid," said the other woman, touching the invalid's hair gently. Then turning to Müller with a look of distrust she continued: "Do you come from there? I know Eva's been writing to the asylum without letting me know, but I tell you now she shall not go. She's to stay here with me. I'll make it possible somehow."

"No, indeed," said Müller, with a friendly smile into the eyes of the agitated woman. "Miss Eva shall stay right on here, and I have a feeling that things will be a little easier for you now. But I must be going home. May I see the presents?"

Eva opened the box her sister brought out. In it lay a carefully folded silk scarf, the miniature and a letter. The picture represented Josephine Beauharnais in winter outdoor dress. The frame was odd and unusual. It was made of pale gold with the imperial eagle at the top. On its inner side a circle of tiny pale crystal points, like icicles, surrounded the painting. It was not altogether attractive. The only reason for it was possibly the suitability of these icicles to the winter garments worn by the Empress.

Müller laid down the picture again and took the letter which Eva handed him.

My Dear Eva,
I hope the possession of this picture, which I have always admired for your sake, will please you. Please accept it, with this scarf which was once worn by the Empress. As you see I have not yet forgotten-those years of our youth which brought us together. It was your wish that we should both remain alone. Was it right? I have forgiven.
Your Leopold

Müller handed the letter back silently. As Eva laid it into the box again, a tear fell unnoticed upon the paper.

"May I come back again if I have anything of importance to tell you?" asked the detective. Both women assented eagerly. He left them, bearing with him the impression that he had just made the acquaintance of two unusual natures. It was a compensation for the fact that his visit had, as he believed, brought him nothing that could be of value to him in his work.

Mrs. Tonner had dinner ready for him when he returned. He told her that he had found Eva and that it was the right Eva.

"Did you know that Erlach possessed two valuable miniatures, representing Napoleon and Josephine?"

"Yes, indeed. I know the pictures well, one of them is still in Mr. Erlach's cabinet."

"I didn't notice it when I was there."

"It's the picture of Napoleon."

"Yes. It must be, for its companion has not been there for some months."

"No, I know that. When I noticed it was missing I imagined it might have been in the package that Mr. Erlach sent to Miss Geiringer."

"It was, she showed it to me. They are charming pictures."

"I was admiring the picture of Napoleon a couple of days before Mr. Erlach's disappearance," continued Mrs. Tonner. "We were working together at cleaning the various valuable curiosities in the glass cabinet in the sitting room. I remember the picture particularly and his speaking about it."

Müller nodded with friendly indifference, his thoughts elsewhere.

"Now can you please tell me the names of all the visitors whom you have ever seen in Erlach's house?" he began.

She was surprised at the question but too sensible to waste any words. She thought a moment and mentioned several names, all of which he wrote down in his book after asking various questions about each. From what she told him Müller saw that Erlach had lived very quietly and that few friends or acquaintances came to his house. He had heard this also from the missing man's nephew, from the gardener Till, and from Plöhn. Till had told him that Erlach's last visitor was the representative of an insurance company. The man had not entered the house, however, for Erlach spoke to him in the garden only for a few moments and then Till had shown him out again. This was on the 6th of September. Mrs. Tonner, who had been indoors at the time, knew nothing of this last visitor. The latest person to enter the house before the disappearance, as far as she knew, was Dr. Maximoff. The Russian had been there on the 2nd or 3rd of September, in the afternoon, and had played chess with Mr. Erlach. The following day Erlach returned the visit and spent the afternoon at Rose Cottage,

CHAPTER 10

Columbus and the Egg

Müller returned to Inzersdorf about five o'clock that afternoon. He did a number of errands in Vienna and among other things that he brought back with him was something to insure his own safety. Years before, business had taken him to Marseilles and in an antiquary shop there he had found a sleeveless vest of fine steel mesh. It was a close metal net of finest workmanship and covered the entire torso. Twice, when out on dangerous errands, Müller had worn this vest as protection under his coat and it had served him well. From the moment that he had seen the huge footprints in the soft earth outside the garden wall, so near to his own habitation he had thought of this vest. For he knew by the traces that the man he had surprised in the Green House was on his trail, might possibly know who he was. The enormous footprints told him also that the nightly visitor to the Erlach mansion was the Unknown who had committed the other crimes in the neighbourhood, was the man with the black cord.

The same huge footprints were found in the opened villa, and around the spot where the more serious attack on the cattle-dealer had taken place. This man was worth considering as a serious opponent. The veteran detective was sure of that, although he was not given to taking seriously any hint of danger to himself.

Müller felt also that it lay in his own interest to push the matter through as quickly as possible. But it was not easy, for he still did not know in which direction to make the advance—he still did not know where to look for the man of whom he had already made an enemy. His own position was a dangerous one. And Karl Tonner was in danger too, for if this unscrupulous rascal realized that Mr. "Hartmann" was a detective, he might easily imagine Mr.

Hartmann's servant to be of the same calling. Müller decided that he would send Karl away to a safer place.

"Anything new?" he asked the young man, as the latter came to take his hat and overcoat.

Tonner shrugged his shoulders. "I don't know whether something I saw today when I went out is still unknown to you," he began.

"You mean the big footprints outside the wall?" asked Müller.

"Yes, but I thought you'd probably seen them yourself."

"And did you think anything else?"

"Well, I thought, sir, that you had better take double care not to meet this man again. He might shoot with better luck next time."

"You're right—partly right. But I may as well tell you it wasn't *he* who fired, it was I. Unfortunately I didn't hit him. It was courageous in you to come to my help, although I'm afraid it rather interfered with the result of my investigation."

"Oh, dear, why didn't I stay where I was!" said Karl. "I'm afraid I only put you into greater danger."

"Oh, no, I'm not so sure about that," said Müller kindly. "Only I'm sorry that I shall have to send you away now, because I might have found you useful for many things."

Karl's eyes opened wide in alarm. "You're going to send me away? Oh, why? Oh, please forgive me for my stupidity—don't send me away—I won't go—I'll stay somewhere near you—for it's my fault that you are in danger now."

"And how about you? Do you think this murderer will spare you either, now that he knows you belong to me?"

Karl's face paled. The thought had not occurred to him. Then he said, in a lower tone: "Is that the reason you are sending me away?" Müller nodded. The young man's fine eyes flashed fire. "I shan't go," he cried. "I'm not afraid. And if anything did happen, what would it matter about me?"

Müller held out his hand. "Very well then, we'll fight together," he said. "But you must not go unarmed now. Do you know how to use a revolver?"

"Oh, yes."

Müller opened his trunk, took out a pistol and handed it to Karl with a box of ammunition. "It's a six shooter and every chamber loaded," he said. "Of course you understand that you're only to use it in extreme need. And now that's settled. But you look as if you wanted to ask a question—well, what is it?"

Müller sat down comfortably, lit a cigar and offered Karl one.

"You said last night the man was partly disguised," began young Tonner timidly. "All I could see was that he had a hood drawn over his head."

"Quite right. But you only saw him in the darkness. I saw him for a moment in the light of my lantern. His cloak was brownish. I don't know how long it was because the light fell upon the upper part of his body only. The hood was stiff, much higher than they usually are, and fitted so close to the head that there wasn't a wrinkle in it. I did not see his face but I knew from the look of the hood at the back that it must close altogether or partially in front. He is masked therefore, and his hood is responsible for part of his unusual height. That's the reason why I told you that you need not bother about very tall men any more. His hood had one other peculiarity also."

"What is it? Please tell me."

"It was cut out over the ears. The man must be able to hear well. It may possibly have left his mouth free also. Or did his voice sound muffled?"

"I don't think so—but I couldn't really tell."

"You couldn't? Oh, well, you'll learn in time. We can't expect to know everything all at once. Now tell me what you were doing with yourself today?"

Karl's report was explicit, but contained very little of value. He had been talking with the people of the village about the various mysterious occurrences, but what he had heard were garbled, incoherent accounts. He met the gardener Till and invited him to drink. Fortunately Till had never seen Karl, for the young man's few visits to his mother had taken place after nightfall, and she herself always let him in and out.

He had quite a conversation with the gardener, chiefly about Mr. Erlach and his disappearance. But as far as he could see there was nothing of value in what he had heard.

"He didn't tell me anything new," concluded Karl. "The man was most interested in the doors that were locked from the inside, and in the three underscored words in the book. Oh, yes—and he mentioned the fact that the candle had spattered so and was surprised that it hadn't set anything on fire, because there was a heavy wind that night and the burning candle was near the open window. Why, what's the matter Mr. Müller? Mr. Hartmann I mean," said Karl, hastily.

Müller had jumped up from his chair and was pacing the room

with long strides. Back and forth he went two or three times, then stopped in front of the astonished Karl and asked: "It was the last window he spoke of? The window near which the table stood? This window was half opened, he said?"

"Yes, that was the window, but it wasn't half open."

"How was it?"

"The right pane of the outside window and the left one of the inside were open."

"Oh, that was it," murmured Müller and repeated once more: "Oh, that was it." A smile flashed across his quiet face and he walked through the room once again. Then he stopped in front of one of the windows and stood for a long time looking out on the dreary stretch of country beyond, over towards the old trees of the Laxenburg Avenue to where beyond them the pointed dark roof of the Green House rose amid the foliage. It stood there, quiet and defiant, as if daring the watcher to penetrate its secrets. And beyond it the sky was a colourless gray. Karl, further back in the room, stood looking at his employer with a growing awe and admiration. He was such a quiet, unassuming little man in mien and bearing and yet how quickly he could make himself the master of any situation. Karl was learning much in these days, and he was changing rapidly from the superficial pleasure-loving youth he had been.

Finally Müller turned back to the room, his face calm as ever. All trace of the excitement into which the mention of the window had thrown him, was gone. He went to the cupboard and took out a book. "Here's something to read," he said, handing it to Karl. "Did you bring in supplies for supper?"

"Yes, sir."

"Well, then, go out into your own room and make yourself comfortable. I shall be busy now for a while and then I'm going over to the house."

When Karl had left him, Müller sat down to another careful study of the official report of the first police visit to the Erlach house, also to a study of the ground plan of the mansion. Towards seven o'clock he joined the Plöhn family at supper and spent a pleasant evening with them.

"Will you take up your studies again tomorrow?" asked the Manager, when Hartmann finally rose to go.

"Oh, indeed I must," was the answer. "Because you see I ran away today. But I don't come to Vienna often and I always have so much to do when I do come."

"Well, the longer you stay with us the better we will like it," said Mrs. Plöhn.

Hartmann bent over her hand politely and then left the house. The next day he appeared in Bauer's office promptly at ten o'clock. He was anxious to learn about the bookkeeping of the factory, about the rates of wages and the method of payment. All this information was given him with a pedantic thoroughness which made him wonder more and more at what Plöhn had told him about Bauer's sentimental proclivities. The bookkeeper, thorough though he was, was quite satisfied with the intelligent interest shown by his listener. No one, except Karl Tonner, knew that this ardent student of brick-making had already passed several hours before the dawn in the Green House. Karl had stood at the window of the pavilion with an excellent field-glass and watched every moving thing that came within the range of his vision. Finally he saw his master coming from the direction of the Erlach property and breathed relieved. Müller seemed in a very good humour and asked for a cup of tea. It had been Hartmann's wish that his own servant should make the morning tea or coffee for both of them, in the pavilion, and Karl had proved himself quite a clever cook. It was a dainty tray before which Müller sat down early this morning. The detective was in an excellent humour and he did not seem to mind the fact that the eggs were a little harder than he usually liked them. Karl was quite upset over his carelessness in the cooking.

"Oh, never mind it," said Müller, "you see I'm taking the second one already." He put it in his egg-cup and was just about to strike the top with his knife. Suddenly he changed his mind, took up the egg again and asked: "Can you make an egg stand on its end?"

Karl Tonner was astonished. He was reckless enough himself, but he was struck dumb with admiration at the man who could joke about trifles while he knew himself to be at the mercy of an unusually clever criminal.

"Oh, yes," said the young man with a smile. "I can do that. It's easy enough. Just break the top of the shell and the egg will stand upright without any trouble."

"That's it exactly, my young friend," replied Müller merrily. "And you know also that Columbus was the first person to do this simple trick?"

"Yes."

"And do you know that that is why we speak about the 'egg of

Columbus' when we mean that a clever brain—a brain such as the man we are looking for must have—manages to accomplish the most apparently difficult feat with the simplest methods?"

"Yes, I've always understood that's what it meant."

"Well, my young friend, there are several sorts of Columbus eggs," laughed Müller, "and now you can give me another cup of tea. It's unusually good this morning."

CHAPTER 11

Müller Visits Rose Cottage

Several days passed. It was already the 28th of September and still no light had been brought into the darkness of the Erlach mystery. This at least was the opinion of the people of Inzersdorf as well as of Lieutenant Erlach and his friend Commissioner Lehr. But Karl, who saw Müller daily and hourly, felt that something of importance had been discovered. The veteran detective wore his armour vest every day, but in spite of the necessity for this precaution he seemed in the best of spirits. He spent more time than before in the brick factory and showed the greatest possible interest in everything connected with it. He had visited the cashier, Gebhart, in his office and had drawn out an invitation from the latter to accompany him to his private rooms, by means of a few casual remarks. As they passed through the halls on this occasion Gebhart pointed to another door with the words: "There's where my colleague Bauer lives." Müller did not need the explanation, for he had already seen the visiting card tacked on the door. Several of the bachelor officials and clerks of the factory were domiciled in one wing of the office building, and the wing itself was connected with the manager's dwelling house by a covered walk. Müller led the conversation around to the subject of the other clerks, with particular interest in Bauer.

Gebhart, as well as all others who came in contact with him, was obliged to admire Bauer's intelligence and capacity for work. But he too, shared the personal antipathy for the man that every one else felt. Even the villagers did not like him. And the jovial innkeeper confessed to Gebhart once that only a stern sense of the business advantage of it enabled him to be as cordial to Bauer as to his other patrons. His pretty little wife was open in her dislike of the "Hamburger," as the villagers called Bauer because of the fact that he had lived for several years in North Germany and was fond of using expressions and words of that locality.

She justified her feelings by the fact that Bauer added an inclination to run after any pretty woman to his other disagreeable qualities. That is, a woman counts such conduct on the part of a man as disagreeable usually only when the man is not attractive.

On his first visit to Gebhart's room the cashier showed him the bit of black cord which he had found there the day after the attack. It was a piece of black horsehair lariat, identical with the bit Müller had found twisted in the carving of Erlach's ebony bed.

Early one bright afternoon, the detective set out to pay his promised call on Dr. Maximoff. The owner of Rose Cottage had evidently seen him coming, for he stood on the threshold, his hands cordially outstretched in welcome. As they walked through the wide hall, little Sonya ran to meet them, for she had already developed a great fondness for Mr. Hartmann on her various visits to the Plöhn house. Maximoff introduced to his guest the dignified elderly lady who took charge of his household and his little girl, and praised her patience with him in spite of what he called his attacks of violent anger. Mrs. Schober smiled in appreciation of the doctor's self-accusation and assured Mr. Hartmann that one could not wish for a more agreeable employer. "Shall I send your tea up to your own room?" she asked.

"Please do," said Maximoff cheerily, running his arm through that of his guest. "I want you to see my sanctum, the room in which I have collected about me everything that gives me inspiration, that enables my soul to lift itself out of the prose of everyday existence."

"And yet our lives have driven such deep roots into this everyday existence that it gives them their chief colour," said Hartmann.

"Yes, you are right," replied the Russian, "and yet you are wrong too. One can carve out a life for oneself, alone, apart from the other, and it is this secret life that makes the other endurable."

"Papa, you're going to show Mr. Hartmann your rings, aren't you?" asked Sonya. "Mimi told me that he liked Aunt Anna's old jewellery so much. Didn't you?" she said, snuggling up to the guest with an air of childish importance.

"Yes, indeed I did, my dear little girl. And I want to see everything that is interesting and strange."

"All right, baby, we'll show Mr. Hartmann all our treasures," said the doctor. "But you run along now and help Mrs. Schober decorate the tea-table."

"Oh, you are expecting guests?"

"The very dearest guests who could come to me—and I include you among them. My betrothed is coming with her relatives."

"But hadn't I better go away?"

"Nonsense, you mustn't think of it for a moment! We have all grown so fond of you, and they will be as glad to see you here as they are to greet you in their own house. You have finished your work for the day, I know, and you must surely stay and be one of the party."

"Really I hadn't an idea that they were coming," continued Hartmann apologetically. "I had letters to write and they kindly sent my dinner for me out to my own room. I have not seen the ladies at all today and I saw Mr. Plöhn only for a moment."

"All the more reason why you should stay and see them now," replied Maximoff, pressing his guest's hand warmly, "and here—now you are about to enter my favourite room."

They stood on the threshold of a large apartment furnished in dark colours, but with great richness and dignity. Heavy, tall bookcases and cabinets in dark wood lined the walls. Behind the glass doors were rows of heavy tomes and a number of scientific instruments. What wall space was still left free was hung with costly rugs on which were placed rare and equally costly weapons of various countries. Between the two windows of the room stood an enormous flat-topped desk covered with books and papers.

"Really, this is delightful," said the guest as his eyes wandered about the attractive room. "I can indeed imagine that it is pleasant to work here and to forget the everyday worries. What a stunning cabinet! That is as handsome a late Empire piece as I have seen." Still speaking, Hartmann went forward to the corner where the round-front cabinet stood.

"Ah, there you see, Sonya—we don't need to show our friend the way!" laughed Maximoff. "He finds out our chiefest treasures at a glance."

"It *was* impolite of me, wasn't it," remarked Hartmann, pausing where he stood. "I ought to be punished. No, don't show me your rings now. I must learn to wait patiently—don't you think so, Sonya? one ought to learn to be patient?"

Sonya was anxious to lead him to the cabinet but he resisted and began the tour of the bookcases.

"You are particularly interested in the subject of mental alienation, I see," he said, as he read through the titles.

"That is my specialty," replied the doctor. "The human soul interests me far more than the human body."

"That's because your body is so healthy," said Hartmann with a smile. "If you knew what it was to be physically ill, you'd find the study of the body more interesting than you do now. However, my argument doesn't hold water. For your soul seems to me to be as healthy as your body. I have seldom met a man who impressed me as so strong and sane and well-proportioned in character as you are."

"You flatter me."

"Not at all. I am merely expressing my opinion. From our pleasant evenings in the Plöhn household I have learned to know you as a delightful conversationalist and a good card player. Now I see on your desk the fat manuscript of what is doubtless a scientific work. I know your fondness for flowers and that you supervise your own garden. Also that you are your little girl's teacher. I have heard of your charities from many of those whom you have helped hereabouts. You must let me tell you that I consider you a very remarkable man,—all that the highly cultivated civilized man *ought* to be, but is not, except in the most unusual cases."

"In the most unusual cases," repeated Maximoff, with a gaze out into space that seemed to forget the presence of his guest.

"Ah, I see you have Pitaval also—and a number more works on Criminal Jurisprudence. Are you particularly interested in that line of study too?"

"Why, yes, very much so," Maximoff nodded smiling. "Pitaval for instance, has given very important contributions on the subject of psychology. Every criminal case interests me because almost every one shows the lack of proportion in the mental make-up of most human beings. But here comes the samovar," he interrupted himself, "now for the lighter things of life. Do the honours, Sonya darling, and then run and help Mrs. Schober. Because if you don't, the flowers won't be nearly as prettily arranged."

The little girl busied herself about the tea-table, arranging the cups and saucers ready to hand, lit the lamp under the kettle, then gave her father a hearty kiss and ran out of the room.

"You are a happy man, indeed," said Maximoff's guest, looking after the charming child.

"Yes, yes, indeed! Is she not a treasure? And I *am* happy now. But there have been hours in my life when I cursed this existence, and such hours may come again," he sighed deeply.

"Now, that is your national melancholy again," said Müller sympathetically. "Is it anything you fear on Sonya's account?"

"Have you noticed anything particular about the child?"

"Only that she is unusually pretty."

"Did you not notice how bright her eyes are and how unnaturally brilliant her skin?"

"Well, what of that?"

"She is the image of her mother, in that as in other ways. Come, I will show you." He led the way into the next room and halted before a life-sized portrait, draped in crepe, of a beautiful woman of fragile, delicate appearance.

Müller looked at the portrait, then spoke, with a trembling in his voice: "Yes, yes, indeed, Sonya bids fair to be as beautiful as her mother was." To himself he thought: "Is the child as delicate also, and will she too die early?" And he understood the sadness in the eyes of the handsome man who stood looking up at the picture.

"As beautiful, yes, and as frail," murmured Maximoff, holding his hands to his eyes. Then he turned quickly and went out of the room, Müller following him more slowly. When he caught up with his host, the latter was already pouring out the tea.

"I don't think that I believe in the theory of heredity as strongly as you do," said the guest casually as he took his cup. "I believe that it is possible to work against the development of an inherited trait, either mental or physical, and sometimes even to exterminate it entirely."

"Do you really think so, dear friend?—do you really think so?" exclaimed the doctor warmly. His face flushed and his eyes gleamed. But the quiet poise of his guest seemed to calm him.

He drank his tea in silence for a few moments. Then he began again: "The book I am writing concerns itself with this very theory of heredity and I will confess to you that what you have just said is my own standpoint. I believe that one can fight inherited tendencies and destroy them—destroy them completely." Again the excitement mastered him. "We must destroy them in whatever way we can,—but it is easy enough—and therefore I don't believe in the power of heredity any more than you do. But you're not drinking your tea. Isn't it to your taste?"

Mr. Hartmann hastened to assure his host that the beverage was in every way satisfactory. He finished his cup and lit one of the tiny cigarettes that lay in a silver dish on the tray. Maximoff began to smoke also and started a new subject of conversation. With no attempt at transition he began to talk of the transmigration of souls. He handled this theme with brilliant originality. And his guest gained the impression that the eccentric Russian had occupied himself intensely with the subject and that he believed in the theory absolutely. The interesting metaphysical conversation was interrupted, however, by the entrance of the Plöhn family and the talk became lighter.

As the weather was so favourable, the company adjourned to the garden after having had their tea, and Mrs. Plöhn and the children led Mr. Hartmann about among the flower-beds, showing him the wonders that Maximoff had wrought since he became master of the property.

The doctor's garden was not very large but was so skilfully planned that it seemed much greater in size than it really was. Artistic groups of trees and shrubs were placed about in such a way as to show the smooth stretches of lawn to greater advantage, gravelled paths twisted in and out among the screening bushes, giving the impression that one might walk some distance before coming out into the open again. Mrs. Plöhn and Hartmann, the children dancing about them, followed one of these paths in its various windings, down towards the lower end of the garden. They passed a round stretch of lawn in the midst of which was a circle of carefully tended box, surrounding a small fir tree.

"There, Aunt Anna," said Sonya catching at Mrs. Plöhn's hand, "there's something new, and papa made it all himself without any help from the gardener. And he's done ever so many things in the conservatory without the gardener too. Anyway the gardener hasn't been here for some time."

"Then you don't have a gardener regularly for all this work?" asked Hartmann. Sonya explained that they did have a gardener formerly, but that he had been dismissed for disobedience during the month of August and that papa found he could get along just as well alone. Then the children led the party into the conservatories, where there was so much to see that they spent quite some time there.

Plöhn himself sat in a comfortable chair on the veranda reading the evening paper. Maximoff and his betrothed strolled up and down in front of the house, arm in arm. They were talking of the various alterations they should make in their home once they were married.

Suzanne Plöhn was an attractive, warm-hearted girl, but her nature was too thoroughly well-poised to be either sentimental or passionate. Her calmness made an excellent and wholesome foil for the brilliant, easily-excited character of the man beside her.

"You mustn't look at me like that, Sergius," she said gently, as she caught the hot glance of his dark eyes resting on her. "I am afraid of you when you look like that. I am afraid of you sometimes anyway—afraid of your passionate nature and—I know you'll laugh at me now—I am afraid of your tremendous physical strength."

"Oh, dearest—dearest," he murmured, drawing her to him in spite of her resistance.

"You mustn't do that, either," she pleaded.

"Not at all—never?" he whispered in her ear. She blushed, with an embarrassed smile.

"You foolish man," she said—"but now, anyway, you must walk beside me quietly and quite demurely."

"Are you really afraid of me?" he asked with a new tone of anxiety in his voice.

She nodded. "Yes, I am, sometimes. It made me shiver to see you break that heavy oak stick the other day. But I know that very strong men have to do that sort of thing occasionally to use up their excess of vigour."

"Well, then, what's the matter?"

"Oh, I don't mean that. But at the time the thought came over me: 'He could break *me* in two like that,' and I shuddered to my very heart—I don't know why. Now don't look so gloomy, dear Sergius. Don't I know how good and how faithful your heart is? Another woman might feel hurt to see that beautiful picture still hanging upstairs there. I like to stand and look at it, for to me it gives an added proof of your power of affection. I like to realize that you cannot and will not forget the woman who first won your heart."

"And it does not offend you—it does not hurt you?" he asked anxiously.

Suzanne shook her head. "We will share your heart as sisters, your dear dead love and I," she replied tenderly, stroking from his brow the furrow her last words had drawn there.

Then they joined the others and an hour later the guests left Rose Cottage. Before his departure Mr. Hartmann had given his solemn promise to return the following day and examine Maximoff's pride, his collection of antique rings.

When Müller retired to his pavilion that evening, he was convinced that Dr. Maximoff was the other of the originals of whom Plöhn had spoken. But the Russian was so much a finished man of the world that his originality was scarcely perceptible outside of his own little kingdom, the home that expressed his rich personality so well. Müller felt surprised again at the thought that this busy and versatile man would even take time to do the actual manual labour in his garden. He knew him also as a philanthropist of astonishing liberality. The Plöhns had told Hartmann, early in his visit, how generous Maximoff was to people of the village. He had built a lodging house and a library for them, and every day ten poor people were given dinners at his expense in the parish house. This afternoon, as they walked back to the manager's home, Plöhn told Hartmann that he had just heard, not from Maximoff himself, but from a friend who was physician in a Viennese hospital, that the Russian had given forty thousand crowns to endow two beds in the establishment. The only condition was that the name of the donator should not be mentioned.

"Of course, I wouldn't let him see that I knew anything about it, and you must promise to do the same." Hartmann promised readily that he would not betray the secret. The veteran detective had taken a great liking to Maximoff and his flattering words when they were alone that afternoon had been only the expression of his sincere admiration.

Next morning Müller spent several hours with Bauer, going over the works. The afternoon found him again in Rose Cottage. Some time was spent in the conservatories in admiration of the doctor's remarkable results in the culture of chrysanthemums, then host and guest went into the house, Sonya running beside them.

"Now you really must see my rings," said the Russian brightly. "Sonya dear, you'll look after the tea, won't you?"

The little girl ran out and the two men, arm in arm, crossed the study and stood before the handsome cabinet which had already attracted Müller's attention. Maximoff's manner was almost ceremonious as he, turned the key in the lock.

"What I have here is not only costly in material and workmanship," he said, "but it has its chief value in the association connected with each piece. Every one of my rings represents as it were a bit of world-history, for each one of them was the property of a person of importance in the history of the world."

While speaking he drew out a drawer of the cabinet. It contained four ebony boxes with glass tops. They were lined with dark blue velvet, and the rings lay resting on little knobs. There were about forty of them, a collection that was indeed of great value. Maximoff pulled up a chair for his guest with the words: "You must sit down and examine these at your ease to thoroughly appreciate them."

Müller settled back comfortably in the chair and examined each piece with great interest, while his host gave the necessary explanation. There was, for instance, a simply-worked golden circlet set with a roughly cut diamond of considerable size which had been worn by Peter the Great A heavy ring set with many pearls of value had once adorned the hand of Anne Boleyn. A peculiarly carved ring of darkened silver had been the property of Count Wallenstein. Maximoff could tell the story of each piece in his collection, and could tell it so well that his listener's enjoyment of the curiosities was enhanced doubly. When the last of the rings had been studied and admired, Maximoff laid the boxes carefully back in the drawer.

"I suppose of course you have documents to prove the truth of the history of this really remarkable collection?" asked Müller.

"Oh, yes, indeed," said the doctor eagerly. "I'll show them to you at once." He fairly tore open the next drawer and took out a large portfolio which lay in it. At the same moment Müller, looking at the open drawer, remarked: "Oh, I see you have all sorts of other beautiful things there. Miniatures too! That is another expensive fad."

"Are you interested in that sort of thing?"

"Very much."

"Then I'll show you what I have. It isn't very much, I've been collecting miniatures only about a year or so."

He took the case out of the drawer and held it so that his guest could look at the little pictures. There were only seven of them, but each one a masterpiece in its way. One of them seemed to interest Müller greatly. He stared at it as if hypnotized, while Maximoff drew out and sorted the papers in the portfolio. A stereotyped smile curved Müller's lips, but the smile did not go deeper than the surface. His heart seemed to stand still and the thoughts whirled through his brain in such a mad rush that he did not hear Maximoff's next remark.

Finally the detective realized that his host was speaking to him. "Why, you're quite lost in the study of my art treasures," said Maximoff with a little laugh. It was a bright and cheery little laugh, but a shiver, icy cold, ran down Müller's spine as he felt the other man's hand on his shoulder.

"Which is it that so absorbs you?" continued the Russian.

Müller rose slowly from his chair and pushed it back. He leaned lightly against the window frame, and his face was pale. But the eyes which met Maximoff's firmly were perfectly calm. And the tone of his voice was quiet and indifferent as he finally spoke.

123

"The Napoleon interests me the most, I think. I've never seen him painted just this way before."

"Yes, isn't it odd," replied Maximoff eagerly. "It isn't the great Emperor we see here, the mighty General, it's just a private individual who feels as cold as we would when the thermometer drops down to zero. The picture interested me because of what I call its *ironical* conception of the subject, and I procured it recently with considerable difficulty."

While the Russian was speaking he held the little picture before him and looked at it, his eyes full of merriment. Another phase of his surprise, scarcely less great than the first, filled the detective's mind. In spirit, he reviewed his visit to Miss Geiringer, and held again in his hand the picture of the Empress Josephine, undoubtedly the companion to this miniature of Napoleon. Then he heard Mrs. Tonner say again: "Mr. Erlach and I cleaned the picture of the Emperor two days before his disappearance." And again: "Doctor Maximoff was the last person to visit Mr. Erlach, he was in our house on the 3rd of September." And again Müller seemed to hear Till's report: "An insurance agent came to the place on the 6th of September but he did not enter the house."

Like succeeding flashes of lightning these sentences shot through the detective's head, bound together as it were by the bits of black cord and the enormous footprints that he had seen in the Erlach garden—footprints which he had seen later in front of the wall surrounding the Plöhn pavilion, a proof that the man with the black cord had followed him there and knew who he was.

And now he was here in the house of the most highly respected man in the neighbourhood, stood opposite this cultivated and greathearted man, and saw him smiling at the little picture of Napoleon, the picture which, as he said, he had "recently procured with considerable difficulty"—the picture which was in Erlach's possession up to two days before his disappearance, after which time no visitor had entered his house. Had Maximoff been there once more, without the knowledge of Mrs. Tonner or the Tills? And had he persuaded the old gentleman to sell him the picture?

But Müller remembered that Maximoff himself had once mentioned that his last meeting with Erlach took place in the very first days of September, the afternoon that he had played chess in the Green House. This agreed with what Mrs. Tonner had said—but might it not have been a lie after all?

All these thoughts circled madly through Müller's head while he stood looking at the smiling Russian. "What was the difficulty of which the other spoke? There are various ways of procuring a treasured masterpiece," he asked himself. His teeth set firmly and a pitiless gleam rose in his eyes, while his hand involuntarily found its way to the pocket of his coat, in the depths of which was his little revolver.

When a man finds himself unexpectedly in the lion's den, the feel of a weapon in his hand is very comforting. But was he in any danger here, here as the guest of this delightfully amiable and quite harmlessly cordial Maximoff?

It did not seem possible to the veteran detective. Still, every single move in this series of crimes had been carried out with a most unusual and unheard-of audacity, carried out in a way that could only have been done by a most unusual type of criminal.

Müller found himself suddenly with a new clue, a new trail opening before him. A false one, perhaps? But however that might be, it was his duty to follow it up, unless he could prove that there was an identical miniature of Napoleon still in the cabinet in Erlach's study. If the picture was not in its place there, then he would have to follow up this new clue. In the course of his long and rich experience he had learned that however utterly improbable a thing may seem, it may yet be a fact.

The detective breathed deeply and a peculiar gleam came into his eyes, a strange smile moved his lips. The stately, handsome host did not seem to notice it. His great dark eyes still rested merrily on the little picture of the shivering Emperor, as he delicately breathed into the air rings of smoke from his tiny cigarette.

"Do you see this, Mr. Hartmann?" he said, cheerily. "The painter has even taken the liberty of putting a tiny touch of red on the Imperial nose." He handed the picture to his guest.

"Yes, really. So it is," answered the other laughing, and added: "You said just now that you had considerable difficulty in obtaining possession of this picture. What was the trouble?"

Müller smiled in harmless friendliness as he asked the question. Not a line of his face, not a quiver in his voice, betrayed the tenseness that held him for the last few moments.

Maximoff was equally calm. In his usual witty manner he began to tell the story of how he had found the miniature in the shop of an antiquary in Vienna, of how he had gone there again and again, to try and buy just this one piece out of a Napoleon collection which the man wanted to sell all together. It had cost Maximoff, so he said, many journeys and considerable money until he finally managed to get possession of this most interesting piece of the entire collection. The Russian did not spare a joke at the expense of his own obstinacy and his awakening collector's mania. His story was easily and naturally told, but when it came to an end Müller noticed that Maximoff had not mentioned the name or the address of the antiquary in question.

At this moment a young serving maid entered with a card on a silver tray. The girl was evidently untrained as yet, for she left the door open behind her and Müller could see a man in the hall outside. A single glance at this visitor and the detective turned to the window, almost burying himself in the heavy curtains that hung there. The gleam in his eye was perceptibly heightened.

He kept his gaze on Maximoff, who, as he read the name on the card, lost his laughing indifference. His face flushed in anger, a deep fold ploughed itself between his brows and his eyes shot fire. He was evidently in the grip of one of the sudden rages of which he himself had spoken.

"You idiot! Don't you know enough to shut the door?" he cried to the girl and then walked quickly to the now entering visitor. "You know your business! Nobody's safe from you, I suppose?"

The stranger, an elegantly dressed gentleman, seemed to be somewhat offended at this reception, for his voice was sharp as he answered: "Dr. Maximoff, I should indeed know very little about my business if it were not possible for me to follow up anyone who has once honoured me with his confidence and his patronage. Why, I am—"

He did not get any further, for on entering the room he had seen the figure of a man in the shadow of the heavy plush curtains at the window. He bowed lightly to this scarcely seen person and Maximoff also turned to the window.

"My dear Mr. Hartmann," said the doctor, "pray excuse me. I'm obliged to talk to this gentleman a few moments, but I will soon return to you."

"You'd better lock up your treasures first," replied Hartmann, from behind the handkerchief which he held to his face, as he was struggling with a fit of coughing. Maximoff motioned the stranger to enter the neighbouring room and shut the door behind him.

"These people are so aggressive," he said indignantly to Müller. "I went to see this man the other day to talk about some changes I want made in my house, a new addition I am desirous of building, and now he comes here without being sent for."

"Well, I'll be off then," said Müller. "For as long as the man is here you might as well have your talk with him without being hurried."

"Are you really going?"

"Yes, I must. But if you permit it I will come soon again."

"Permit it? Why, I shall be delighted to see you here, delighted! I confess that I'm growing very fond of you."

"Is that really true?"

"Haven't you noticed that I seem to enjoy your company?"

"At least you have not avoided me, but seemed rather to seek me out."

"Well, then?"

"Then I may be equally frank? and tell you that I find myself taking a great liking to you."

"Why do you speak so low?"

"It isn't necessary that your architect should know everything, is it? But now you must go to him. Good afternoon, doctor. We will meet soon again, I hope."

A few moments later Müller was outside, walking along the dreary highroad. He looked at his watch, then changed his direction suddenly and walked rapidly towards the little railway station. He was just in time to spring into a train for Vienna. He found himself alone in the compartment.

"What was that man doing there?" he asked half aloud. Then he burst out into a hearty laugh. "Did he send for him to spy on the dwellers in the pavilion?"

But his sudden merriment did not last long. It gave way to the graver thoughts that absorbed him completely, that dazed him with their swing and rush.

"It is absolutely mysterious—incomprehensible—if it is *he,* why am I still alive? And if it is not he, why these two lies today? For I know that this Napoleon miniature is the one that belonged to Erlach. The manner of painting, even the odd frame might be repeated on two pictures. But the peculiar pattern of the paper that is pasted over the back of this little masterpiece and of the picture of Josephine, could hardly be repeated in a copy. Well, I'll know before nightfall whether there is a picture of Napoleon in Erlach's cabinet. But I very much fear that Maximoff's story of how he got the picture was as much a lie as his assertion that his visitor was an architect. I am greatly afraid of it," thought the veteran detective, "for I really and truly had begun to like the man."

In the city Müller went to his own home first. An hour and a half later he entered the office of a well-known private detective agency.

He was ushered into a cosily-furnished little room, hardly larger than a good-sized closet. All the reception rooms of the establishment were on this order. For the customers who came here desired secrecy beyond everything else. Müller was well known to the attendants and was shown into the little room which adjoined the manager's private office.

"The manager may be here any moment," said the attendant who showed him in. "Is there anything I can do for you until he comes?"

"No, thank you," said Müller. "I don't mind being alone as I have a great deal to think over."

"There, I think he's in there now," said the attendant, listening towards the door of the private office. Müller rose and knocked at this door. As he passed a long mirror to reach it, he smiled at the reflection he saw there, the reflection of his own slender figure. For he had left all that made up Mr. Hartmann in his own home.

"Ah, good afternoon, my dear Mr. Müller," cried Manager Greng, as Müller entered the room.

Greng was engaged in hanging up his overcoat on a hat rack. He stopped just where he was, flung the coat over his arm, and came forward with his free hand outstretched. *"Deus ex machina,"* he exclaimed, evidently greatly pleased to see the old detective.

"And why?" asked Müller with a cheery laugh, as the other led him to a soft corner of the sofa and piled up the cushions invitingly. "My—my! you're treating me as if I were Her Royal Highness, who was here on the 24th," he continued, leaning back in the corner.

Greng walked over to the hat tree, hung up his coat and now came back hastily. "What do you know about the Princess?" he asked in astonishment, not altogether pleased.

Müller pointed to the cigar box that stood on the table and remarked with a smile: "Why don't you say as usual, 'Help yourself, old man'?"

"Sure, help yourself, old man." Greng pushed the box over to Müller. "But then you'll answer my question, won't you?"

Greng took a seat, too, and his momentary displeasure was soon gone. In fact he was glad that "this Müller" seemed to know everything, for the last two hours Müller had been the principal figure in a scheme of his. The veteran detective took so much time to light his cigar that Greng decided it were better not to say anything about the Princess and to talk to Müller about his own scheme. This was the gist of his first remark.

"As you like," replied the other. "Well, then, what sort of a scheme is it that you have woven around my worthy personality?"

Greng rose, went over to a cupboard and brought out a bottle of brandy and two glasses. "We'll drink a glass to your very good health first," he said.

"My health *is* excellent just at present, thank you," answered Müller.

"I'm very glad to hear it."

"Why, particularly?"

"First for your sake and then for my own."

"Nothing the matter with this brandy," said the guest as he sipped it slowly. "But what does it matter to you how I am feeling?"

"It awakens a hope."

"What hope?"

Greng looked at his guest carefully. "You certainly look fine."

"Do you think so?"

"Yes, I do. I notice the difference possibly, because it's two years since I saw you last."

"Yes, that was in Pegli, wasn't it? It was certainly awfully good of you to come over from Genoa just to see me."

"It was quite natural. I was living in hopes then, too."

"Concerning me? You didn't say anything about it."

"No. I didn't dare mention the subject"

"Mercy! I had no idea you were so shy."

"Well, you see, when one man wants to suggest a partnership to another and the other begins the conversation by saying that he never intends to work again—it doesn't look very hopeful."

"I was having so much trouble with my liver just then."

"Is it all right now? You certainly look it. And you certainly look very enterprising today."

"I not only *look* enterprising, but just at present I feel very much so."

"And you feel like working again?" Greng bent forward eagerly.

"Yes, I feel quite like working again. That's the reason I'm here today."

"Oh, that's fine! Then I may ask you something?"

"Certainly, what is it?"

"Would you be ready for a journey?"

"Out of the country?"

"To Russia."

Müller drank his second glass of brandy slowly and carefully, weighing each drop of the amber liquid on his tongue as if he hadn't another thought in the world. The younger man waited until his impatience got the better of him. "Well, my dear Müller, do answer?"

"To Russia, you say?" remarked the old detective indifferently. "And what am I to do there?"

Greng shrugged his shoulders and answered with a slight embarrassment: "I don't know."

"You *don't know?*"

"No. My client is very distrustful."

"But he must have confided in you to *some* extent."

"He has told me only that he wants an independent, preferably unmarried, highly intelligent and discreet detective to go on a journey to Russia with him."

"Is that all? And you're to find this treasure for him?"

"Yes, that's it."

"He came here about it? And you haven't let him get out of your sight since then, have you?"

"Müller! What do you know about it?"

"I know that you were in Dr. Maximoff's house this afternoon."

"Well, that beats all!"

" 'You know your business! No one is safe from you, I suppose.' These were the words with which he welcomed you."

"The devil! Now how the mischief did you know that? Are you omnipresent?"

"No. I'm only in one place at one time. But the place I happened to be at that time was in the window of the study at Rose Cottage."

"Oh, then you were the man who stood there?"

"You have hit it exactly."

"Incredible! Arid yet I don't know, it's not so surprising. I had to tell the Russian that I hadn't the sort of a man he wanted at liberty just now and that he might have to wait some little time before I could send him the right person. So I suppose he may have heard of you and sent for you himself. That explains his anger at my coming. If he needed me he wouldn't have considered it an intrusion. Still I don't know then, why he should have lied to me? Why didn't he tell me that he had the man he wanted instead of insisting that I was to find someone right away? That's what I don't understand."

"But I understand it."

"Then do tell me."

"Dr. Maximoff does not know that I am a detective and he must not know it for some time yet," said Müller, believing in his heart that what he had just said was a lie. "So you see he couldn't very well engage me for this journey, and he had to trust to you further."

"Oh, that's it, is it? Have you been friends with him for some time?"

"For several weeks now. I'm rather surprised that he should not have spoken of this journey to anybody."

"Would you be in a position to know if he did speak of it?"

"Certainly. I see him very often in the presence of his best friends in that neighbourhood."

"And you hadn't a suspicion that there was a secret in this man's life? There must be, judging from what he demands of me."

"No. I hadn't the faintest suspicion of it until today," answered Müller truthfully. Then he added: "There are secrets—*political* secrets in the lives of most Russians who live outside their own country. I suppose this is another one of the same kind."

"Probably. Anyway, he pays very well. He has promised me an unusually large commission for finding the man he wants. And the salary the latter will earn will be equally munificent. So I thought of you, Müller."

"That was kind of you. But you know that I haven't worked merely for money for some time now."

"Pardon me, that wasn't what I meant. I had thought of you, for it struck me that the case promised to be interesting."

"Interesting politically, probably—but I'm not interested in politics. No, I'm afraid you can't depend upon me here. I don't want to enter Maximoff's service and thus lose him as a friend."

"Oh, confound it!" complained Greng, "and I thought it was my special good fortune that brought you to me today. Because to be honest with you, if you don't want to do it I'll have to lose the good job."

"Oh, no, you won't. You can take this case."

"My dear Müller! What do you mean?"

"Now don't get excited. You'll get your commission and save the reputation of your house. I have a young friend, his name is George Münzer, who I think is just the man. I will be responsible for him and you can recommend him to Maximoff without fear."

"George Münzer? The name is quite new to me," said Greng.

"Not to me," thought Müller, "for I had an uncle by that name." Then he said aloud: "There was a time, you know, when the name of Napoleon Bonaparte was new to most people. If I say that I'll be responsible for this young man, you needn't fear recommending him to anybody."

"Oh, certainly—certainly," said Greng hastily. "When can you send him to me?"

"In the course of the next two or three days. I think he is in Vienna now and at liberty."

"Not for two or three days? Oh, dear!"

"What's the matter now? Are you in such a hurry?"

"I'm not, but the Russian seems to be. By what he says, he'd like to start the man off tomorrow."

"Oh, I don't believe a day or two will make such a difference." Müller rose slowly from his chair and continued: "Well, for your sake, I'll see if I can't find Münzer today. If he is free you will have word by tomorrow morning."

"Oh, thank you ever so much. That's really nice of you." Greng shook Müller's hand warmly. But not until the latter had taken up his hat did it occur to the manager of the establishment to inquire the reason for his guest's coming to him.

"Why, you see," replied Müller with a show of candour. "I was greatly interested in knowing what you and Maximoff had to do with one another. That's the only reason I came."

Then Müller left the office after another hearty handshake with the man from whom he had easily learned something which might be of value to him. He was very glad now to realize that Greng had not recognized the change in his figure, or had not noticed that Maximoff had addressed him by a strange name. For otherwise, the really very clever manager of the private detective agency, who knew his business although he was in some respects a little too credulous, might have noticed that Müller was playing a part out in Inzersdorf. Quite satisfied with the result of his visit to the agency, the veteran detective stepped into a printer's shop, ordered some visiting cards and sat down to wait for them. The cards were printed with the name: George Münzer.

Müller stayed in his own house only long enough to return to the outer contour and the apparel of Mr. Hartmann. His servant Conrad mounted the box of the carriage beside the coachman and drove out with him. The stars were already showing clear in the sky when they reached the secluded spot on the Black Moor where Müller usually let his carriage wait while he visited the Erlach house. He carried the keys with him in his pocket so as to be ready to go there whenever necessity required. Once in Erlach's study he lit a candle and searched carefully in every corner of the cabinet where Erlach kept his curiosities. The miniature of Napoleon was not there, nor was it anywhere else in the room. When Müller was quite sure of this fact, he pressed his hands to his forehead a moment, and sighed deeply. Then he went out, leaving the Green House to its undisturbed quiet again.

Conrad had been doing sentry duty at the garden gate and reported that no one had passed anywhere within the range of his vision. Müller sent him back to the carriage with orders for the coachman to drive further up the street towards the brick factory. He himself walked towards the Plöhn house and let himself in unseen at the garden gate. Karl was waiting for him anxiously in the pavilion.

"Shall I get supper ready for you?" he asked. "It's nearly ten o'clock. I've had mine already."

"No, my dear Tonner. I'll fix what I need for myself later. I want you now to listen carefully to what I have to say to you."

"Yes sir."

"How many times do you think that Dr. Maximoff has seen you? Think it over carefully."

Karl pondered a minute. "Not more than three times at most," he said decidedly.

"Did he ever speak to you?"

"No. And I don't believe he really ever saw me. The doctor is a little bit haughty. I don't think a servant really exists for him."

"Possibly. I never noticed it myself."

"I felt it, sir."

"All the better then. For then he has never noticed you particularly. That's a very becoming beard you're wearing. Thus far I've had no objection to it but now I'm afraid it's in the way."

"I'll have it shaved off, sir," replied Karl willingly.

Müller nodded. "Yes, have it taken off before eleven o'clock tomorrow morning."

"It'll be gone by that time, sir."

"Here are three hundred crowns. Now let me see, you've been wearing a gray suit here, haven't you?—Now you go and buy yourself a dark blue or a black suit and a heavy winter overcoat. Also get anything else you may think you would need for a journey to Russia. It must all be done before eleven o'clock tomorrow."

133

"You can depend upon me, sir."

"Then from eleven o'clock on you must stay at home."

"Here?"

"No, in my house in the city. We'll dine there tomorrow noon and then I'll explain everything to you. Here are your visiting cards. You will need to use two of them tomorrow, so don't lose them and don't forget what your name is."

Karl threw a glance at the little pasteboards. "Then my name is George Münzer?"

"Yes, you are George Münzer, a private detective by profession. I'll tell you all the rest tomorrow. And now get ready to go back to town. You will find my carriage waiting for you by the railroad bridge. Good night, George Münzer."

"Good night, Mr. Hartmann."

Ten minutes later Müller heard a wagon driving slowly past the garden wall, the noise of the wheels dying away in the distance. He stood at the window for some time. He knew there was no danger in doing so, for the room behind him was in darkness. While his eyes wandered up to the gleaming star-points in the blackness of the space above, his mind went over in review all he had experienced that eventful afternoon and evening.

"No," he murmured half aloud. "There is no picture of Napoleon in Erlach's cabinet." Then after a little while he added, with a deep sigh: "And this Maximoff is such a really delightful and sympathetic personality."

CHAPTER 12

The Embarrassment of Bauer

Next day the ladies Plöhn found occasion for one of those dissertations on the shortcomings of servants so dear to the feminine heart. Mr. Hartmann told them that he had been obliged to dismiss his young valet without notice, because of insubordination and impertinence. "I lost my patience and told him to get out of my sight at once," reported the indignant landowner, his soft heart reproaching him all the while for the calumny he was obliged to heap on the head of his faithful Karl.

Müller reached his own house in the city exactly at eleven o'clock. He was greeted by his former housekeeper, whom he had recalled as there was now no further reason for secrecy as far as Mrs. Tonner was concerned. The latter seemed so disappointed at the change in the household that the soft hearted Müller hastened to reassure her. He told her that his home was hers until she could get another good position, or until Karl was able to make a home for himself and his mother. "Is he able to do anything for himself yet?" asked the anxious mother timidly. "It is your kindness alone that gives him the opportunity to be honest at least."

Müller shook his head. "It's not such very great kindness on my part. I need your son, and he is proving himself very useful to me. You need have no anxiety about him, if you have no objection to his following my profession. He may do well at it, if he makes good in this detective work I am now testing him with."

"Why should I have any objection to it?"

"There are people who do not think highly of the profession."

"I am not one of them," replied Mrs. Tonner warmly. "How could I be, now that I know you and know what sort of a man you are. It isn't the work that makes the man, but the man that makes or mars the profession he adopts. If Karl should become ever so little like you I will be proud of him—more proud of him than I thought possible—of late years."

"Has he told you that he is going to Russia?" asked Müller, changing the subject.

Mrs. Tonner shook her head. "That was wise of him," continued Müller in a tone of approval. "In our profession a man must say as little as possible even to those who are nearest to him. But there is no harm in your knowing where he is going. If he is away longer than now planned, it will be perfectly safe for him to write you if you wish it."

"It shall be just as you think best," said Mrs. Tonner calmly.

Müller gave her a slip of paper with a few lines written on it. "In case Karl is not here at the time, I want you to send this telegram to me as soon as you receive one which I will send you. My message will be a perfectly indifferent one, let us say, something about buying flowers for me. As soon as it comes, get this off at once. And now I want to talk to Karl. Has he come home yet?"

"Yes. He came in half an hour ago. Now I understand why he had all that shopping to do."

"He had to get ready for his trip. Please have dinner served at half-past twelve and order the carriage for one o'clock."

Müller nodded to Mrs. Tonner, and went upstairs to the little room he had assigned to Karl. The door was half open, and the young man sat by the window reading. He was so absorbed in his book that he did not hear Müller's entrance, nor the closing of the door. The detective smiled as if pleased at his protégé's power of concentration, and spoke gently. "George Münzer," was all he said.

Karl started, and sprang up from his chair, "Oh, Mr. Müller, I didn't hear you come in!"

"Well, I'm glad to see you know your new name when you hear it," replied Müller with a glance at the book in Karl's hands. "That's right, you know how to go about it, I see," he continued. For the book was the familiar red-covered Baedeker, with the word "Russia" in gold letters on the cover. Inside the book, however, covering the open pages was a sheet of white paper on which was written, many dozen times, the name, "George Münzer."

Karl stood blushing in embarrassment, still holding his lead pencil. "Wasn't it. foolish of me?" he asked.

"Not at all. It was a very good exercise for you, and the best thing you could have done. The most important thing for you the first few days will be to make no slip as to your name, and you can't be too familiar with it. Now sit down, and I will give you your instructions."

The two men sat in earnest consultation until dinner time, Müller talking and Karl listening carefully, answering only now and then to show that he understood. As they went down to the dining-room Karl's cheeks were flushed and his eyes shone with pleasurable excitement. The meal passed quietly and at one o'clock they entered the carriage and drove to Greng's agency. The manager of the establishment was already waiting for them in his inner office, as Müller had announced their coming by messenger.

Greng studied the young stranger carefully, and could find no fault in his outer appearance at least. This tall clean-shaven good-looking young man, with his slender, graceful figure and his well-cut, simple dark suit looked more like a young Englishman of leisure than anything else, and Greng was greatly pleased with Müller's protégé. The modest and unassuming, but thoroughly well-poised manners of the young man pleased him also. George Münzer said little during the interview, and Müller, who was present, remained strictly impartial. Greng was anxious to have Münzer go to see Maximoff at once, but the new young detective refused to do so. It was finally arranged that the introduction to Greng's wealthy client should take place on the following day, at an hour determined by Münzer.

****

Mr. Hartmann spent the rest of the afternoon, after his return to Inzersdorf, in the society of the Plöhn family. He strolled over to the house just as the twilight had fallen, and found his hosts in the cosy sitting-room. Maximoff was there also, seated at the piano, accompanying Suzanne's singing. The Russian was an excellent pianist, and a particularly skilful accompanist. With delicate understanding of every shading of the mood of the song, his playing melted into the voice, lifting it into clearer prominence, giving it a background of gentle-hued harmonies. He was playing without notes, improvising from time to time, letting his soul speak in the soft flow of harmony his fingers awoke from the ivory keys. His great dark eyes with their glance of gentle melancholy, that hung like a veil of mystery over the velvet-soft depths, were raised in tender affection to the sweet calm face of the girl who stood beside him. Her eyes answered his, as she looked down at him. She too had no notes, singing free from memory.

She sang for him alone. The quiet little group that sat beyond the radius of light thrown by the tall lamp near the piano had been forgotten by the man and woman whose souls met in the consciousness of one another's nearness, in the harmonies that floated around them like a clinging screen, shutting them in a delicious solitude.

Suzanne's slender figure in her pale coloured gown swayed gently as she sang. The lamp gleamed on her fair hair and delicate skin, surrounding her head like an aureole. The simple Scotch ballad that she sang seemed to her an expression of her own happiness as she looked down at this handsome gifted man, this man with the great heart and the wonderful brain, who had yet chosen her for his beloved, although she was but a simple country girl. The glow of her feeling illumined her wrapt face as she sang the simple tale of the prince who plucked a floweret from the hedgerow, to wear next his heart, beating with his heartbeats, happy in his love. What though the floweret was happy but for a brief hour, to wither then and die! Happier still was she than if left on her bush, to blossom free in wind and sunshine. Better a moment's brief joy than a life of loveless security!

The gentle reproachful sadness of the old ballad melted away in the happiness that shown in Suzanne's eyes and curved her pure lips. When her eyes met those of her beloved there was no room in her soul for aught but the joy of being his.

Müller sat back in the shade, watching the couple at the piano. His busy brain twisted and turned a thousand possibilities in the crucible of his highly trained intelligence, sharpened to keenness by rich experience. All the while an undercurrent of suppressed emotion welled up from his heart, keeping up a running commentary of doubt to all the suggestions offered by the brain. "It can't be true ... it simply can't be true," he thought. "I'm off on a false trail again, and it's not for the first time either. There'll be some reasonable explanation as to the Napoleon portrait ... I know there will. If there is any secret in this man's life, it has something to do with politics, I know."

Again he lost himself in the study of Maximoff's features. The Russian's handsome face, with its clear colourless skin framed in curly dark hair, wore an expression of calm content. It was a content back of which the warm blood and vitality of the man were beating, there was nothing ox-like in the easy repose of the face. But it was the face of a man who was at peace with himself and the world, for this hour at least. His hands too, drew Müller's eyes to them, slender white hands which yet, even in their easy movement over the ivory keys, showed complete muscular control and great strength. They seemed to suit the man's fine figure with the broad shoulders and slender hips, and to complete the picture of virile manhood at its very finest in the prime of early maturity.

The veteran detective, with his deep knowledge of the world and the human heart, wondered that there was not more passion in the grave happiness in Suzanne's eyes. It must be, he thought, that there is no place for sensual passion in her clear soul, or surely this man would be capable of awakening it.

A slight movement beside him made him turn and he saw that Bauer had slipped in and taken the chair to his left. With his mind still full of the charm and strength of the Russian, Müller noticed as never before the utter lack of attraction in this other man. Here too were height and evident strength in a human frame, but where in the one case all was grace and easy elasticity, in the other the strength took the shape of awkward bulk. Maximoff had never been more fascinating, more brilliant than he was this evening. In the radiance which seemed to go out from him the ugliness of the unfortunate bookkeeper was thrown into greater prominence. Bauer sat hunched together on his chair, evidently not listening to the music, but absorbed in his own thoughts. They were not pleasant thoughts, for his hands twitched nervously, he bit at his lips and swallowed hard every now and then. The detective looked at him more carefully. He knew that this man had been acquainted with Erlach and had been inside the Green House more than once.

Mrs. Tonner had told Müller that during the two years of her service there Bauer visited her employer about ten or a dozen times. Like all the others who spoke about the bookkeeper, she was willing to acknowledge that the man seemed to be a faithful worker, a capable business man, reserved and unobtrusive, but—there was always a "but" when people spoke of Bauer. They seemed to distrust some secret behind his quiet. No one had confidence in him nor liking for him. The men servants complained of his exacting haughtiness, the women were afraid of him, as he evinced a desire to become aggressive in his attentions whenever he was sure that he would not be found out.

The ladies of the Plöhn family, even the manager's wife, who was anxious always to be just to every one, made no pretence of liking Bauer. Mrs. Plöhn was always the cordial hostess to her husband's employees, but Müller saw that it took an effort sometimes for her to overlook Bauer's unpleasant manners. Suzanne was more outspoken and frankly said that it was not so much the man's lack of good looks that bothered her, but the fact that, as she expressed it,

"there's a certain type of ugliness which comes only from inward vulgarity."

Müller remembered all these things now, for he knew that it was worth while giving a certain amount of attention to the intuition of cultivated fine-minded women. He had been watching the book-keeper lately and had won the man's confidence sufficiently to draw out an invitation to visit him in his room. Here he gained still more the impression of the man's pettiness and meanness, "vulgarity" as Suzanne called it But he realized also that behind this vulgarity there was not enough bigness of heart or soul to make possible the commission of such crimes as had been perpetrated by the Unknown with the black cord. By this time Müller had become convinced that Bauer was not this Unknown, although he was not quite sure that the bookkeeper might not in some way have been connected with the occurrences in the Green House. For there was something on this man's mind, Müller saw that. And a little incident that occurred on this very evening increased his suspicion, and reawoke his interest in the bookkeeper.

During the singing Mr. Plöhn, who had been in one of the other rooms, came to the door and beckoned his wife to him. The couple passed through the next room, into the drawing-room and a subdued sound of voices was heard from there. Müller recognized a strange voice—a man's. They spoke softly, too softly at least to hear at that distance and through the music the words that were said. With a curiosity which was one of his unpleasant qualities Bauer leaned forward as if anxious to see who the stranger was. Suddenly he turned pale, bit his lips nervously and arose from his chair. He took a step or two towards the door between the rooms, then turned in the direction of the hall door. Here he halted for a moment and came up to Müller.

"Mr. Hartmann, will you please make my excuses?" he said hastily. "I have a very bad headache and think I'd better not wait for supper."

"Certainly. I'll tell Mr. and Mrs. Plöhn you're not feeling well," Müller replied, taking the hand the other held out to him. Bauer's hand was cold and moist and trembled perceptibly. "You certainly do look wretched," continued Müller. "Why, you are trembling all over."

"I—I don't feel well—I had better go to my room," murmured Bauer.

The man was quite upset and Müller followed him closely with his eye. The bookkeeper reached the door in a few long strides and closed it gently behind him. Scarcely was the door fully shut before Müller stood beside it.

The two at the piano were so absorbed in their music and in one another, that they paid no attention to what was going on behind them. And even if they had, there would have been nothing particularly noticeable in the fact that Bauer left the room because he was not feeling well and that Hartmann should have followed him in case he needed help. But the latter did not leave the room at once. He stood at the door for some few minutes, then turned the knob very softly. He opened the door quickly and looked out into the hall.

He saw what he was expecting to see. Ferdinand Bauer stood close to the drawing room door listening at the crack. When Müller opened the door of the music room, the sound of the singing came out into the hall so much louder that Bauer started and looked around. Müller closed the door, shutting off the sound, and walked down the hall. Bauer stood waiting for him with an evil gleam in his eye. "I—I was dizzy," he said sharply.

"Is there anything I can do for you? Can I assist you to your room?" asked Mr. Hartmann with a tone of friendly sympathy. "Just think how embarrassing if this door should suddenly open while you were leaning against it. You wouldn't like to tumble into the drawing room like that."

"These doors open to the outside," remarked the other in the same sharp tone. Then he turned without another word and walked on towards the covered passageway which led from the main house to the office building.

"Miss Suzanne is right," thought Müller. "It *is* inner vulgarity that makes this man so unpleasant and has given him this particular type of ugliness. Yes, a man of that kind might easily be led into committing a crime. But this man seems to me to be too petty for the series of crimes that I am following up here. Or—I have been mistaken before in my life, may he not be deeper than I think? They call me infallible, but the world doesn't realize how many mistakes I have made, how many failures I have to my record. They see only my victories. I must be careful here and not go ahead too fast. If this man has not the brain to have planned these crimes, might he not have been the instrument used by another? The only thing here is that there was no robbery committed in the most of these cases,— and I do not think that this man would become a criminal without some pecuniary advantage to himself. Or is this only another mistake of mine? Can a soul like his hate enough to murder—or murder for the joy of it?—I saw him kick an unoffending dog one day. And yet he is a coward, as was shown by his action just now. Whoever it is inside there, frightened him so that he fairly ran away,—for the strides he took could almost be called running."

Here Müller's thoughts came to a standstill again and went off in another direction. Again he saw himself in the Erlach house in the dead of night and saw the tall figure running away with long strides that carried it into the darkness with astonishing rapidity.— He *must* find out what it was, who it was, that had so frightened Bauer just now.

He returned to the music room just as Suzanne was gathering up the loose sheets that lay on the piano. Maximoff whirled round on the piano stool and said laughingly: "Our music has driven you all away, hasn't it? You at least have had the courage to come back."

Hartmann laughed in answer to the joke but his mind was on the drawing room behind him. He walked casually through the music room to where he could see the door. But this did him no good, for the only person within his range of vision now was Plöhn himself who stood leaning against a table, smoking. He could catch a glimpse of Mrs. Plöhn's light dress but that was all. He had just made up his mind to go into the drawing room even without being asked, when he heard Suzanne say: "We seem to have a caller." At the same moment there was a sound of chairs being shoved back in the drawing room and Mrs. Plöhn came forward through the intervening apartment. At her side was a cheery-faced, very young lieutenant in the uniform of an Infantry regiment. Suzanne gave an exclamation of pleasure and walked forward to meet the stranger.

"Why, if it isn't Cousin Fritz," she exclaimed brightly. "And how nice we look in our new uniform! I suppose you've been up to some mischief and have been sent to Vienna to be punished, eh?"

The young man drew himself up for a formal salute as he answered with mock gravity: "Quite right, fair cousin. I've been in Vienna since the 20th of the month, sentenced to attend the coming carnival!"

"Thinking of pleasure as usual," continued Suzanne with a merry laugh. "But you haven't met my betrothed yet. Sergius, permit me to present to you my cousin, this extremely undignified Lieutenant of Imperial Infantry, Fritz von Seilern—Lieutenant von Seilern—Dr. Maximoff."

The gentlemen shook hands and then Mrs. Plöhn introduced the young officer to Hartmann. The manager asked where Bauer was and Hartmann gave the latter's excuses for his absence. A few moments later, supper was announced.

Mr. Hartmann-Müller could not imagine what it was in the appearance of the harmless young warrior that had so upset Bauer. Apparently absorbed in the enjoyment of his supper, the detective listened to the conversation carefully and learned that Fritz von Seilern had not been in Inzersdorf for three years. Therefore he could not have met Bauer in this place at least. But might they not have met somewhere else? Some connection there must be between the two men. For Bauer was no fool. He would not have run away for nothing in such excitement. Müller spoke of Bauer two or three times, mentioning his first name, as it was much more unusual than the surname. But the young lieutenant did not seem to have the faintest interest in this absent Ferdinand Bauer. Müller was puzzled. Suddenly the conversation took a turn that interested him greatly.

"What's this I hear about a crime that was committed in this neighbourhood recently?" asked the visitor unexpectedly, in the midst of another topic. "I heard some men talking about it in the train. They seemed to think that the police were showing their usual stupidity in not discovering anything yet Something about an old man wasn't it? Was it a murder?"

Müller volunteered no information, but while the others were talking he watched Maximoff with the greatest interest. Suzanne was first to speak: "It was old Mr. Erlach who lived alone in the Green House," she said. "He was mysteriously missing one morning, and they have not yet found him, either dead or alive."

"Erlach, Erlach?" repeated the young lieutenant. "I wonder if that's any relation to my comrade Paul Erlach? It's his regiment I've changed to—it seems to me I heard that he has relatives hereabouts."

"Lieutenant Paul Erlach was the nephew of the missing man," answered Plöhn,—"and is his sole heir if the death is proven."

"Is there much money there?"

"Yes, quite some, I believe."

"Well, I hope Erlach will get it," said Lieutenant Fritz. "He's a nice chap, we all like him. It's hell to be poor in the Army, you know."

Plöhn and the ladies continued to give their new guest the details of the affair, and Mr. Hartmann threw in an observation occasionally, stray questions, which, although the others did not notice it, were calculated to keep the conversation to this one topic. All the while the detective was watching Maximoff, who sat opposite him. But the man on whom Müller's keen gray eyes were so closely fixed was the most harmless-seeming of the entire company. He ate his supper slowly with the delicate enjoyment of a connoisseur in well prepared food, he was constantly on the watch for some courtesy to the ladies of the family, he threw in a remark about the excellent wine, and then bent his entire attention towards putting together a new combination of fruits for Suzanne. Everything about the man seemed to point to a perfect calm, and a peaceful enjoyment of the moment. There was not a single glance of the eye, not the faintest fleeting shade of expression in his face to show that the subject of the conversation had any interest for him whatever.

"Hasn't it occurred to anyone yet that the disappearance of the old gentleman, and the other mysterious crimes which have been committed in this neighbourhood might all have been carried out by the same person?" remarked Müller, when he thought the interest in the subject was flagging.

Mrs. Plöhn looked up surprised. "Why, no, I hadn't thought of it," she said.

Suzanne shook her head. "If it were so, they would have found the black cord in the Erlach house."

"Yes, exactly," said her brother. "We spoke of that possibility once before, you remember."

Maximoff was occupied in peeling a pear. Under his strong supple fingers the little knife moved slowly and delicately.

"You know you really ought never to peel a pear," he said to Suzanne, "because the very sweetest part of it lies directly under the skin."—At this point he stopped and looked right at Hartmann, continuing eagerly: "That's an idea that ought to be followed up. It occurred to me once before and I forgot to mention it." He returned to Suzanne again: "Who knows whether the great Unknown has not left his usual reminder behind him in the Green House. Our local authorities have discovered so little in this matter that one carelessness more or less would not be surprising. They may have simply overlooked the uncanny 'visiting card,' as Mr. Hartmann calls it." Maximoff returned to his pear, cut it carefully in pieces and ate it slowly. He seemed to be pondering over something and did not take part in the conversation for some few minutes.

Fritz was interested in hearing about the other crimes and they told him the principal details. He too, was lost in admiration of the reckless courage and the uncanny cleverness of the man with the black cord.

When Maximoff had finished eating his pear he wiped his beard carefully, then remarked, in a pause in the talk: "Your idea has taken complete possession of me, Mr. Hartmann. I think I'll have a chat with our Constable Kern tomorrow, and start him on another investigation of the Erlach house. The detective whose coming was announced to us some time ago seems—either not to have come at all, or like the other brilliant police minds, not to have discovered any thing worthy of notice."

"Possibly," replied Hartmann returning the other's smile frankly. Müller had noticed something in Maximoff's speech, the little pause which he put in after the word "seems"—to the others it meant nothing but to Müller it seemed like a sudden change of idea due to caution. Might not a man have said that, in just that way, who knew perfectly well that the detective of whom he spoke had been in the Green House? And who else could have known of the detective's presence there except the masked man who had taken flight so hastily that night? But this masked man knew also that the guest in the pavilion was the expected detective. The trace of the footprints right up to his garden gate showed Hartmann that he had been recognized.

If this man had indeed been Maximoff, who now sat smiling so cordially at "Mr. Hartmann," then he must believe that he could play with this Mr. Hartmann as a cat plays with a mouse. His eyes shone brightly, his well-cut mouth curved in cheery lines, as he continued: "I would not be at all surprised if the black cord could be found somewhere in that house. Ws all know how short-sighted the eye of the law is." Was it mere chance that the man's great dark eyes rested on Hartmann at the moment?

"Or is he only looking at me so fixedly because it is my thought that he is carrying out at length?" asked Müller of himself. He was conscious of a growing inner excitement, of animation, particularly now that he knew that Maximoff had engaged a detective for some secret work. His talk of a journey to Russia might have been merely a blind to throw Greng off the track. For it was quite possible that this new detective was to be set to spy upon "Mr. Hartmann." But all this could only be true, if it were also true that Sergius Maximoff was one of the greatest criminals of his day—and this was a thought that Müller could not yet take seriously.

All his years of experience had taught the veteran detective that criminals are to be found in every class and in any period of life, had taught him that the most attractive outward appearance may often be a cover for deepest inner depravity. With his brain, his keen working brain, Joseph Müller believed in no one, trusted no one. But with his *heart*, he was always believing and trusting. He knew that in the mental make-up of every criminal there is some insecure point, some crack as it were through which one can at times look into the carefully hidden horrors concealed there. But Maximoff, this highly intelligent, goodhearted man, whose life was so full of work and study, and philanthropy, so rich in harmless enjoyment of the beauty of nature, in his love for his art treasures,—how could this man bury such horrors in his soul. There are things which are possible if not probable—but there are other things which are not even possible.

While Joseph Müller, the experienced detective, was revolving all these thoughts in his brain, Mr. Robert Hartmann, Polish landowner, was smiling at Dr. Maximoff and repeating his own word: "Possibly." He said it once more and this time it sounded like a question.

Soon after this Mr. Hartmann rose and made his farewells for the evening. Back in his own room he took out his notebook and on its last page wrote the one word: "Collar."

CHAPTER 13

Mr. Hartmann is Called Away

Very early next morning the guest in the pavilion took a train for the city and drove in a cab to his own house. He was here only a few moments and one of his errands was to tell Karl to wear a turnover collar when he came to visit Maximoff that morning. Then Müller took the cab again and drove back to the station.

As he passed a cigar store it suddenly occurred to him that he hadn't anything to smoke. He called to the driver and the cab stopped in front of the shop. When the. detective had bought his cigars and come out onto the sidewalk again, his eyes fell on some books in a neighbouring window. They were scientific works, dealing mainly with modern developments in medicine. Müller paused for a moment, read several of the titles, then returned to his cab, which rolled onward through the streets.

Before the station was reached something peculiar happened. Müller took the burning cigar from his mouth and pulled off his hat. A wave of hot blood flushed his face up to his very hair, and his eyes gleamed brightly. It was but a few seconds, however, before he had regained his usual calm. He gave a short laugh, put on his hat again and resumed his smoking. Soon his cab stopped at the station and he walked up and down in front of the entrance, after looking at his watch and ascertaining that there was still eighteen minutes before the departure of the train. A few moments later his own carriage drove up to the sidewalk. Karl Tonner got out, looking very smart in his new clothes. He wore a turnover collar instead of the high standing collar that he had put on early that morning. Müller and his young companion entered an empty compartment just as the train rolled out of the station.

"I nearly forgot the collar," said Müller, looking at the young man with careful scrutiny.

"Is it so very important?" asked Karl with a laugh.

"Yes, it is very important to change the minor lines of one's appearance, as we cannot change the main contours. With your smooth-shaven face, the turnover collar, a different hat and different coloured clothes, you look so different altogether that Maximoff is not likely to have the faintest suspicion that he has ever seen you before."

When the train stopped at an intervening station Müller changed compartments. He had looked about him on the station in Vienna and was almost certain that no one from Inzersdorf was on the train, still he thought it better that he and Karl should not be seen together. When he returned to the village he went straight to the factory and spent an hour or so studying the ground plan of the works, and investigating the details of the machine installation. No one in the works had any idea that he had made this hasty expedition to the city. If anyone had noticed his absence in the early morning hours at all, it was probably only to think that he had gone for a walk.

Most of Müller's time in the factory was spent in Bauer's company. The latter had quite recovered from his upset of the day before, although Müller was still in the dark as to the reason for it. Finally, a little after twelve, Hartmann bade goodbye to his instructor, saying that he had to take a train for the city to keep an appointment there at two o'clock. He reached his own house in time for dinner and sat there waiting until Karl returned.

It was nearly four o'clock before the young man arrived. His visit with Maximoff had stretched itself out to such length because the doctor had invited him to lunch. The serious interview concerning the service demanded of him did not take place until after the meal. The Russian had evidently exerted all the spell of his very great fascination, perhaps with a design of binding this young man all the more closely to him. Karl was simply delighted with his new employer. He could not say enough about his wonderful cleverness, his deep learning and his cordiality. As far as he could make out the whole thing concerned a quite harmless little service, which, however, might not be without its difficulties.

Maximoff had told his visitor that he was politically compromised and did not dare to return to Russia himself. He needed some documents from there, which must be in his possession before his approaching marriage. There were personal papers only, a certificate of baptism, marriage certificate of his parents and various more of similar kinds. Had it not been for his political leanings he could have sent for these papers through the Russian Embassy. But under the circumstances he did not wish to draw the attention of the official representative of the Russian government to his whereabouts. Therefore he needed the services of someone else, who must be discreet and quick-witted. He would pay a very large sum for the work and it might be worth it. Bribes must be given and complications might arise which would need a clear head and quick wits to meet them.

But the principal thing, Maximoff assured the young man, was the matter of discretion. Even these preliminary revelations must remain a deep secret between them. The doctor did not wish the lady who was to become his wife ever to suspect even that he was in danger of arrest in his own country. As he was never likely to return there he saw no necessity of putting her under the hanging dread of a danger that might never reach him. He would, he said, make the journey together with the young detective, until they reached the Russian border. Before he left him there, he would give him the final details which no one else was ever to know. In a hotel which he would designate, in the little town of Oswieçim, they would meet after the work had been done. Maximoff would take his papers, Münzer receive his salary and then they would part, never to meet again,

This was the main content of the conversation which Karl Tonner had had with the Russian that afternoon. Maximoff evidently had not the faintest suspicion that he was talking to the man who had lived in the Plöhn house for a week or so as Mr. Hartmann's servant. The arrangements had been easily made and Karl's engagement for the work was settled before the luncheon was over.

Maximoff was pleased with this serious-minded, quiet young man, who had such excellent manners and who spoke so little, who seemed also to attach so little importance to what might prove a dangerous errand. The young man's poise and ease seemed to show that he was brave and quick-witted, and the gleam that lit up his blue eyes when the Russian named the sum he was to receive for the work, told the latter that his new employee would surely do his best. The two men parted in mutual satisfaction, after arranging how they should meet the following evening at the Northern station in Vienna.

Müller listened carefully to what Karl told him, asked many questions and finally announced that he would take part in this expedition himself. Karl was surprised at this but greatly relieved. In spite of his careless manner he felt the responsibility of what he was undertaking.

Before he left his home Müller had another little talk with Mrs. Tonner about the Napoleon miniature. She was firm in her assertion that it had been in Erlach's cabinet two days before his disappearance and that no one had entered the house since then. Then Müller repeated his instructions about the telegram which Mrs. Tonner was to send to him to reach him at six o'clock on the afternoon of the following day. He did some shopping in the city and he himself packed both his own and Karl's grips and ordered them left ready in the hall.

****

The next afternoon, a little after four o'clock, the usual group gathered around the tea table in the Plöhn sitting-room. Maximoff was there also and Suzanne sat at his side, apparently in a more tender mood than was her custom. She let her hand rest in his and gazed up into his eyes more often than usual.

When Mr. Hartmann joined the circle he said to the doctor: "Do you know that I have just come from Rose Cottage? I dropped in there in the hope of seeing you, and asking you to lend me one of your Lombroso books?"

"Oh, why didn't you take what you wanted? Anything in the house is yours, as you know."

"I didn't like to take any without telling you first," answered Hartmann, sitting down and taking his cup.

"I'll send over all I have of Lombroso as soon as I get home," said Maximoff cordially.

"Oh, no, don't think of it," replied Hartmann hastily. "I don't want to burden your brain with anything more today. For Mrs. Schober and your dear little girl told me that you are going away on a journey, this very evening."

"Yes, I am going, but—"

"May I ask where you are going?"

"Just think, he's going to Russia!" interrupted Suzanne. "The very thought frightens me."

Maximoff laughed and raised her hand affectionately to his lips. "Why should it frighten you, dear? I'm not likely to get in the way of any bomb-throwers. It's only the suddenness of this that has upset you. You see I did not know until this morning that I would have to go." He turned to Hartmann as he said the last words.

"Indeed!"

150

"It concerns some papers which I need before we can be married. Unexpected difficulties in the getting of them have arisen."

"Difficulties that require your own presence, I suppose."

"Exactly. And as any hindrance to my wishes always makes me nervous—"

"You want to lay them at once? I understand your impatience. I cannot endure the slowness of official red tape myself."

"There you see, my dear Suzanne, Mr. Hartmann would do the same in my case."

"Yes, yes, I understand. I know—but I can't help feeling so strangely uneasy." Suzanne's voice shook as she spoke. Then she smiled with a touch of mockery at her own fears and continued: "My nerves seem to be playing me tricks lately, anyway. There is a presentiment of evil hanging over me. But it's ridiculous and I will not give way to it. Don't let my foolishness worry you, Sergius. I wouldn't for the world rob you of the good spirits you are in just at present. Get your business attended to as quickly as you can and come back to us safe and well." The girl endeavoured to give brightness to her tone, but underneath the forced cheeriness was a shade of anxiety quite unusual in Suzanne's well-poised nature. Her sister-in-law changed the subject in the hope of cheering Suzanne's melancholy and the men seconded her nobly. Suzanne herself sat quiet, listening with polite attention but taking no part in the conversation.

Shortly after five o'clock Maximoff rose. "You're going already?" asked Suzanne, her eyes dimming.

"Yes, I must, dearest," he replied tenderly. "I've had so little time for this thing and as I do not know how long I will be gone, there is much I must see to in the house. I must get the half-past six train from here too. For the express from the Northern station in Vienna leaves at 10:05 and the evening service on our slow little road here is not very reliable."

"Yes, that's true. Then I see you must hurry," said Suzanne, accompanying him out of the room. When she returned she sat down beside the others, but seemed still struggling with the unknown dread that was oppressing her usually calm spirits. Müller wondered at it, pondering again over the mystery of the intuition of those who love. The girl's depression awoke an answering melancholy in his own soul, and it took all his strength of will to keep up the conversation.

The clock struck six and the telegram which he expected had not arrived. Mr. Hartmann continued to chat about all sorts of indifferent things, apparently careless and easy in his mind. Half-past six sounded. Mr. Hartmann was in the midst of an interesting hunting story and one would not have thought that he had a worry in the world. And indeed Müller was not worried. He knew that his own carriage was waiting for him at the next crossroad, and that his horses, although quite ordinary in appearance, were speedy and reliable, and that if necessary he could make the long distance from Inzersdorf to the Northern station in Vienna in less than two hours.

So he had quite some time yet and could afford to be calm about it.

At quarter to seven the door bell rang. "There it is," thought Müller. But when the butler came in, it was only a package of books he brought. Maximoff had sent all the works of Lombroso that he possessed. Hartmann was delighted at this friendliness and began to talk of the doctor's active interest in psychology. Plöhn spoke of the Russian as an expert in the field. In the midst of an eager discussion on this interesting topic, the clock struck seven.

"I don't need to go really until quarter to eight," thought Müller. "I'll complain of my rheumatism and say that a cup of tea in bed and a good book will cheer me up. While they believe me in the pavilion settling myself for a quiet evening, my carriage will be on its way to the Northern station. But I hate to think of the unpleasant surprise these dear people will have tomorrow morning."

Just then the door bell rang again and the maid brought in a telegram for Mr. Hartmann. He signed the accompanying book and the girl left the room.

Hartmann opened the telegram. "From the Baron," he said. "Goodness! Well! what do you think—there has been a robbery in my house, I must go home at once! My housekeeper sent me word on a postal card,—did you ever hear of such stupidity? Fortunately all my mail goes to the Baron's office and he saw that at once and telegraphed me." He let the paper fall from his hand onto the table amid the general condolences of the family, "I won't be able to catch the train that our friend has just taken," he said looking at his watch.

"Must you leave this evening?" asked Mrs. Plöhn.

"Indeed I must, kind hostess. My people appear to have lost their heads entirely, or they would have written more definitely what the trouble is."

He took up the telegram again and read it aloud this time, with a tone of anger in his voice. The dispatch read:

Your people send word on postal card of robbery in your house. Ask you to return at once.

Wouldn't you think they could have said a few more words? In an establishment like mine it makes considerable difference what part of the house is entered. Well I'll have to pack up at once. I think I'll just throw a few things in a bag and leave the rest here. For I want to come again if you will permit it. I feel that I need a little more time here for my work.

His host assured him that he would always be welcome whenever he might come.

"Too bad that you can't be with Sergius on the train," said Suzanne. But Hartmann replied it would only be a case of going as far as the Prater with him. "I take the North-Western Railway to reach my home. But I must hurry now, for I have only forty minutes to pack my bag and take the next train. Many, many thanks for all your kindness to me. I shall miss this pleasant family group, particularly the dear children. But then I hope to see you all soon again. Now let me see when the Baron sent this telegram." Mr. Hartmann was quite indignant now in his excitement. He looked at the paper again. "3:10 p. m." he read. "Well, it took long enough to reach here, didn't it?"

"I'll send Wilhelm to you to help you pack. In the meantime they will be getting the carriage ready," said Plöhn.

"Oh, no, please don't bother about the carriage," replied Hartmann, "but I'd be very glad of Wilhelm's help, he can carry my bag to the station."

Another warm handshake and Mr. Hartmann left the house. He hurried through the garden, and when he reached his pavilion he opened a window and leaning far out he gave a long, sharp, peculiartoned whistle which was answered from somewhere in the neighbourhood. Then he closed the window and turned on the electric light. When Wilhelm entered two minutes later, he found Mr. Hartmann already busy at his packing.

"Did you hear that whistling, sir?" asked the man. Mr. Hartmann replied that he had been so absorbed in his packing that he had paid no attention to anything else.

"There was a whistle, a long queer whistle, and then it was answered from across the moor. That's no way for decent people to act after nightfall," said the servant, who, as Müller had already noticed, was not particularly valorous. The man was undoubtedly troubled in his mind about his coming back from the Station alone. This suited Müller exactly. He closed his bag and locked it, locked the cupboards in which he had left his things and put the key in his pocket. Then he turned out the light and left the pavilion, Wilhelm carrying his bags for him.

"Run up to the house and give the key of the pavilion to Mr. Plöhn," said Müller, "their you can follow me to the station." But when they reached the front door they found Mr. Plöhn already there, talking to the driver of a carriage which stood in the road outside.

"Here's a lucky chance for you, Mr. Hartmann! Here's an empty cab which will save you a few moments in getting to the station. The man has been to Laxenburg and his horses are tired, but you have time enough and it will be more convenient than walking. He's been paid for the journey, so he'll take you there for the tip."

Mr. Hartmann got into the carriage and the men parted with another handshake. The wagon rolled off and Plöhn returned to the house, followed by Wilhelm who was heartily glad to be spared the trip to the station.

In the cosy well-lighted sitting-room Mrs. Plöhn was reading the telegram which their guest had left on the table. It read just as he had told them:

Your people send word on postal card of robbery in your house. Ask you to return at once. Greeting.
Stein

Then she laid the paper down and turned to her sister-in-law.

"Did you see how his hand trembled?" she asked. "He seemed quite upset about it"

"No wonder," replied Suzane, "a message like that is apt to upset anybody. I feel so sorry for him. He's such a nice man."

"Yes, we shall miss him," said Mrs. Plöhn. "It was a pleasing change in our quiet life."

"Oh, dear, it'll be very quiet now that both Mr. Hartmann and Sergius are away, goodness knows for how long."

"They seemed to get on so well together," said, Mrs. Plöhn, taking up her sewing.

"Yes, yes, indeed!" Suzanne spoke eagerly. "Sergius told me that he had seldom met a man for whom He felt such an instant sympathy and liking as he did for Mr. Hartmann."

"Mr. Hartmann speaks very well of Sergius, too."

"Ah, yes, we'll be very lonely without them."

****

One of the men of whom they were speaking rolled through the dreary country towards the little station, his mind quite at ease. As they neared the railway he bent out of the closed wagon and called to the driver. The carriage stopped and the man on the box sprang down and came around to the window.

"You managed that very well, Heberlein. Now you can give me my bags inside here and then let me see what your watch says."

"Seven forty-two," replied Heberlein, and Müller continued: "Seven thirty-eight is the exact time. You must get me to a quiet, badly-lighted place in the immediate neighbourhood of the Northern station at nine-forty at the very latest. You have two full hours to make it in. That will be easy. But you'd better be moving now."

CHAPTER 14

Muller And Karl Go on a Journey

At half past nine that evening, a two-horse carriage stopped a few steps from a side entrance of the Northern station, at the corner of an illy-lighted and little-used street. A quiet appearing, slender man, with heavy spectacles, long gray beard and gray hair, alighted from the carriage. He wore a light-brown cape overcoat and a wide-brimmed soft felt hat. After a short conversation with the driver of the carriage, the gentleman took up his bags himself and carried them into the hall where the ticket offices were. Here he left his luggage with a porter and went to buy his ticket. The office had just been opened and there was a crowd of people, thirty at least, who were pushing their way up to the narrow space in front of the window. The little old gentleman was interested in one person only in this crowd, and that person was Dr. Maximoff. He edged his way up until he stood in the line immediately behind the Russian and heard the latter ask for two first-class tickets to Granica. While he was getting his change the old gentleman noticed that immediately behind him in the line was a very impatient lady. Just as Maximoff left the window, the old gentleman stepped back with a deep bow and let the lady go up ahead of him. She acknowledged the courtesy with a smile, bought her ticket and hurried off. Then the old gentleman's turn came and he bought a ticket for Granica, first-class. He turned and followed Maximoff, who was leisurely mounting the broad steps that led up to the waiting room and the restaurant of the Northern station. The old gentleman and his porter walked up equally leisurely. There were but a few people in the roomy, attractive restaurant hall of the first class waiting room. Müller, who now looked like a man nearing seventy, sat down at a table quite near the one at which Maximoff had taken his place and at which George Münzer was already sitting. There was a glass partition between the two tables and Müller sat so that he could not be seen by Maximoff. The two men at the other table were talking in French. Easily as he spoke German, Maximoff preferred French and Karl handled the language very well. This was one of the things which had so pleased the Russian and decided him in favour of the young detective. Their conversation now was quite unimportant, dealing mainly with the supper they had just eaten. Müller smiled at the ease with which his protégé chatted about indifferent things on the eve of what might prove a hazardous undertaking. He was greatly pleased at his choice of Karl for this work. But he was also pleased with his own disguise. For Karl, as he could see, had been quietly making a scrutiny of all the other men in the restaurant, and his eyes had once or twice rested on the old gentleman who sat beyond the glass wall, but there was no sign of recognition in them.

When there were but fourteen minutes left before the departure of the night express, Maximoff rose from the table. "They've probably put our luggage in our compartment already," he said, "but you might go and have a look at it. I'll follow you when I have bought some cigarettes. We have a long night before us and I don't sleep well on the train." The Russian left the room, but Karl sat motionless for a moment or two, his eyes now openly making a tour of the hall.

"Why that sigh?" asked Müller, who had risen and come up behind the young man. The latter wheeled around quickly. "Oh, I didn't recognize you. I was afraid something might have prevented you coming with us," he exclaimed with a sigh of undeniable relief.

"Are you in a corridor car?" asked Müller.

"Yes, we have a small compartment reserved for us."

"You'd better go now. I'll follow you and try to get a seat as near you as I can. At all events I'll be in the same car."

Karl went out in the direction towards the trains, and Müller followed him, picking up the porter with his luggage outside the restaurant. A few minutes later Müller had secured a seat in the compartment immediately adjoining one on which hung a card "Reserved," the compartment into which he had seen Karl disappear. Müller's compartment was also a small one with room for only three people altogether. When the train left the station he was glad to see that he was still alone. He drew the curtains over the two windows that looked out into the corridor, and when the conductor had punched his ticket, he also drew the shade over the lamp on the ceiling.

It was a very heavy shade and the little compartment was now completely dark. The corridor outside was brilliantly lighted. Müller could easily see Maximoff's face through the crack where the curtains met on the windows. The doctor was leaning against one of the outer windows in the corridor and smoking. He was talking to Karl, who stood so that Müller could only see his one shoulder. They were not talking loud enough for the listener to understand what they said, but it must have been something pleasant, for Maximoff's face was merry, and both men were laughing heartily. A few moments later Karl's shoulder disappeared from Müller's range of vision. The young man must have gone back into the compartment, for Maximoff evidently felt certain that the other was no longer looking at him.

How did the old ferret in the dark compartment know this? Something odd that happened just then revealed it to him. Maximoff's face had changed suddenly and remarkably. There was a peculiar set look to it, although his mouth still smiled and his eyes shone. It was a victorious smile and the brilliancy of his eyes suited it well. Was this merriment called forth by the conversation just closed? Müller had not heard the words, so he did not know. But for that fleeting moment the brightness and the laughter had taken on something that made them terrible, an ugly gleam as of mocking cruelty. Before the old detective had time to know whether he really saw it, or only thought he saw it, Maximoff's face regained its former expression. Karl had returned from the compartment and stood now so that Müller could see his face also. It was smiling and content.

The great train thundered on through the night. The two men left the corridor and went into their compartment to make themselves comfortable for the hours of rest. Müller followed their example, for he did not intend to stay on watch that night as he knew it would be quite unnecessary. It was some time however, before he could lose himself in sleep. For ever and again there arose before his mental vision the picture of the sudden change on Maximoff's handsome, smiling face. It was a change so subtle, so quickly come and so quickly gone, that only a trained eye such as Müller's, watching this man with intensity, could have seen it. And yet even *he* asked himself again and again: "Did I really see it or did I mistake? Is it possible that I have at last caught a glimpse, through the weak spot in this man's armour, of the horrors that may lie beneath his charm and fascination?"

Before Müller finally fell asleep he started up once more with a jerk. He had been dozing and had lost the consciousness that he was in a moving train. A sudden swaying of the car aroused him. "What am I doing here? Why am I on a train?" he asked himself. Then the cloud cleared from his senses and he remembered where he was and why he was there.

"I don't like this idea of Maximoff going with Karl," he murmured. "And still less do I like the plan for them to meet in Oswieçim and finish up their business in this out-of-the-way, obscure little place. There's something decidedly suspicious in that scheme and that's the reason I'm going along with them. But there's no reason why I shouldn't sleep quietly tonight. There's no danger for the boy thus far, because this mysterious doctor wants his papers and he hasn't got them yet. So why not sleep as long as I can?" Having thus reasoned himself back into a drowsy frame of mind, Müller tried his door again to see that it was locked, put his head down on the cushion and soon fell fast asleep.

He slept so soundly that he did not wake up until the train stopped in Oderberg. He looked at his watch and saw it was three o'clock. From then on he did not permit himself to do more than doze, and heard the names of various stations called out, Petrovitch, Dzieditz, and Oswieçim. When they got to the last station, Müller rose from his couch, and looked out into the landscape, still indistinct in the gray morning twilight. Only a few isolated points of light showed where the little town lay. But against the nebulous horizon rose the outlines of the ruined castle which overlooks the town. A great factory which Müller remembered from a former journey, shone out at the foot of the hill, with its rows of lighted windows.

"And this is the place where Maximoff intends to wait for Karl and pay him off," thought Müller, with a look back at the little town as the train rolled on. "Why doesn't he pay him in Vienna? I don't understand this thing at all and I don't like it."

On and on, through the brightening twilight, through the early gray of a foggy morning, the heavy express thundered, rocking and swaying. Lazy white streaks of mist hung over the many little ponds and lakes lying with their still waters like uncut jewels between the dark fringe of the forest. Müller dressed slowly, making sure that the curtains of the corridor windows were carefully drawn. It took him some time to complete his toilet, and he spent considerable care in the combing of the long gray beard which had apparently grown during his drive from Inzersdorf to the Northern station in Vienna. He smiled to himself as he saw his own slender figure in the glass, for he had left Mr. Hartmann's comfortable curves in his carriage.

Long before they reached Granica, the Russian border station, where the train was timed to arrive at six o'clock, Müller had completed his disguise as the quiet elderly gentleman. He was the last to leave the train in Granica. The inspection of baggage and passes of those travellers who were going on into Russia, took quite some time, although it went off smoothly enough. Müller kept at a distance from the two men he was following. He did not need to be near them now, for he knew what the next move was to be. As Karl went past him, in the wake of Maximoff, he utilized a moment of crowding pressure on the part of a group of passengers coming through a doorway, and thrust a bit of paper into Müller's hand. On the paper was written the word "Riga." A meaning glance from the young man's eyes seemed to say that he had heard something of importance which he was anxious to communicate.

Karl had indeed heard things which interested him greatly and which he was desirous of talking over with his wise friend and mentor. Shortly after Maximoff and George Münzer had retired into their compartment the evening before, the young man gently reminded his employer that the latter had promised him important details of the work during this first part of the journey. The brightness vanished from the Russian's face at this, and a melancholy gravity took its place. He leaned back in his corner and let his eyes rest in serious sharp scrutiny on the young man opposite. He did not speak for some time.

"Does it not occur to you that I am paying a very high sum for what appears to be a simple service?" he asked finally.

Münzer nodded. "You spoke of possible complications," he replied. "I judge that you took these into consideration and therefore I was not surprised at your generosity." The young man made his reply easily, with a careless little smile. Maximoff laid down his cigarette and leaned forward.

"You need not be surprised at it," he continued in a low voice. "For I took into consideration that you might have to overcome very great difficulties."

"That is what we are here for, to overcome great difficulties," answered the young man, thinking to himself that it was not he who could be depended upon, but the quiet little man in the neighbouring compartment. But he continued calmly: "Please, Dr. Maximoff, do not be afraid to tell me everything. I am here to do your bidding."

The Russian leaned over, looked at him keenly, and whispered: "Are you ready, for—anything?"

Münzer answered the gaze with steady eyes and after a moment's pause, replied: "Yes, for *anything.*"

Maximoff's eyes gleamed. The set look which had given his face the appearance of a mask for a moment, vanished. "That is good—that is very good—it is a good thing for you, too," he said with a peculiar smile. His words and his smile struck Karl and he wondered at them, but he did not let the other see it.

"Tell me what is it you want," he said again, and Maximoff's peculiar smile faded.

"Listen to me," he began. "My name is not Maximoff. I borrowed this name from a relative who in all probability has been dead many years. I say in all probability, for I do not know for a certainty that the man is dead. Now there are three possible contingencies for this case of ours. The one that will make it easiest for you is that in the city of this man's home they have had no news from him whatever, and will therefore hand you out the papers without any trouble. The difficulty will arise if he should by any possibility have returned to his home, or if a certificate of death has reached there. Will you know how to manage the matter in either of these cases?"

Münzer paused for a moment as if he was thinking it over. Then he gave the answer that he had been ready at once to give. "Everything can be had in Russia for money and as you are willing to spare no expense—"

The doctor nodded as if satisfied. Then he said, the tone of his voice as chill as steel and his eyes shining oddly: "For money, yes, or with cunning—or by force." But before the other could wonder at the words, his voice was gentle again and he continued calmly, quite the amiable companion as before: "Of course, it goes without saying, that you will be provided with sufficient money to *buy* the documents if necessary. Ah, how true it is that one can never know until life is over, into what queer situations one may come. Not so very many years ago I should have been greatly astonished if anyone had told me that it would be necessary for me to steal my cousin's name in order to live a comfortable life undisturbed by the Russian government."

Münzer nodded meditatively."

"Did you borrow his professional title also, or have you a right to it?" he asked finally.

"I'm a doctor of medicine in my own right. Sergius and I studied and graduated together at the University in Vienna. Then he went to South Africa and has not been heard of since. I married, became a widower, and settled in Austria. It is eight years now since I had the last news of Sergius."

"I don't believe he can have any objection to your use of his name, as he is doubtless dead," remarked Münzer. And Maximoff replied eagerly: "Yes, don't you think so? Even the most honest man can find himself driven into deceit at times. When I fled from Russia, hounded by the spies of the government, and hid myself in Austria under the cloak of my cousin's name, I never dreamed that I would marry again, never dreamed that my life's happiness would depend on those papers that I want you to get for me, papers without which the ceremony cannot take place under the laws of my adopted land." With a sigh he sank back into his cushions again.

"I can't see anything wrong in what you are doing," declared Münzer calmly. "You do not harm anybody-by using this name. You can depend upon me, I will do all that lies in my power, in your interest and in my own, to get you the papers. I feel sure that it can be done. You say that I can get along very well in the places where I have to be, with German or French?"

"Yes. It was not necessary for me to find someone who spoke Russian," answered Maximoff. "But you want to ask something else, I can see it in your face. What is it that you still want to know?"

"I merely wanted to ask why you didn't tell me what you've just told me now, when we were together in Inzersdorf?"

Maximoff made a considerable pause before he answered. "I feared that if you knew the truth about the matter you might not undertake the job. Once started on the journey, you would not care to break it off and turn back."

Münzer felt that the doctor was not telling the truth now and it made a disagreeable impression upon him, an impression that was not removed by anything that was said further. For Maximoff declared that he was sleepy and made his preparations for rest, rather hurriedly it seemed to his companion. He really did fall asleep very soon, into a sleep that was so deep and sound that Karl could have no doubt as to its reality. The young man sat for some time looking at his companion, and it was not the regular deep breathing nor the loosely-hanging arms that told him that the man on the other seat was really asleep,—it was the expression of his face. Maximoff was dreaming. His soul, untrammelled, went on its own free way through the ether. Through what paths did it wander? Karl drew back into his corner, and young and strong as he was he shivered as if with a severe chill. The Russian had smiled in his sleep. But the smile that drew his lips apart and distorted the usually agreeable lines of his face was the smile of a fiend incarnate.

"Do I only think so?" thought Karl, shuddering. "Is it the wavering light on his face and my own imagination that makes me think so?" He could not come to a decision about it, for Maximoff turned over suddenly and his face was hidden from his companion.

It was long before Karl could fall asleep. He did not know the reason of Müller's interest in the Russian doctor. His patron had told him no more than that they must keep an eye on Maximoff. And before they parted he had reminded him to watch every movement, every expression of the other, and to remember every word of the conversation.

The veteran detective had not given his young protégé the faintest hint of his belief, of his suspicion rather, that Maximoff was the man who had fled before him that night in the Green House and who had followed them in their wanderings over the moor back to the gate in front of the pavilion.

And yet Karl in his heart had an inkling of Müller's suspicion and of the fact that this suspicion was the reason for their present journey. But he too asked himself why this mysterious and terrible man with the black cord, who now knew for some time that the supposed Hartmann was a detective who was on his trail, could have left them so undisturbed. And he too found no answer to the question.

The young man sat for hours watching the sleeping Russian. Again and again a shudder ran through his frame, when he recalled the mysterious words the other had said, accompanied by a smile that was equally mysterious, the words—"that is good—that is very good—that is very good for you also."

And more and more did the certainty come to him that he himself would have been in great danger, after hearing the other's secret, if he had not declared himself ready for whatever might happen. It was some time after midnight before the young man fell into an uneasy slumber. When the train rolled out of the station of Trzebinia, he sprang up again and saw Maximoff standing in front of him, smiling cheerily down at him.

"Had a good sleep?" asked the doctor who was already fully dressed and just about to take a roll of banknotes out of his pocket-book. In spite of the varied experiences of his life Karl was still too new at his present work not to be surprised at his own changing sensations. At the present moment he could not understand how, in the stillness of the night on the sleeping train, he could for one moment have imagined that Maximoff and that terrible Unknown were one and the same person. How was it possible that these great melancholy eyes, this sympathetic face, so serious and yet so cordial, should belong to such an unscrupulous criminal? It was quite impossible! With a feeling of remorse the young man pressed the hand the other held out to him.

"We will soon part," said the doctor with a sigh. "And when we meet again, I hope you will bring to me the papers that I need so greatly, the papers upon which the happiness of my life will depend. You are young yet, Münzer, your heart beats warm with sympathy as the heart of youth should beat. I hope that you really understand what your success in this matter means to a man who has gone further along life's weary pathway than you have. And I hope that you will have the courage, if need be, to force fate and put through your will, no matter what difficulties may occur."

He pressed the young man's hand firmly as he spoke and looked at him with a glance of ardent pleading. Then straightening himself up he continued in a calm and business-like tone: "Here are four thousand *rubles* in notes, and in this little bag you will find a large sum in gold and silver, Russian currency. I know the conditions into which I am sending you and I know that the money I am giving you will be sufficient, I am relying on your intelligence and your discretion, and I hope to meet you in less than a week in Oswieçim. I will not appear to know you in the station in Granica, it is better that we should not be seen together there at all. I will wait on the street outside the railway station and you can wave to me from the train. This will show me that you have passed the frontier without trouble. In Riga you must buy yourself another ticket to Wenden, your last destination. And now good luck to you."

Another warm clasp of the hand, then the doctor took up his grip and went out into the corridor. Two or three minutes later the train halted in the frontier station of Granica.

When the luggage and the passports had been examined, the passengers who were crossing the border into Russia were allowed to enter the waiting train. Müller and Karl were together in a compartment. The latter stood at the window watching Maximoff who,

164

plainly visible, was strolling up and down the street. When the train began to move Karl waved his handkerchief and Maximoff took off his hat and whirled it around his head two or three times.

"Well, what's your report?" asked Müller as Karl sat down opposite him.

The young man gave him a detailed account, reciting word for word what had happened since he and the doctor set forth on their trip the evening before, and everything that had been said between them. He showed Müller the papers and the money which had been given him. The veteran detective took charge of both. There was only one document of importance, an official paper stating that the physician and house-owner, Sergius Maximoff, had been a member of the community of Inzersdorf for six years.

Müller was not surprised at the important points in Karl's report. He knew already that there was something wrong in the doctor's past. And now he felt certain that it was not a political matter. There must be some other reason why Maximoff did not dare return to his own country. The remark: "That is very good for you also," that Maximoff had made to Karl, seemed to corroborate Müller's suspicions. What would have happened if Karl, once started on this mysterious journey, had not been willing to agree to any schemes the other should unfold? In all likelihood he would never have returned to Austria, would have disappeared somewhere en route. Was it not possible that Maximoff intended to let him disappear when he handed him the papers in Oswięçim? Was it for this reason that an obscure little town near the Polish frontier had been chosen for a meeting that might just as well take place anywhere else along the route, or better than all, in Vienna? A great many things can happen in these obscure little Polish towns. A stranger, particularly when registered under a false name in a hotel, can disappear and never be heard of again. Müller thought of all this and remembered the peculiar fleeting change in Maximoff's face the evening before when the Russian was alone in the corridor.

The travellers took a short rest in Warsaw. When they entered the train to continue their journey to Riga, Müller had already laid aside his false beard and wig. They spent the night in Riga, and the next day about noon they arrived in the little county-seat of Wenden. They took rooms in the best hotel in the place, freshened themselves up a bit, ate dinner, and then walked over to the principal square of the town to make inquiries in the main post office for the address of Dr. Sergius Maximoff.

But there was no Dr. Maximoff in this little town of about five thousand inhabitants. The friendly official behind the window, an elderly man who had served at his present post for many years, told them he was quite certain that in all the city of Wenden there was only one Maximoff and this was not Sergius Maximoff, but Andreas. Also he was not a doctor, but was an elderly retired government official who lived with his wife on the edge of the town near the great park belonging to the palace of Count Sievers. But the postmaster remembered now that some years ago letters were sent to Prätoria, in Africa—yes, it was Prätoria, letters addressed to a Dr. Maximoff. He supposed this to be the son of Andreas Maximoff. Letters had come from this far-away son and he had noticed them because of the postage stamp. But it was some years since any of these letters had come, and in fact as far as the official knew the correspondence had stopped altogether. This was all he could say about the matter, and it was all that Müller wanted to know.

****

The worst contingency, the possibility that the real Sergius Maximoff was alive and in his home, had not occurred. The only danger now was that there might be a certificate of his death in existence in Wenden. This possibility did not worry Müller much. He knew that he would be able to cope with it, as he had funds at his disposal and his own quick wits to rely upon. It was his intention really to obtain the papers for Maximoff—even if they would never be used in the way the Russian wanted to use them. They would be ready for Karl to hand to him in Oswięçim as arranged. Müller was very anxious to know what would happen then, and he did not intend to lose the opportunity of finding out. Possibly nothing would happen at all. It may have been a mere chance that this obscure little town was chosen as the meeting-place. Maximoff had to stay away from his home for a certain length of time anyway, as those he left behind supposed him in Russia. He would have to meet his representative somewhere along the line of the journey, so why not Oswięçim as well as any place? Whether this was the case, or whether Müller's darker suspicions were justified—well, he would be on hand if necessary to protect the young man whom he had sent forth on this mysterious errand.

"And now," said Müller to his pupil as they left the post office, "what would be your next move?"

"Why, I think that even if the government offices are open at this hour, and the papers could be obtained, it would be better not to go there first, but rather to make the journey to the outskirts of the city, to the park of Count Sievers," answered Karl.

"Quite right."

"And then I would have a chat with Mr. Andreas Maximoff, if I could find the gentleman at home."

"Quite right," repeated Müller, "that would be the best thing to do. But now, as I am taking for granted that you will have more interest in looking about you in a strange town than I have, suppose you play the part of a distinguished tourist today and take a stroll through this place with your Baedeker very much in evidence? I will meet you in our hotel at seven o'clock. There's no need for more than one of us to call upon Mr. Andreas Maximoff." Müller handed Karl the red-covered book, raised his hat and walked on down the street.

It was not a long walk to the outskirts of the little town. One or two inquiries along the way and Müller soon found the park and the home of the elder Maximoff at its gate. It was a pretty little house, set in a pretty little garden. Its walls were gray with age and its overhanging roof, darkened by wind and weather of decades, made it look like some old bird spreading out its wings and crouching close to the ground to escape the cold. A couple of fine old pine trees towered above it, and although it was still October the frost lay thick on the ground in this northern land and the attractive scenery wore its winter dress.

Müller rang the bell, and when the door was opened by a simple-looking peasant woman he asked if he might see Mr. Maximoff. The card he handed the girl bore the name of George Münzer.

The master of the house, a comfortable-looking elderly gentleman wrapped in a voluminous woollen dressing-gown, came to meet him cordially. Müller announced himself as an Austrian who had been a college mate of the old gentleman's son in Vienna twelve years before. He had found himself in Wenden on business and stopped in to see Sergius in case the latter might be at home. The old man shook his head sadly. He could not tell his visitor, he said mournfully, whether his son was still alive even. Sergius had been lost to him for many years, no news had come of his fate anywhere. The last he knew was that his boy had gone to South Africa, to the Boer colony, and then he had heard no more.

Müller's sympathy with the kind old man's sorrow was quite genuine, and was so soothing to his host that the latter was evidently anxious his visitor should remain for a more lengthy chat. Interesting strangers from elsewhere, particularly those who had known his son, were a rarity in old Maximoff's quiet existence. Fortunately for Müller, however, the garrulity of old age and of those who live a quiet life in the country, was stronger than the natural interest to hear tales of the college life of his lost son. The old man wanted to talk, not to listen. So it was easy for Müller to get him started on family affairs, on a discussion of his few other relatives. Among these was a nephew, by the name of Nikolai Simirenko, of whom the old man seemed to have a good deal to tell. What he did say about this nephew was so interesting that Müller kept the conversation confined to this topic for the rest of his visit, for the better part of an hour in fact.

Twilight had fallen as Müller returned to the centre of town. He walked through the quiet streets, wrapped in the hush of the early northern night, his own thoughts spreading a cloud about him heavier than the leaden pall on the sky above. When he met Karl and they had retired to their own rooms after supper, he told the story of his afternoon. The recital of what he had learned so excited the young man that he tossed restlessly for the greater part of the night.

Before noon the following day Karl handed Müller the three documents that were the official reason for their journey. There was no difficulty in getting them and it was only to hasten the deliberation of governmental procedure that Karl was obliged to expend some of the money Maximoff had given him for the purpose.

The two men left Wenden that same afternoon, taking the express to St. Petersburg. But Karl arrived alone in the Imperial city. His patron had given him two days' leave to look about him in this famous town, the second city of importance in the Russian Empire. Müller himself left the train at Dorpat, after arranging that Karl should meet him there on the third day following. Left alone, Müller went to his hotel and retired early. Next morning a two-horse carriage which he had ordered was waiting for him as soon as the tardy northern day had broken. Far out into the country he drove, all through the short hours of daylight, past many little villages and wayside lakes with quiet black waters, over rough wooden bridges crossing streams already quieting down for their winter sleep, through miles and miles of dreary moorland and gloomy pine forests. Finally as the sun was already setting in the west, the horses stopped their tireless trot in front of a modest little wayside inn, where Müller spent the night.

Next morning the journey began again. This time, however, the drive lasted only two hours, then a halt was made at another wayside inn, where the horses were unharnessed and led to the stable to rest, and Müller went on foot His destination was a large building, almost a castle in size and appearance, which lay in the midst of a beautiful wide-stretching park. But in spite of its impressiveness there was a gloom about the handsome structure. High brick walls and heavy iron gates surrounded the carefully kept park, and on all the windows of the great house massive iron bars were firmly set in the stone walls.

Müller remained here for a long time. Then he returned to the inn, took dinner there and drove back to his quarters of the night before. He slept uneasily, waking from time to time and murmuring incoherent sentences. The old detective chided himself for his distress of mind, for he knew that he should have been greatly satisfied with what he had discovered. He knew that he was about to add another achievement to his record, one which perhaps would be counted among his finest.

Then the following day the long drive began again, all through the hours of daylight until Dorpat was reached. By this time the conflict in his heart had calmed down and he knew that he would do as he had always done, resign himself to the inevitable and accept the success which he purchased with such a wrench to his nerves and to his soft heart. He slept quite well that night, and next morning Karl arrived punctually at the pre-arranged hour. The young man was fairly bubbling over with the enjoyment of his two days' sight-seeing in the beautiful Russian capital. Müller let him have his say about it first, because he knew that what he had to tell would darken his young friend's mind as it had his own. And indeed it did. Müller told his story as they sat alone in the compartment on their way to Riga. And Karl sat quiet, subdued and depressed by the terrible narrative.

When they reached Riga, they despatched a telegram at once. The message read:

Will arrive tomorrow, Monday evening, 8:39. Should recommend immediate continuing of journey. *G. M.*

The telegram was addressed to:

Adam Kucinsky
Station Hotel
Oswieçim, Gallicia

Then the travellers sought a comfortable hotel and did not resume their journey until the following day. They stopped in Warsaw long enough for Müller to disguise himself as a heavily-bearded elderly gentleman. This time, however, his cape-overcoat was not light brown but dark gray. It was buttoned its full length so that a wilful breeze could not reveal the fact that its lining was light brown. The majority of Müller's outer garments were arranged in this way to play a double part The hair, beard and hat he wore now had all quite another colour than those in evidence on the hitherward journey. His eyes were covered with smoked glasses, and it would have been quite impossible to recognize him as the white-haired tourist on the Viennese express two or three days back.

When they were on the last stretch of their journey, Müller rose from his seat, gathered up his luggage, and said: "Now my dear Tonner, I shall have to leave you to yourself. It is a difficult game you will have to play, a game in which your very life may be at stake. You must carefully calculate every word you say, every expression of your face, and be ready for even the most cleverly put questions. If this man gets the faintest suspicion that you know about his past, then your life is in the greatest possible danger, even if you do not leave the train in Oswieçim. I will be in the next compartment but even then, if he knew the truth, I might not be able to reach you soon enough to save you."

He pressed Karl's hand warmly and went into the next compartment, which already bore a placard "Reserved" on its door.

As the train drew in, Maximoff stood on the platform, his luggage carried by a porter behind him, ready for the journey.

George Münzer waved his hat from the door of the train.

"Everything all right?" cried Maximoff as he saw him.

"Everything all right," answered the young man. "Come aboard, I have a reserved compartment."

Maximoff jumped on the train, paid off his porter, arranged his luggage and then shook his employee's hand warmly.

"Your wish is fulfilled," said Münzer. "Settle yourself comfortably and I'll tell you my story and give you the papers."

"Did you have any trouble?" Maximoff was so eager to ask this question that he did not even wait to take off his overcoat.

Münzer helped him make himself comfortable in the corner of the seat and then handed him the documents and the rest of the money. He reported that there had been no trouble about two of the papers, but that the usual bureaucratic deliberation had made it necessary for him to wait three days in Wenden before he could come into possession of them. He had utilized his spare time in a careful inquiry as to whether Sergius Maximoff had returned home, or whether it was known that he were married or dead elsewhere. When the three days had passed he got the papers. But there had been a lot of red tape and bother about it, particularly about the fact that Maximoff had not come himself, or taken the usual political routine through the Consulate.

"In short, I had to dip into your purse a bit and relieve it of some of its contents," the young man concluded. "But you were ready for that contingency and the main thing is that you have your papers."

"And a great burden is lifted from my mind," said the doctor cheerfully. "I cannot tell you how happy it makes me. Thanks—hearty thanks, that you carried out the affair so cleverly. Here is the money you were to receive for your services. But now tell me, why did you want to continue the journey at once? Why didn't you want to stop over night in Oswieçim?"

"Why, I suddenly remembered that if I went right on, it would give me time to stop off at Prerau and visit dear friends of mine whom I haven't seen for some time. Business calls me back to Vienna, but if I save twenty-four hours now I would still have a little time with them."

"That was a good idea," observed the doctor. "Then we will part in Prerau—forever probably."

"That will be entirely as you wish it, sir," replied Münzer, modestly.

Then they lit their cigars and chatted for a while about indifferent subjects. But Karl noticed that Maximoff seemed uneasy about something. Knowing what he did, it was not difficult for him to guess what was troubling the other. He was anxious to get the dangerous moment over with, so he began himself to speak of the subject that might lead to the question he was waiting for. He began to talk of Wenden, what a quaint little town it was, and how there wasn't much to see there, but that the country was pretty, and that the days spent there had not been unenjoyable. Then he paused, puffed lazily at his cigar and waited.

The doctor made some remarks about Wenden, then continued casually: "Oh, by the way, didn't you say that as you were making inquiries about Sergius you learned that his parents still lived in the city?"

"Yes, that was what they told me in Wenden."

"Well, then, it seems to me that a simpler method of getting the information you wanted would have been to visit the old people and ask about their son."

"Surely," replied Münzer, "that was my intention. But Andreas Maximoff was on a trip to St. Petersburg, was not expected back for a week or two and his wife was ill in bed. Under the circumstances I thought it better not to disturb the old lady, particularly as I gathered all the information necessary from other sources."

"Yes, that's true—it *was* quite unnecessary, you are right."

The relief he could not control gave a brightness of tone to Maximoff's voice, and cleared the shadow from his face, the look of anxious cunning from his eyes. Karl, on the watch for every little sign, recognized this and felt a corresponding ease at his own heart. He was not lacking in courage, but he knew that if he had failed to recognize the proper moment or to give the right answer to this question, even the few years of youth in which he had the advantage of Maximoff might have availed him little against the other's remarkable quickness of brain and physical strength and against his almost devilish ingenuity in mischief.

The parting in Prerau was most cordial. Maximoff remained at the window of his compartment waving his hand to the young man, who himself stood on the platform until the train was out of sight Left alone, Maximoff took out the documents again and read them through. A tender smile illumined his eyes and curved his lips. As he put the papers back into his pocket, he murmured gently: "Suzanne— my darling Suzanne."

His heart was light and free, a thousand rosy visions flashed through his brain,—life was opening Out before him at its fairest.

And yet only a thin partition lay between him and his fate, for in the next compartment sat Joseph Müller.

CHAPTER 15

On the Eve of Action

One beautiful moonlit October evening, brilliant with the clear atmosphere of late autumn, a jolly company sat together at the supper table in the Plöhn house. The guests who had been together at that hospitable board so often were all there again, Bauer and Gebhart, Maximoff and Hartmann. The doctor had returned two days before, but Hartmann did not reach Inzersdorf until that very afternoon. During the early part of the meal, Maximoff gave a witty account of how he had discovered, on his journey to his home country, that he had grown completely out of touch with the habits and customs there, that even the food did not taste the same to him; As he intended to spend the rest of his life in Austria, he was glad to recognize that he had become such a thoroughly good Austrian. He also told them that he was sending Mrs. Schober and Sonya to Vienna the following day to have the little girl fitted for a coat made from some valuable sealskins he had brought with him. The latter half of the supper was devoted to a report by Hartmann of the robbery in his house and the damage done there. The Polish landowner had recovered from the depressing effect of his loss and was ready to look at the matter from, the humorous side. More especially as he had recovered most of the really valuable property that had been taken.

"And since they found the robber," began Gebhart slowly, and Bauer who seemed greatly interested, interrupted and finished the sentence himself, "then there's nothing more to be done in the matter."

"No," repeated Mr. Hartmann, "there's nothing more to be done in the matter, it's all quite clear now—absolutely clear." He said the words very slowly and very thoughtfully. There was a sad gravity in his eyes for which the amusing account he had just given did not supply the motive in any way.

These sad, dark eyes rested quietly on the charming group of Suzanne and Maximoff. The man was bending gracefully forward as the girl turned the soft oval of her cheek up to him and he fastened an earring into the delicately tinted lobe of her ear. They were a pair of unusually shaped ornaments which Maximoff had brought his betrothed as a reminder of his Russian journey. One of the earrings would not stay closed, which was the reason of the doctor's present occupation with it Müller's eyes, dimmed and darkened by the thoughts within as he looked at the attractive couple, suddenly grew sharp and keen and focused immediately on the ornament in Suzanne's ear. He realized first that he had seen these earrings in Maximoff's cabinet of curiosities and wondered that Suzanne had not seen them too. They were a rather peculiar setting, the French *fleur de lys* in diamonds hanging from a single jewel of considerable size which was inserted in the ear. He knew, of course, that Maximoff had not been to Russia but that he was obliged to make those around him believe that he had taken the journey. This first little deception about the earrings was clear to Müller, but under it was a dim memory of something else connected with the jewel.

Suddenly he knew what it was, and the quick vibration of every nerve through Müller's frame translated itself into such a violent movement of Mr. Hartmann's left hand that he had almost upset his wine glass. Fortunately only "almost," otherwise the claret in the glass would have made an ugly stain on the snowy cloth. The hand lay quiet on the table now, and the fingers, which had been drawn together as if in a cramp, slowly straightened themselves out again.

"You are not well?" asked Mrs. Plöhn gently and sympathetically, so that he alone could hear. "Or have you lost more than you are willing to tell us?"

Mr. Hartmann bowed his thanks to the gentle hostess and replied: "No, that is not it, kind friend. But it was a sudden shock, a painful surprise that upset me for a moment."

"Why, how strange," said the lady. "A painful surprise? Here? Now?"

Mr. Hartmann drew her hand gallantly to his lips. "Don't let us speak of it," he pleaded. "Some little incident, unimportant in itself, will often bring up a painful memory. I need not assure you that what I said a moment back had nothing whatever to do with—" Hartmann stopped as if seeking for words to finish his sentence and turned his attention rather too markedly to the dish of fruit handed him at this moment by the maid. "Oh, how beautiful!" he exclaimed, "what a charming arrangement of form and colour." It took him some time to sufficiently admire the attractive dish and to choose what he wanted himself. This enabled him to forget to finish his sentence.

"Then you too are nervous sometimes," said Plöhn, who sat at his other side. "Even *you* cannot always control your feelings? I thought you one of the most perfectly poised natures I have ever met."

"I'm afraid you overestimate me," returned Hartmann smiling. "Although of course you could not know the struggles I have had to learn outer composure at least."

"Only outer composure? Then you *are* upset sometimes, even if you have learned how to conceal it? Then *your* soul can lose its poise?" It was Maximoff who spoke now. He looked into Hartmann's eyes with kindly interest as he continued: "It is as psychiater that I ask, and also as such, that I would really like to know what excited you a moment back. For I know it could not have been a petty or unimportant matter."

"No, it was not a petty nor an unimportant matter," replied Hartmann, and his eyes, again deepened by melancholy gravity, rested sadly on the doctor's handsome face. "The thing that suddenly came to my mind, that so upset me, concerns the downfall of a human destiny. You are psychiater, I can well believe that you would find my mental trouble of a few moments back interesting as a study. If you wish, we can talk it over tomorrow. Will it be convenient to you if I come at eleven o'clock? I have important business to attend to later."

"Oh, please come, surely," said Maximoff. "I am glad to see you at any hour."

"Then he is to know the secret?" pouted Suzanne, "but we aren't worthy of it? I don't think that's nice of you."

"You'll hear it later, Miss Plöhn," replied Hartmann, "but not now. It's too long and sad a story to tell at such a time."

The girl's eyes met his as he spoke. Suddenly the smile on her lips faded and her eyes widened while she gazed as if hypnotized into the intelligent keen gray eyes of the man who had spoken. A shudder ran down her spine, all unconsciously something in her heart asked the question which his eyes feared to answer, and he turned away. Suzanne shivered, then laughed a forced laugh and made some indifferent remark. No one had noticed the little scene, but Müller was startled to his very heart by it. It was as if his thoughts had taken visible form and shape in his eyes, and this sensitive woman-soul had seen the picture, the doom that would so terribly change her own life.

Mrs. Plöhn rose from the table and her guests followed her example. Still under the impression made by the conversation of a moment or two before, the company bowed to one another silently as if not in the mood for the usual spoken greetings which are a pleasant habit of the close of a meal in all Teutonic countries. One person alone, Bauer, not quite fine-feeling enough to recognize the mood of the others, broke the little pause with a loud, harsh: *"Prost Mahlseit."*

Then something happened which gave a second and more severe surprise to the little gathering. Mr. Hartmann lost control of his nerves again. And this time Bauer's remark was the cause of it. The bookkeeper was in the habit of joining in the usual Austrian expression used on such occasions. But once in a very great while, and this happened to be one of the times, he would affect the travelled man and use the North German *"Prost Mahlseit."* Hartmann wheeled around as he heard it, stared right in Bauer's face and then gave a loud short laugh. It was a laugh full of scorn and the glance of Hartmann's eyes, which seemed to run the bookkeeper through and through, was equally scornful. The two ladies were startled out of their usual composure by this astonishing impoliteness on the part of their polished and considerate guest. Gebhart shook his head and Plöhn and Maximoff exchanged surprised glances. Bauer flushed and moved a step forward towards the man whose laugh had sounded like a deliberate insult.

"What do you mean?" he said, in a tone that was like a hiss of anger.

Then Hartmann laughed again, but this time quite naturally and cheerily as he replied: *"One who knows* had to laugh at your 'Prost Mahlseit.'"

The others exchanged glances again. They would have begun to doubt Hartmann's sanity, had not Bauer's changing expression proved that he at least understood the sense of these incomprehensible words. The bookkeeper's angry surprise had given way to a start of embarrassment. His face was deadly pale, his lips drawn back and he looked as he wished the ground would open and swallow him up.

"Well, you needn't lose your head about it completely," said Hartmann with a somewhat forced gayety. "We can talk over the matter in all calmness tomorrow morning. You'll honour me with a visit to my charming retreat, will you not?" Then turning to the others he continued easily: "Dear friends, you will forgive me if I leave you now? My nerves seem to be quite out of my control tonight, and I think it will be better for me to retire and get a good sleep. I will be no loss to you the way I am feeling now." He bowed again and left the room.

A few moments later he locked himself in his pavilion, and without turning up the light, walked to the window and stood looking out on the moonlit moor beyond.

"I'm glad to hear that Sonya and Mrs. Schober will be in the city tomorrow," he murmured. "I believe I have a fever tonight. My pulse is beating at an unnatural rate. It's the same old story—no matter how old I grow I cannot control my excitement at this stage of the game. And this case—this case—But I want to hear from his own lips the truth about his own condition. And therefore I must be calmer and more clear-headed than ever tomorrow. It is not only that my success will be in doubt, but my very life will be in danger if I do not play my part well. About noon tomorrow my life will be hanging on a thread. There isn't an insurance company in the world that would take the risk if they knew the particulars. But even at *this* price there is nothing in the whole world that would compensate me for the loss of that hour that is to come—it will be the most interesting experience of my life. And he lets her wear those earrings! When I suddenly realized where they came from it upset me completely. I must be growing old to lose my grip on myself like that. And then this '*Prost Mahlseit*! Such a ridiculous, such a silly affair as that other is, but it was just the straw that broke the camel's back. I don't know what those dear people will think of me. Well, we'll get through somehow till tomorrow, and tomorrow the bomb will burst Tomorrow—! And those enormous footprints that I saw down there by the gate? They have added another sensation to this case. Every day I ask myself why he does not kill 'Mr. Hartmann,' for he must have recognized the latter as his enemy. That is the biggest riddle of all. I hope that tomorrow I will find the solution for it also. Provided I am alive tomorrow, that is—for it's not at all certain. My conduct was foolish tonight under the circumstances,—why I directly challenged the man to end it all himself. It would be easy enough to put a bomb under this little house here, still—the man's recklessness and audacity are so great that it probably affords him the keenest pleasure to play with me as a cat plays with a mouse. No, on second thoughts, I doubt if my sleep will be disturbed tonight."

All these thoughts passed through the old detective's mind as his eyes wandered over the dreary sweep of the Black Moor, to which the moonlight gave a veiled charm it did not possess by day. Müller's pulses beat hastily, the blood throbbed at his temples, but his inmost soul was calm and the brain behind the quiet gray eyes was keen as steel.

Suddenly he started back from the window, for he had just heard the sound of a footfall outside. Someone was walking about the pavilion, inside the wall. Müller listened for a moment, then crept out of the room and opened the front door softly. He slipped down the steps unseen and hid himself behind the bush that stood at the foot of the stairs. But he had scarcely found his position before he left it again and came out into the moonlight, saying with a light laugh: "Oh, it's you is it? Then you couldn't wait till tomorrow? You absolutely *had* to know today how I found out your secret?"

The man who stood before him was Bauer, the moonlight lying full on his pale ugly face, which was less repulsive than usual because it bore so clearly an expression of fear and shame. The soft heart of the old detective awoke again. "Poor soul! what a petty coward it is anyway," he thought to himself. Then he said aloud, with a calm severe voice: "But you are quite mistaken if you think that I intend to answer any questions of yours. It will be quite the other way around."

"I—I am ready for anything you wish," stammered Bauer. "I will answer any questions—and give any satisfaction that may be demanded of me."

Müller smiled scornfully. "All that is demanded of you is that you make an humble apology, a *written* apology stating that you were the sender of the two stupid and malicious anonymous letters received by Lieutenant Erlach. If you do this, I'll promise you that the affair is closed forever."

"I'll—I'll do it," stammered the poor coward again. And Müller answered: "Very well then, and now you can go home and go to sleep."

He turned towards his own door again but Bauer threw out a hand to stop him. "Well, what more do you want?" grumbled the detective.

"Will—will Nellie—Cornelia—read my letter?" gasped the book-keeper, his face flushed.

"Miss von Feldern, you mean," corrected Müller "Miss von Feldern," repeated Bauer obediently.

"Who now, I hope, will never be annoyed again by your poems and flowers."

"Never again," declared Bauer hanging his head. He looked so entirely repentant and miserable that Müller's anger was lost in pity.

"You know Lieutenant Erlach personally, do you not?" asked the detective. Bauer nodded and Müller continued: "And you didn't realize that *you* could have no possible chance to supplant him in the affections of the lady?"

"Miss von Feldern did not know from whom the letters and flowers came."

"But you knew her personally?"

"Yes, I met her in my mother's house."

"Did she ever notice you particularly?"

The amorous bookkeeper sighed deeply as only answer.

"There you see," said the other more good-naturedly, "when a man knows that the lady has no interest in him whatever, then, if he *is* a man, he will not annoy her with his attentions and only make himself ridiculous by doing so. And above all it is an unmanly thing to play an ugly trick on the more fortunate one who has honestly and fairly won the lady's heart. There, that's all I have to say. Is there anything more that occurs to you?"

"Why, Mr. Hartmann, I would like to know how you—"

"Oh, how I recognized you as the writer of those wretched letters? Well, I'll allow you to suppose that I know Lieutenant Erlach, that he showed me the letters, that I suggested jealousy as a motive for writing them, furthermore, that Miss von Feldern was questioned and told us that some unknown admirer sent her poems and flowers while she was living in the country—also that her landlady there had a son who—appears to have been something like you. Furthermore, you may also suppose that Mr. Plöhn happened one day to mention that you are a poet in secret and that you send flowers to a lady whose name he does not know. I scarcely noticed what he told me about you for my head was full of a more important matter. Besides which, your name is Bauer and the mother of the man Miss von Feldern mentioned is a Mrs. von Probst."

"*Was,*" interrupted the bookkeeper. "My mother has been dead for nearly two years now. Mr. von Probst was her second husband."

"Oh, indeed!"

Now it was Müller's turn to blush hotly as he realized that he had been caught in a bit of carelessness.

He should have known long ago that Bauer was the writer of those two letters. A few simple questions or one look at the police records would have told him what he wanted to know. Of course from the very beginning he had treated the matter of the letters as of little importance and it had had nothing whatever to do with his coming to Inzersdorf. But it was a mistake on his part to forget any detail that might in any way be connected with the principal matter in hand. Müller was very much dissatisfied with himself and whenever this happened he was always extremely considerate of others. He laid his hand now on Bauer's arm and spoke in a tone of fatherly kindness.

"We are all liable to err," he said. "But try not to let yourself be dragged into any such meanness again. A repentant apology will make good what you have done, that is all than anyone can demand of you. But do not be offended if I warn you that you will not gain your own respect, nor any inward peace if you go on in this way. And self respect is what every man needs who would be a man worthy the name. Oh, one thing more, why did you run away that night?—you know, when you had the headache several days ago?"

"I—I thought it was Erlach in the parlour. I could only see his shoulder, his arm and back—it was the same uniform."

"Oh," said Müller, "very well then, now goodnight, I am very sleepy. Remember what I have told you, you will find it is for your own good."

Bauer stood motionless, his head drooping, his arms at his side. He looked very unhappy. When he realized that Müller was no longer speaking, he raised his head heavily and with difficulty and looked at the older man with dim eyes.

"Well, won't you give me your hand for goodnight?" Müller's tone was quite gentle and friendly.

Bauer started, stretched out both hands and a sob wrung itself up out of his heart. Müller's eyes were dim in sympathy and for quite some little time he endured the heavy pressure of the bookkeeper's strong hand. Finally he said, with his usual great good nature: "Hadn't you better let go now? I think one thumb is gone, and besides you know we really can't stand here all night like a couple of women saying goodbye after a coffee party."

Bauer dropped the other's hand.

"Oh, how kind you are," he stammered. "You are so gentle with me. You even give me your hand. You don't think I am quite impossible. I thank you, oh, I thank you for what you have done!"

"Oh, come, come! What a very romantic-minded person you are!"

Bauer set his teeth hard and spoke haltingly, but more as if trying to hold back the words than as if forcing them out. "If only any human being in all the world had ever really loved me, then I wouldn't be so filled up with envy and hatred and bitterness and malice. Even my own mother never loved me. She was always cold and hard and perfectly pitiless towards the very faults that I had inherited from her—and the rest of the world paid no attention to me, of if they did it was only to laugh at me."

"Oh, no, you are mistaken," interrupted Müller "Have I not seen every day now, how kind the Plöhns are to you and how they appreciate your good qualities?"

"Yes—yes, that is really true," murmured Bauer, and his face brightened as if he had made a pleasant discovery. Then he asked another question. "But how did you ever recognize me just from the '*Prost Mahlseit*'?"

"That's not so astonishing," replied Müller with a smile. "We use the phrase very little in this part of the country and it just so happened that I haven't heard it since I saw it in your letters. Then I suddenly recollected, and although the name was still wrong, I remembered the signature of your letter and your fright showed me that my conclusions were justified. But don't let us talk about it any more, and don't look so unhappy. You realize that the Plöhns are fond of you—is it not a good deal when kind, intelligent people, such as they are, think well of you? But you'd better go now. They might notice your long absence. Tomorrow they will see that the little difficulty between us is quite settled. I give you my word no one will ever know what the reason for this little difference was. Oh, and please remember that no one here must suspect I am acquainted with Lieutenant Erlach. Do you understand? You must never give even a hint of it!"

Bauer looked at him seriously. The peculiarity of this circumstance, that Hartmann knew Erlach well enough to have seen the letters, and yet that he had never mentioned the fact of his acquaintance with the young officer in the house of mutual friends, suddenly struck him as odd. He stood silent for a moment, thinking it over. Then a flash came up in his eyes as if he had realized the significance. A question rose to his lips but he did not dare utter it. He held out his hands again, saying gravely: "I will not mention it. Good-night." Then he walked slowly back through the moonlit garden to the house.

When Müller returned to his own room and went to bed his sleep was deep and untroubled. The little diversion from the more strenuous current of his thoughts had done him good. When he awoke the next morning his pulse was calm and regular, he was in excellent condition mentally and physically. The maid who brought his breakfast tray at eight o'clock found him standing at the open window, gazing into the sunny morning landscape. In Fanny's opinion there was nothing particularly inspiring about the Black Moor. But it seemed to have put

Mr. Hartmann into the very best of spirits as he came up to the table on which she had just set the abundantly spread tray.

"Why, my dear child," he laughed, "you bring me more every day. Do you expect me to eat all that? What would happen to my waistline if I did? You're too kind to me, you and Mistress cook. It's time I showed my gratitude. Here, this is yours and take the other to the presiding goddess of our kitchen."

Fanny blushed in pleasure as she took up the two twenty-crown notes that the guest laid on the table. When she had shut the door behind her, Müller said to himself: "Well, that's settled. Now I'll put something for Wilhelm under the brush there. When you're going into battle as I am, it's best to arrange these little things beforehand."

Müller enjoyed his breakfast thoroughly, then packed his trunk and his grip, looking out of the window from time to time as he did so. When everything was in its place and there was nothing more to be done, Müller could devote himself entirely to the inspection of the surrounding scenery, and it appeared to interest him more than ever that morning. It was nearly ten o'clock when he saw a pedlar coming towards him along the street, quite an ordinary pedlar such as might be seen anywhere along the country roads. Müller's eyes watched this pedlar carefully. When the man came along the road to a point right under the window of the pavilion, he stopped, doffed his hat and said respectfully: "Can I show the gentleman some cuff buttons or an eyeglass cord? And I have some fine new suspenders too."

Müller replied that he did not need anything just now, and asked the man how business was these days.

"Very good, thank you, sir. Everything is in order, and arranged as well as anyone could wish."

Müller seemed pleased to find someone who did not complain of poor business, for he waved a friendly hand to the man before he left the window. As he turned back into the room he smiled as if content. "This former ne'er-do-weel is turning out quite a useful lad," he thought. Then he repeated the words with sudden gravity: "Everything is in order and all is arranged—I can leave here in three-quarters of an hour."

For a span he stood motionless, lost in his thoughts.

Then, seeming to awake again to the exigencies of the present, he walked over to a little table that stood between the windows, and took up three articles that lay there. They were a small but wicked looking revolver, a little silver whistle, and a small bottle with a very wide mouth. The bottle was closed with a metal cap and contained a clear liquid.

Müller put the revolver in his right coat pocket and hid the whistle in his vest. Before he put the little bottle in its place he tried its stopper. This was, as has just been said, a metal cap, a rather deep cap for the size of the bottle and its outer surface was roughened to make it the more easily handled. With a single scarcely perceptible turn of his fingers Müller opened this cap, but he shut it again equally quickly. For in the fleeting instant it was open, the sharp fumes that arose with deadly vigour betrayed the fact that the bottle was filled with chloroform. When Müller had assured himself that the cap was in good working order, he put the bottle in another coat pocket. The pockets of Müller's coats were all of unusual capacity, were lined with leather, and had little inner compartments, so that heavy objects carried in these pockets could not move about as he walked, and attract attention from the outside.

Now that he had equipped himself for the serious business of this day, he left his room and went over to the factory. He sought out the manager, chatted with him a while and asked casually whether Plöhn intended to remain in his office the rest of the morning. Plöhn replied in the affirmative. While Müller was in the office, Bauer entered on some business errand.

"Say, what was the matter with you two last evening?" Plöhn asked at once. Bauer blushed hotly but Hartmann answered calmly: "It was a little matter that concerned no one but ourselves. Mr. Bauer came to my room last evening and we talked it over and settled it quite satisfactorily."

This might not have been an explanation, but it was a decided hint in protest of further curiosity. Plöhn understood, but he was not offended, for he knew that Hartmann was saving Bauer some embarrassment. The bookkeeper's expression of the evening before had plainly shown that whatever it was, he was at fault. Müller stayed in the office until quarter to eleven, then he bade farewell to the manager and walked down the road to Rose Cottage. He walked slowly, his head bowed and at times a deep breath that was almost a sigh welled up from his very heart.

CHAPTER 16

"I Am the Man With the Black Cord"

Rose Cottage lay on a main road, and not far from it was a neat little country inn. The inn was an old building with a wide courtyard and a large garden stretching far away from the back of the house. One end of this garden, with its fencing of high green hedge, was separated only by a small strip of grassy meadow from Maximoff's property.

Just as Müller passed the inn two closed cabs drove in under the archway of the old-fashioned building. There was nothing remarkable in this, for although the inn was little used by the more well-to-do inhabitants of the neighbourhood, it was quite a gathering place for cabmen who had brought a fare out into the country and were rest-ing a bit before returning to town. One thing however was noticeable on this occasion and that was that the two wagons did not stop in the courtyard as usual, but drove right through down to the furthest end of the garden. Also the observer might have seen that the curtains on all the windows of the cabs were drawn. But there was no one to no-tice this, for there was no one in the courtyard of the inn except the host of the Eagle himself, who stood in his doorway.

"Drive right on in, there's no one in the courtyard nor in the garden and the key is in the gate." This was what he said to the leading driver. The two cabs drove on unseen, down to the gate in the fence which was hidden by the thick hedge. Through this gate one could pass out onto the meadows which lay between the inn and Rose Cottage. The latter was protected from the outer world by a very high brick wall, having a handsome entrance gate on the street side. But there was a smaller gate at the back opening onto the meadow.

No one living in Rose Cottage knew that this back gate had been unlocked since early morning, that it had been opened from the out-side and that the garden was now accessible to anyone. When the cabs stopped in front of the inn garden gate, five men alighted from the closed wagons, slipped through the gate, across the grassy lane and into the garden of Rose Cottage. One of these men was Constable Kern, a second wore the uniform of a city police official. The three other men in plain clothes were heavily built individuals with calm eyes and in-different mien. The five men slipped from one bush to another, safely hidden from the house, until they had come several yards from the gate. Here they stopped on the near side of the circle of peculiarly-cut box which surrounded a young cedar. One of the men carried a spade and immediately began to dig at the earth with it. The two other men in plain clothes continued their creeping progress toward the house. With a little care they could come quite near the dwelling without being seen as Maximoff's fondness for arrangements of evergreens gave them sufficient cover. There was no dog in Rose Cottage and the two maid servants were busy in the house. When the two men had come quite close to the dwelling house they stood watching and listening, without going further.

The bell of the front garden gate shrilled through the quiet air. The long window opening on to the terrace was thrown back, and a carefully dressed gentleman came out, whistling a merry tune. He laid down the magazine he carried onto a little table and walked on down the few steps from the terrace.

"That's him," whispered one of the listeners to his companion. They crouched down the more carefully behind the evergreens. Maximoff turned on the top step and looked back to the house. "Stay where you are," he called to the woman who appeared at the door. "I'll open the gate. But don't forget to bring us in something to eat. I am very hungry."

"No, sir, I'll attend to it. Mrs. Schober told me what to get for you," answered the woman, who was evidently the cook, before she disap-peared from the doorway. The doctor had turned the corner of the house and the men behind the evergreens could no longer see him. But in a few moments he returned arm in arm with his guest.

"Don't you want to look at my newly blossoming chrysanthe-mums?" asked Maximoff. "They are white as milk and most unusually beautiful." He pulled his guest gently in the direction of the conserva-tory, but the latter did not follow the pressure.

"No, my dear doctor," he said, "I want to talk to you about something much more serious today. Can't we go into the house? It will be easier for me to talk to you in your attractive study. And I have something to tell you that will surprise you greatly."

"Oh, indeed!"

"Yes, it is the physician I come to see today, not the friend alone."

The two men stood on the terrace now, in front of the long open window.

"You aren't well?" the men behind the bushes heard Maximoff say. "I noticed it yesterday—at least you are not as calm as usual."

"No," replied Hartmann, leaning on the railing as if for support. "I was very restless yesterday, as I have been for several days. There is a crisis coming on again.—I know it in this unnatural excitement, this fear that is on me. Can't we leave this window open, when we are in the room? I need the air." Hartmann passed through into the study as he spoke. The doctor followed him with a shake of the head. But he hospitably fulfilled his guest's wishes at once, threw open the other half of the window, drew a light table and two comfortable armchairs up to the threshold, and invited his friend to make himself comfortable.

"Well then, doctor," began Mr. Hartmann. Then he paused and looked about distrustfully. "No one can overhear us?"

"No, no one."

"Could not Mrs. Schober or Sonya suddenly come in?"

"They are in Vienna today."

"Oh, yes, you told me about it I remember now. But your servants?"

"The coachman is in the city with the ladies. The code has just returned to the kitchen and the other maid is busy upstairs." The doctor smiled at his guest's nervousness.

"Well, if you are really sure that no one can hear us."—Mr. Hartmann looked very anxious and nervous. Maximoff's face grew grave. He laid his hand on his visitor's arm and spoke gently and soothingly.

"You are really very nervous today, dear friend," he said. "We all have these little troubles now and then. Tell me frankly what the matter is? But first of all we will quiet your nerves by giving you something good to eat. It's the best thing in the world." He touched an electric bell on the wall near him. "The cook will bring us a light lunch and when she has gone we can lock the doors behind her, draw our chairs quite close together, and talk while we are enjoying the refreshments. Does that program appeal to you?"

Mr. Hartmann took the hand that was stretched out to him and pressed it warmly. "There is no reason why it shouldn't," he said. "I feel calmer already. You have something that is almost like hypnotism in your strength. I feel as if you could force me to believe you whether I wanted to or not."

"Is that really true?" asked the doctor and his eyes gleamed. "But here's our lunch," he said as the door opened. He rose from his chair and examined the contents of the various plates and dishes on the big silver tray.

"There, this looks all right—now bring us over those cigars," said the doctor to the cook, "and then you can vanish again. And see that I am not disturbed under any circumstances. I am not at home to anyone now."

"Very well, sir."

When the woman had brought over the cigars and cigarettes and had left the room, Maximoff locked the three inner doors of the study and came back to the table. He sought out the choicest morsels for his guest, but Mr. Hartmann seemed to have very little appetite that morning.

He had scarcely taken a few bites when he pushed back his plate and said, in a voice that was not natural with him, "You are very kind, doctor, but I cannot eat it, I really cannot. My throat seems closed up."

This was the actual truth. The soft-hearted Müller was really suffering from some of the symptoms of excitement and anxiety which he had described. Maximoff himself was quite alarmed now. He put down his knife and fork, took a hasty swallow of brandy, then reached over the table and caught at his guest's hand.

"Why, your hand's like ice," he said, "and your pulse is beating unnaturally fast. It's time we looked into this matter. Do you think you would have confidence in me as a physician, although I have practiced general medicine very little. I am really only a specialist in mental troubles—"

Mr. Hartmann wiped his brow, which was bedewed with sweat and answered hoarsely: "That is why I come to you."

"What? I do not understand." The doctor looked up.

"It is not my body that is sick."

"But I never should have thought—"

"That my soul is sick?—" Hartmann straightened up in his chair with a short laugh, while a look of cunning brightened his eyes. His arms lay on the side rests of the chair and his fingers drummed the measure of a merry march, as if he were in the very best of spirits. He looked just a little malicious and decidedly mischievous. The doctor was leaning towards him and looking at him with the greatest interest. Finally he said slowly: "And now, Mr. Hartmann, tell me all about it."

"That's why I'm here."

"Well, then?"

"You'll probably think me a fool."

"No, you are quite mistaken."

"Oh, yes—yes, you will," insisted the guest with a threatening look.

Maximoff had spent years in the study of mental alienation. It had been his chief interest since his youth. The unbalanced mind, the sick soul, was the one thing which absorbed all his mental powers. He possessed almost every important work written on this subject and had had many an opportunity to study actual cases. It was natural, therefore, that he should be most curious at this sudden turn in the behaviour of a man whom he had known quite intimately now for several weeks, and who had always appeared to him absolutely normal and sane.

And now this man came to him acting in a way that was decidedly not normal, telling him himself that there was something wrong with his mind, and certainly looking it. Maximoff knew all the symptoms, particularly this sudden cunning, this unmotivated merriment. He was certain that he was in the presence of a man whose mind was affected. He was very sorry for Hartmann, whom he had grown to like. But his love for the study of the sick mind overcame his pity for his friend. He pulled his chair nearer to his visitor and began his questioning.

"Well, suppose you are right?" began the doctor with a delicate smile. "What do you say now?"

"I say that you are still mistaken."

"Indeed! Then you mean to say—"

"I mean to say that I know what the matter with me is and who I really am—and I know that there are moments like those yesterday when I come near betraying myself."

"Oh, I see, you are afraid that although you are mentally quite normal, others will think you insane."

"That is it exactly."

"And why do you fear that?"

"Because I cannot always control myself. Because every now and then I am forced to do what *They* insist upon."

"Who are *They*?"

"Had I better tell you that?" Hartmann's eyes took on a renewed look of sly cunning.

"You are quite safe in telling me," said Maximoff, lighting a cigarette and handing his guest the box of cigars. Hartmann took one and smoked so hastily that he was soon surrounded by a pale cloud. The doctor pulled his chair still nearer. He did not want to lose the changing expressions on the other's face.

"Well, aren't you going to tell me," he said, as Hartmann sat staring ahead of him and smiling weirdly.

"I can't tell you," he murmured finally.

"Why can't you?"

"Because *They*—have no names."

"I don't understand."

"You'll understand as soon as I tell you more. But first I want to know if you can give me some medicine."

"What sort of medicine do you want?"

"I want something to quiet my nerves. Something to give me back the control over myself, so that I do not draw people's attention to me by some ridiculous stupidity."

"What stupidity do you mean?"

"Why, yesterday for instance. You saw how absurdly I acted. And didn't you notice how they all looked at me when I nearly upset the wineglass and then when I laughed at Bauer's remark and said such stupid things."

"Yes, I did notice it."

"Well, there you see! And I do not want to draw people's attention to me."

"Why not?"

"Because if I do attract too much attention—then I'm done for."

"Now I don't understand you at all."

"I believe that. You haven't the faintest idea who I really am."

"Aren't you Robert Hartmann, landowner from Poland?"

Maximoff's guest laughed heartily. He beat his hands on his knees and choked in the violence of his merriment. "Robert Hartmann," he repeated and could scarcely say the words clearly, so shaken was he by his fits of laughter. Finally, he had controlled himself and now it was he who pulled his chair nearer to the other.

"You're quite sure no one can hear us," he whispered.

The doctor shook his head. "No one. We are quite undisturbed here," he replied soothingly.

"You are such a versatile man," continued the other. "You are not only a physician, you are a philosopher as well and I understand you are interested, as a philosopher, in every phase of mental abnormality."

"Yes, certainly, certainly."

"And among other things, in one branch of the science of the soul which is the most illuminating."

"What do you mean by that?"

"I mean that you are greatly interested, or I have understood that you are, in crime and criminals. Or rather—" Hartmann punctuated his remarks with a scornful gesture. "Or rather, in that which the weaklings, and the cowards, *call* crime."

A golden gleam shot up in the doctor's dark eyes and a peculiar smile curved his well-cut mouth.

"A great many of the books in your splendid library concern this fascinating chapter of human existence." Hartmann continued to speak without waiting for any answer. "And I noticed that for years you have been collecting all those copies of our leading newspapers which give reports of important criminal cases of recent times."

"Yes, you are right, but why do you speak of that now?"

"I will explain in a few moments. You believe then that I am Robert Hartmann from Poland? Landed proprietor and respectable house owner?"

"Well?" Maximoff's face expressed great interest. The golden gleams in his dark eyes clustered to brilliant points of light.

"But I'm not—I'm somebody else," said his guest, looking about anxiously. "But you're the only person I shall tell the truth to."—His eyes closed to narrow slits and his voice took on a threatening tone as he continued: "Professional etiquette demands that you should hold my confidence an absolute secret—therefore I am going to make you a confession—a confession that I must make to someone or I shall go mad. I know that I would really become insane if I could not tell somebody who I am."

The doctor breathed quicker. His face flushed and his voice was hoarse as he asked: "Who are you, then?"

His guest bent over until their faces almost touched and whispered: "If you look over the files of your newspapers from 1892 until 1906, you will see that during these years thirty-one murder cases occurred in Vienna, murder cases of which robbery was the motive. Twenty-four of the criminals were caught, notice this—only twenty-four. Seven remained undiscovered and free. On the 15th of

April, 1892, the woman Schramm, keeper of a little tap-room in the fifteenth district, was murdered. On the 8th of August, 1897, Thomas Brabenec was discovered stabbed to death in a grove outside the city. On the 26th of May, 1904, an old woman by the name of Faron, widow of a railway switchman, was found dead in her house. Please notice how easily these figures come to me. There are certain dates one does not forget."

"Well, go on—go on," said Maximoff eagerly. His face had regained its usual clear pallor, but the gleam in his eyes had grown wilder and a wicked smile played about his half-open mouth. His strong white hand held his guest's arm as if in a vice, and his voice sank to a hoarse whisper.

Mr. Hartmann smiled also; he was now quite calm, and seemed absolutely cold and indifferent as to the effect of his narrative on the other. There was a tone of scorn in his voice as he took up his story.

"The murderers—or rather the murderer of these three unfortunates has never been found. The police and the public are still labouring under the delusion that it was a case of murder for robbery." Maximoff's guest laughed aloud, as his eyes, bright with mocking merriment, met the Russian's wild gaze. "Absurd isn't it! As if *we*, who can make thousands by one blow if we want to, would murder for the sake of a few crowns! Why, I can tell you that the Schramm woman had exactly seven crowns, eighteen *hellars* in her till! Brabenec had less than six crowns in his pocket, and the poor old Faron creature hadn't enough money in her whole little hut for me to pay the cab back to my home. But the rest of the world don't understand. The herd of ordinary weaklings can't understand the keen sensation that lies in killing for the sheer sake of killing."

Maximoff's hand tightened on the arm of his guest with a grip of iron. His face was terrible. It was frozen into a smile that might have expressed the evil of a fiend in hell. His eyes alone were alive—they rested greedily, with a sort of devilish satisfaction on the man who sat there, telling him these things. Müller's hand still held the cigar which had gone out.

"My dear doctor, won't you give me a light?" said the detective calmly. In spite of his self-control he was anxious to get rid of that deadly grasp on his arm. He lit the cigar again, took a few puffs and continued:

"Now you know my secret. But you don't know my name yet. It isn't really necessary that you should know it. It's enough that you know

now that I am the mysterious murderer who has given the authorities so many difficult riddles to solve—riddles they have not yet solved."

A smile of easy self-satisfaction illumined Müller's face. It was reflected from Maximoff's eyes, although the Russian had now become noticeably uneasy. The sympathetic objectiveness with which he listened to the beginning of his guest's recital, had vanished entirely. His lips moved as if to speak, and yet he did not speak, while his mouth twitched and his hands clenched and unclenched nervously. The veteran detective on the other hand had now regained his habitual self-control and he was so calm that it was easy for him to continue to play his part thoroughly well.

"What worries me now," he began again, "is the way my nerves are going back on me. As you saw yourself, I draw people's attention by my stupid behaviour. I was very much annoyed that it should have happened yesterday in a house where I wish to remain unknown."

Maximoff started as if a sudden thought had occurred to him. "What are you doing there?" he exclaimed suspiciously. "You forced your way into that house under a false name—and it can't be for a good purpose."

"Oh, be easy about that," replied the other. "No harm will come to any of the Plöhn family, particularly not to Miss Plöhn if that is what is worrying you, through my presence there."

"But what do you want there, anyway?" repeated Maximoff. His guest smiled and sank his voice to a whisper. "I want to look on at the bunglers who are still fussing around, breaking their stupid heads over my last deed, and—naturally not finding out anything. Why, they haven't even found the—"

"What last deed do you mean?" interrupted the doctor vehemently.

For the last few minutes Müller had held his cigar in his left hand. Now with a casual unobtrusive movement, he dropped his right hand into the coat pocket which contained the bottle of chloroform. Then he answered in a tone of astonishment: "Why, haven't you understood yet? Of course it's the Erlach case I mean."

Maximoff sprang from his chair, a hot wave of blood rushing up to his very temples. He looked dazed, bewildered. He pressed both hands to his forehead, measured the length of the room a few times with long strides, then halted suddenly in front of his guest and burst into an uproarious fit of laughter. He put out his hand to a chair as if for support, so greatly was he shaken by the violence of his merriment. Hartmann looked up at him in indignant surprise.

"Have you gone mad?" he exclaimed.

Maximoff pulled himself together and controlled his laughter with an effort. "No, I am not mad, my dear friend—but now I know what's the matter with you."

Now it was Müller's turn to spring up. "What do you mean by that?" he cried harshly. But the doctor patted him on the shoulder and answered soothingly. "Oh, nothing—nothing at all to offend you. I was simply overcome by the idea that you, Erlach's murderer, should deliberately come here to watch the people who are hunting for him in vain."

Müller bowed as if flattered. "The best joke of all happened on a Sunday two weeks ago," he began again.

The doctor went back to his chair and sat down. The inward merriment against which he was still fighting shone from his eyes and played about his handsome mouth. "Oh, please, do tell me about it," he asked, biting his lips to keep back the laughter. "What happened two weeks ago then?"

"It was Sunday night. I went back to the Green House as I did several times before. And what do you suppose? One of those spying bunglers was there also, a detective I mean—must have been the detective you mentioned a little while ago."

"Oh, that was a detective, was it?"

"I put him out in short order I can tell you. I fired at him twice, but I'm sorry to say I didn't hit him."

"Oh, then it was *you* who did the shooting that night?"

"Then my valet, who had come to my help, and I, walked back and forth, twisting and curving about the moor. I wanted to cover our trail, for I knew that the fool would be waiting for me and I didn't want him to see where I was living. But I must say he was cleverer than I thought. We didn't see him again, but he must have followed us."

"What? why do you believe that?" cut in Maximoff, greatly surprised.

"I found his footprints in the mud outside the garden gate next morning. Since then I have been in a constant state of surprise that I should have been left so undisturbed."

"I don't believe that you would have been left undisturbed if the man had come there in pursuit of you," replied Maximoff, emphasizing each word sharply, with a rolling anger in his voice. Then he said, more brightly: "I give you my word the man was there by pure accident. But now I want you to tell me how. you did that trick in the

Green House. The whole thing is such a mystery that I am naturally very curious to hear the explanation of it." He smiled at Müller ironically as he spoke.

"It took me many weeks to think it out, to plan it all beforehand, as you may imagine," began the detective. "I hung about the garden wall in the disguise of a pedlar and took a wax impression of the three keyholes which barred the way to Erlach's room, the garden gate and the two front doors, the iron one and the inner one. Then I waited for a stormy evening, when the noise of the wind should deaden everything else, climbed over the garden wall, opened the gate from the inside and opened the house doors. I entered the house and Erlach's Study, the door of which I knew was never locked, for the old gentleman might at any moment need the help of his housekeeper. He was aged and feeble, and worried about his health." Müller stopped talking and took a long puff from his cigar.

"Well, go on—tell me about it," insisted the doctor.

Müller's eyes lit up again in cruel cunning. "Well, then—then I shot Erlach," he remarked with a smile.

The doctor gave a short hard laugh, then spoke gently: "Well, my friend, go on, tell me the rest."

"Then I carried the body out onto the moor," narrated Müller, losing himself again in the enjoyment of his cigar. But Maximoff bent over and almost tore it from his hand as he said: "I want you to talk, not to smoke."

"Why, what else is there to talk about?"

"The greatest mystery of all—the mystery that no one has as yet solved." Maximoff was quite calm as he said this, his only sensation seemed to be an over-weening curiosity.

"Oh, you mean the garden door bolted on the inside? Well, when I carried the body out, I went back into the garden, locked and bolted the door and climbed over the wall. That's simple enough."

"Yes, that—and the strangling of an old man, that's all very simple," mocked Maximoff. "Any fool can do that."

"Oh now, see here," exclaimed Müller angrily.

"Any fool," repeated Maximoff sharply. Then with kaleidoscopic suddenness he was once more the friendly soothing physician. "Of course I don't mean you when I say 'any fool,'" he continued. "For you have outdone the cleverest criminal I know, the Man with the Black Cord. He himself might be proud of this crime." The doctor's eyes fairly sparkled and his smile was triumphant.

"Why, yes, I *am* the Man with the Black Cord," remarked Müller, his eyes shining also and his lips curved in a victorious smile.

The doctor sprang up from his chair, ran back and forth through the study with his hands pressed to his temples, then halted again before his guest, and again his uproarious laughter echoed from the walls of the handsome room.

"Oh, that's great," he cried merrily. "That's the most delicious thing I've heard in many a day. You then—*you* are this genius of crime, the Unknown whom you yourself first called the 'Man with the Black Cord!'"

Again his laughter rang through the room, then with another one of his sudden changes his voice quieted down to gentleness and he continued: "Well, then, you great man, do explain to me the riddle of the doors locked from the inside, and the disappearance of the strangled victim from the closed room."

"Of the *shot* victim you mean?"

"No, he was *strangled,* first chloroformed and then strangled, if you want to know the particulars," declared Maximoff in a tone of conviction.

"All right, just as you like," replied Müller with a smile as of satisfied vanity. "Well, first I underscored the three words in the old book on the table, then I left it open there, and locked the bedroom from the inside. Then I turned the key in the lock of the study door in such a way that it only needed the least little touch to snap the lock."

"Well, and then?" Maximoff's breath came quickly and Müller's hand was clasped tightly around the neck of the chloroform bottle in his pocket.

"Then," he went on, "then I took a long thin iron rod with a hook on the end, which I had brought with me, and when I had left the house, locking both front doors, I went around in front of the sitting room windows, and stood on the bench that is there. I pushed the rod into the room through the open window and with its hook I could easily catch the key of the door and turn it, snapping the lock. So that you see in this way both doors were locked from the inside and their keys were in the proper place. That was no such great trick. But I committed a blunder here. I had to leave a burning candle on the little table so that I could see the lock distinctly. I wanted to put out this candle with the end of the rod but it was difficult to manage it, and I hit the burning wick with such violence that the wax spattered all over the table. Well, doctor, why don't you say something?"

Maximoff had sunk down in a heap in his chair, completely absorbed in his thoughts. Finally he raised his head, doubt, anxiety and scorn striving for the mastery in his face. "And *that's* why you claim to be the Man with the Black Cord?" he murmured, rising and beginning again his uneasy pacing of the room.

Müller rose also. He pushed his chair back so that the door onto the terrace was free, and the heavy armchair stood between him and Maximoff. He had already taken the little bottle of chloroform from his pocket and held it in his closed hand, thumb and first finger in place on the nickel top. Then he waited.

At first Maximoff's anger seemed to gain the victory over his warring emotions, then a moment later he controlled himself and his scorn came uppermost again. He stopped still in the middle of the room, both hands in his pockets, his voice hushed to a quiet calm tone, while his eyes rested mockingly on those of his guest. "But you haven't finished your story. Where did you hide Erlach's body?"

Müller pretended embarrassment. He stared at the doctor as if quite bewildered. "The body—the body? Where did I hide it?" he murmured, then after a pause: "I—I hid it—"

"Well, where did you hide it?" came from between the doctor's set teeth.

Müller looked quite helpless. "I—I don't know—I can't remember."

"Then you hold your tongue," screamed Maximoff, but Müller persisted obstinately: "All the same I'm the Man with the Black Cord—here look at this. I carry a piece of it with me wherever I go-He held out the bit of cord he had found on Erlach's bed, so that the other could see it. Maximoff stared at it, his face reddened, the veins on his temples pulsed audibly—"You are a fool," he cried—"an impertinent insolent idiot—how dare you usurp the credit for a genius that you never possessed! Why you fool—*I* am the Man with the Black Cord, I—and I'll crush the life out of you—you—"

He could get no further. He choked and gasped and bent forward towards the slight figure of the man who stood opposite him, his powerful hands clenched threateningly, the great muscles of his shoulders stiffening visibly through his coat. Müller made a sudden movement of his right hand, then slipped through the open door onto the terrace.

In the same instant, a sharp whistle rang out and the two men from behind the fir tree dashed into the study. They found the room full of the odour of chloroform and Maximoff already half overcome by the fumes. He still raged and screamed, striking out with his hands and snapping at his captors with his teeth. But the chloroform had already robbed him of most of his great strength.

The frightened women servants rushed to the window and stood there cowering in terror at the noise, and at the unexpected sight of several uniformed policemen in the garden. The Viennese official and Constable Kern entered the study, while Mr. Hartmann walked rapidly towards the lower end of the garden.

The terrifying shrieks still rang through the house, then finally all was still. Sergius Maximoff, bound hand and foot, was thrown down into an armchair by his captors. Even then it took all their strength to hold him, until the violence of his outbreak spent itself in the reaction of utter exhaustion. He sat quite still, a sly smile wreathed his lips and in his eyes shone a satanic determination.

The police commissioner stood before him. "Doctor, we are here to arrest you. We have a wagon waiting back of your garden. You can be driven away quietly without being seen. I am taking for granted therefore, that you will come with me voluntarily, that you will walk there yourself."

"If you will take these cords off my feet," replied Maximoff proudly, "I will follow you wherever you say. But you will find, my dear sir, that before this day is over, it will be up to you to ask my pardon humbly. You have made a mistake in your prisoner. The man you are looking for has been living in Mr. Plöhn's-house under the name of Hartmann. It was I who discovered his identity, and I was about to take him prisoner when he overcame me with chloroform and escaped."

"We'll find him," remarked the commissioner calmly. And Maximoff continued: "But you must lose no time. I will hold you responsible if he escapes entirely. You may better understand the importance of what I say when I tell you that this Hartmann is the Man with the Black Cord, who has Erlach's murder to his credit as well as the others."

The commissioner bowed in silence. At a gesture from him, the attendants loosened the fetters on the Russian's feet.

"Very well, we can go now," said Maximoff, rising from the chair. He was so exhausted that the attendants had to support him as they walked from the house and through the garden. A weird smile brightened the Russian's gloomy face as the little group moved slowly over the lawn towards the rear fence. Then they turned the corner of a group of fir trees and the quiet of the pleasant spot was broken by a terrific scream. Maximoff stood still, his eyes widened, staring at the devastated bed of box which he himself had arranged a few weeks before. The little cedar lay cut down and thrown to one side. The rounded heads of box were torn ruthlessly out and cast in a disorderly heap. Where they had been the earth was removed from a long shallow trough and in this trough lay the body of Leopold Erlach, fully dressed, his nightshirt spread across his legs.

"Come, Doctor, the cabs are waiting," said the commissioner.

But Maximoff did not move. One more gasping shriek and he fell unconscious to the ground.

At this moment Müller was already out in the road, walking towards the factory. He walked very slowly, his head sunk deep on his breast, his face ghastly pale. When that horrible scream rang through the quiet morning air he stopped in his walk and turned to look behind him. His fingers worked as if in a cramp, his teeth set firm and his breath came in a gasp that was a sobbing sigh.

CHAPTER 17

Where the Blow Falls

About an hour after the catastrophe in Rose Cottage, General-Manager Plöhn had already eaten his lunch and was back in his office. He had not taken up the burden of his work yet but sat leaning back in a comfortable armchair reading a paper and smoking. His servant Wilhelm hurried in with a card on a salver.

"This gentleman asks to see you at once," said the man.

Plöhn looked at him in astonishment and asked: "Why, what's the matter? You're shaking all over."

"It's so like him, sir—and yet it isn't him," stammered Wilhelm.

Plöhn shook his head and touched his forehead with one finger. "There's a screw loose with you somewhere," he said laughing. He looked at the card before him. It bore the name of Joseph Müller "Show the gentleman in," said Plöhn, laying aside his paper. The manager was prepared for some surprise after seeing his servant's bewilderment. He watched the door with interest, but when it opened and his visitor entered Plöhn himself appreciated what had happened to Wilhelm. The man who stood before him was an inch or so shorter than Hartmann and weighed considerably less. Also he was quite differently dressed, but apart from this the resemblance was astonishing. Plöhn put his hand to his forehead as if fearing for his own brain now, and looked down again at the name on the card.

"Joseph Müller? Joseph Müller?" he murmured. "I never saw such a likeness before."

"Nor did I," said Joseph Müller in Hartmann's voice as he closed the door.

The manager, who had risen at the other's entrance, sat down again and stared up at his caller. He shook his head and seemed too bewildered to find words.

"May I sit down?" asked Joseph Müller, pulling a chair near to the desk.

"Please do," murmured Plöhn, wondering to himself whether he were not taking his afternoon nap at the moment and dreaming all this. Then Joseph Müller spoke:

"It was under the name of Robert Hartmann from Poland, that I enjoyed your delightful hospitality."

"Then you are not the man you let us believe you to be?" questioned the manager slowly, as if trying to understand.

Müller put his tall hat down on the edge of the table, unbuttoned his black coat and took a portfolio from his pocket. From this he drew a large card and handed it to Plöhn.

"This is who, and what, I am," he said.

Plöhn looked at the photograph on the card and the official statement of the police department that accompanied it. His face was very grave as he handed the paper back to Müller.

"Then you are a detective?" he said.

"Yes, I am a detective. I think I need not tell you that I came here to investigate the Erlach case."

"I imagined that was it. But my chief, the Baron, knows who it is that he sent to me?"

"Naturally. I could not have come without his assistance. This may be some excuse for my presence here."

"You need no excuse Mr.—Müller. You were a welcome guest— and you have endeared yourself to us all."

Müller bowed and pressed the other's hand warmly. "And now I have come to thank you for all your kindness, your sincere cordiality."

Plöhn looked down at the little man before him, whose face was so grave and who seemed struggling to suppress a sadness which threatened to overcome him. "Then you are going away?" the manager asked. "You have not been successful here? They're going to send another detective?"

"I am going away because there is nothing more to do here."

"What do you mean?"

"I mean that Erlach's murderer has been discovered and is already in security."

"At last! oh, but wait a minute. I mustn't be the only one to hear that. Let's go over and join the ladies." Plöhn rose from his chair but Müller shook his head.

"Please sit down again, Mr. Plöhn. I cannot tell the ladies what I have to tell you."

"Why not?"

"Please, won't you sit down?"

There are moments in the lives of all of us when we have the instant recognition that something terrible is nearing us. We do not know what it is, nor from what side it is coming, but we know that it *is* coming, and that it is something horrible. For the first time in his life, the robust, good-natured and easy-going Plöhn realized that such a moment had come for him. He sat down, drew a deep breath and looked up anxiously at his visitor.

"I could not tell your sister especially,—not at least until you know," said Müller low.

Plöhn bent forward in his chair, in evident excitement. He swallowed hard several times, then spoke with difficulty: "What—what do' you mean—"

"It is you who must tell Miss Suzanne." Müller too was hoarse.

"I—I don't understand you," murmured Plöhn.

"Oh, yes, you understand me perfectly well."

"Mr. Hartmann—Mr. Müller—"

"I left Rose Cottage less than an hour ago."

"It's some mistake—some horrible mistake," gasped the manager.

"Unfortunately—there is no mistake possible here."

"Sergius—"

"Sergius is not his name."

"Maximoff—"

"That is not his name."

"If it is thought that he killed Erlach—"

"It is *known* that he killed Erlach."

"Then he did it in anger. He is easily aroused—and passionate—and he is so strong—a death blow might be given before he thought it—"

"It was a murder—a carefully prearranged murder, a crime that was carried out with the same care, the same cleverness and the same daring as the—"

"As the—" Plöhn's icy hand caught at Müller's fingers, scarcely less icy, his eyes seemed starting from their sockets. Müller finished his sentence: "As were the other crimes that he has committed."

Plöhn tried to speak but only gasped.

"For he is the Man with the Black Cord."

Plöhn's face was ghastly, and on Müller's brow the great beads of perspiration stood out. He wiped them away, then he continued sadly: "You see how I am obliged to reward all your hospitality. But I have one comfort for you."

"A comfort? How could there be any comfort here."

"Maximoff is insane."

Plöhn looked up, startled afresh.

"Is not that some comfort to you?" asked the detective.

He did not know whether Plöhn had even heard him. The poor man sat there frozen to stone, looking out into blankness with eyes that were dumb in grief. In this horrible moment, he first realized how fond he had grown of Maximoff. Then he thought of his sister and a shudder ran through every fibre of his robust frame. For he realized that it was he who must tell this girl so dear to him, this woman happy in her love, dreaming of how a few weeks more would make her a happy wife,—he must tell her that the man she loved was the monster who had held the entire neighbourhood in terror for so long. When he realized what the truth had meant to him, the strong man, he shuddered to think of the crushing blow it would be to her. He groaned aloud and covered his face with his hands. He sat thus for many minutes, and Müller too, was quite still. He understood the other's suffering, and he gave him time to recover from the first shock.

It was very quiet in the comfortable little office. A soft hum of distant noises came from the direction of the factory, but within the room nothing was heard except the ticking of the clock and the deep gasping breath of the stricken man. Finally Plöhn raised his head and straightened himself up in his chair. He had conquered the first dreadful moment of the shock; a certain frozen calm came into his face.

"Now—now you can tell me what you have to tell." His voice sounded hard.

Müller told his story. He told of how he had received the first hint when he saw the picture of Napoleon which Maximoff had shown him as one of his art treasures, and of which he already knew that it had been in Erlach's possession up to two days before the latter's disappearance. He spoke of the visit of the detective Greng at Rose Cottage and told the story of the journey to Russia. He described his visit to old Andreas Maximoff in Wenden and that it was there he had first heard about Nikolai Simirenko, which was the true name of the man who was betrothed to Suzanne. Old Maximoff had told him much of the past of this nephew, and had told him also that Simirenko came of a family in which the trait of insanity was hereditary.

When he reached this part of the story Plöhn gave a sigh of relief. "Oh, thank God! thank God!" he exclaimed, "then at least he is not responsible for his terrible deeds."

Müller nodded. "You are right," he continued. "Nikolai Simirenko is an unfortunate man, his mind is held in bondage by a terrible delusion. Listen now. He knew of the hereditary taint in his blood and even as a youth, although he was strong and well, he suffered tortures in the thought that he might fall a victim to the curse, to the curse that had weighed so long upon his family. He took up the study of medicine, hoping that through his knowledge in this field he would be able to save himself from the threatened disaster. It was natural under the circumstances that the specialty to attract him should be mental alienation. He was an excellent student, too much so for his own good. About twelve years ago he and his cousin, whose name he is now bearing, took their degree at the University of Vienna,—then they both returned home.

"Sergius Maximoff brought his own people the good news that his cousin Nikolai had returned to his home in the best of health and spirits. Then the real Maximoff went on a tour of the world and settled down in South Africa, where all news from him soon ceased. Nikolai Simirenko remained in Russia, married and lived happily with his wife for about three years. He devoted himself to his studies, alas too deeply! He had always been well-to-do and now, through a legacy, he had become a very rich man. But he did not spend his days in the usual enjoyments indulged in by other rich young men.

"He was always of a reserved disposition and he became more so as time passed on. He had few friends and seemed interested only in his studies. He and his wife travelled much until Sonya was born. Then the young couple were obliged to remain at home, for Sonya's mother never recovered her health after the birth of the child. Her husband scarcely left her bedside. He sent for the most renowned specialists from St. Petersburg and Berlin, but none of them could bring relief to the sufferer. It was he himself who finally put an end to his wife's pain—she was found one morning in her bed, strangled. Around her throat was a bit of black cord which had literally put an end to her suffering. The family curse had fallen, the hereditary insanity had broken out in Simirenko.

"There was no doubt about it, for he himself quite calmly acknowledged that he had deliberately killed the wife whom he loved more than anything else in the world, because he could not bear to see her suffer. He was proud of what he had done—and who shall say that his pride was altogether unjustified? It was this attitude of his that seemed so abnormal to those around him, and they committed him to an asylum."

"I visited this asylum," continued Müller, "and I soon convinced myself that it would not take any great cunning to escape from it. Simirenko had been there scarcely a year before he got away, doubtless helped by a judicious use of money. On the night of his flight he stopped in at his own house, took his little girl and the two disappeared from Russia. How he ever managed to pass the frontier with the child will perhaps never be explained. And there is something else equally important which is equally likely to remain a mystery. He had no immediate relatives, and when he was put in the asylum the state took charge of his fortune. To the surprise of everyone there was no money there, his entire fortune seemed to have disappeared entirely."

The narrator paused and took a sip from a glass of water that stood on the table.

"Had that anything to do with Maximoff—I mean with that man's insanity?" asked Plöhn.

Müller shrugged his shoulders. "What I think," he replied, "is that Maximoff—*I* cannot get away from the name either—utilized his various journeyings to invest his fortune quietly in some other country. Russia is very uncertain financially as well as politically, and his actions in this respect would seem to show a sane and normal mind."

"Was he—insane when he killed his wife?" asked Plöhn again.

Again the detective shrugged his shoulders and he answered this question with another: "Is it a sign of insanity when a physician decides to end the suffering of a patient whom he knows to be in acute pain and incurable?"

Again there was silence in the room until Müller took up his story: "Since his flight from the asylum all knowledge of Nikolai Simirenko was lost in Russia. But the physicians of the institution have not lost interest in their unfortunate colleague. I did not tell them the reason for my inquiries for I wanted unbiased information. I called myself a former Viennese acquaintance of his, who came into that neighbourhood by chance, had heard of Simirenko's sad case and now wished to know more about it One of the physicians, a kindly, elderly gentleman, told me that Dr. Simirenko's insanity was of an unusual sort It concerned one corner of his brain alone as it were, and as such it might be considered as having started fresh with him, although he said it was not possible to doubt the existence of an inherited inclination to mental abnormality. But it was fear of the dread fate, his ardent wish to escape it, his hot desire to shield himself through knowledge, the mental overwork and constant occupation with one train of thought—these were the stages of the journey made by Simirenko until he reached the dread goal of broken nerves and outspoken insanity. Psychiatry, and its allied branches of study had made Simirenko a madman. And the, worst misfortune that befell him was that while in Vienna he had had as a classmate a Hindu student with whom he had become warm friends. This man taught him to believe in the doctrine of the transmigration of souls."

"Oh, yes—yes. He used to speak of it sometimes," threw in Plöhn. "Has that anything to do with his madness?"

"A great deal. It is the most important factor connected with the crimes he has committed here."

"Please tell me what you mean."

"As a natural connection with his studies of psychology, Nikolai Simirenko came to take a great interest in the soul of the criminal. I don't know whether you have noticed that there were so many books on Criminal Psychology in his library. He himself told me, on one of my visits to Rose Cottage, that what interested him most along the wide field of medical science, was what the unthinking mass called 'The Sinister Perversities of the Human Soul.' Even then his expression, 'As the unthinking mass call it' struck me, for it was evident that he did not consider himself one of the mass. The old Russian doctor in the asylum told me that while he was there Simirenko openly avowed his admiration for several of the famous criminals of history, those types of men who had learned to kill for the pure joy of killing."

"Oh, this is terrible!"

"Ezzelino di Romano, Nero, and men of that stamp seemed to be the ideal of this gifted young man, who in his *normal* moments represented the best type of warm-hearted and highly intelligent modern scholar. He also took the greatest possible interest in that half mythical character, the Court Jeweller Cardillac, who is said to have lived in the time of Louis XIV and to have perpetrated a long series of mysterious crimes. What seemed to particularly interest him in Cardillac was his love for strange and odd pieces of jewellery. He seemed to believe that the souls of these great criminals of history entered by turn into his own in his sick moments, and ordered all his doings, for which he was not otherwise responsible.

"One of the patients in the institution wore an odd and beautiful ring to which Simirenko seemed greatly attracted. The man was found dead in bed one morning and his ring missing. At first the cause of death was not apparent, but at the autopsy it was discovered that a tiny nail was driven deep into the victim's skull. After Simirenko's flight from the asylum the missing ring, also a miniature portrait of the head doctor's son, were discovered in the mattress of his bed."

"Oh, this is terrible—terrible," cried Plöhn shuddering.

"Yes, it is indeed, terrible," repeated Müller, "and I think it was high time that the man was discovered and rendered harmless—high time for Miss Suzanne and for his own little girl, Sonya."

Plöhn looked up with a horror in his eyes that seemed to rob him of words. The detective continued: "Those earrings which Simirenko gave Miss Suzanne—you remember he said that he had brought them from Russia—they had formerly belonged to Erlach. You remember my excitement at the moment? I had found a description and a drawing of the jewels among the dead man's papers, and the earrings themselves were not in his cabinet, nor was there any clue to their whereabouts. With his mania for murder Simirenko combined a tendency here and there to make away with property of others. But it was never for any other reason than to obtain some cherished art treasure—or in some cases to make up for the niggardliness of his victim."

"I don't understand—what do you mean?"

"On my secret visits to the Green House," explained Müller, "I found reason to think that about twenty thousand crowns were missing from Erlach's capital. I learned accidentally that immediately after Erlach's disappearance Maximoff had given forty thousand crowns to endow two free beds in a Viennese hospital. Yesterday I made an official investigation of this matter and discovered that one of the beds was registered under 'Endowed by L. E.,' and the other 'N. S.' Old Erlach, as you know, was very close with his money and anything but generous. His murderer set the old miser a monument which the other scarcely deserved. And at the same time he gave a neat little sum out of his own property. But I must say that I did not like his giving his future wife the earrings which had belonged to his latest victim."

"Yes, yes I understand—I feel the same way myself. But are you sure—absolutely sure—that those were Erlach's earrings?"

"Yes, there is no doubt possible. They were a very odd design and besides the description and drawing which I told you I found in some old family papers—you can see another picture of them yourself in the family portrait hanging in the drawing room of the Erlach house."

"Have they—have they found Erlach's body?"

"Yes, Simirenko had buried it in his garden."

"Then they have arrested him already?" Plöhn sighed deeply as he spoke, and Müller's voice was sad as he answered the question.

"They took him away about two hours ago. Just before I came here the commissioner, who remained in Rose Cottage some little while after the arrest, told me he had made interesting discoveries in the little room which the doctor called his photographing dark room. It *was* used for this purpose, but for other purposes as well. In a cupboard in this room the commissioner found a long dark cloak with a high stiff-lined hood in which holes were cut for the ears, also several pairs of gloves of remarkably fine and flexible kid, and boots with very high heels and heavy soles which were fastened into felt slippers. Also there was a little strong box in the cupboard which contained a paper missing among Erlach's securities. And something more was found there. A big coil of horsehair lariat, bits of which we have already seen."

"Oh, yes—yes, the black cord—why did he use that in his crimes?"

"Who can tell the vagaries a sick soul may have? He had bought a lariat once as a curiosity for his collection of foreign weapons. The strength and flexibility of the narrow cord seemed to appeal to him and it was with this that he strangled his wife. It became afterward a sort of a fad with him, a vanity as it were, that he should leave his trademark behind him whenever he had committed a crime."

"But I still don't understand why none of us ever recognized the man's condition! Just think how often he was in our house, how intimate our friendship was!"

"But you told me yourself that you had never seen much of him until he became interested in your sister, and that you were never really intimate with him until the two were engaged. That is but little over two months now, I believe."

"Yes, you are right," said Plöhn, "before that he lived like a hermit. None of us really knew anything about him."

"And madmen of his stamp are wonderful actors. It is hardly to be called acting even, for I feel assured that in the man's normal moments he had but very little realization of what he did when the fit was on him. His really unusual and well-trained mind asserted its sovereignty even in his hours of madness. Therefore all his crimes were carefully planned and carried out with an audacity which proved the man of great intelligence. It did not seem possible that he could sit and talk to us so calmly about these very crimes if he were always, when normal, conscious of what his other self had done. And in his normal moments he was certainly a man of most unusual ability and charm, one of those rare beings whom one does not meet very often."

"Yes, that's what makes it so dreadful," cut in Plöhn. "I have seldom seen a man who combined so many good qualities."

"All the more terrible that such a brain should have been over-thrown," continued Müller "In fact it did not occur to me that the man was actually mad—when I first began to suspect him I thought myself obliged to believe him one of the greatest criminals of modern times. Then one day I happened by accident to see the title of a well-known book on Criminal Psychology and I remembered its contents, which were well-known to me. There have been other cases similar to his,—but they are to be found at rare intervals. I myself didn't realize how terrible they could be until I had it brought home to me."

"You're going already?" asked Plöhn hastily as Müller rose from his chair.

"There are some more details which might interest you," said the detective, "but we can postpone the telling of them for another time. I am very tired now and I must make up my official report."

Plöhn realized that his guest looked tired and he touched the bell on his desk. "Let me order you something to eat," he said, going to the door as the attendant came. They sat in silence until the tray was brought and as Müller ate the cold meat and drank the wine, it seemed to restore and rest him. Plöhn waited on him anxiously, with a request in his eyes which he dared not yet make.

Müller looked up suddenly from the tray and remarked: "One thing I must tell you in justice to my valet Karl—who is not my valet, but a professional assistant. I did not dismiss him from my service as I had to tell you that I did. I wanted to get him out of the way so that I could send him on the Russian journey with Simirenko."

"You feel better now—more rested?" asked Plöhn, handing his guest the box of cigars.

"Yes, thank you, I think it was partly hunger. Although I *am* tired. But I generally find that I can keep up when there is some-thing to do."

"If your profession brings you many such experiences as you have gone through today, it must be hard on mind and body."

Müller sighed. "Yes, this did touch me deeply; I had grown very fond of the man. It's this fool heart of mine that gives me so much trouble. It steps in when I want to be most professional and if it doesn't actually lead me into doing unprofessional things, it makes me suffer as I have done today."

"It's just this kind heart of yours—and your wide experience that makes me—that gives me the courage to ask something of you." Plöhn spoke hesitatingly as if trying to find the words. Müller looked up without answering. Plöhn took a fresh start: "I want you to help me—to help me tell Suzanne," he almost groaned.

"Oh—no—no."

"Yes, you must—I am helpless here. She is all I have left besides my own family—she is very dear to me. I am awkward and clumsy. These things are beyond me—I don't know how to put it so that it would not kill her at once. You would know. You have been through so many cases of suffering and sorrow that your own work must have brought about. She likes you and has confidence in you. She knows that you liked—him—you must tell her—you must help me tell her." Plöhn's voice sank to a pathetic note of pleading that was touching in the contrast of its helplessness with his robust frame and fresh wholesome face.

Müller paused a moment, then rose heavily and slowly from his chair. "Very well, then," he said, "if you wish it I will do what I can."

Plöhn seized his hand and wrung it hard, stammering incoherent thanks. Together the men walked from the office through the covered passageway to the house. As they entered the cheerful sitting room Suzanne was there alone, sewing at a window. She sprang up and came to meet them with a merry welcome.

"Why, this is delightful! I hardly expected you two this hour of the day—why, I beg your pardon—I thought it was Mr. Hartmann—"

"It is—the man you have known as Hartmann," said Müller slowly.

"But what—but you are so different today. I don't understand." Suzanne turned her eyes towards her brother as if to ask explanation from him. When she saw his drawn and haggard face, she gasped, pressed her hands to her heart and then exclaimed, low: "Oh, what is it—what is the matter?—what is it?"

The keen-sensed girl felt that some tragedy was in the air. All the gloom of the presentiment that had been hanging over her for the last week or two, in strange contrast to her usually sane and wholesome nature, came back with a rush. It had disappeared the last few days. Her lover's return in such good spirits, their mutual happy plans for the approaching marriage, all the sweet preparations for it that mean so much to a true woman, had served to restore Suzanne to her usual habitude of looking on the brighter side of life only. But at this moment she passed through the hideous ache of anticipation that had, a short time back, so crushed her brother's more material spirit. Suzanne was a woman of character and accustomed to self-control. She did not cry out now, but stood there quietly waiting.

Plöhn put out his hand and she laid hers in it, drawing close to him and looking up in his face.

"Suzanne," he began, trying to control his own emotion, "this gentleman whom we have known as Mr. Hartmann, is the detective Joseph Müller. He has been our guest because his professional duty demanded it."

"Detective—here on duty?"

"He came to find the monster who has terrorized our neighbourhood—whom he himself called 'The Man with the Black Cord.'"

Suzanne drew a step off from her brother. A sound that was almost like a short laugh came from her lips, so great was her sudden relief.

"And have you found him?" she exclaimed. "Oh, yes, you have, I see—but I don't see why—why you should both look so—upset! What's that to you, Richard? It seems to have touched you—was it— was it one of your men?"

"No, not one of my men."

"Well, who was it then? Who was it? Was it someone we knew? Why you ought to be glad that he is found—that our homes here are safe once more."

"It was someone—we all knew," began Plöhn haltingly.

"Oh, who—who—?" Again the black pall of some approaching evil seemed to sink down on Suzanne's heart.

Müller came forward a step and spoke: "Miss Plöhn, this man with the black cord, who is the perpetrator of all these mysterious crimes, including Erlach's disappearance—Erlach's *murder* I should say, is not so much a criminal as an unfortunate. He is a madman."

"Madman?" asked Suzanne. "Oh, how terrible! And we have had a madman in our midst all this time without knowing it?"

"Yes, without knowing it," said Müller, "and I myself was as much surprised by the truth as any of you could have been."

"But who is it—who?" Suzanne's insistence bore a note of fear. Her brother took her hands again and drew her in the shelter of his arms. "Why Richard," she continued, "I'm not so frightened—I'm no weakling you know—of course the thought is unpleasant, but now that the man has been found we are quite safe—why, you foolish boy."

"No one suspected the truth," said Müller in the moment's pause that ensued, "because this madman, in his lucid intervals, was one of the most remarkably intelligent and attractive men I have ever met."

Suzanne had been looking at the detective even as she spoke to her brother. Now she turned her head to look at the man whose arms still encircled her protectingly. A low, inarticulate note of fear broke involuntarily from her lips as she saw her brother's face. "Richard! who is it—who is it he is talking about—what is it that you know—why do you look so horrified—why do you hold me so? Who is this man he is talking about—tell me—do tell me." Plöhn only held her closely and looked helplessly at Müller.

"You will have need of all your courage, Miss Suzanne," said the detective, "to bear this shock which is to come to you. It has almost crushed your brother. He has not yet recovered. This—madman was dear to us all—and to you—very dear to you—"

"To me!" her voice rose to a higher note. "To me!" she repeated. "Oh—" Here she looked at them both again, a quick, comprehending glance. "Oh, my God!—not—not—"

"Yes," said Plöhn, very low. "It is he."

"Sergius?" Suzanne scarcely breathed the name as she swayed in her brother's protecting arms. "Oh, no, no, no. Oh, it is ridiculous—I don't believe you—you are both gone crazy—it is you who are madmen."

Her brother only held her tighter as Müller spoke very gravely.

"No, it is no mistake, unfortunately,. This man who had won all our hearts, this highly-gifted man of great talent was the victim of a taint of hereditary insanity which took a homicidal course."

Suzanne gave a low moan and covered her face with her hands. She would have fallen had not Plöhn held her tightly. "My poor Suzanne," he murmured. "My poor dear girl!"

"Let me think," she said very slowly. "I can't grasp it. Then—if he did all these terrible things—oh, but I can't believe it, I can't."

"You must, dear," said Plöhn. "It is only too true—"

"But then—hereditary insanity you say? Then he was not responsible?"

"No, thank God, no," exclaimed Plöhn. "His better self—the man we loved, scarcely realized what he did in his moments of madness. Is it not so?" he turned to Müller with a look of pleading.

"Yes, I believe it was so," said the detective. "It made the horror of what I had to do a little less poignant."

"*You—you* did it—" Suzanne shook herself free from her brother's arm and straightened up. "Then you came here to hound him down? You came to us under a false name to watch him?—oh, it was cruel—cruel!"

Müller shook his head sadly, and Plöhn took his sister's hands. "Be just, dear," he said. "He has done only his duty—and he has saved your life possibly."

"What?"

"His first wife died—" Plöhn did not finish the sentence, but Suzanne understood. With a scream she threw herself into his arms again and buried her face on his shoulder, shuddering violently.

"He did it to end her sufferings—she was in great pain and her malady was incurable," said Müller quickly, feeling the horror in the girl's soul. "He knew it was only a question of time—he was a physician—and he ended it. *This* crime at least, terrible as it is in our eyes, has much to excuse it."

"Because he loved her so greatly," came in smothered tones from Suzanne.

"Yes, because he loved her so greatly," repeated Müller.

"Then his *love* at least was not madness?" the girl continued mechanically, tonelessly.

"No, that was genuine, as were all his good qualities."

Suzanne wheeled round suddenly. "Where is he now?" There was a sudden unnatural calm about her.

"They have taken him—to the city."

"To prison?"

"No—to the asylum."

"I must go to him—my place is at his side—he loved me—if my love is of any value it must show itself now. Take me to him."

"No—no, dear, you must not think of it," murmured Plöhn. "Your presence would be of no good to him just now—it might only serve to excite him dangerously—" Again she broke from her brother's restraining grasp.

"But I *must*, it is my duty."

"There is another duty which calls for you," said Müller. "That poor little girl—now doubly orphaned, so terribly orphaned—"

"Sonya! Poor little Sonya!—then she too—she too—"

"Yes, she too was in danger." Müller completed the sentence which the girl did not dare think out.

"Oh—it is horrible—let me think—I must have time to think—"
Suzanne stood between them, looking at them in another moment of
deadly calm. Then suddenly, even before her brother could catch her,
she fell to the floor unconscious.

CHAPTER 18

Epilogue

On Christmas day a thick covering of snow lay over the wide stretches of country around Inzersdorf and gave the charm of beauty even to the desolate Black Moor. The Erlach garden was a picture with its snowy spaces of lawn, and the trees and bushes sparkling in a covering of many-facetted crystals. In the midst of the white radiance the handsome old house stood dark in its ivy covering. But there was no longer the gloom of emptiness in its darkness, and the quiet old structure seemed to smile with the gayety within.

For about two weeks now the Green House had been again a home. Miss Eva Geiringer and her sister lived there, and Mrs. Tonner, with a young serving maid as assistant, took care of them. That the two sisters had found such a beautiful home was due to Müller. But like many another of his good deeds he did not consider it anything of importance. It seemed quite natural to him that he should speak of the two forsaken women to Paul Erlach, and the lieutenant thought it equally natural that the woman who might have been his uncle's wife, should in her old days at least be an inmate of the home which might have been hers altogether. It was no charity in his eyes, particularly as Eva's sister had undertaken the preparation of Nellie von Feldern's trousseau. The two ladies were to live in the Green House for the rest of their lives, thus keeping it open for the young officer and his wife whenever they could make them selves free for a visit to the country. This Christmas day, every room in the old house was thrown open and a merry company roamed in and out through all its nooks and corners. "Colonel von Feldern, Nellie's father, with his wife and younger daughter, had come out for the day with the young couple. Commissioner Lehr, Müller and Karl were also invited. The warm-hearted young officer could not forget those to whom his gratitude was due on this, his first day of hospitality in his heritage. While all was in busy bustling preparation for a hearty Christmas dinner, Müller sat in a corner room, chatting quietly with Miss Eva. His warm heart rejoiced at the look of calm happiness on the pale face of the gentle little invalid.

"He's been here several times then?" he asked.

"Three times already," she answered eagerly. "He brought your letter the first time, the letter in which you asked him to come and see us occasionally. And we found him a pleasant visitor."

"Then you haven't taken a dislike to him?" asked Müller. "I don't want to make it too much of a sacrifice for you. But your kindness will do the poor man so much good."

The invalid smiled sadly as she replied: "For me! How can a poor worthless cripple like myself feel any superiority over a man who has all his faculties, and a man who does his duty in life so thoroughly well as Mr. Bauer does. No, indeed, we will always be glad to see him and to do what we can towards banishing his distrust of the world. Besides, he's braver than you think, he did not write his apology to Lieutenant Erlach, but he came in person. But now, Mr. Müller, do tell me about Simirenko and his unfortunate betrothed."

Müller sighed deeply. "Miss Suzanne is out of danger now. But I fear she will not shake off the deep sorrow in her heart as quickly as she did the brain fever. Simirenko is safely guarded in the asylum. He has violent moments every now and then when it takes great force to subdue him. But in his lucid intervals he is very quiet. I went to the asylum to ask about him yesterday, and they tell me that he has spoken of me frequently, spoken of me kindly. Oh, and another thing they told me. When he was brought to the asylum he had to undergo a physical examination and it was discovered that he had three broken ribs. He acknowledged calmly that they were broken by Gebhart's blow the night of his attack on the latter, you remember the story."

"Yes, yes, you told me. What a terrible man he is—and yet I am sorry for him."

"Yes, as I am," said the detective sadly. "To think that just *this* soul should be darkened by madness!"

****

Several years had passed and summer was on the land again.

A man sat at the window of a great house outside Vienna. There were strong bars at the window and the door was securely locked. The man was tall but gaunt, his clothes hung loosely from his broad shoulders. His beautiful supple hands had lost their look of strength and were almost transparent and waxen. His hair was quite white.

After the ravings of the first few terrible weeks, Nikolai Simirenko had been one of the most quiet patients of the asylum. Although kept in the strongest cell under safe watch he had never attempted an escape. The absolute stillness that seemed to have come over the man made him the most unusual case which the physicians of the institution had ever known. He seemed quite lucid, was again the finely educated, intelligent man of the world, the sympathetic scholar. In spite of the longing for his little girl which was revealed in an occasional moment, he had expressly asked that Sonya should be kept safely guarded and never allowed to see him.

It seemed to make him happy to know that Sonya was in Suzanne's care, being brought up as her own child. The news which came two or three years after his incarceration, that Suzanne had married, did not distress him. It seemed a relief to him to know that she could overcome the tragedy he had brought into her life.

He spoke very little, most of his time was spent in reading, studying. He was quite contented, but his great physical strength, his magnificent health, were slowly fading. He grew daily thinner and weaker.

He has a visitor every now and then, one visitor only. The first time that Müller asked to see Simirenko he did it hesitatingly, fearing that if the patient would receive him at all, his presence might have a bad effect. But the Russian came to the door to meet him, quite calm, although his eyes were moist A couple of strong attendants were waiting outside, watching through a secret peephole in case the detective should be in danger. But after this first visit he asked that the watching be discontinued, as he knew it was quite unnecessary.

Sitting at the window this summer day, Simirenko was awaiting his one friend. Awaiting him impatiently, for he looked out of the window now and then to see if the carriage was not yet in sight. Then he turned to the table in front of him. On it stood three photographs. One of them was a picture of his wife, whose fate he took into his own hands, then a portrait of her little daughter and beside them Suzanne's picture. He gathered them up and locked them away in the drawer, for he did not wish even his one faithful friend to look into this sanctuary of his heart. He did not wish even this one friend to know the hours that he spent in hopeless torturing longing. Then he went back to the window and stood watching.

Finally he heard the wheels of a carriage on the road and the sound of the doorbell. The pale man's eyes brightened and a faint smile curved his well-cut lips.

The Pocket Diary Found
in the Snow

CHAPTER 1

The Discovery in the Snow

A quiet winter evening had sunk down upon the great city. The clock in the old clumsy church steeple of the factory district had not yet struck eight, when the side door of one of the large buildings opened and a man came out into the silent street.

It was Ludwig Amster, one of the working-men in the factory, starting on his homeward way. It was not a pleasant road, this street along the edge of the city. The town showed itself from its most disagreeable side here, with malodorous factories, rickety tenements, untidy open stretches and dumping grounds offensive both to eye and nostril.

Even by day the street that Amster took was empty; by night it was absolutely quiet and dark, as dark as were the thoughts of the solitary man. He walked along, brooding over his troubles. Scarcely an hour before he had been discharged from the factory because of his refusal to submit to the injustice of his foreman.

The yellow light of the few lanterns show nothing but high board walls and snow drifts, stone heaps, and now and then the remains of a neglected garden. Here and there a stunted tree or a wild shrub bent their twigs under the white burden which the winter had laid upon them. Ludwig Amster, who had walked this street for several years, knew his path so well that he could take it blindfolded. The darkness did not worry him, but he walked somewhat more slowly than usual, for he knew that under the thin covering of fresh-fallen snow there lay the ice of the night before. He walked carefully, watching for the slippery places.

He had been walking about half an hour, perhaps, when he came to a cross street. Here he noticed the tracks of a wagon, the trace still quite fresh, as the slowly falling flakes did not yet cover it. The tracks led out towards the north, out on to the hilly, open fields.

Amster was somewhat astonished. It was very seldom that a carriage came into this neighbourhood, and yet these narrow wheel-tracks could have been made only by an equipage of that character. The heavy trucks which passed these roads occasionally had much wider wheels. But Amster was to find still more to astonish him.

In one corner near the cross-roads stood a solitary lamp-post. The light of the lamp fell sharply on the snow, on the wagon tracks, and—on something else besides.

Amster halted, bent down to look at it, and shook his head as if in doubt.

A number of small pieces of glass gleamed up at him and between them, like tiny roses, red drops of blood shone on the white snow. All this was a few steps to one side of the wagon tracks.

"What can have happened here—here in this weird spot, where a cry for help would never be heard? where there would be no one to bring help?"

So Amster asked himself, but his discovery gave him no answer. His curiosity was aroused, however, and he wished to know more. He followed up the tracks and saw that the drops of blood led further on, although there was no more glass. The drops could still be seen for a yard further, reaching out almost to the board fence that edged the sidewalk. Through the broken planks of this fence the rough bare twigs of a thorn bush stretched their brown fingers. On the upper side of the few scattered leaves there was snow, and blood.

Amster's wide serious eyes soon found something else. Beside the bush there lay a tiny package. He lifted it up. It was a small, light, square package, wrapped in ordinary brown paper. Where the paper came together it was fastened by two little lumps of black bread, which were still moist. He turned the package over and shook his head again. On the other side was written, in pencil, the lettering uncertain, as if scribbled in great haste and in agitation, the sentence, "Please take this to the nearest police station."

The words were like a cry for help, frozen on to the ugly paper. Amster shivered; he had a feeling that this was a matter of life and death.

The wagon tracks in the lonely street, the broken pieces of glass and the drops of blood, showing that some occupant of the vehicle had broken the window, in the hope of escape, perhaps, or to throw out the package which should bring assistance—all these facts grouped themselves together in the brain of the intelligent working-man to form some terrible tragedy where his assistance, if given at once, might be of great use. He had a warm heart besides, a heart that reached out to this unknown who was in distress, and who threw out the call for help which had fallen into his hands.

He waited no longer to ponder over the matter, but started off at a full run for the nearest police station. He rushed into the room and told his story breathlessly.

They took him into the next room, the office of the commissioner for the day. The official in charge, who had been engaged in earnest conversation with a small, frail-looking, middle-aged man, turned to Amster with a question as to what brought him there.

"I found this package in the snow."

"Let me see it."

Amster laid it on the table. The older man looked at it, and as the commissioner was about to open it, he handed him a paper-knife with the words: "You had better cut it open, sir."

"Why?"

"It is best not to injure the seals that fasten a package."

"Just as you say, Müller," answered the young commissioner, smiling. He was still very young to hold such an office, but then he was the son of a Cabinet Minister, and family connections had obtained this responsible position for him so soon. Kurt von Mayringen was his name, and he was a very good-looking young man, apparently a very good-natured young man also, for he took this advice from a subordinate with a most charming smile. He knew, however, that this quiet, pale-faced little man in the shabby clothes was greater than he, and that it was mere accident of birth that put him, Kurt von Mayringen, instead of Joseph Müller, in the position of superior.

The young commissioner had had most careful advice from headquarters as to Müller, and he treated the secret service detective, who was one of the most expert and best known men in the profession, with the greatest deference, for he knew that anything Müller might say could be only of value to him with his very slight knowledge of his business. He took the knife, therefore, and carefully cut open the paper, taking out a tiny little notebook, on the outer side of which a handsome monogram gleamed up at him in golden letters.

"A woman made this package," said Müller, who had been looking at the covering very carefully; "a blond woman."

The other two looked at him in astonishment. He showed them a single blond hair which had been in one of the bread seals.

"How I was murdered." Those were the words that Commissioner von Mayringen read aloud after he had hastily turned the first few pages of the notebook, and had come to a place where the writing was heavily underscored.

The commissioner and Amster were much astonished at these words, but the detective still gazed quietly at the seals of the wrapping.

"This heading reads like insanity," said the commissioner. Müller shrugged his shoulders, then turned to Amster. "Where did you find the package?"

"In Garden street."

"When?"

"About twenty minutes ago."

Amster gave a short and lucid account of his discovery. His intelligent face and well-chosen words showed that he had observation and the power to describe correctly what he had observed. His honest eyes inspired confidence.

"Where could they have been taking the woman?" asked the detective, more of himself than of the others.

The commissioner searched hastily through the notebook for a signature, but without success. "Why do you think it is a woman? This writing looks more like a man's hand to me. The letters are so heavy and—"

"That is only because they are written with broad pen," interrupted Müller, showing him the writing on the package; "here is the same hand, but it is written with a fine hard pencil, and you can see distinctly that this is a woman's handwriting. And besides, the skin on a man's thumb does not show the fine markings that you can see here on these bits of bread that have been used for seals."

The commissioner rose from his seat. "You may be right, Müller. We will take for granted, then, that there is a woman in trouble. It remains to be seen whether she is insane or not."

"Yes, that remains to be seen," said Müller dryly, as he reached for his overcoat.

"You are going before you read what is in the notebook?" asked Commissioner von Mayringen.

Müller nodded. "I want to see the wagon tracks before they are lost; it may help me to discover something else. You can read the book and make any arrangements you find necessary after that."

Müller was already wrapped in his overcoat. "Is it snowing now?" He turned to Amster.

"Some flakes were falling as I came here."

"All right. Come with me and show me the way." Müller nodded carelessly to his superior officer, his mind evidently already engrossed in thoughts of the interesting case, and hurried out with Amster. The commissioner was quite satisfied with the state of affairs. He knew the case was in safe hands. He seated himself at his desk again and began to read the little book which had come into his hands so strangely. His eyes ran more and more rapidly over the closely written pages, as his interest grew and grew.

When, half an hour later, he had finished the reading, he paced restlessly up and down the room, trying to bring order into the thoughts that rushed through his brain. And one thought came again and again, and would not be denied in spite of many improbabilities, and many strange things with which the book was full; in spite, also, of the varying, uncertain handwriting and style of the message. This one thought was, "This woman is not insane."

While the young official was pondering over the problem, Müller entered as quietly as ever, bowed, put his hat and cane in their places, and shook the snow off his clothing. He was evidently pleased about something. Kurt von Mayringen did not notice his entrance. He was again at the desk with the open book before him, staring at the mysterious words, "How I was murdered."

"It is a woman, a lady of position. And if she is mad, then her madness certainly has method." Müller said these words in his usual quiet way, almost indifferently. The young commissioner started up and snatched for the fine white handkerchief which the detective handed him. A strong sweet perfume filled the room. "It is hers?" he murmured.

"It is hers," said Müller. "At least we can take that much for granted, for the handkerchief bears the same monogram, A. L., which is on the notebook."

Commissioner von Mayringen rose from his chair in evident excitement. "Well?" he asked.

It was a short question, but full of meaning, and one could see that he was waiting in great excitement for the answer. Müller reported what he had discovered. The commissioner thought it little enough, and shrugged his shoulders impatiently when the other had finished.

Müller noticed his chief's dissatisfaction and smiled at it. He himself was quite content with what he had found.

"Is that all?" murmured the commissioner, as if disappointed.

"That is all," repeated the detective calmly, and added, "That is a good deal. We have here a closely written notebook, the contents of which, judging by your excitement, are evidently important. We have also a handkerchief with an unusual perfume on it. I repeat that this is quite considerable. Besides this, we have the seals, and we know several other things. I believe that we can save this lady, of if it be too late, we can avenge her at least."

The commissioner looked at Müller in surprise. "We are in a city of more than a million inhabitants," he said, almost timidly.

"I have hunted criminals in two hemispheres, and I have found them," said Müller simply. The young commissioner smiled and held out his hand. "Ah, yes, Müller—I keep forgetting the great things you have done. You are so quiet about it."

"What I have done is only what any one could do who has that particular faculty. I do only what is in human power to do, and the cleverest criminal can do no more. Besides which, we all know that every criminal commits some stupidity, and leaves some trace behind him. If it is really a crime which we have found the trace of here, we will soon discover it." Müller's editorial "we" was a matter of formality. He might with more truth have used the singular pronoun.

"Very well, then, do what you can," said the commissioner with a friendly smile.

The older man nodded, took the book and its wrappings from the desk, and went into a small adjoining room.

The commissioner sent for an attendant and gave him the order to fetch a pot of tea from a neighbouring saloon. When the tray arrived, he placed several good cigars upon it, and sent it in to Müller. Taking a cigar himself, the commissioner leaned back in his sofa corner to think over this first interesting case of his short professional experience. That it concerned a lady in distress made it all the more romantic.

In his little room the detective, put in good humour by the thoughtful attention of his chief, sat down to read the book carefully. While he studied its contents his mind went back over his search in the silent street outside.

He and Amster had hurried out into the raw chill of the night, reaching the spot of the first discovery in about ten or fifteen minutes. Müller found nothing new there. But he was able to discover in which direction the carriage had been going. The hoof marks of the single horse which had drawn it were still plainly to be seen in the snow.

"Will you follow these tracks in the direction from which they have come?" he asked of Amster. "Then meet me at the station and report what you have seen."

"Very well, sir," answered the workman. The two men parted with a hand shake.

Before Müller started on to follow up the tracks in the other direction, he took up one of the larger pieces' of glass. "Cheap glass," he said, looking at it carefully. "It was only a hired cab, therefore, and a one-horse cab at that."

He walked on slowly, following the marks of the wheels. His eyes searched the road from side to side, looking for any other signs that might have been left by the hand which had thrown the package out of the window. The snow, which had been falling softly thus far, began to come down in heavier flakes, and Müller quickened his pace. The tracks would soon be covered, but they could still be plainly seen. They led out into the open country, but when the first little hill had been climbed a drift heaped itself up, cutting off the trail completely.

Müller stood on the top of this knoll at a spot where the street divided. Towards the right it led down into a factory suburb; towards the left the road led on to a residence colony, and straight ahead the way was open, between fields, pastures and farms, over moors, to another town of considerable size lying beside a river. Müller knew all this, but his knowledge of the locality was of little avail, for all traces of the carriage wheels were lost.

He followed each one of the streets for a little distance, but to no purpose. The wind blew the snow up in such heaps that it was quite impossible to follow any trail under such conditions.

With an expression of impatience Müller gave up his search and turned to go back again. He was hoping that Amster might have had better luck. It was not possible to find the goal towards which the wagon had taken its prisoner—if prisoner she was—as soon as they had hoped. Perhaps the search must be made in the direction from which she had been brought.

Müller turned back towards the city again. He walked more quickly now, but his eyes took in everything to the right and to the left of his path. Near the place where the street divided a bush waved its bare twigs in the wind. The snow which had settled upon it early in the day had been blown away by the freshening wind, and just as Müller neared the bush he saw something white fluttering from one twig. It was a handkerchief, which had probably hung heavy and lifeless when he had passed that way before. Now when the wind held it out straight, he saw it at once. He loosened it carefully from the thorny twigs. A delicate and rather unusual perfume wafted up to his face. There was more of the odour on the little cloth than is commonly used by people of good taste. And yet this handkerchief was far too fine and delicate in texture to belong to the sort of people who habitually passed along this street. It must have something to do with the mysterious carriage. It was still quite dry, and in spite of the fact that the wind had been playing with it, it had been but slightly torn. It could therefore have been in that position for a short time only. At the nearest lantern Müller saw that the monogram on the handkerchief was the same in style and initials as that on the notebook. It was the letters A. L.

The Story of the Notebook

It was warm and comfortable in the little room where Müller sat. He closed the windows, lit the gas, took off his overcoat—Müller was a pedantically careful person—smoothed his hair and sat down comfortably at the table. Just as he took up the little book, the attendant brought the tea, which he proceeded at once to enjoy. He did not take up his little book again until he had lit himself a cigar. He looked at the cover of the dainty little notebook for many minutes before he opened it. It was a couple of inches long, of the usual form,.and had a cover of brown leather. In the left upper corner were the letters A. L. in gold. The leaves of the book, about fifty in all, were of a fine quality of paper and covered with close writing. On the first leaves the writing was fine and delicate, calm and orderly, but later on it was irregular and uncertain, as if penned by a trembling hand under stress of terror. This change came in the leaves of the book which followed the strange and terrible title, "How I was murdered."

Before Müller began to read he felt the covers of the book carefully. In one of them there was a tiny pocket, in which he found a little piece of wall paper of a noticeable and distinctly ugly pattern. The paper had a dark blue ground with clumsy lines of gold on it. In the pocket he found also a tramway ticket, which had been crushed and then carefully smoothed out again. After looking at these papers, Müller replaced them in the cover of the notebook. The book itself was strongly perfumed with the same odour which had exhaled from the handkerchief.

The detective did not begin his reading in that part of the book which followed the mysterious title, as the commissioner had done. He began instead at the very first words.

"Ah! she is still young," he murmured, when he had read the first lines. "Young, in easy circumstances, happy and contented."

These first pages told of pleasure trips, of visits from and to good friends, of many little events of every-day life. Then came some accounts, written in pencil, of shopping expeditions to the city. Costly laces and jewels had been bought, and linen garments for children by the dozen. "She is rich, generous, and charitable," thought the detective, for the book showed that the considerable sums which had been spent here had not been for the writer herself. The laces bore the mark, "For our church"; behind the account for the linen stood the words, "For the charity school."

Müller began to feel a strong sympathy for the writer of these notices. She showed an orderly, almost pedantic, character, mingled with generosity of heart. He turned leaf after leaf until he finally came to the words, written in intentionally heavy letters, "How I was murdered."

Müller's head sank down lower over these mysterious words, and his eyes flew through the writing that followed. It was quite a different writing here. The hand that penned these words must have trembled in deadly terror. Was it terror of coming death, foreseen and not to be escaped? or was it the trembling and the terror of an overthrown brain? It was undoubtedly, in spite of the difference, the same hand that had penned the first pages of the book. A few characteristic turns of the writing were plainly to be seen in both parts of the story. But the ink was quite different also. The first pages had been written with a delicate violet ink, the later leaves were penned with a black ink of uneven quality, of the kind used by poor people who write very seldom. The words of this later portion of the book were blurred in many places, as if the writer had not been able to dry them properly before she turned the leaves. She therefore had had neither blotting paper nor sand at her disposal.

And then the weird title!

Was it written at the dictation of insanity? or did A. L. know, while she wrote it, that it was too late for any help to reach her? Did she see her doom approaching so clearly that she knew there was no escape?

Müller breathed a deep breath before he continued his reading. Later on his breath came more quickly still, and he clinched his fist several times, as if deeply moved. He was not a cold man, only thoroughly self-controlled. In his breast there lived an unquenchable hatred of all evil. It was this that awakened the talents which made him the celebrated detective he had become.

I fear that it will be impossible for any one to save me now, but perhaps I may be avenged. Therefore I will write down here all that has happened to me since I set out on my journey.

These were the first words that were written under the mysterious title. Müller had just read them when the commissioner entered.

"Will you speak to Amster; he has just returned?" he asked.

Müller rose at once. "Certainly. Did you telegraph to all the railway stations?"

"Yes," answered the commissioner, "and also to the other police stations."

"And to the hospitals?—asylums?"

"No, I did not do that." Commissioner von Mayringen blushed, a blush that was as becoming to him as was his frank acknowledgment of his mistake. He went out to remedy it at once, while Müller heard Amster's short and not particularly important report. The working-man was evidently shivering, and the detective handed him a glass of tea with a good portion of rum in it.

"Here, drink this; you are cold. Are you ill?" Amster smiled sadly. "No, I am not ill, but I was discharged today and am out of work now—that's almost as bad."

"Are you married?"

"No, but I have an old mother to support."

"Leave your address with the commissioner. He may be able to find work for you; we can always use good men here. But now drink your tea." Amster drank the glass in one gulp. "Well, now we have lost the trail in both directions," said Müller calmly. "But we will find it again. You can help, as you are free now anyway. If you have the talent for that sort of thing, you may find permanent work here."

A gesture and a look from the working-man showed the detective that the former did not think very highly of such occupation. Müller laid his hand on the other's shoulder and said gravely: "You wouldn't care to take service with us? This sort of thing doesn't rate very high, I know. But I tell you that if we have our hearts in the right place, and our brains are worth anything, we are of more good to humanity than many an honest citizen who wouldn't shake hands with us. There— and now I am busy. Goodnight."

With these words Müller pushed the astonished man out of the room, shut the door, and sat down again with his little book. This is what he read:

Wednesday—is it Wednesday? They brought me a newspaper to-day which had the date of Wednesday, the 20th of November. The ink still smells fresh, but it is so damp here, the paper may have been older. I do not know surely on what day it is that I begin to write this narrative. I do not know either whether I may not have been ill for days and weeks; I do not know what may have been the matter with me—I know only that I was unconscious, and that when I came to myself again, I was here in this gloomy room. Did any physician see me? I have seen no one until today except the old woman, whose name I do not know and who has so little to say. She is kind to me otherwise, but I am afraid of her hard face and of the smile with which she answers all my questions and entreaties. 'You are ill.' These are the only words that she has ever said to me, and she pointed to her forehead as she spoke them. She thinks I am insane, there-fore, or pretends to think so.

What a hoarse voice she has. She must be ill herself, for she coughs all night long. I can hear it through the wall—she sleeps in the next room. But I am not ill, that is I am not ill in the way she says. I have no fever now, my pulse is calm and regular. I can remember everything, until I took that drink of tea in the rail-way station. What could there have been in that tea? I suppose I should have noticed how anxious my travelling companion was to have me drink it.

Who could the man have been? He was so polite, so fa-therly in his anxiety about me. I have not seen him since then. And yet I feel that it is he who has brought me into this trap, a trap from which I may never escape alive. I will describe him. He is very tall, stout and blond, and wears a long heavy beard, which is slightly mixed with grey. On his right cheek his beard only partly hides a long scar. His eyes are hidden by large smoked glasses. His voice is low and gentle, his manners most correct—except for his giving people poison or what-ever else it was in that tea.

I did not suffer any—at least I do not remember anything except becoming unconscious. And I seem to have felt a pain like an iron ring around my head. But I am not insane, and this fear that I feel does not spring from my imagination, but from the real danger by which I am surrounded. I am very hungry, but I do not dare to eat anything except eggs, which cannot be tampered with. I tasted some soup yesterday, and it seemed to me that it had a queer taste. I will eat nothing that is at all suspicious. I will be in my full senses when my murderers come; they shall not kill me by poison at least.

When I came to my senses again—it was the evening of the day before yesterday—I found a letter on the little table beside my bed. It was written in French, in a handwriting that I had never seen before, and there was no signature.

This strange letter demanded of me that I should write to my guardian, calmly and clearly, to say that for reasons which I did not intend to reveal, I had taken my own life. If I did this my present place of sojourn would be exchanged for a far more agreeable one, and I would soon be quite free. But if I did not do it, I would actually be put to death. A pen, ink and paper were ready there for the answer.

'Never,' I wrote. And then despair came over me, and I may have indeed appeared insane. The old woman came in. I entreated and implored her to tell me why this dreadful fate should have overtaken me. She remained quite indifferent and I sank back, almost fainting, on the bed. She laid a moist cloth over my face, a cloth that had a peculiar odour. I soon fell asleep. It seemed to me that there was someone else besides the woman in the room with me. Or was she talking to herself? Next morning the letter and my answer had disappeared. It was as I thought; there was someone else in my room. Someone who had come on the tramway. I found the ticket on the carpet beside my bed. I took it and put it in my notebook!

I believe that it is Sunday today. It is four days now since I have been conscious. The first sound that I remember hearing was the blast of a horn. It must come from a factory very near me. The old windows in my room rattle at the sound. I hear it mornings and evenings and at noon, on week days. I did not hear it today, so it must be Sunday. It was Monday, the 18th of November, that I set out on my trip, and reached here in the evening—(here? I do not know where I am), that is, I set out for Vienna, and I know that I reached the Northern Railway station there in safety.

I was cold and felt a little faint—and then he offered me the tea—and what happened after that? Where am I? The paper that they gave me may have been a day or two old or more. And today is Sunday—is it the first Sunday since my departure from home? I do not know. I know only this, that I set out on the 18th of November to visit my kind old guardian, and to have a last consultation with him before my coming of age. And I know also that I have fallen into the hands of someone who has an interest in my disappearance.

There is someone in the next room with the old woman. I hear a man's voice and they are quarrelling. They are talking of me. He wants her to do something which she will not do. He commands her to go away, but she refuses. What does he mean to do? I do not want her to leave me alone. I do not hate her any more; I know that she is not bad. When I listened I heard her speaking of me as of an insane person. She really believes that I am ill. When the man went away he must have been angry. He stamped down the stairs until the steps creaked under his tread: I know it is a wooden staircase therefore.

I am safe from him today, but I am really ill of fright. Am I really insane? There is one thing that I have forgotten to write down. When I first came to myself I found a bit of paper beside me on which was written, 'Beware of calling in help from outside. One scream will mean death to you.' It was written in French like the letter. Why? Was it because the old woman could not read it? She knew of the piece of paper, for she took it away from me. It frightens me that I should have forgotten to write this down. Am I really ill? If I am not yet ill, this terrible solitude will make me so.

What a gloomy room this is, this prison of mine. And such a strange ugly wall-paper. I tore off a tiny bit of it and hid it in this little book. Someone may find it some day and may discover from it this place where I am suffering, and where I shall die, perhaps. There cannot be many who would buy such a pattern, and it must be possible to find the factory where it was made. And I will also write down here what I can see from my barred window. Far down below me there is a rusty tin roof, it looks like as if it might belong to a sort of shed. In front and to the right there are windowless walls; to the left, at a little distance, I can see a slender church spire, greenish in colour, probably covered with copper, and before the church there are two poplar trees of different heights.

Another day has passed, a day of torturing fear! Am I really insane? I know that I see queer things. This morning I looked towards the window and I saw a parrot sitting there! I saw it quite plainly. It ruffled up its red and green feathers and stared at me. I stared back at it and suddenly it was gone. I shivered. Finally I pulled myself together and went to the window. There was no bird outside nor was there a trace of any in the snow on the window sill. Could the wind have blown away the tracks so soon, or was it really my sick brain that appeared to see this tropical bird in the midst of the snow? It is Tuesday today; from now on I will carefully count the days—the days that still remain to me.

This morning I asked the old woman about the parrot. She only smiled and her smile made me terribly afraid. The thought that this thing which is happening to me, this thing that I took to be a crime, may be only a necessity—the thought fills me with horror! Am I in a prison? or is this the cell of an insane asylum? Am I the victim of a villain? or am I really mad? My pulse is quickening, but my memory is quite clear; I can look back over every incident in my life.

"She has just taken away my food. I asked her to bring me only eggs as I was afraid of everything else. She promised that she would do it.

Are they looking for me? My guardian is Theodore Fellner, Cathedral Lane, 14. My own name is Asta Langen.

They took away my travelling bag, but they did not find this little book and the tiny bottle of perfume which I had in the pocket of my dress. And I found this old pen and a little ink in a drawer of the writing table in my room.

Wednesday. The stranger was here again today. I recognised his soft voice. He spoke to the woman in the hall outside my room. I listened, but I could catch only a few words. 'Tomorrow evening—I will come myself—no responsibility for you.' Were these words meant for me? Are they going to take me away? Where will they take me? Then they do not dare to kill me here? My head is burning hot. I have not dared to drink a drop of liquid for four days. I dare not take anything into which they might have put some drug or some poison.

Who could have such an interest in my death? It cannot be because of the fortune which is to be mine when I come of age; for if I die, my father has willed it to various charitable institutions. I have no relatives, at least none who could inherit my money. I had never harmed any one; who can wish for my death?

There is somebody with her, somebody was listening at the door. I have a feeling as if I was being watched. And yet—I examined the door, but there is no crack anywhere and the key is in the lock. Still I seem to feel a burning glance resting on me. Ah! the parrot! is this another delusion? Oh God, let it end soon! I am not yet quite insane, but all these unknown dangers around me will drive me mad. I must fight against them.

Thursday. They brought me back my travelling bag. My attendant is uneasy. She was longer in cleaning up the room than usual today. She seemed to want to say something to me, and yet she did not dare to speak. Is something to happen today then? I did not close my eyes all night. Can one be made insane from a distance? hypnotised into it, as it were? I will not allow fear alone to make me mad. My enemy shall not find it too easy. He may kill my body, but that is all—

These were the last words which Asta Langen had written in her notebook, the little book which was the only confidant of her terrible need. When the detective had finished reading it, he closed his eyes for a few minutes to let the impression made by the story sink into his mind.

Then he rose and put on his overcoat. He entered the commissioner's room and took up his hat and cane.

"Where are you going, Müller?" asked Herr Von Mayringen.

"To Cathedral Lane, if you will permit it."

"At this hour? it is quarter past eleven! Is there any such hurry, do you think? There is no train from any of our stations until morning. And I have already sent a policeman to watch the house. Besides, I know that Fellner is a highly respected man.

"There is many a man who is highly respected until he is found out," remarked the detective.

"And you are going to find out about Fellner?" smiled the commissioner. "And this evening, too?"

"This very evening. If he is asleep I shall wake him up. That is the best time to get at the truth about a man."

The commissioner sat down at his desk and wrote out the necessary credentials for the detective. A few moments later Müller was in the street. He left the notebook with the commissioner. It was snowing heavily, and an icy north wind was howling through the streets. Müller turned up the collar of his coat and walked on quickly. It was just striking a quarter to twelve when he reached Cathedral Lane. As he walked slowly along the moonlit side of the pavement, a man stepped out of the shadow to meet him. It was the policeman who had been sent to watch the house. Like Müller, he wore plain clothes.

"Well?" the latter asked.

"Nothing new. Mr. Fellner has been ill in bed several days, quite seriously ill, they tell me. The janitor seems very fond of him."

"*H'm*—we'll see what sort of a man he is. You can go back to the station now, you must be nearly frozen standing here."

Müller looked carefully at the house which bore the number 14. It was a handsome, old-fashioned building, a true patrician mansion which looked worthy of all confidence. But Müller knew that the outside of a house has very little to do with the honesty of the people who live in it. He rang the bell carefully, as he wished no one but the janitor to hear him.

The latter did not seem at all surprised to find a stranger asking for the owner of the house at so late an hour. "You come with a telegram, I suppose? Come right up stairs then, I have orders to let you in."

These were the words with which the old janitor greeted Müller. The detective could see from this that Mr. Theodore Fellner's conscience must be perfectly clear. The expected telegram probably had something to do with the non-appearance of Asta Langen, of whose terrible fate her guardian evidently as yet knew nothing. The janitor knocked on one of the doors, which was opened in a few moments by an old woman.

"Is it the telegram?" she asked sleepily.

"Yes," said the janitor.

"No," said Müller, "but I want to speak to Mr. Fellner."

The two old people stared at him in surprise.

"To speak to him?" said the woman, and shook her head as if in doubt. "Is it about Miss Langen?"

"Yes, please wake him."

"But he is ill, and the doctor—"

"Please wake him up. I will take the responsibility."

"But who are you?" asked the janitor.

Müller smiled a little at this belated caution on the part of the old man, and answered. "I will tell Mr. Fellner who I am. But please announce me at once. It concerns the young lady." His expression was so grave that the woman waited no longer, but let him in and then disappeared through another door. The janitor stood and looked at Müller with half distrustful, half anxious glances.

"It's no good news you bring," he said after a few minutes.

"You may be right."

"Has anything happened to our dear young lady?"

"Then you know Miss Asta Langen and her family?"

"Why, of course. I was in service on the estate when all the dreadful things happened."

"What things?"

"Why the divorce—and—but you are a stranger and I shouldn't talk about these family affairs to you. You had better tell me what has happened to our young lady."

"I must tell that to your master first."

The woman came back at this moment and said to Müller, "Come with me, please. Berner, you are to stay here until the gentleman goes out again."

Müller followed her through several rooms into a large bed-chamber where he found an elderly man, very evidently ill, lying in bed.

"Who are you?" asked the sick man, raising his head from the pillow. The woman had gone out and closed the door behind her.

"My name is Müller, police detective. Here are my credentials."

Fellner glanced hastily at the paper. "Why does the police send to me?"

"It concerns your ward."

Fellner sat upright in bed now. He leaned over towards his visitor as he said, pointing to a letter on the table beside his bed, "Asta's overseer writes me from her estate that she left home on the 18th of November to visit me. She should have reached here on the evening of the 18th, and she has not arrived yet. I did not receive this letter until today."

"Did you expect the young lady?"

"I knew only that she would arrive sometime before the third of December. That date is her twenty-fourth birthday and she was to celebrate it here."

"Did she not usually announce her coming to you?"

"No, she liked to surprise me. Three days ago I sent her a telegram asking her to bring certain necessary papers with her. This brought the answer from the overseer of her estate, an answer which has caused me great anxiety. Your coming makes it worse, for I fear—" The sick man broke off and turned his eyes on Müller; eyes so full of fear and grief that the detective's heart grew soft. He felt Fellner's icy hand on his as the sick man murmured: "Tell me the truth! Is Asta dead?"

The detective shrugged his shoulders. "We do not know yet. She was alive and able to send a message at half past eight this evening."

"A message? To whom?"

"To the nearest police station." Müller told the story as it had come to him.

The old man listened with an expression of such utter dazed terror that the detective dropped all suspicion of him at once.

"What a terrible riddle," stammered the sick man as the other finished the story.

"Would you answer me several questions?" asked Müller. The old gentleman answered quickly, "Any one, every one."

"Miss Langen is rich?"

"She has a fortune of over three hundred thousand *guldens*, and considerable land."

"Has she any relatives?"

"No," replied Fellner harshly. But a thought must have flashed through his brain for he started suddenly and murmured, "Yes, she has one relative, a step-brother."

The detective gave an exclamation of surprise.

"Why are you astonished at this?" asked Fellner.

"According to her notebook, the young lady does not seem to know of this step-brother."

"She does not know, sir. There was an ugly scandal in her family before her birth. Her father turned his first wife and their son out of his house on one and the same day. He had discovered that she was deceiving him, and also that her son, who was studying medicine at the time, had stolen money from his safe. What he had discovered about his wife made Langen doubt whether the boy was his son at all. There was a terrible scene, and the two disappeared from their home forever. The woman died soon after. The young man went to Australia. He has never been heard of since and has probably come to no good."

"Might he not possibly be here in Europe again, watching for an opportunity to make a fortune?"

Fellner's hand grasped that of his visitor. The eyes of the two men gazed steadily at each other. The old man's glance was full of sudden helpless horror, the detective's eyes shone brilliantly. Müller spoke calmly: "This is one clue. Is there no one else who could have an interest in the young lady's death?"

"No one but Egon Langen, if he bear this name by right, and if he is still alive."

"How old would he be now?"

"He must be nearly forty. It was many years before Langen married again."

"Do you know him personally?"

"Have you a picture of Miss Langen?"

Fellner rang a bell and Berner appeared. "Give this gentleman Miss Asta's picture. Take the one in the silver frame on my desk;" the old gentleman's voice was friendly but faint with fatigue. His old servant looked at him in deep anxiety. Fellner smiled weakly and nodded to the man. "Sad news, Berner! Sad news and bad news. Our poor Asta is being held a prisoner by some unknown villain who threatens her with death."

"My God, is it possible? Can't we help the poor young lady?"

"We will try to help her, or if it is—too late, we will at least avenge her. My entire fortune shall be given up for it. But bring her picture now."

Berner brought the picture of a very pretty girl with a bright intelligent face. Müller took the picture out of the frame and put it in his pocket.

"You will come again? soon? And remember, I will give ten thousand *guldens* to the man who saves Asta, or avenges her. Tell the police to spare no expense—I will go to headquarters myself tomorrow."

Fellner was a little surprised that Müller, although he had already taken up his hat, did not go. The sick man had seen the light flash up in the eyes of the other as he named the sum. He thought he understood this excitement, but it touched him unpleasantly and he sank back, almost frightened, in his cushions as the detective bent over him with the words "Good. Do not forget your promise, for I will save Miss Langen or avenge her. But I do not want the money for myself. It is to go to those who have been unjustly convicted and thus ruined for life. It may give the one or the other of them a better chance for the future."

"And you? what good do you get from that?" asked the old gentleman, astonished. A soft smile illumined the detective's plain features and he answered gently, "I know then that there will be some poor fellow who will have an easier time of it than I have had."

He nodded to Fellner, who had already grasped his hand and

pressed it hard. A tear ran down his grey beard, and long after Müller had gone the old gentleman lay pondering over his last words.

Berner led the visitor to the door. As he was opening it, Müller asked: "Has Egon Langen a bad scar on his right cheek?"

Berner's eyes looked his astonishment. How did the stranger know this? And how did he come to mention this forgotten name.

"Yes, he has, but how did you know it?" he murmured in surprise. He received no answer, for Müller was already walking quickly down the street. The old man stared after him for some few minutes, then suddenly his knees began to tremble. He closed the door with difficulty, and sank down on a bench beside it. The wind had blown out the light of his lantern; Berner was sitting in the dark without knowing it, for a sudden terrible light had burst upon his soul, burst upon it so sharply that he hid his eyes with his hands, and his old lips murmured, "Horrible! Horrible! The brother against the sister."

The next morning was clear and bright. Müller was up early, for he had taken but a few hours sleep in one of the rooms of the station, before he set out into the cold winter morning. At the next corner he found Amster waiting for him. "What are you doing here?" he asked in astonishment.

"I have been thinking over what you said to me yesterday. Your profession is as good and perhaps better than many another."

"And you come out here so early to tell me that?"

Amster smiled. "I have something else to say."

"Well?"

"The commissioner asked me yesterday if I knew of a church in the city that had a slender spire with a green top and two poplars in front of it."

Müller looked his interest.

"I thought it might possibly be the Convent Church of the Grey Sisters, but I wasn't quite sure, so I went there an hour ago. It's all right, just as I thought. And I suppose it has something to do with the case of last night, so I thought I had better report at once. I was on my way to the station."

"That will do very well. You have saved us much time and you have shown that you are eminently fitted for this business."

"If you really will try me, then—"

"We'll see. You can begin on this. Come to the church with me now." Müller was no talker, particularly not when, as now, his brain was busy on a problem.

The two men walked on quickly. In about half an hour they found themselves in a little square in the middle of which stood an old church. In front of the church, like giant sentinels, stood a pair of tall poplars. One of them looked sickly and was a good deal shorter than its neighbour. Müller nodded as if content.

"Is this the church the commissioner was talking about?" queried Amster.

"It is," was the answer. Müller walked on toward a little house built up against the church, which was evidently the dwelling of the sexton.

The detective introduced himself to this official, who did not look over-intelligent, as a stranger in the city who had been told that the view from the tower of the church was particularly interesting. A bright silver piece banished all distrust from the soul of the worthy man. With great friendliness he inquired when the gentlemen would like to ascend the tower. "At once," was the answer.

The sexton took a bunch of keys and told the strangers to follow him. A few moments later Müller and his companion stood in the tiny belfry room of the slender spire. The fat sexton, to his own great satisfaction, had yielded to their request not to undertake the steep ascent. The cloudless sky lay crystal clear over the still sleeping city and the wide spread snow-covered fields which lay close at hand, beyond the church. On the one side were gardens and the low rambling buildings of the convent, and on the other were huddled high-piled dwellings of poverty.

Müller looked out of each of the four windows in turn. He spent some time at each window, but evidently without discovering what he looked for, for he shook his head in discontent. But when he went once more to the opening in the East, into which the sun was just beginning to pour its light, something seemed to attract his attention. He called Amster and pointed from the window.

"Your eyes are younger than mine, lend them to me. What do you see over there to the right, below the tall factory chimney?" Müller's voice was calm, but there was something in his manner that revealed excitement. Amster caught the infection without knowing why. He looked sharply in the direction towards which Müller pointed, and began: "There is a tall house near the chimney, to the right of it, one wall touching it. The house is crowded in between other newer buildings, and looks to be very old and of a much better sort than its neighbours. The other houses are plain stone, but this

242

house has carvings and statues on it, which are white with snow. But the house is in bad condition, one can see cracks in the wall."

"And its windows?"

"I cannot see them. They must be on the other side of the house, towards the courtyard which seems to be hemmed in by the blank walls of the other houses."

"And at the front of the house?"

"There is a low wall in front which shuts off the courtyard from a narrow, ill-kept street."

"Yes, I see it myself now. The street is bordered mainly by gardens and vacant lots."

"Yes, sir, that is it." Müller nodded as if satisfied. Amster looked at him in surprise, still more surprised, however, at the excitement he felt himself. He did not understand it, but Müller understood it. He knew that he had found in Amster a talent akin to his own, one of those natures who once having taken up a trail cannot rest until they reach their goal. He looked for a few moments in satisfaction at the assistant he had found by such chance, then he turned and hastened down the stairs again.

"We're going to that house?" asked Amster when they were down in the street. Müller nodded.

Without hesitation the two men made their way through a tangle of dingy, uninteresting alleys, between modern tenements, until about ten minutes later they stood before an old three-storied building, which had a frontage of four windows on the street. "This is our place," said the detective, looking up at the tall, handsome gateway and the rococo carvings that ornamented the front of this decaying dwelling. It was very evidently of a different age and class from those about it.

Müller had already raised his hand to pull the bell, when he stopped and let it sink again. His eye caught sight of a placard pasted up on the wall of the next house, and already half torn off by the wind. The detective walked over, and raising the placard with his cane, read the words on it. "That's right," he said to himself. Amster gave a look on the paper. But he could not connect the contents of the notice with the case of the kidnapped lady, and he shook his head in surprise when Müller turned to him with the words: "The lady we are looking for is not insane." On the paper was announced in large letters that a reward would be offered to the finder of a red and green parrot which had escaped from a neighbouring house.

Müller rang the bell and they had to wait some few minutes before the door opened with great creakings, and the tousled head of an old woman peered out.

"What do you want?" she asked hoarsely, with distrustful looks.

"Let us in, and then give us the keys of the upstairs rooms." Müller's voice was friendly, but the woman grew perceptibly paler.

"Who are you?" she stammered. Müller threw back his overcoat and showed her his badge. "But there is nobody here, the house is quite empty."

"There were a lady and gentleman here last evening." The woman threw a frightened look at Müller, then she said hesitatingly: "The lady was insane and has been taken to an asylum."

"That is what the man told you. He is a criminal and the police are looking for him."

"Come with me," murmured the woman. She seemed to understand that further resistance was useless. She carefully locked the outside door. Amster remained down stairs in the corridor, while Müller followed the old woman up the stairs. The staircase to the third story was made of wood. The house was evidently very old, with low ceilings and many dark corners.

The woman led Müller into the room in which she had cared for the strange lady at the order of the latter's "husband." He had told her that it was only until he could take the lady to an asylum. One look at the wall paper, a glance out of the window, and Müller knew that this was where Asta Langen had been imprisoned. He sat down on a chair and looked at the woman, who stood frightened before him.

"Do you know where they have taken the lady?"

"No, sir.

"Do you know the gentleman's name?"

"No, sir.

"You did not send the lady's name to the authorities?"*

"No, sir."

"Were you not afraid you would get into trouble?"

"The gentleman paid me well, and I did not think that he meant anything bad, and—and—"

"And you did not think that it would be found out?" said Müller sternly.

"I took good care of the lady."

---

* Any stranger taking rooms in a hotel or lodging house must be registered with the police authorities by the proprietor of the house within forty-eight hours of arrival.

"Yes, we know that."

"Did she escape from her husband?"

"He was not her husband. But now tell me all you know about these people; the more truthful you are the better it will be for you."

The old woman was so frightened that she could scarcely find strength to talk. When she finally got control of herself again she began: "He came here on the first of November and rented this room for himself. But he was here only twice before he brought the lady and left her alone here. She was very ill when he brought her—so ill that he had to carry her upstairs. I wanted to go for a doctor, but he said he was a doctor himself, and that he could take care of his wife, who often had such attacks. He gave me some medicine for her after I had put her to bed. I gave her the drops, but it was a long while before she came to herself again.

"Then he told me that she had lost her mind, and that she believed everybody was trying to harm her. She was so bad that he was taking her to an asylum. But he hadn't found quite the right place yet, and wanted me to keep her here until he knew where he could take her. Once he left a revolver here by mistake. But I hid it so the lady wouldn't see it, and gave it to the gentleman the next time he came. He was angry at that, though I couldn't see why, and said I shouldn't have touched it."

The woman had told her story with much hesitation, and stopped altogether at this point. She had evidently suddenly realised that the lady was not insane, but only in great despair, and that people in such a state will often seek death, particularly if any weapon is left conveniently within their reach.

"What did this gentleman look like?" asked Müller, to start her talking again. She described her tenant as very tall and stout with a long beard slightly mixed with grey. She had never seen his eyes, for he wore smoked glasses.

"Did you notice anything peculiar about his face?"

"No, nothing except that his beard was very heavy and almost covered his face."

"Could you see his cheeks at all?"

"No, or else I didn't notice."

"Did he leave nothing that might enable us to find him?"

"No, sir, nothing. Or yes, perhaps, but I don't suppose that will be any good."

"What was it? What do you mean?"

"It gave him a good deal of trouble to get the lady into the wagon, because she had fainted again. He lost his glove in doing it. I have it down stairs in my room, for I sleep down stairs again since the lady has gone."

Müller had risen from his chair and walked over to the old writing desk which stood beside one window. There were several sheets of ordinary brown paper on it and sharp pointed pencil and also something not usually found on writing desks, a piece of bread from which some of the inside had been taken. "Everything as I expected it," he said to himself. "The young lady made up the package in the last few moments that she was left alone here."

He turned again to the old woman and commanded her to lead him down stairs. "What sort of a carriage was it in which they took the lady away?" he asked as they went down.

"A closed coupe."

"Did you see the number?"

"No, sir. But the carriage was very shabby and so was the driver."

"Was he an old man?"

"He was about forty years old, but he looked like a man who drank. He had a light-coloured overcoat on."

"Good. Is this your room?"

"Yes, sir."

They were now in the lower corridor, where they found Amster walking up and down. The woman opened the door of the little room, and took a glove from a cupboard. Müller put it in his pocket and told the woman not to leave the house for anything, as she might be sent for to come to the police station at any moment. Then he went out into the street with Amster. When they were outside in the sunlight, he looked at the glove. It was a remarkably small size, made for a man with a slender, delicate hand, not at all in accordance with the large stout body of the man described by the landlady. Müller put his hand into the glove and found something pushed up into the middle finger. He took it out and found that it was a crumpled tramway ticket.

"Look out for a shabby old closed coupe, with a driver about forty years old who looks like a drunkard and wears a light overcoat. If you find such a cab, engage it and drive in it to the nearest police station. Tell them there to hold the man until further notice. If the cab is not free, at least take his number. And one thing more, but you will know that yourself,—the cab we are looking for will have new glass in the right-hand window." Thus Müller spoke to his companion as he put the glove into his pocket and unfolded the tramway ticket. Amster understood that they had found the starting point of the drive of the night before.

"I will go to all coupe stands," he said eagerly.

"Yes, but we may be able to find it quicker than that." Müller took the little notebook, which he was now carrying in his pocket, and took from it the tramway ticket which was in the cover. He compared it with the one he had just found. They were both marked for the same hour of the day and for the same ride.

"Did the man use them?" asked Amster. The detective nodded. "How can they help us?"

"Somewhere on this stretch of the street railroad you will probably find the stand of the cab we are looking for. The man who hired it evidently arrived on the 6:30 train at the West Station—I have reason to believe that he does not live here,—and then took the street car to this corner. The last ticket is marked for yesterday. In the car he probably made his plans to hire a cab. So you had better stay along the line of the car tracks. You will find me in room seven, police headquarters, at noon today. The authorities have already taken up the case. You may have something to tell us then. Good luck to you."

Müller hurried on, after he had taken a quick breakfast in a little cafe. He went at once to headquarters, made his report there and then drove to Fellner's house. The latter was awaiting him with great impatience. There the detective gathered much valuable information about the first marriage of Asta Langen's long-dead father. It was old Berner who could tell him the most about these long-vanished days.

When he reached his office at headquarters again, he found telegrams in great number awaiting him. They were from all the hospitals and insane asylums in the entire district. But in none of them had there been a patient fitting the description of the vanished girl. Neither the commissioner nor Müller was surprised at this negative result. They were also not surprised at all that the other branches of the police department had been able to discover so little about the disappearance of the young lady. They were aware that they had to deal with a criminal of great ability who would be careful not to fall into the usual slips made by his kind.

There was no news from the cab either, although several detectives were out looking for it. It was almost nightfall when Amster ran breathlessly into room number seven. "I have him! he's waiting outside across the way!" This was Amster's report.

Müller threw on his coat hastily. "You didn't pay him, did you? On a cold day like this the drivers don't like to wait long in any one place."

"No danger. I haven't money enough for that," replied Amster with a sad smile. Müller did not hear him as he was already outside. But the commissioner with whom he had been talking and to whom Müller had already spoken of his voluntary assistant, entered into a conversation with Amster, and said to him finally: "I will take it upon myself to guarantee your future, if you are ready to enter the secret service under Müller's orders. If you wish to do this you can stay right on now, for I think we will need you in this case."

Amster bowed in agreement. His life had been troubled, his reputation darkened by no fault of his own, and the work he was doing now had awakened, an interest and an ability that he did not know he possessed. He was more than glad to accept the offer made by the official.

Müller was already across the street and had laid his hand upon the door of the cab when the driver turned to him and said crossly, "Someone else has ordered me. But I am not going to wait in this cold, get in if you want to."

"All right. Now tell me first where you drove to last evening with the sick lady and her companion?" The man looked astonished but found his tongue again in a moment. "And who are you?" he asked calmly.

"We will tell you that upstairs in the police station," answered Müller equally calmly, and ordered the man to drive through the gateway into the inner courtyard. He himself got into the wagon, and in the course of the short drive he had made a discovery. He had found a tiny glass stopper, such as is used in perfume bottles. He could understand from this why the odour of perfume which had now become familiar to him was still so strong inside the old cab. Also why it was so strong on the delicate handkerchief. Asta Langen had taken the stopper from the bottle in her pocket, so as to leave a trail of odour behind her.

CHAPTER 3

The Lonely Cottage

Fifteen minutes after the driver had made his report to Commissioner Von Mayringen, the latter with Amster entered another cab. A well-armed policeman mounted the box of this second vehicle. "Follow that cab ahead," the commissioner told his driver. The second cab followed the one-horse coupe in which Müller was seated. They drove first to No. 14 Cathedral Lane, where Müller told Berner to come with him. He found Mr. Fellner ready to go also, and it was with great difficulty that he could dissuade the invalid, who was greatly fatigued by his morning visit to the police station, from joining them.

The carriages then drove off more quickly than before. It was now quite dark, a gloomy stormy winter evening. Müller had taken his place on the box of his cab and sat peering out into the darkness. In spite of the sharp wind and the ice that blew against his face the detective could see that they were going out from the more closely built up portions of the city, and were now in new streets with half-finished houses. Soon they passed even these and were outside of the city. The way was lonely and dreary, bordered by wooden fences on both sides. Müller looked sharply to right and to left.

"You should have become alarmed here," he said to the driver, pointing to one part of the fence.

"Why?" asked the man.

"Because this is where the window was broken."

"I didn't know that—until I got home."

"*H'm*; you must have been nicely drunk."

The driver murmured something in his beard.

"Stop here, this is your turn, down that street," Müller said a few moments later, as the driver turned the other way.

"How do you know that?" asked the man, surprised.

"None of your business."

"This street will take us there just the same."

"Probably, but I prefer to go the way you went yesterday."

"Very well, it's all the same to me." They were silent again, only the wind roared around them, and somewhere in the distance a fog horn moaned.

It was now six o'clock. The snow threw out a mild light which could not brighten the deep darkness around them. About half an hour later the first cab halted. "There's the house up there. Shall I drive to the garden gate?"

"No, stop here." Müller was already on the ground. "Are there any dogs here?" he asked.

"I didn't hear any yesterday."

"That's of no value. You didn't seem to hear much of anything yesterday." Müller opened the door of the cab and helped Berner out. The old man was trembling. "That was a dreadful drive!" he stammered.

"I hope you will be happier on the drive back," said the detective and added, "You stay here with the commissioner now."

The latter had already left his cab with his companion. His sharp eyes glanced over the heavily shaded garden and the little house in its midst. A little light shone from two windows of the first story. The men's eyes looked toward them, then the detective and Amster walked toward a high picket fence which closed the garden on the side nearest its neighbours. They shook the various pickets without much caution, for the wind made noise enough to kill any other sound. Amster called to Müller, he had found a loose picket, and his strong young arms had torn it out easily. Müller motioned to the other three to join them. A moment later they were all in the garden, walking carefully toward the house.

The door was closed but there were no bars at the windows of the ground floor. Amster looked inquiringly at the commissioner and the latter nodded and said, "All right, go ahead."

The next minute Amster had broken in through one pane of the window and turned the latch. The inner window was broken already so that it was not difficult for him to open it without any further noise. He disappeared into the dark room within. In a few seconds they heard a key turn in the door and it opened gently. The men entered, all except the policeman, who remained outside. The blind of his lantern was slightly opened, and he had his revolver ready in his hand.

Müller had opened his lantern also, and they saw that they were in a prettily furnished corridor from which the staircase and one door led out.

The four men tiptoed up the stairway and the commissioner stepped to the first of the two doors which opened onto the upper corridor. He turned the key which was in the lock, and opened the door, but they found themselves in a room as dark as was the corridor. From somewhere, however, a ray of light fell into the blackness. The official stepped into the room, pulling Berner in after him. The poor old man was in a state of trembling excitement when he found himself in the house where his beloved young lady might already be a corpse. One step more and a smothered cry broke from his lips. The commissioner had opened the door of an adjoining room, which was lighted and handsomely furnished. Only the heavy iron bars across the closed windows showed that the young lady who sat leaning back wearily in an arm-chair was a prisoner.

She looked up as they entered. The expression of utter despair and deep weariness which had rested on her pale face changed to a look of terror; then she saw that it was not her would-be murderer who was entering, but those who came to rescue. A bright flush illumined her cheeks and her eyes gleamed. But the change was too sudden for her tortured soul. She rose from her chair, then sank fainting to the floor.

Berner threw himself on his knees beside her, sobbing out, "She is dying! She is dying!"

Müller turned on the instant, for he had heard the door on the other side of the hall open, and a tall slender man with a smooth face and a deep scar on his right cheek stood on the threshold looking at them in dazed surprise. For an instant only had he lost his control. The next second he was in his room again, slamming the door behind him. But it was too late. Amster's foot was already in the crack of the door and he pushed it open to let Müller enter. "Well done," cried the latter, and then he turned to the man in the room. "Here, stop that. I can fire twice before you get the window open."

The man turned and walked slowly to the centre of the room, sinking down into an arm-chair that stood beside the desk. Neither Amster nor Müller turned their eyes from him for a moment, ready for any attempt on his part to escape. But the detective had already seen something that told him that Langen was not thinking of flight. When he turned to the desk, Müller had seen his eyes glisten while a scornful smile parted his thin, lips. A second later he had let his handkerchief fall, apparently carelessly, upon the desk. But in this short space of time the detective's sharp eyes had seen a tiny bottle upon which was a black label with a grinning skull. Müller could not see whether the bottle was full or empty, but now he knew that it must hold sufficient poison to enable the captured criminal to escape open disgrace. Knowing this, Müller looked with admiration at the calmness of the villain, whose intelligent eyes were turned towards him in evident curiosity.

"Who are you and who else is here with you?" asked the man calmly.

"I am Müller of the Secret Service," replied his visitor and added, "You must put up with us for the time being, Mr. Egon Langen. The police commissioner is occupied with your step-sister, whom you were about to murder."

Langen put his hand to his cheek, looking at Müller between his lashes as he said, "To murder? Who can prove that?"

"We have all the proofs we need."

"I will acknowledge only that I wanted Asta to disappear."

Müller smiled. "What good would that have done you? You wanted her entire fortune, did you not? But that could have come to you only after thirty years, and you are not likely to have waited that long. Your plan was to murder your step-sister, even if you could not get a letter from her telling of her intention to commit suicide."

Langen rose suddenly, but controlled himself again and sank back easily in his chair. "Then the old woman has been talking?" he asked.

Müller shook his head. "We knew it through Miss Langen herself."

"She has spoken to no one for over ten days."

"But you let her throw her notebook out of the window of the cab."

"Ah—"

"There, you see, you should not have let that happen."

Drops of perspiration stood out on Langen's forehead. Until now, perhaps, he had had some possible hope of escape. It was useless now, he knew.

As calmly as he had spoken thus far Müller continued. "For twenty years I have been studying the hearts of criminals like yourself. But there are things I do not understand about this case and it interests me very much."

Langen had wiped the drops from his forehead and he now turned on Müller a face that seemed made of bronze. There was but one expression on it, that of cold scorn.

"I feel greatly flattered, sir, to think that I can offer a problem to one of your experience," Langen began. His voice, which had been slightly veiled before, was now quite clear. "Ask me all you like. I will answer you."

Müller began: "Why did you wait so long before committing the murder? and why did you drag your victim from place to place when you could have killed her easily in the compartment of the railway train?"

"The windows of the compartment were open, my honoured friend, and it was a fine warm evening for the season, because of which the windows in the other compartment were also open. There was nothing else I could do at that time then, except to offer Asta a cup of tea when she felt a little faint upon leaving the train. I am a physician and I know how to use the right drugs at the right time. When Asta had taken the tea, she knew nothing more until she woke up a day later in a room in the city."

"And the piece of paper with the threat on it? and the revolver you left so handy for her? oh, but I forgot, the old woman took the weapon away before the lady could use it in her despair," said Müller.

"Quite right. I see you know every detail."

"But why didn't you complete your crime in the room in the old house?" persisted Müller.

"Because I lost my false beard one day upon the staircase, and I feared the old woman might have seen my face enough to recognise me again. I thought it better to look for another place."

"And then you found this house."

"Yes, but several days later."

"And you hired it in the name of Miss Asta Langen? Who would then have been found dead here several days after you had entered the house?"

"Several days, several weeks perhaps. I preferred to wait until the woman who rented the house had read in the papers that Asta Langen had disappeared and was being sought for. Somebody would have found her here, and her identity would have easily been established, for I knew that she had some important family documents with her."

Müller was silent a moment, with an expression of deep pity on his face. Then he continued: "Yes, someone would have found her, and her suicide would have been a dark mystery, unless, of course, malicious tongues would have found ugly reasons enough why a beautiful young lady should hide herself in a lonely cottage to take her own life."

Müller had spoken as if to himself. Egon Langen's lips, parted in a smile so evil that Amster clenched his fists.

"And you would not have regretted this ruining the reputation as well as taking the life of an innocent girl?" asked the detective low and tense.

"No, for I hated her."

"You hated her because she was rich and innocent. She was very charitable and would gladly have helped you if you were in need. Beside this, you were entitled to a portion of your father's estate. It is almost thirty thousand *guldens*, as Mr. Fellner tells me. Why did you not take that?"

"Fellner did not know that I had already received twenty thousand of this when my father turned me out. He probably would have heard of it later, for Berner was the witness. I did not care for the remaining ten thousand because I would have the entire fortune after Asta's death. I would have seen the official notice and the call for heirs in Australia, and would have written from there, announcing that I was still alive. If you had come several days later I should have been a rich man within a year."

His clenched fist resting on his knee, the rascal stared out ahead of him when he ended his shameless confession. In his rage and disappointment he had not noticed that Müller's hand dropped gently to the desk and softly took a little bottle from under the handkerchief. Langen came out of his dark thoughts only when Müller's voice broke the silence.

"But you miscalculated, if you expected to inherit from your sister. She is still a minor and your father's will would have given you only ten thousand *guldens*.

"But you forget that Asta will be twenty-four on the third of December."

"Ah, then you would have kept her alive until then."

"You understand quickly," said Langen with a mocking smile.

"But she disappeared on the eighteenth of November. How could you prove that she died after her birthday, therefore in full possession of her fortune and without leaving any will?"

"That is very simple. I buy several newspapers every day. I would have taken them up to the fourth and fifth of December and left them here with the body."

"You are more clever even than I thought," said the detective dryly as he heard the commissioner's steps behind him. Müller put a whistle to his lips and its shrill tone ran through the house, calling up the policeman who stood by the door.

Egon Langen's face was grey with pallor, his features were distorted, and yet there was the ghost of a smile on his lips as he saw his captors enter the door. He put his hand out, raised his handkerchief hastily and then a wild scream echoed through the room, a scream that ended in a ghastly groan.

"I have taken your bottle, you might as well give yourself up quietly," said Müller calmly, holding his revolver near Langen's face. The prisoner threw himself at the detective but was caught and overpowered by Amster and the policeman.

A quarter of an hour later the cabs drove back toward the city. Inside one cowered Egon Langen, watched by the policeman and Amster. Berner was on the box beside the driver, telling the now interested man the story of what had happened to his dear young lady. In the other cab sat Asta Langen with Kurt von Mayringen and Müller.

"Do you feel better now?" asked the young commissioner in sincere sympathy that was mingled with admiration for the delicate beauty of the girl beside him, an admiration heightened by her romantic story and marvellous escape.

Asta nodded and answered gently: "I feel as if some terrible weight were lifted from my heart and brain. But I doubt if I will ever forget these horrible days, when I had already come to accept it as a fact that—that I was to be murdered."

"This is the man to whom you owe your escape," said the commissioner, laying his hand on Müller's knee. Asta did not speak, but she reached out in the darkness of the cab, caught Müller's hand and would have raised it to her lips, had not the little man drawn it away hastily. "It was only my duty, dear young lady," he said. "A duty that is not onerous when it means the rescue of innocence and the preventing of crime. It is not always so, unfortunately—nor am I always so fortunate as in this case."

This indeed is what Müller calls a "case with a happy ending," for scarcely a year later, to his own great embarrassment, he found himself the most honoured guest, and a centre of attraction equally with the bridal couple, at the marriage of Kurt von Mayringen and Asta Langen. Müller asserts, however, that he is not a success in society, and that he would rather unravel fifty difficult cases than again be the "lion" at a fashionable function.

The Case of the Pool of
Blood in the Pastor's Study

The Case of the Pool of Blood in the Pastor's Study

The sun rose slowly over the great bulk of the Carpathian mountains lying along the horizon, weird giant shapes in the early morning mist. It was still very quiet in the village. A cock crowed here and there, and swallows flew chirping close to the ground, darting swiftly about preparing for their higher flight. Janci the shepherd, apparently the only human being already up, stood beside the brook at the point where the old bridge spans the streamlet, still turbulent from the mountain floods. Janci was cutting willows to make his Margit a new basket.

Once the shepherd raised his head from his work, for he thought he heard a loud laugh somewhere in the near distance. But all seemed silent and he turned back to his willows. The beauty of the landscape about him was much too familiar a thing that he should have felt or seen its charm. The violet hue of the distant woods, the red gleaming of the heather-strewn moor, with its patches of swamp from which the slow mist arose, the pretty little village with its handsome old church and attractive rectory—Janci had known it so long that he never stopped to realise how very charming, in its gentle melancholy, it all was.

Also, Janci did not know that this little village of his home had once been a flourishing city, and that an invasion of the Turks had razed it to the ground leaving, as by a miracle, only the church to tell of former glories.

The sun rose higher and higher. And now the village awoke to its daily life. Voices of cattle and noises of poultry were heard about the houses, and men and women began their accustomed round of tasks. Janci found that he had gathered enough willow twigs by this time. He tied them in a loose bundle and started on his homeward way.

His path led through wide-stretching fields and vineyards past a little hill, some distance from the village, on which stood a large house. It was not a pleasant house to look at, not a house one would care to live in, even if one did not know its use, for it looked bare and repellent, covered with its ugly yellow paint, and with all the windows secured with heavy iron bars. The trees that surrounded it were tall and thick-foliaged, casting an added gloom over the forbidding appearance of the house. At the foot of the hill was a high iron fence, cutting off what lay behind it from all the rest of the world. For this ugly yellow house enclosed in its walls a goodly sum of hopeless human misery and misfortune. It was an insane asylum.

For twenty years now, the asylum had stood on its hill, a source of superstitious terror to the villagers, but at the same time a source of added income. It meant money for them, for it afforded a constant and ever-open market for their farm products and the output of their home industry. But every now and then a scream or a harsh laugh would ring out from behind those barred windows, and those in the village who could hear, would shiver and cross themselves. Shepherd Janci had little fear of the big house. His little hut cowered close by the high iron gates, and he had a personal acquaintance with most of the patients, with all of the attendants, and most of all, with the kind elderly physician who was the head of the establishment. Janci knew them all, and had a kind word equally for all. But otherwise he was a silent man, living much within himself.

When the shepherd reached his little home, his wife came to meet him with a call to breakfast. As they sat down at the table a shadow moved past the little window. Janci looked up. "Who was that?" asked Margit, looking up from her folded hands. She had just finished her murmured prayer.

"Pastor's Liska," replied Janci indifferently, beginning his meal. (Liska was the local abbreviation for Elizabeth.)

"In such a hurry?" thought the shepherd's wife. Her curiosity would not let her rest. "I hope His Reverence isn't ill again," she remarked after a while. Janci did not hear her, for he was very busy picking a fly out of his milk cup.

"Do you think Liska was going for the old man?" began Margit again after a few minutes.

The "old man" was the name given by the people of the village, more as a term of endearment than anything else, to the generally loved and respected physician who was the head of the insane asylum.

He had become general mentor and oracle of all the village and was known and loved by man, woman and child.

"It's possible," answered Janci.

"His Reverence didn't look very well yesterday, or maybe the old housekeeper has the gout again."

Janci gave a grunt which might have meant anything. The shepherd was a silent man. Being alone so much had taught him to find his own thoughts sufficient company. Ten minutes passed in silence since Margit's last question, then some one went past the window. There were two people this time, Liska and the old doctor. They were walking very fast, running almost. Margit sprang up and hurried to the door to look after them.

Janci sat still in his place, but he had laid aside his spoon and with wide eyes was staring ahead of him, murmuring, "It's the pastor this time; I saw him—just as I did the others."

"Shepherd, the inn-keeper wants to see you, there's something the matter with his cow." Count —— a young man, coming from the other direction and pushing in at the door past Margit, who stood there staring up the road.

Janci was so deep in his own thoughts that he apparently did not hear the boy's words. At all events he did not answer them, but himself asked an unexpected question—a question that was not addressed to the others in the room, but to something out and beyond them. It was a strange question and it came from the lips of a man whose mind was not with his body at that moment—whose mind saw what others did not see.

"Who will be the next to go? And who will be our pastor now?" These were Janci's words.

"What are you talking about, shepherd? Is it another one of your visions?" exclaimed the young fellow who stood there before him. Janci rubbed his hands over his eyes and seemed to come down to earth with a start.

"Oh, is that you, Ferenz? What do you want of me?"

The boy gave his message again, and Janci nodded good-humouredly and followed him out of the house. But both he and his young companion were very thoughtful as they plodded along the way. The boy did not dare to ask any questions, for he knew that the shepherd was not likely to answer. There was a silent understanding among the villagers that no one should annoy Janci in any way, for they stood in a strange awe of him, although he was the most good-natured mortal under the sun.

While the shepherd and the boy walked toward the inn, the old doctor and Liska had hurried onward to the rectory. They were met at the door by the aged housekeeper, who staggered down the path wringing her hands, unable to give voice to anything but inarticulate expressions of grief and terror. The rest of the household and the farm hands were gathered in a frightened group in the great courtyard of the stately rectory which had once been a convent building. The physician hurried up the stairs into the pastor's apartments. These were high sunny and airy rooms with arched ceilings, deep window seats, great heavy doors and handsomely ornamented stoves. The simple modern furniture appeared still more plain and common-place by contrast with the huge spaces of the building.

In one of the rooms a *gendarme* was standing beside the window. The man saluted the physician, then shrugged his shoulders with an expression of hopelessness. The doctor returned a silent greeting and passed through into the next apartment.

The old man was paler than usual and his face bore an expression of pain and surprise, the same expression that showed in the faces of those gathered downstairs. The room he now entered was large like the others, the walls handsomely decorated, and every corner of it was flooded with sunshine. There were two men in this room, the village magistrate and the notary. Their expression, as they held out their hands to the doctor, showed that his coming brought great relief. And there was something else in the room, something that drew the eyes of all three of the men immediately after their silent greeting.

This was a great pool of blood which lay as a hideous stain on the otherwise clean yellow-painted floor. The blood must have flowed from a dreadful wound, from a severed artery even, the doctor thought, there was such a quantity of it. It had already dried and darkened, making its terrifying ugliness the more apparent.

"This is the third murder in two years," said the magistrate in a low voice.

"And the most mysterious of all of them," added the clerk.

"Yes, it is," said the doctor. "And there is not a trace of the body, you say?—or a clue as to where they might have taken the dead—or dying man?"

With these words he looked carefully around the room, but there was no more blood to be seen anywhere. Any spot would have been clearly visible on the light-coloured floor. There was nothing else to

262

tell of the horrible crime that had been committed here, nothing but the great, hideous, brown-red spot in the middle of the room.

"Have you made a thorough search for the body?" asked the doctor.

The magistrate shook his head. "No, I have done nothing to speak of yet. We have been waiting for you. There is a *gendarme* at the gate; no one can go in or out without being seen."

"Very well, then, let us begin our search now."

The magistrate and his companion turned towards the door of the room but the doctor motioned them to come back. "I see you do not know the house as well as I do," he said, and led the way towards a niche in the side of the wall, which was partially filled by a high bookcase.

"Ah—that is the entrance of the passage to the church?" asked the magistrate in surprise.

"Yes, this is it. The door is not locked."

"You mean you believe—"

"That the murderers came in from the church? Why not? It is quite possible."

"To think of such a thing!" exclaimed the notary with a shake of his head.

The doctor laughed bitterly. "To those who are planning a murder, a church is no more than any other place. There is a bolt here as you see. I will close this bolt now. Then we can leave the room knowing that no one can enter it without being seen."

The simple furniture of the study, a desk, a sofa, a couple of chairs and several bookcases, gave no chance of any hiding place either for the body of the victim or for the murderers. When the men left the room the magistrate locked the door and put the key in his own pocket. The *gendarme* in the neighbouring apartment was sent down to stand in the courtyard at the entrance to the house. The sexton, a little hunchback, was ordered to remain in the vestry at the other end of the passage from the church to the house.

Then the thorough search of the house began. Every room in both stories, every corner of the attic and the cellar, was looked over thoroughly. The stable, the barns, the garden and even the well underwent a close examination. There was no trace of a body anywhere, not even a trail of blood, nothing which would give the slightest clue as to how the murderers had entered, how they had fled, or what they had done with their victim.

The great gate of the courtyard was closed. The men, reinforced by the farm hands, entered the church, while Liska and the dairy-maids huddled in the servants' dining-room in a trembling group around the old housekeeper. The search in the church as well as in the vestry was equally in vain. There was no trace to be found there any more than in the house.

Meanwhile, during these hours of anxious seeking, the rumour of another terrible crime had spread through the village, and a crowd that grew from minute to minute gathered in front of the closed gates to the rectory, in front of the church, the closed doors of which did not open although it was a high feast day. The utter silence from the steeple, where the bells hung mute, added to the spreading terror. Finally the doctor came out from the rectory, accompanied by the magistrate, and announced to the waiting villagers that their venerable pastor had disappeared under circumstances which left no doubt that he had met his death at the hand of a murderer. The peasants listened in shuddering silence, the men pale-faced, the women sobbing aloud with frightened children hanging to their skirts. Then at the magistrate's order, the crowd dispersed slowly, going to their homes, while a messenger set off to the near-by county seat.

It was a weird, sad Easter Monday. Even nature seemed to feel the pressure of the brooding horror, for heavy clouds piled up towards noon and a chill wind blew fitfully from the north, bending the young corn and the creaking tree-tops, and moaning about the straw-covered roofs. Then an icy cold rain descended on the village, sending the children, the only humans still unconscious of the fear that had come on them all, into the houses to play quietly in the corner by the hearth.

There was nothing else spoken of wherever two or three met together throughout the village except this dreadful, unexplainable thing that had happened in the rectory. The little village inn was full to overflowing and the hum of voices within was like the noise of an excited beehive. Everyone had some new explanation, some new guess, and it was not until the notary arrived, looking even more important than usual, that silence fell upon the excited throng. But the expectations aroused by his coming were not fulfilled. The notary knew no more than the others although he had been one of the searchers in the rectory. But he was in no haste to disclose his ignorance, and sat wrapped in a dignified silence until some one found courage to question him.

"Was there nothing stolen?" he was asked.

"No, nothing as far as we can tell yet. But if it was the gypsies—as may be likely—they are content with so little that it would not be noticed."

"Gypsies?" exclaimed one man scornfully. "It doesn't have to be gypsies, we've got enough tramps and vagabonds of our own. Didn't they kill the pedlar for the sake of a bag of tobacco, and old Katiza for a couple of hens?"

"Why do you rake up things that happened twenty years ago?" cried another over the table. "You'd better tell us rather who killed Red Betty, and pulled Janos, the smith's farm hand, down into the swamp?"

"Yes, or who cut the bridge supports, when the brook was in flood, so that two good cows broke through and drowned?"

"Yes, indeed, if we only knew what band of robbers and villains it is that is ravaging our village."

"And they haven't stopped yet, evidently."

"This is the worst misfortune of all! What will our poor do now that they have murdered our good pastor, who cared for us all like a father?"

"He gave all he had to the poor, he kept nothing for himself."

"Yes, indeed, that's how it was. And now we can't even give this good man Christian burial."

"Shepherd Janci knew this morning early that we were going to have a new pastor," whispered the landlord in the notary's ear. The latter looked up astonished. "Who said so?" he asked.

"My boy Ferenz, who went to fetch him about seven o'clock. One of my cows was sick."

Ferenz was sent for and told his story. The men listened with great interest, and the smith, a broad-shouldered elderly man, was particularly eager to hear, as he had always believed in the shepherd's power of second sight. The tailor, who was more modern-minded, laughed and made his jokes at this. But the smith laid one mighty hand on the other's shoulder, almost crushing the tailor's slight form under its weight, and said gravely: "Friend, do you be silent in this matter. You've come from other parts and you do not know of things that have happened here in days gone by. Janci can do more than take care of his sheep. One day, when my little girl was playing in the street, he said to me, 'Have a care of Maruschka, smith!' and three days later the child was dead. The evening before Red Betty was murdered he saw her in a vision lying in a coffin in front of her door. He told it to the sexton, whom he met in the fields; and next morning they found Betty dead. And there are many more things that I could tell you, but what's the use; when a man won't believe it's only lost talk to try to make him. But one thing you should know: when Janci stares ahead of him without seeing what's in front of him, then the whole village begins to wonder what's going to happen, for Janci knows far more than all the rest of us put together."

The smith's grave, deep voice filled the room and the others listened in a silence that gave assent to his words. He had scarcely finished speaking, however, when there was a noise of galloping hoofs and rapidly rolling wagon wheels. A tall brake drawn by four handsome horses dashed past in a whirlwind.

"It's the count—the count and the district judge," said the landlord in a tone of respect. The notary made a grab at his hat and umbrella and hurried from the room. "That shows how much they thought of our pastor," continued the landlord proudly. "For the count himself has come and with four horses, too, to get here the more quickly. His Reverence was a great friend of the countess."

"They didn't make so much fuss over the pedlar and Betty," murmured the cobbler, who suffered from a perpetual grouch. But he followed the others, who paid their scores hastily and went out into the streets that they might watch from a distance at least what was going on in the rectory. The landlord bustled about the inn to have everything in readiness in case the gentlemen should honour him by taking a meal, and perhaps even lodgings, at his house. At the gate of the rectory the coachman and the maid Liska stood to receive the newcomers, just as five o'clock was striking from the steeple.

It should have been still quite light, but it was already dusk, for the clouds hung heavy. The rain had ceased, but a heavy wind came up which tore the delicate petals of the blossoms from the fruit trees and strewed them like snow on the ground beneath. The count, who was the head of one of the richest and most aristocratic families in Hungary, threw off his heavy fur coat and hastened up the stairs at the top of which his old friend and confidant, the venerable pastor, usually came to meet him. Today it was only the local magistrate who stood there, bowing deeply.

"This is incredible, incredible!" exclaimed the count.

"It is, indeed, sir," said the man, leading the magnate through the dining-room into the pastor's study, where, as far as could be seen, the murder had been committed. They were joined by the district judge, who had remained behind to give an order sending a carriage to the nearest railway station. The judge, too, was serious and deeply shocked, for he also had greatly admired and revered the old pastor. The stately rectory had been the scene of many a jovial gathering when the lord of the manor had made it a centre for a day's hunting with his friends. The bearers of some of the proudest names in all Hungary had gathered in the high-arched rooms to laugh with the venerable pastor and to sample the excellent wines in his cellar. These wines, which the gentlemen themselves would send in as presents to the master of the rectory, would be carefully preserved for their own enjoyment. Not a landed proprietor for many leagues around but knew and loved the old pastor, who had now so strangely disappeared under such terrifying circumstances.

"Well, we might as well begin our examination," remarked the count. "Although if Dr. Orszay's sharp eyes did not find anything, I doubt very much if we will. You have asked the doctor to come here again, haven't you?"

"Yes, your Grace! As soon as I saw you coming I sent the sexton to the asylum." Then the men went in again into the room which had been the scene of the mysterious crime. The wind rattled the open window and blew out its white curtains. It was already dark in the corners of the room, one could see but indistinctly the carvings of the wainscoting. The light backs of the books, or the gold letters on the darker bindings, made spots of brightness in the gloom. The hideous pool of blood in the centre of the floor was still plainly to be seen.

"Judging by the loss of blood, death must have come quickly."

"There was no struggle, evidently, for everything in the room was in perfect order when we entered it."

"There is not even a chair misplaced. His Bible is there on the desk, he may have been preparing for today's sermon."

"Yes, that is the case; because see, here are some notes in his handwriting."

The count and Judge von Kormendy spoke these sentences at intervals as they made their examination of the room. The local magistrate was able to answer one or two simpler questions, but for the most part he could only shrug his shoulders in helplessness. Nothing had been seen or heard that was at all unusual during the night in the rectory. When the old housekeeper was called up she could say nothing more than this. Indeed, it was almost impossible for the old woman to say anything, her voice choked with sobs at every second word. None of the household force had noticed anything unusual, or could remember anything at all that would throw light on this mystery.

"Well, then, sir, we might just as well sit down and wait for the detective's arrival," said the judge.

"You are waiting for some one besides the doctor?" asked the local magistrate timidly.

"Yes, His Grace telegraphed to Budapest," answered the district judge, looking at his watch. "And if the train is on time, the man we are waiting for ought to be here in an hour. You sent the carriage to the station, didn't you? Is the driver reliable?"

"Yes, sir, he is a dependable man," said the old housekeeper.

Dr. Orszay entered the room just then and the count introduced him to the district judge, who was still a stranger to him.

"I fear, count, that our eyes will serve but little in discovering the truth of this mystery," said the doctor.

The nobleman nodded. "I agree with you," he replied. "And I have sent for sharper eyes than either yours or mine."

The doctor looked his question, and the count continued: "When the news came to me I telegraphed to Pest for a police detective, telling them that the case was peculiar and urgent. I received an answer as I stopped at the station on my way here. This is it: 'Detective Joseph Müller from Vienna in Budapest by chance. Have sent him to take your case.'"

"Müller?" exclaimed Dr. Orszay. "Can it be the celebrated Müller, the most famous detective of the Austrian police? That would indeed be a blessing."

"I hope and believe that it is," said the count gravely. "I have heard of this man and we need such a one here that we may find the source of these many misfortunes which have overwhelmed our peaceful village for two years past. It is indeed a stroke of good luck that has led a man of such gifts into our neighbourhood at a time when he is so greatly needed. I believe personally that it is the same person or persons who have been the perpetrators of all these outrages and I intend once for all to put a stop to it, let it cost what it may."

"If any one can discover the truth it will be Müller," said the district judge. "It was I who told the count how fortunate we were that this man, who is known to the police throughout Austria and far beyond the borders of our kingdom, should have chanced to be in

Budapest and free to come to us when we called. You and I"—he turned with a smile to the local magistrate—"you and I can get away with the usual cases of local brutality hereabouts. But the cunning that is at the bottom of these crimes is one too many for us."

The men had taken their places around the great dining-table. The old housekeeper had crept out again, her terror making her forget her usual hospitality. And indeed it would not have occurred to the guests to ask or even to wish for any refreshment. The maid brought a lamp, which sent its weak rays scarcely beyond the edges of the big table. The four men sat in silence for some time.

"I suppose it would be useless to ask who has been coming and going from the rectory the last few days?" began the count.

"Oh, yes, indeed, sir," said the district judge with a sigh. "For if this murderer is the same who committed the other crimes he must live here in or near the village, and therefore must be known to all and not likely to excite suspicion."

"I beg your pardon, sir," put in the doctor. "There must be at least two of them. One man alone could not have carried off the farm hand who was killed to the swamp where his body was found. Nor could one man alone have taken away the bloody body of the pastor. Our venerable friend was a man of size and weight, as you know, and one man alone could not have dragged his body from he room without leaving an easily seen trail."

The judge blushed, but he nodded in affirmation to the doctor's words. This thought had not occurred to him before. In fact, the judge was more notable for his good will and his love of justice rather than for his keen intelligence. He was as well aware of this as was any one else, and he was heartily glad that the count had sent to the capital for reinforcements.

Some time more passed in deep silence. Each of the men was occupied with his own thoughts. A sigh broke the silence now and then, and a slight movement when one or the other drew out his watch or raised his head to look at the door. Finally, the sound of a carriage outside was heard. The men sprang up.

The driver's voice was heard, then steps which ascended the stairs lowly and lightly, audible only because the stillness was so great.

The door opened and a small, slight, smooth-shaven man with a gentle face and keen grey eyes stood on the threshold. "I am Joseph Müller," he said with a low, soft voice.

The four men in the room looked at him in astonishment.

269

"This simple-looking individual is the man that every one is afraid of?" thought the count, as he walked forward and held out his hand to the stranger.

"I sent for you, Mr. Müller," said the magnate, conscious of his stately size and appearance, as well as of his importance in the presence of a personage who so little looked what his great fame might have led one to expect.

"Then you are Count ——?" answered Müller gently. "I was in Budapest, having just finished a difficult case which took me there. They told me that a mysterious crime had happened in your neighbourhood, and sent me here to take charge of it. You will pardon any ignorance I may show as a stranger to this locality. I will do my best and it may be possible that I can help you."

The count introduced the other gentlemen in order and they sat down again at the table.

"And now what is it you want me for, count?" asked Müller.

"There was a murder committed in this house," answered the count.

"When?"

"Last night."

"Who is the victim?"

"Our pastor."

"How was he killed?"

"We do not know."

"You are not a physician, then?" asked Müller, turning to Orszay.

"Yes, I am," answered the latter.

"Well?"

"The body is missing," said Orszay, somewhat sharply.

"Missing?" Müller became greatly interested. "Will you please lead me to the scene of the crime?" he said, rising from his chair.

The others led him into the next room, the magistrate going ahead with a lamp. The judge called for more lights and the group stood around the pool of blood on the floor of the study. Müller's arms were crossed on his breast as he stood looking down at the hideous spot. There was no terror in his eyes, as in those of the others, but only a keen attention and a lively interest.

"Who has been in this room since the discovery?" he asked.

The doctor replied that only the servants of the immediate household, the notary, the magistrate, and himself, then later the count and the district judge entered the room.

"You are quite certain that no one else has been in here?"

"No, no one else."

"Will you kindly send for the three servants?" The magistrate left the room.

"Who else lives in the house?"

"The sexton and the dairymaid."

"And no one else has left the house today or has entered it?"

"No one. The main door has been watched all day by a gendarme."

"Is there but one door out of this room?"

"No, there is a small door beside that bookcase."

"Where does it lead to?"

"It leads to a passageway at the end of which there is a stair down into the vestry."

Müller gave an exclamation of surprise.

"The vestry as well as the church have neither of them been opened on the side toward the street."

"The church or the vestry, you mean," corrected Müller. "How many doors have they on the street side?"

"One each."

"The locks on these doors were in good condition?"

"Yes, they were untouched."

"Was there anything stolen from the church?"

"No, nothing that we could see."

"Was the pastor rich?"

"No, he was almost a poor man, for he gave away all that he had."

"But you were his patron, count."

"I was his friend. He was the confidential adviser of myself and family."

"This would mean rich presents now and then, would it not?"

"No, that is not the case. Our venerable pastor would take nothing for himself. He would accept no presents but gifts of money for his poor."

"Then you do not believe this to have been a murder for the sake of robbery?"

"No. There was nothing disturbed in any part of the house, no drawers or cupboards broken open at all."

Müller smiled. "I have heard it said that your romantic Hungarian bandits will often be satisfied with the small booty they may find in the pocket or on the person of their victim."

"You are right, Mr. Müller. But that is only when they can find nothing else."

"Or perhaps if it is a case of revenge.

"It cannot be revenge in this case!"

"The pastor was greatly loved?"

"He was loved and revered."

"By every one?"

"By every one!" the four men answered at once.

Müller was still a while. His eyes were veiled and his face thoughtful. Finally he raised his head. "There has been nothing moved or changed in this room?"

"No—neither here nor anywhere else in the house or the church," answered the local magistrate.

"That is good. Now I would like to question the servants."

Müller had already started for the door, then he turned back into the room and pointing toward the second door he asked: "Is that door locked?"

"Yes," answered the count. "I found it locked when I examined it myself a short time ago."

"It was locked on the inside?"

"Yes, locked on the inside."

"Very well. Then we have nothing more to do here for the time being. Let us go back into the dining-room."

The men returned to the dining-room, Müller last, for he stopped to lock the door of the study and put the key in his pocket. Then he began his examination of the servants.

The old housekeeper, who, as usual, was the first to rise in the household, had also, as usual, rung the bell to waken the other servants. Then when Liska came downstairs she had sent her up to the pastor's room. His bedroom was to the right of the dining-room. Liska had, as usual, knocked on the door exactly at seven o'clock and continued knocking for some few minutes without receiving any answer. Slightly alarmed, the girl had gone back and told the housekeeper that the pastor did not answer.

Then the old woman asked the coachman to go up and see if anything was the matter with the reverend gentleman. The man returned in a few moments, pale and trembling in every limb and apparently struck dumb by fright. He motioned the women to follow him, and all three crept up the stairs. The coachman led them first to the pastor's bed, which was untouched, and then to the pool of blood in his study. The sight of the latter frightened the servants so much that they did not notice at first that there was no sign of the pastor himself, whom they now knew must have been murdered. When they finally came to themselves sufficiently to take some action, the man hurried off to call the magistrate, and Liska ran to the asylum to fetch the old doctor; the pastor's intimate friend. The aged housekeeper, trembling in fear, crept back to her own room and sat there waiting the return of the others.

This was the story of the early morning as told by the three servants, who had already given their report in much the same words to the count on his arrival and also to the magistrate. There was no reason to doubt the words of either the old housekeeper or of Janos, the coachman, who had served for more than twenty years in the rectory and whose fidelity was known. The girl Liska was scarcely eighteen, and her round childish face and big eyes dimmed with tears, corroborated her story. When they had told Müller all they knew, the detective sat stroking, his chin, and looking thoughtfully at the floor. Then he raised his head and said, in a tone of calm friendliness: "Well, good friends, this will do for tonight. Now, if you will kindly give me a bite to eat and a glass of some light wine, I'd be very thankful. I have had no food since early this morning."

The housekeeper and the maid disappeared, and Janos went to the stable to harness the count's trap.

The magnate turned to the detective. "I thank you once more that you have come to us. I appreciate it greatly that a stranger to our part of the country, like yourself, should give his time and strength to this problem of our obscure little village."

"There is nothing else calling me, sir," answered Müller. "And the Budapest police will explain to headquarters at Vienna if I do not return at once."

"Do you understand our tongue sufficiently to deal with these people here?"

"Oh, yes; there will be no difficulty about that. I have hunted criminals in Hungary before. And a case of this kind does not usually call for disguises in which any accent would betray one."

"It is a strange profession," said the doctor.

"One gets used to it—like everything else," answered Müller, with a gentle smile. "And now I have to thank you gentlemen for your confidence in me."

"Which I know you will justify," said the count.

Müller shrugged his shoulders: "I haven't felt anything yet—but it will come—there's something in the air."

The count smiled at his manner of expressing himself, but all four of the men had already begun to feel sympathy and respect for this quiet-mannered little person whose words were so few and whose voice was so gentle. Something in his grey eyes and in the quiet determination of his manner made them realise that he had won his fame honestly. With the enthusiasm of his race the Hungarian count pressed the detective's hand in a warm grasp as he said: "I know that we can trust in you. You will avenge the death of my old friend and of those others who were killed here. The doctor and the magistrate will tell you about them tomorrow. We two will go home now. Telegraph us as soon as anything has happened. Every one in the village will be ready to help you and of course you can call on me for funds. Here is something to begin on." With these words the count laid a silk purse full of gold pieces on the table. One more pressure of the hand and he was gone. The other men also left the room, following the count's lead in a cordial farewell of the detective. They also shared the nobleman's feeling that now indeed, with this man to help them, could the cloud of horror that had hung over the village for two years, and had culminated in the present catastrophe, be lifted.

The excitement of the count's departure had died away and the steps of the other men on their way to the village had faded in the distance. There was nothing now to be heard but the rustling of the leaves and the creaking of the boughs as the trees bent before the onrush of the wind. Müller stood alone, with folded arms, in the middle of the large room, letting his sharp eyes wander about the circle of light thrown by the lamps. He was glad to be alone—for only when he was alone could his brain do its best work. He took up one of the lamps and opened the door to the room in which, as far as could be known, the murder had been committed. He walked in carefully and, setting the lamp on the desk, examined the articles lying about on it. There was nothing of importance to be found there. An open Bible and a sheet of paper with notes for the day's sermon lay on top of the desk. In the drawers, none of which were locked, were official papers, books, manuscripts of former sermons, and a few unimportant personal notes.

The flame of the lamp flickered in the breeze that came from the open window. But Müller did not close the casement. He wanted to leave everything just as he had found it until daylight. When he saw that it was impossible to leave the lamp there he took it up again and left the room.

"What is the use of being impatient?" he said to himself. "If I move about in this poor light I will be sure to ruin some possible clue. For there must be some clue left here. It is impossible for even the most practiced criminal not to leave some trace of his presence."

The detective returned to the dining-room, locking the study door carefully behind him. The maid and the coachman returned, bringing in an abundant supper, and Müller sat down to do justice to the many good things on the tray. When the maid returned to take away the dishes she inquired whether she should put the guest chamber in order for the detective. He told her not to go to any trouble for his sake, that he would sleep in the bed in the neighbouring room.

"You going to sleep in there?" said the girl, horrified.

"Yes, my child, and I think I will sleep well tonight. I feel very tired." Liska carried the things out, shaking her head in surprise at this thin little man who did not seem to know what it was to be afraid. Half an hour later the rectory was in darkness. Before he retired, Müller had made a careful examination of the pastor's bedroom. Nothing was disturbed anywhere, and it was evident that the priest had not made any preparations for the night, but was still at work at his desk in the study when death overtook him. When he came to this conclusion, the detective went to bed and soon fell asleep.

In his little hut near the asylum gates, shepherd Janci slept as sound as usual. But he was dreaming and he spoke in his sleep. There was no one to hear him, for his faithful Margit was snoring loudly. Snatches of sentences and broken words came from Janci's lips: "The hand—the big hand—I see it—at his throat—the face—the yellow face—it laughs—"

Next morning the children on their way to school crept past the rectory with wide eyes and open mouths. And the grown people spoke in lower tones when their work led them past the handsome old house. It had once been their pride, but now it was a place of horror to them. The old housekeeper had succumbed to her fright and was very ill. Liska went about her work silently, and the farm servants walked more heavily and chattered less than they had before. The hump-backed sexton, who had not been allowed to enter the church and therefore had nothing to do, made an early start for the inn, where he spent most of the day telling what little he knew to the many who made an excuse to follow him there.

The only calm and undisturbed person in the rectory household was Müller. He had made a thorough examination of the entire scene of the murder, but had not found anything at all. Of one thing alone was he certain: the murderer had come through the hidden passageway from the church. There were two reasons to believe this, one of which might possibly not be sufficient, but the other was conclusive.

The heavy armchair before the desk, the chair on which the pastor was presumably sitting when the murderer entered, was half turned around, turned in just such a way as it would have been had the man who was sitting there suddenly sprung up in excitement or surprise. The chair was pushed back a step from the desk and turned towards the entrance to the passageway. Those who had been in the room during the day had reported that they had not touched any one of the articles of furniture, therefore the position of the chair was the same that had been given it by the man who had sat in it, by the murdered pastor himself.

Of course there was always the possibility that some one had moved the chair without realising it. This clue, therefore, could not be looked upon as an absolutely certain one had it stood alone. But there was other evidence far more important. The great pool of blood was just half-way between the door of the passage and the armchair. It was here, therefore, that the attack had taken place. The pastor could not have turned in this direction in the hope of flight, for there was nothing here to give him shelter, no weapon that he could grasp, not even a cane. He must have turned in this direction to meet and greet the invader who had entered his room in this unusual manner. Turned to meet him as a brave man would, with no other weapon than the sacredness of his calling and his age.

But this had not been enough to protect the venerable priest. The murderer must have made his thrust at once and his victim had sunk down dying on the floor of the room in which he had spent so many hours of quiet study, in which he had brought comfort and given advice to so many anxious hearts; for dying he must have been—it would be impossible for a man to lose so much blood and live.

"The struggle," thought the detective, "but was there a struggle?" He looked about the room again, but could see nothing that showed disorder anywhere in its immaculate neatness. No, there could have been no struggle. It must have been a quick knife thrust and death at once. "Not a shot?" No, a shot would have been heard by the night watchman walking the streets near the church. The night was quiet, the window open. Some one in the village would have heard the noise of a shot. And it was not likely that the old housekeeper who slept in the room immediately below, slept the light sleep of the aged would have failed to have heard the firing of a pistol.

Müller took a chair and sat down directly in front of the pool of blood, looking at it carefully. Suddenly he bowed his head deeper. He had caught sight of a fine thread of the red fluid which had been drawn out for about a foot or two in the direction towards the door to the dining-room. What did that mean? Did it mean that the murderer went out through that door, dragging something after him that made this delicate line? Müller bent down still deeper. The sun shone brightly on the floor, sending its clear rays obliquely through the window. The sharp eyes which now covered every inch of the yellow-painted floor discovered something else. They discovered that this red thread curved slightly and had a continuation in a fine scratch in the paint of the floor. Müller followed up this scratch and it led him over towards the window and then back again in wide curves, then out again under the desk and finally, growing weaker and weaker, it came back to the neighbourhood of the pool of blood, but on the opposite side of it. Müller got down on his hands and knees to follow up the scratch. He did not notice the discomfort of his position, his eyes shone in excitement and a deep flush glowed in his cheeks. Also, he began to whistle softly.

Joseph Müller, the bloodhound of the Austrian police, had found a clue, a clue that soon would bring him to the trail he was seeking. He did not know yet what he could do with his clue. But this much he knew; sooner or later this scratch in the floor would lead him to the murderer. The trail might be long and devious; but he would follow it and at its end would be success. He knew that this scratch had been made after the murder was committed; this was proved by the blood that marked its beginning. And it could not have been made by any of those who entered the room during the day because by that time the blood had dried. This strange streak in the floor, with its weird curves and spirals, could have been made only by the murderer. But how? With what instrument? There was the riddle which must be solved.

And now Müller, making another careful examination of the floor, found something else. It was something that might be utterly unimportant or might be of great value. It was a tiny bit of hardened lacquer which he found on the floor beside one of the legs of the desk. It was rounded out, with sharp edges, and coloured grey with a tiny zigzag of yellow on its surface. Müller lifted it carefully and looked at it keenly. This tiny bit of lacquer had evidently been knocked off from some convex object, but it was impossible to tell at the moment just what sort of an object it might have been. There are so many different things which are customarily covered with lacquer. However, further examination brought him down to a narrower range of subjects. For on the inside of the lacquer he found a shred of reddish wood fibre. It must have been a wooden object, therefore, from which the lacquer came, and the wood had been of reddish tinge.

Müller pondered the matter for a little while longer. Then he placed his discovery carefully in the pastor's emptied tobacco-box, and dropped the box in his own pocket. He closed the window and the door to the dining-room, lit a lamp, and entered the passageway leading to the vestry. It was a short passageway, scarcely more than a dozen paces long.

The walls were whitewashed, the floor tiled and the entire passage shone in neatness. Müller held the light of his lamp to every inch of it, but there was nothing to show that the criminal had gone through here with the body of his victim.

"The criminal"—Müller still thought of only one. His long experience had taught him that the most intricate crimes were usually committed by one man only. The strength necessary for such a crime as this did not deceive him either. He knew that in extraordinary moments extraordinary strength will come to the one who needs it.

He now passed down the steps leading into the vestry. There was no trace of any kind here either. The door into the vestry was not locked. It was seldom locked, they had told him, for the vestry itself was closed by a huge carved portal with a heavy ornamented iron lock that could be opened only with the greatest noise and trouble. This door was locked and closed as it had been since yesterday morning. Everything in the vestry was in perfect order; the priest's garments and the censers all in their places. Müller assured himself of this before he left the little room. He then opened the glass door that led down by a few steps into the church.

It was a beautiful old church, and it was a rich church also. It was built in the older Gothic style, and its heavy, broad-arched walls, its massive columns would have made it look cold and bare had not handsome tapestries, the gift of the lady of the manor, covered the walls. Fine old pictures hung here and there above the altars, and handsome stained glass windows broke the light that fell into the high vaulted interior. There were three great altars in the church, all of them richly decorated. The main altar stood isolated in the choir. In the open space behind it was the entrance to the crypt, now veiled in a mysterious twilight. Heavy silver candlesticks, three on a side, stood on the altar. The pale gold of the tabernacle door gleamed between them.

Müller walked through the silent church, in which even his light steps resounded uncannily. He looked into each of the pews, into the confessionals, he walked around all the columns, he climbed up into the pulpit, he did everything that the others had done before him yesterday. And as with them, he found nothing that would indicate that the murderer had spent any time in the church. Finally he turned back once more to the main altar on his way out. But he did not leave the church as he intended. His last look at the altar had showed him something that attracted his attention and he walked up the three steps to examine it more closely.

What he had seen was something unusual about one of the silver candlesticks. These candlesticks had three feet, and five of them were placed in such a way that the two front feet were turned toward the spectator. But on the end candlestick nearest Müller the single foot projected out to the front of the altar. This candlestick therefore had been set down hastily, not placed carefully in the order of things as were the others.

And not only this. The heavy wax candle which was in the candlestick was burned down about a finger's breadth more than the others, for these were all exactly of a height. Müller bent still nearer to the candlestick, but he saw that the dim light in the church was not sufficient. He went to one of the smaller side altars, took a candle from there, lit it with one of the matches that he found in his own pocket and returned with the burning candle to the main altar. The steps leading up to this altar were covered by a large rug with a white ground and a pattern of flowers. Looking carefully at it the detective saw a tiny brown spot, the mark of a burn, upon one of the white surfaces. Beside it lay a half used match.

Walking around this carefully, Müller approached the candlestick that interested him and holding up his light he examined every inch of its surface. He found what he was looking for. There were dark red spots between the rough edges of the silver ornamentation.

"Then the body is somewhere around here," thought the detective and came down from the steps, still holding the burning candle.

He walked slowly to the back of the altar. There was a little table there such as held the sacred dishes for the communion service, and the little carpet-covered steps which the sexton put out for the pastor when he took the monstrance from the high-built tabernacle. That was all that was to be seen in the dark corner behind the altar. Holding his candle close to the floor Müller discovered an iron ring fastened to one of the big stone flags. This must be the entrance to the crypt.

Müller tried to raise the flag and was astonished to find how easily it came up. It was a square of reddish marble, the same with which the entire floor of the church was tiled. This flag was very thin and could easily be raised and placed back against the wall. Müller took up his candle, too greatly excited to stop to get a stick for it. He felt assured that now he would soon be able to solve at least a part of the mystery. He climbed down the steps carefully and found that they led into the crypt as he supposed. They were kept spotlessly clean, as was the entire crypt as far as he could see it by the light of his flickering candle. He was not surprised to discover that the air was perfectly pure here. There must be windows or ventilators somewhere, this he knew from the way his candle behaved.

The ancient vault had a high arched ceiling and heavy massive pillars. It was a subterranean repetition of the church above. There had evidently been a convent attached to this church at one time; for here stood a row of simple wooden coffins all exactly alike, bearing each one upon its lid a roughly painted cross surrounded by a wreath. Thus were buried the monks of days long past.

Müller walked slowly through the rows of coffins looking eagerly to each side. Suddenly he stopped and stood still. His hand did not tremble but his thin face was pale—pale as that face which looked up at him out of one of the coffins. The lid of the coffin stood up against the wall and Müller saw that there were several other empty ones further on, waiting for their silent occupants.

The body in the open coffin before which Müller stood was the body of the man who had been missing since the day previous. He lay there quite peacefully, his hands crossed over his breast, his eyes closed, a line of pain about his lips. In the crossed fingers was a little bunch of dark yellow roses. At the first glance one might almost have thought that loving hands had laid the old pastor in his coffin. But the red stain on the white cloth about his throat, and the bloody disorder of his snow-white hair contrasted sadly with the look of peace on the dead face. Under his head was a white silk cushion, one of the cushions from the altar.

Müller stood looking down for some time at this poor victim of a strange crime, then he turned to go.

He wanted to know one thing more: how the murderer had left the crypt. The flame of his candle told him, for it nearly went out in a gust of wind that came down the opening right above him. This was a window about three or four feet from the floor, protected by rusty iron bars which had been sawed through, leaving the opening free. It was a small window, but it was large enough to allow a man of much greater size than Müller to pass through it. The detective blew out his candle and climbed up onto the window sill. He found himself outside, in a corner of the churchyard. A thicket of heavy bushes grown up over neglected graves completely hid the opening through which he had come. There were thorns on these bushes and also a few scattered roses, dark yellow roses.

Müller walked thoughtfully through the churchyard. The sexton sat huddled in an unhappy heap at the gate. He looked up in alarm as he saw the detective walking towards him. Something in the stranger's face told the little hunchback that he had made a discovery. The sexton sprang up, his lips did not dare utter the question that his eyes asked.

"I have found him," said the detective gravely.

The hunchback sexton staggered, then recovered himself, and hurried away to fetch the magistrate and the doctor.

An hour later the murdered pastor lay in state in the chief apartment of his home, surrounded by burning candles and high-heaped masses of flowers. But he still lay in the simple convent coffin and the little bunch of roses which his murderer had placed between his stiffening fingers had not been touched.

Two days later the pastor was buried. The count and his family led the train of numerous mourners and among the last was Müller.

A day or two after the funeral the detective sauntered slowly through the main street of the village. He was not in a very good humour, his answer to the greeting of those who passed him was short. The children avoided him, for with the keenness of their kind they recognised the fact that this usually gentle little man was not in possession of his habitual calm temper. One group of boys, playing with a top, did not notice his coming and Müller stopped behind them to look on. Suddenly a sharp whistle was heard and the boys looked up from their play, surprised at seeing the stranger behind them. His eyes were gleaming, and his cheeks were flushed, and a few bars of a merry tune came in a keen whistle from his lips as he watched the spirals made by the spinning top.

Before the boys could stop their play the detective had left the group and hastened onward to the little shop. He left it again in eager haste after having made his purchase, and hurried back to the rectory. The shop-keeper stood in the doorway looking in surprise at this grown man who came to buy a top. And at home in the rectory the old housekeeper listened in equal surprise to the humming noise over her head. She thought at first it might be a bee that had got in some-how. Then she realised that it was not quite the same noise, and having already concluded that it was of no use to be surprised at anything this strange guest might do, she continued reading her scriptures.

Upstairs in the pastor's study, Müller sat in the armchair attentively watching the gyrations of a spinning top. The little toy, started at a certain point, drew a line exactly parallel to the scratch on the floor that had excited his thoughts and absorbed them day and night.

"It was a top—a top" repeated the detective to himself again and again. "I don't see why I didn't think of that right away. Why, of course, nothing else could have drawn such a perfect curve around the room, unhindered by the legs of the desk. Only I don't see how a toy like that could have any connection with this cruel and purposeless murder. Why, only a fool—or a madman—"

Müller sprang up from his chair and again a sharp shrill whistle came from his lips. "A madman!—" he repeated, beating his own forehead. "It could only have been a madman who committed this murder! And the pastor was not the first, there were two other murders here within a comparatively short time. I think I will take advantage of Dr. Orszay's invitation."

Half an hour later Müller and the doctor sat together in a summerhouse, from the windows of which one could see the park surrounding the asylum to almost its entire extent. The park was arranged with due regard to its purpose. The eye could sweep through it unhindered. There were no bushes except immediately along the high wall. Otherwise there were beautiful lawns, flower beds and groups of fine old trees with tall trunks.

As would be natural in visiting such a place Müller had induced the doctor to talk about his patients. Dr. Orszay was an excellent talker and possessed the power of painting a personality for his listeners. He was pleased and flattered by the evident interest with which the detective listened to his remarks.

"Then your patients are all quite harmless?" asked Müller thoughtfully, when the doctor came to a pause.

"Yes, all quite harmless. Of course, there is the man who strangely enough considers himself the reincarnation of the famous French murderer, the goldsmith Cardillac, who, as you remember, kept all Paris in a fervour of excitement by his crimes during the reign of Louis XIV. But in spite of his weird mania this man is the most good-natured of any. He has been shut up in his room for several days now. He was a mechanician by trade, living in Budapest, and an unsuccessful invention turned his mind."

"Is he a large, powerful man?" asked Müller.

Dr. Orszay looked a bit surprised. "Why do you ask that? He does happen to be a large man of considerable strength, but in spite of it I have no fear of him. I have an attendant who is invaluable to me, a man of such strength that even the fiercest of them cannot overcome him, and yet with a mind and a personal magnetism which they cannot resist. He can always master our patients mentally and physically—most of them are afraid of him and they know that they must do as he says. There is something in his very glance which has the power to paralyse even healthy nerves, for it shows the strength of will possessed by this man."

"And what is the name of this invaluable attendant?" asked Müller with a strange smile which the doctor took to be slightly ironical.

"Gyuri Kovacz. You are amused at my enthusiasm? But consider my position here. I am an old man and have never been a strong man. At my age I would not have strength enough to force that little woman there—she thinks herself possessed and is quite cranky at times—to go to her own room when she doesn't want to. And do you see that man over there in the blue blouse? He is an excellent gardener but he believes himself to be Napoleon, and when he has his acute attacks I would be helpless to control him were it not for Gyuri."

"And you are not afraid of Cardillac?" interrupted Müller.

"Not in the least. He is as good-natured as a child and as confiding. I can let him walk around here as much as he likes. If it were not for the absurd nonsense that he talks when he has one of his attacks, and which frightens those who do not understand him, I could let him go free altogether."

"Then you never let him leave the asylum grounds?

"Oh, yes. I take him out with me very frequently. He is a man of considerable education and a very clever talker. It is quite a pleasure to be with him. That was the opinion of my poor friend also, my poor murdered friend."

"The pastor?"

"The pastor. He often invited Cardillac to come to the rectory with me."

"Indeed. Then Cardillac knew the inside of the rectory?"

"Yes. The pastor used to lend him books and let him choose them himself from the library shelves. The people in the village are very kind to my poor patients here. I have long since had the habit of taking some of the quieter ones with me down into the village and letting the people become acquainted with them. It is good for both parties. It gives the patients some little diversion, and it takes away the worst of the senseless fear these peasants had at first of the asylum and its inmates. Cardillac in particular is always welcome when he comes, for he brings the children all sorts of toys that he makes in his cell."

The detective had listened attentively and once his eyes flashed and his lips shut tight as if to keep in the betraying whistle. Then he asked calmly: "But the patients are only allowed to go out when you accompany them, I suppose?"

"Oh, no; the attendants take them out sometimes. I prefer, however, to let them go only with Gyuri, for I can depend upon him more than upon any of the others."

"Then he and Cardillac have been out together occasionally?"

"Oh, yes, quite frequently. But—pardon me—this is almost like a cross-examination."

"I beg your pardon, doctor, it's a bad habit of mine. One gets so accustomed to it in my profession."

"What is it you want?" asked Doctor Orszay, turning to a fine-looking young man of superb build, who entered just then and stood by the door.

"I just wanted to announce, sir, that No. 302 is quiet again!"

"302 is Cardillac himself, Mr. Müller, or to give him his right name, Lajos Varna," explained the doctor turning to his guest. "He is the 302nd patient who has been received here in these twenty years. Then Cardillac is quiet again?" he asked, looking up at the young giant. "I am glad of that. You can announce our visit to him. This gentleman wants to inspect the asylum."

Müller realised that this was the attendant Gyuri, and he looked at him attentively. He was soon clear in his own mind that this remarkably handsome man did not please him, in fact awoke in him a feeling of repulsion. The attendant's quiet, almost cat-like movements were in strange contrast to the massivity of his superb frame, and his large round eyes, shaped for open, honest glances, were shifty and cunning. They seemed to be asking "Are you trying to discover anything about me?" coupled with a threat. "For your own sake you had better not do it."

When the young man had left the room Müller rose hastily and walked up and down several times. His face was flushed and his lips tight set. Suddenly he exclaimed: "I do not like this Gyuri."

Dr. Orszay looked up astonished. "There are many others who do not like him—most of his fellow-warders for instance, and all of the patients. I think there must be something in the contrast of such quiet movements with such a big body that gets on people's nerves. But consider, Mr. Müller, that the man's work would naturally make him a little different from other people. I have known Gyuri for five years as a faithful and unassuming servant, always willing and ready for any duty, however difficult or dangerous. He has but one fault—if I may call it such—that is that he has a mistress who is known to be mercenary and hard-hearted. She lives in a neighbouring village."

"For five years, you say? And how long has Cardillac been here?"

"Cardillac? He has been here for almost three years."

"For almost three years, and is it not almost three years—" Müller interrupted himself. "Are we quite alone? Is no one listening?" The doctor nodded, greatly surprised, and the detective continued almost in a whisper, "and it is just about three years now that there have been committed, at intervals, three terrible crimes notable from the cleverness with which they were carried out, and from the utter impossibility, apparently, of discovering the perpetrator."

Orszay sprang up. His face flushed and then grew livid, and he put his hand to his forehead. Then he forced a smile and said in a voice that trembled in spite of himself: "Mr. Müller, your imagination is wonderful. And which of these two do you think it is that has committed these crimes—the perpetrator of which you have come here to find?"

"I will tell you that later. I must speak to No. 302 first, and I must speak to him in the presence of yourself and Gyuri."

The detective's deep gravity was contagious. Dr. Orszay had sufficiently controlled himself to remember what he had heard in former days, and just now recently from the district judge about this man's marvellous deeds. He realised that when Müller said a thing, no matter how extravagant it might sound, it was worth taking seriously. This realisation brought great uneasiness and grief to the doctor's heart, for he had grown fond of both of the men on whom terrible suspicion was cast by such an authority.

Müller himself was uneasy, but the gloom that had hung over him for the past day or two had vanished. The impenetrable darkness that had surrounded the mystery of the pastor's murder had gotten on his nerves. He was not accustomed to work so long over a problem without getting some light on it. But now, since the chance watching of the spinning top in the street had given him his first inkling of the trail, he was following it up to a clear issue. The eagerness, the blissful vibrating of every nerve that he always felt at this stage of the game, was on him again. He knew that from now on what was still to be done would be easy. Hitherto his mind had been made up on one point; that one man alone was concerned in the crime. Now he understood the possibility that there might have been two, the harmless mechanician who fancied himself a dangerous murderer, and the handsome young giant with the evil eyes.

The two men stood looking at each other in a silence that was almost hostile. Had this stranger come to disturb the peace of the refuge for the unfortunate and to prove that Dr. Orszay, the friend of all the village, had unwittingly been giving shelter to such criminals?

"Shall we go now?" asked the detective finally.

"If you wish it, sir," answered the doctor in a tone that was decidedly cool.

Müller held out his hand. "Don't let us be foolish, doctor. If you should find yourself terribly deceived, and I should have been the means of proving it, promise me that you will not be angry with me."

Orszay pressed the offered hand with a deep sigh. He realised the other's position and knew it was his duty to give him every possible assistance. "What is there for me to do now?" he asked sadly.

"You must see that all the patients are shut up in their cells so that the other attendants are at our disposal if we need them. Varna's room has barred windows, I suppose?"

"Yes."

"And I suppose also that it has but one door. I believe you told me that your asylum was built on the cell system."

"Yes, there is but one door to the room."

"Let the four other attendants stand outside this door. Gyuri will be inside with us. Tell the men outside that they are to seize and hold whomever I shall designate to them. I will call them in by a whistle. You can trust your people?"

"Yes, I think I can."

"Well, I have my revolver," said Müller calmly, "and now we can go."

They left the room together, and found Gyuri waiting for them a little further along the corridor. "Aren't you well, sir?" the attendant asked the doctor, with an anxious note in his voice.

The man's anxiety was not feigned. He was really a faithful servant in his devotion to the old doctor, although Müller had not misjudged him when he decided that this young giant was capable of anything. Good and evil often lie so close together in the human heart.

The doctor's emotion prevented him from speaking, and the detective answered in his place. "It is a sudden indisposition," he said. "Lead me to No. 302, who is waiting for us, I suppose. The doctor wants to lie down a moment in his own room."

Gyuri glanced distrustfully at this man whom he had met for the first time today, but who was no stranger to him—for he had already learned the identity of the guest in the rectory. Then he turned his eyes on his master. The latter nodded and said: "Take the gentleman to Varna's room. I will follow shortly."

The cell to which they went was the first one at the head of the staircase. "Extremely convenient," thought Müller to himself. It was a large room, comfortably furnished and filled now with the red glow of the setting sun. A turning-lathe stood by the window and an elderly man was at work at it. Gyuri called to him and he turned and rose when he saw a stranger.

Lajos Varna was a tall, loose-jointed man with sallow skin and tired eyes. He gave only a hasty glance at his visitor, then looked at Gyuri. The expression in his eyes as he turned them on those of the warder was like the look in the eyes of a well-trained dog when it watches its master's face. Gyuri's brows were drawn close together and his mouth set tight to a narrow line. His eyes fairly bored themselves into the patient's eyes with an expression like that of a hypnotiser.

Müller knew now what he wanted to know. This young man understood how to bend the will of others, even the will of a sick mind, to his own desires. The little silent scene he had watched had lasted just the length of time it had taken the detective to walk through the room and hold out his hand to the patient.

"I don't want to disturb you, Mr. Varna," he said in a friendly tone, with a motion towards the bench from which the mechanician had just arisen. Varna sat down again, obedient as a child. He was not always so apparently, for Müller saw a red mark over the fingers of one hand that was evidently the mark of a blow. Gyuri was not very choice in the methods by which he controlled the patients confided to his care.

"May I sit down also?" asked Müller.

Varna pushed forward a chair. His movements were like those of an automaton.

"And now tell me how you like it here?" began the detective. Varna answered with a low soft voice, "Oh, I like it very much, sir." As he spoke he looked up at Gyuri, whose eyes still bore their commanding expression.

"They treat you kindly here?"

"Oh, yes."

"The doctor is very good to you?"

"Ah, the doctor is so good!" Varna's dull eyes brightened.

"And the others are good to you also?"

"Oh, yes." The momentary gleam in the sad had vanished again.

"Where did you get this red scar?"

The patient became uneasy, he moved anxiously on his chair and looked up at Gyuri. It was evident that he realised there would be more red marks if he told the truth to this stranger.

Müller did not insist upon an answer. "You are uneasy and nervous sometimes, aren't you?"

"Yes, sir, I have been—nervous—lately."

"And they don't let you go out at such times?"

"Why, I—no, I may not go out at such times."

"But the doctor takes you with him sometimes—the doctor or Gyuri?" asked the detective.

"Yes."

"I haven't had him out with me for weeks," interrupted the attendant. He seemed particularly anxious to have the "for weeks" clearly heard by this inconvenient questioner.

Müller dropped this subject and took up another. "They tell me you are very fond of children, and I can see that you are making toys for them here."

"Yes, I love children, and I am so glad they are not afraid of me." These words were spoken with more warmth and greater interest than anything the man had yet said.

"And they tell me that you take gifts with you for the children every time you go down to the village. This is pretty work here, and it must be a pleasant diversion for you." Müller had taken up a dainty little spinning-wheel which was almost completed. "Isn't it made from the wood of a red yew tree?"

"Yes, the doctor gave me a whole tree that had been cut down in the park."

"And that gave you wood for a long time?"

"Yes, indeed; I have been making toys from it for months." Varna had become quite eager and interested as he handed his visitor a number of pretty trifles. The two had risen from their chairs and were leaning over the wide window seat which served as a store-house for the wares turned out by the busy workman. They were toys, mostly, all sorts of little pots and plates, dolls' furniture, balls of various sizes, miniature bowling pins, and tops. Müller took up one of the latter.

"How very clever you are, and how industrious," he exclaimed, sitting down again and turning the top in his hands. It was covered with gray varnish with tiny little yellow stripes painted on it. Towards the lower point a little bit of the varnish had been broken off and the reddish wood underneath was visible. The top was much better constructed than the cheap toys sold in the village. It was hollow and contained in its interior a mechanism started by a pressure on the upper end. Once set in motion the little top spun about the room for some time.

"Oh, isn't that pretty! Is this mechanism your own invention?" asked Müller smiling. Gyuri watched the top with drawn brows and murmured something about "childish foolishness."

"Yes, it is my own invention," said the patient, flattered. He started out on an absolutely technical explanation of the mechanism of tops in general and of his own in particular, an explanation so lucid and so well put that no one would have believed the man who was speaking was not in possession of the full powers of his mind.

Müller listened very attentively with unfeigned interest.

"But you have made more important inventions than this, haven't you?" he asked when the other stopped talking. Varna's eyes flashed and his voice dropped to a tone of mystery as he answered: "Yes indeed I have. But I did not have time to finish them. For I had become some one else."

"Some one else?"

"Cardillac," whispered Varna, whose mania was now getting the best of him again.

"Cardillac? You mean the notorious goldsmith who lived in Paris 200 years ago? Why, he's dead."

Varna's pale lips curled in a superior smile. "Oh, yes—that's what people think, but it's a mistake. He is still alive—I am—I have—although of course there isn't much opportunity here—"

Gyuri cleared his throat with a rasping noise.

"What were you saying, friend Cardillac?" asked Müller with a great show of interest.

"I have done things here that nobody has found out. It gives me great pleasure to see the authorities so helpless over the riddles I have given them to solve. Oh, indeed, sir, you would never imagine how stupid they are here."

"In other words, friend Cardillac, you are too clever for the authorities here?

"Yes, that's it," said the insane man greatly flattered. He raised his head proudly and smiled down at his guest. At this moment the doctor came into the room and Gyuri walked forward to the group at the window.

"You are making him nervous, sir," he said to Müller in a tone that was almost harsh.

"You can leave that to me," answered the detective calmly. "And you will please place yourself behind Mr. Varna's chair, not behind mine. It is your eyes that are making him uneasy."

The attendant was alarmed and lost control of himself for a moment. "Sir!" he exclaimed in an outburst.

"My name is Müller, in case you do not know it already, Joseph Müller, detective. Gyuri Kovacz, you will do what I tell you to! I am master here just now. Is it not so, doctor?"

"Yes, it is so," said the doctor.

"What does this mean?" murmured Gyuri, turning pale.

"It means that the best thing for you to do is to stand up against that wall and fold your arms on your breast," said Müller firmly. He took a revolver from his pocket and laid it beside him on the turning-lathe. The young giant, cowed by the sight of the weapon, obeyed the commands of this little man whom he could have easily crushed with a single blow.

Dr. Orszay sank down on the chair beside the door. Müller, now completely master of the situation, turned to the insane man who stood looking at him in a surprise which was mingled with admiration.

"And now, my dear Cardillac, you must tell us of your great deeds here," said the detective in a friendly tone.

The unfortunate man bent over him with shining eyes and whispered: "But you'll shoot him first, won't you?"

"Why should I shoot him?"

"Because he won't let me say a word without beating me. He is so cruel. He sticks pins into me if I don't do what he wants."

"Why didn't you tell the doctor?"

"Gyuri would have treated me worse than ever then. I am a coward, sir, I'm so afraid of pain and he knew that—he knew that I was afraid of being hurt and that I'd always do what he asked of me. And because I don't like to be hurt myself I always finished them off quickly."

"Finished who?"

"Why, there was Red Betty, he wanted her money."

"Who wanted it?"

"Gyuri."

The man at the wall moved when he heard this terrible accusation. But the detective took up his revolver again. "Be quiet there!" he called, with a look such as he might have thrown at an angry dog. Gyuri stood quiet again but his eyes shot flames and great drops stood out on his forehead.

"Now go on, friend Cardillac," continued the detective. "We were talking about Red Betty."

"I strangled her. She did not even know she was dying. She was such a weak old woman, it really couldn't have hurt her."

"No, certainly not," said Müller soothingly, for he saw that the thought that his victim might have suffered was beginning to make the madman uneasy. "You needn't worry about that. Old Betty died a quiet death. But tell me, how did Gyuri know that she had money?"

"The whole village knew it. She laid cards for people and earned a lot of money that way. She was very stingy and saved every bit. Somebody saw her counting out her money once, she had it in a big stocking under her bed. People in the village talked about it. That's how Gyuri heard of it."

"And so he commanded you to kill Betty and steal her money?"

"Yes. He knew that I loved to give them riddles to guess, just as I did in Paris so long ago."

"Oh, yes, you're Cardillac, aren't you? And now tell us about the smith's swineherd."

"You mean Janos? Oh, he was a stupid lout," answered Varna scornfully.

"He had cast an eye on the beautiful Julcsi, Gyuri's mistress, so of course I had to kill him."

"Did you do that alone?"

"No, Gyuri helped me."

"Why did you cut the bridge supports?"

"Because I enjoy giving people riddles, as I told you. But Gyuri forbade me to kill people uselessly. I liked the chance of getting out though. The doctor's so good to me and the others too. Gyuri is good to me when I have done what he wanted. But you see, Mr. Müller, I am like a prisoner here and that makes me angry. I made Gyuri let me out nights sometimes."

"You mean he let you out alone, all alone?"

"Yes, of course, for I threatened to tell the doctor everything if he didn't."

"You wouldn't have dared do that."

"No, that's true," smiled Varna slyly. "But Gyuri was afraid I might do it, for he isn't always strong enough to frighten me with his eyes. Those were the hours when I could make him afraid—I liked those hours—"

"What did you do when you were out alone at night?"

"I just walked about. I set fire to a tree in the woods once, then the rain came and put it out. Once I killed a dog and another time I cut through the bridge supports. That took me several hours to do and made me very tired. But it was such fun to know that people would be worrying and fussing about who did it."

Varna rubbed his hands gleefully. He did not look the least bit malicious but only very much amused. The doctor groaned. Gyuri's great body trembled, his arms shook, but he did not make a single voluntary movement. He saw the revolver in Müller's hand and felt the keen grey eyes resting on him in pitiless calm.

"And now tell us about the pastor?" said the detective in a firm clear voice.

"Oh, he was a dear, good gentleman," said No. 302 with an expression of pitying sorrow on his face. "I owed him much gratitude; that's why I put the roses in his hand."

"Yes, but you murdered him first."

"Of course, Gyuri told me to."

"And why?"

"He hated the pastor, for the old gentleman had no confidence in him."

"Is this true?" Müller turned to the doctor.

"I did not notice it," said Orszay with a voice that showed deep sorrow.

"And you?" Müller's eyes bored themselves into the orbs of the young giant, now dulled with fear.

Gyuri started and shivered. "He looked at me sharply every now and then," he murmured.

"And that was why he was killed?"

The warder's head sank on his breast.

"No, not only for that reason," continued No. 302. "Gyuri needed money again. He ordered me to bring him the silver candlesticks off the altar."

"Murder and sacrilege," said the detective calmly.

"No, I did not rob the church. When I had buried the reverend gentleman I heard the cock crowing. I was afraid I might get home here too late and I forgot the candlesticks. I had to stop to wash my hands in the brook. While I was there I saw shepherd Janci coming along and I hid behind the willows. He almost discovered me once, but Janci's a dreamer, he sees things nobody else sees—and he doesn't see things that everybody else does see. I couldn't help laughing at his sleepy face. But I didn't laugh when I came back to the asylum. Gyuri was waiting for me at the door. When he saw that I hadn't brought the candlesticks he beat me and tortured me worse than he'd ever done before."

"And you didn't tell anyone?"

"Why, no; because I was afraid that if I told on him, I'd never be able to go out again."

"And you, quite alone, could carry the pastor's body out of his room?"

"I am very strong."

"How did you arrange it that there should be no traces of blood to betray you?"

"I waited until the body had stiffened, then I tied up the wound and carried him down into the crypt."

"Why did you do that?"

"I didn't want to leave him in that horrid pool of blood."

"You were sorry for him then?"

"Why, yes; it looked so horrid to see him lying there—and he had always been so good to me. He was so good to me that very evening when I entered his study.

"He recognised you?

"Certainly. He sprang up from his chair when I came in through the passage from the church. I saw that he was startled, but he smiled at me and reached out his hand to me and said: 'What brings you here, my dear Cardillac?' And then I struck. I wanted him to die with that smile on his lips. It is beautiful to see a man die smiling, it shows that he has not been afraid of death. He was dead at once. I always kill that way—I know just how to strike and where. I killed more than a hundred people years ago in Paris, and I didn't leave one of them the time for even a sigh. I was renowned for that—I had a kind heart and a sure hand."

Müller interrupted the dreadful imaginings of the madman with a question. "You got into the house through the crypt?"

"Yes, through the crypt. I found the window one night when I was prowling around in the churchyard. When I knew that the pastor was to be the next, I cut through the window bars. Gyuri went into the church one day when nobody was there and found out that it was easy to lift the stone over the entrance to the crypt. He also learned that the doors from the church to the vestry were never locked. I knew how to find the passageway, because I had been through it several times on my visits to the rectory. But it was a mere chance that the door into the pastor's study was unlocked."

"A chance that cost the life of a worthy man," said the detective gravely.

Varna nodded sadly. "But he didn't suffer, he was dead at once."

"And now tell me what this top was doing there?" No. 302 looked at the detective in great surprise, and then laid his hand on the latter's arm. "How did you know that I had the top there?" he asked with a show of interest.

"I found its traces in the room, and it was those traces that led me here to you," answered Müller.

"How strange!" remarked Varna. "Are you like shepherd Janci that you can see the things others don't see?"

"No, I have not Janci's gift. It would be a great comfort to me and a help to the others perhaps if I had. I can only see things after they have happened."

"But you can see more than others—the others did not see the traces of the top?"

"My business is to see more than others see," said Müller. "But you have not told me yet what the top was doing there. Why did you take a toy like that with you when you went out on such an errand?"

"It was in my pocket by chance. When I reached for my handkerchief to quench the flow of blood the top came out with it. I must have touched the spring without knowing it, for the top began to spin. I stood still and watched it, then I ran after it. It spun around the room and finally came back to the body. So did I. The pastor was quite still and dead by that time."

"You have heard everything, Dr. Orszay?" asked the detective, rising from his chair.

"Yes, I have heard everything," answered the venerable head of the asylum. He was utterly crushed by the realisation that all this tragedy and horror had gone out from his house.

Varna rose also. He understood perfectly that now Gyuri's power was at an end and he was as pleased as a child that has just received a present. "And now you're going to shoot him?" he asked, in the tone a boy would use if asking when the fireworks were to begin.

Müller shook his head. "No, my dear Cardillac," he replied gravely. "He will not be shot—that is a death for a brave soldier—but this man has deserved—" He did not finish the sentence, for the warder sank to the floor unconscious.

"What a coward!" murmured the detective scornfully, looking down at the giant frame that lay prostrate before him. Even in his wide experience he had known of no case of a man of such strength and such bestial cruelty, combined with such utter cowardice.

Varna also stood looking down at the unconscious warder. Then he glanced up with a cunning smile at the other two men who stood there. The doctor, pale and trembling with horror, covered his face with his hands. Müller turned to the door to call in the attendants waiting outside. During the moment's pause that ensued the madman bent over his worktable, seized a knife that lay there and dropped on one knee beside the prostrate form. His hand was raised to strike when a calm voice said: "Fie! Cardillac, for shame! Do not belittle yourself. This man here is not worthy of your knife, the hangman will look after him."

Varna raised his loose-jointed frame and looked about with glistening eyes and trembling lips. His mind was completely darkened once more. "I must kill him—I must have his blood—there is no one to see me," he murmured. "I am a hangman too—he has made a hangman of me," and again he bent with uplifted hand over the man who had utilised his terrible misfortune to make a criminal of him. But two of the waiting attendants seized his arms and threw him back on the floor, while the other two carted Gyuri out. Both unfortunates were soon securely guarded.

"Do not be angry with me, doctor," said Müller gravely, as he walked through the garden accompanied by Orszay.

Doctor Orszay laughed bitterly. "Why should I be angry with you—you who have discovered my inexcusable credulity?"

"Inexcusable? Oh, no, doctor; it was quite natural that you should have believed a man who had himself so well in hand, and who knew so well how to play his part. When we come to think of it, we realise that most crimes have been made possible through some one's credulity, or over-confidence, a credulity which, in the light of subsequent events, seems quite incomprehensible. Do not reproach yourself and do not lose heart. Your only fault was that you did not recognise the heart of the beast of prey in this admirable human form."

"What course will the law take?" asked Orszay. "The poor unfortunate madman—whose knife took all these lives—cannot be held responsible, can he?"

"Oh, no; his misfortune protects him. But as for the other, though his hands bear no actual bloodstains, he is more truly a murderer than the unhappy man who was his tool. Hanging is too good for him. There are times when even I could wish that we were back in the Middle Ages, when it was possible to torture a prisoner.

"You do not look like that sort of a man," smiled the doctor through his sadness.

"No, I am the most good-natured of men usually, I think—the meekest anyway," answered Müller. "But a case like this—. However, as I said before, keep a stout heart, doctor, and do not waste time in unnecessary self-reproachings." The detective pressed the doctor's hand warmly and walked down the hill towards the village.

He went at once to the office of the magistrate and made his report, then returned to the rectory and packed his grip. He arranged for its transport to the railway station, as he himself preferred to walk the inconsiderable distance. He passed through the village and had just entered the open fields when he met Janci with his flock. The shepherd hastened his steps when he saw the detective approaching.

"You have found him, sir?" he exclaimed as he came up to Müller. The men had come to be friends by this time. The silent shepherd with the power of second sight had won Müller's interest at once.

"Yes, I found him. It is Gyuri, the warder at the asylum."

"No, sir, it is not Gyuri—Gyuri did not do it."

"But when I tell you that he did?"

"But I tell you, sir, that Gyuri did not do it. The man who did it—he has yellowish hands—I saw them—I saw big yellowish hands. Gyuri's hands are big, but they are brown."

"Janci, you are right. I was only trying to test you. Gyuri did not do it; that is, he did not do it with his own hands. The man who held the knife that struck down the pastor was Varna, the crazy mechanician."

Janci beat his forehead. "Oh, I am a foolish and useless dreamer!" he exclaimed; "of course it was Varna's hands that I saw. I have seen them a hundred times when he came down into the village, and yet when I saw them in the vision I did not recognise them."

"We're all dreamers, Janci—and our dreams are very useless generally."

"Yours are not useless, sir," said the shepherd. "If I had as much brains as you have, my dreams might be of some good."

Müller smiled. "And if I had your visions, Janci, it would be a powerful aid to me in my profession."

"I don't think you need them, sir. You can find out the hidden things without them. You are going to leave us?"

"Yes, Janci, I must go back to Budapest, and from there to Vienna. They need me on another case."

"It's a sad work, this bringing people to the gallows, isn't it?"

"Yes, Janci, it is sometimes. But it's a good thing to be able to avenge crime and bring justice to the injured. Goodbye, Janci."

"Goodbye, sir, and God speed you."

The shepherd stood looking after the small, slight figure of the man who walked on rapidly through the heather. "He's the right one for the work," murmured Janci as he turned slowly back towards the village.

An hour later Müller stood in the little waiting-room of the railway station writing a telegram. It was addressed to Count ——.

Do you know the shepherd Janci? It would be a good thing to make him the official detective for the village. He has high qualifications for the profession. If I had his gifts combined with my own, not one could escape me. I have found this one however. The guards are already taking him to you. My work here is done. If I should be needed again I can be found at Police Headquarters, Vienna.

Respectfully,

Joseph Müller

While the detective was writing his message—it was one of the rare moments of humour that Müller allowed himself, and he wondered mildly what the stately Hungarian nobleman would think of it—a heavy farm wagon jolted over the country roads towards the little county seat. Sitting beside the driver and riding about the wagon were armed peasants. The figure of a man, securely bound, his face distorted by rage and fear, lay in the wagon. It was Gyuri Kovacz, who had murdered by the hands of another, and who was now on his way to meet the death that was his due.

And at one of the barred windows in the big yellow house stood a sallow-faced man, looking out at the rising moon with sad, tired eyes. His lips were parted in a smile like that of a dreaming child, and he hummed a gentle lullaby.

In his compartment of the express from Budapest to Vienna, Joseph Müller sat thinking over the strange events that had called him to the obscure little Hungarian village. He had met with many strange cases in his long career, but this particular case had some features which were unique. Müller's lips set hard and his hands tightened to fists as he murmured: "I've met with criminals who used strange tools, but never before have I met with one who had the cunning and the incredible cruelty to utilise the mania of an unhinged human mind. It is a thousand times worse than those criminals who, now and then throughout the ages, have trained brute beasts to murder for them. Truly, this Hungarian peasant, Gyuri Kovacz, deserves a high place in the infamous roll-call of the great criminals of history. A student of crime might almost be led to think that it is a pity his career has been cut short so soon. He might have gone far.

"But for humanity's sake" (Müller's eyes gleamed), "I am thankful that I was able to discover this beast in human form and render him innocuous; he had done quite enough."

The Case of the
Registered Letter

The Case of the Registered Letter

"Oh, sir, save him if you can—save my poor nephew! I know he is innocent!"

The little old lady sank back in her chair, gazing up at Commissioner von Riedau with tear-dimmed eyes full of helpless appeal. The commissioner looked thoughtful. "But the case is in the hands of the local authorities, madam," he answered gently, a strain of pity in his voice. "I don't exactly see how we could interfere."

"But they believe Albert guilty! They haven't given him a chance!"

"He cannot be sentenced without sufficient proof of his guilt."

"But the trial, the horrible trial—it will kill him—his heart is weak. I thought—I thought you might send some one—some one of your detectives—to find out the truth of the case. You must have the best people here in Vienna. Oh, my poor Albert—"

Her voice died away in a suppressed sob, and she covered her face to keep back the tears.

The commissioner pressed a bell on his desk. "Is Detective Joseph Müller anywhere about the building?" he asked of the attendant who appeared at the door.

"I think he is, sir. I saw him come in not long ago."

"Ask him to come up to this room. Say I would like to speak to him." The attendant went out.

"I have sent for one of the best men on our force, madam," continued the commissioner, turning back to the pathetic little figure in the chair. "We will go into this matter a little more in detail and see if it is possible for us to interfere with the work of the local, authorities in G——."

The little old lady gave her eyes a last hasty dab with a dainty handkerchief and raised her head again, fighting for self-control. She was a quaint little figure, with soft grey hair drawn back smoothly from a gentle-featured face in which each wrinkle seemed the seal of some loving thought for others. Her bonnet and gown were of excellent material in delicate soft colours, but cut in the style of an earlier decade. The capable lines of her thin little hands showed through the fabric of her grey gloves. Her whole attitude bore the impress of one who had adventured far beyond the customary routine of her home circle, adventured out into the world in fear and trembling, impelled by the stress of a great love.

A knock was heard at the door, and a small, slight man, with a kind, smooth-shaven face, entered at the commissioner's call. "You sent for me, sir?" he asked.

"Yes, Müller, there is a matter here in which I need your advice, your assistance, perhaps. This is Detective Müller, Miss—" (the commissioner picked up the card on his desk) "Miss Graumann. If you will tell us now, more in detail, all that you can tell us about this case, we may be able to help you."

"Oh, if you would," murmured Miss Graumann, with something more of hope in her voice. The expression of sympathetic interest on the face of the newcomer had already won her confidence for him. Her slight figure straightened up in the chair, and the two men sat down opposite her, prepared to listen to her story.

"I will tell you all I know and understand about this matter, gentlemen," she began. "My name is Babette Graumann, and I live with my nephew, Albert Graumann, engineering expert, in the village of Grunau, which is not far from the city of G——. My nephew Albert, the dearest, truest—" sobs threatened to overcome her again, but she mastered them bravely. "Albert is now in prison, accused of the murder of his friend, John Siders, in the latter's lodgings in G——."

"Yes, that is the gist of what you have already told me," said the commissioner. "Müller, Miss Graumann believes her nephew innocent, contrary to the opinion of the local authorities in G——. She has come to ask for some one from here who could ferret out the truth of this matter. You are free now, and if we find that it can be done without offending the local authorities—"

"Who is the commissioner in charge of the case in G——?" asked Müller.

"Commissioner Lange is his name, I believe," replied Miss Graumann.

"*H'm!*" Müller and the commissioner exchanged glances.

"I think we can venture to hear more of this," said the commissioner, as if in answer to their unspoken thought. "Can you give us the details now, madam? Who is, or rather who was, this John Siders?"

"John Siders came to our village a little over a year ago," continued Miss Graumann. "He came from Chicago; he told us, although he was evidently a German by birth. He bought a nice little piece of property, not far from our home, and settled down there. He was a quiet man and made few friends, but he seemed to take to Albert and came to see us frequently. Albert had spent some years in America, in Chicago, and Siders liked to talk to him about things and people there. But one day Siders suddenly sold his property and moved to G———. Two weeks later he was found dead in his lodgings in the city, murdered, and now—now they have accused Albert of the crime."

"On what grounds?—oh, I beg your pardon, sir; I did not mean—"

"That's all right, Müller," said the commissioner. "As you may have to undertake the case, you might as well begin to do the questioning now."

"They say"—Miss Graumann's voice quavered—"they say that Albert was the last person known to have been in Siders' room; they say that it was his revolver, found in the room. That is the dreadful part of it—it was his revolver. He acknowledges it, but he did not know, until the police showed it to him, that the weapon was not in its usual place in his study. They tell me that everything speaks for his guilt, but I cannot believe it—I cannot. He says he is innocent in spite of everything. I believe him. I brought him up, sir; I was like his own mother to him. He never knew any other mother. He never lied to me, not once, when he was a little boy, and I don't believe he'd lie to me now, now that he's a man of forty-five. He says he did not kill John Siders. Oh, I know, even without his saying it, that he would not do such a thing."

"Can you tell us anything more about the murder itself?" questioned Müller gently. "Is there any possibility of suicide? Or was there a robbery?"

"They say it was no suicide, sir, and that there was a large sum of money missing. But why should Albert take any one else's money? He has money of his own, and he earns a good income besides—we have all that we need. Oh, it is some dreadful mistake! There is the newspaper account of the discovery of the body. Perhaps Mr. Müller might like to read that." She pointed to a sheet of newspaper on the desk. The commissioner handed it to Müller. It was an evening paper, dated G——, September 24th, and it gave an elaborate account, in provincial journalese, of the discovery that morning of the body of John Siders, evidently murdered, in his lodgings. The main facts to be gathered from the long-winded story were as follows:

John Siders had rented the rooms in which he met his death about ten days before, paying a month's rent in advance. The lodgings consisted of two rooms in a little house in a quiet street. It was a street of simple two-story, one and two family dwellings, occupied by artisans and small tradespeople. There were many open spaces, gardens and vacant lots in the street. The house in which Siders lodged belonged to a travelling salesman by the name of Winter. The man was away from home a great deal, and his wife, with her child and an old servant, lived in the lower part of the house, while the rooms occupied by Siders were in the upper story. Siders lived very quietly, going out frequently in the afternoon, but returning early in the evening. He had said to his landlady that he had many friends in G——. But during the time of his stay in the house he had had but one caller, a gentleman who came on the evening of the 23rd of September. The old maid had opened the door for him and showed him to Mr. Siders' rooms. She described this visitor as having a full black beard, and wearing a broad-brimmed grey felt hat. Nobody saw the man go out, for the old maid, the only person in the house at the time, had retired early. Mrs. Winter and her little girl were spending the night with the former's mother in a distant part of the city. The next morning the old servant, taking the lodger's coffee up to him at the usual hour, found him dead on the floor of his sitting-room, shot through the heart. The woman ran screaming from the house and alarmed the neighbours. A policeman at the corner heard the noise, and led the crowd up to the room where the dead man lay. It was plain to be seen that this was not a case of suicide. Everywhere were signs of a terrible struggle. The furniture was overturned, the dressing-table and the cupboard were open and their contents scattered on the floor, one of the window curtains was torn into strips, as if the victim had been trying to escape by way of the window, but had been dragged back into the room by his murderer. An overturned ink bottle on the table had spattered wide, and added to the general confusion. In the midst of the disorder lay the body of the murdered man, now cold in the rigour of death.

The police commissioner arrived soon, took possession of the rooms, and made a thorough examination of the premises. A letter found on the desk gave another proof, if such were needed, that this was not a case of suicide. This letter was in the handwriting of the dead man, and read as follows:

Dear Friend,

I appreciate greatly all the kindness shown me by yourself and your good wife. I have been more successful than I thought possible in overcoming the obstacles you know of. Therefore, I shall be very glad to join you day after tomorrow, Sunday, in the proposed excursion. I will call for you at 8 a.m.—the cab and the champagne will be my share of the trip. We'll have a jolly day and drink a glass or two to our plans for the future.

With best greetings for both of you,

Your old friend,

John

G——, Friday, Sept. 23rd

An envelope, not yet addressed, lay beside this letter. It was clear that the man who penned these words had no thought of suicide. On the contrary, he was looking forward to a day of pleasure in the near future, and laying plans for the time to come. The murderer's bullet had pierced a heart pulsing with the joy of life.

This was the gist of the account in the evening paper. Müller read it through carefully, lingering over several points which seemed to interest him particularly. Then he turned to Miss Babette Graumann. "And then what happened?" he asked.

"Then the police Commissioner came to Grunau and questioned my nephew. They had found out that Albert was Mr. Siders' only friend here. And late that evening the Mayor and the Commissioner came to our house with the revolver they had found in the room in G——, and they—they—" her voice trembled again, "they arrested my dear boy and took him away."

"Have you visited him in prison? What does he say about it himself?"

"He seems quite hopeless. He says that he is innocent—oh, I know he is—but everything is against him. He acknowledges that it was he who was in Mr. Siders' room the evening before the murder. He went there because Siders wrote him to come. He says he left early, and that John acted queerly. He knows they will not believe his story. This worry and anxiety will kill him. He has a serious heart trouble; he has suffered from it for years, and it has been growing steadily worse. I dare not think what this excitement may do for him." Miss Graumann broke down again and sobbed aloud. Müller laid his hands soothingly on the little old fingers that gripped the arm of the chair.

"Did your nephew send you here to ask for help?" he inquired very gently.

"Oh, no"The old lady looked up at him through her tears."No, he would not have done that. I'm afraid that he'll be angry if he knows that I have come. He seemed so hopeless, so dazed. I just couldn't stand it. It seemed to me that the police in G—— were taking things for granted, and just sitting there waiting for an innocent man to confess, instead of looking for the real murderer, who may be gone, the Lord knows where, by now!" Miss Graumann's faded cheeks flushed a delicate pink, and she straightened up in her chair again, while her eyes snapped defiance through the tears that hung on their lashes.

A faint gleam twinkled up in Müller's eyes, and he did not look at his chief. Doctor von Riedau's own face glowed in a slowly mounting flush, and his eyes drooped in a moment of conscious embarrassment at some recollection, the sting of which was evidently made worse by Müller's presence. But Commissioner von Riedau had brains enough to acknowledge his mistakes and to learn from them. He looked across the desk at Miss Graumann. "You are right, madam, the police have made that mistake more than once. And a man with a clear record deserves the benefit of the doubt. We will take up this case. Detective Müller will be put in charge of it. And that means, madam, that we are giving you the very best assistance the Imperial Police Force affords."

Miss Babette Graumann did not attempt to speak. In a wave of emotion she stretched out both little hands to the detective and clasped his warmly. "Oh, thank you," she said at last. "I thank you. He's just like my own boy to me; he's all the child I ever had, you know."

"But there are difficulties in the way," continued the commissioner in a business-like tone. "The local authorities in G—— have not asked for our assistance, and we are taking up the case over their heads, as it were. I shall have to leave that to Müller's diplomacy. He will come to G—— and have an interview with your nephew. Then he will have to use his own judgment as to the next steps, and as to how far he may go in opposition to what has been done by the police there."

"And then I may go back home?" asked Miss Graumann. "Go home with the assurance that you will help my poor boy?"

"Yes, you may depend on us, madam. Is there anything we can do for you here? Are you alone in the city?"

"No, thank you. There is a friend here who will take care of me. She will put me on the afternoon express back to G——."

"It is very likely that I will take that train myself," said Müller. "If there is anything that you need on the journey, call on me."

"Oh, thank you, I will indeed! Thank you both, gentlemen. And now goodbye, and God bless you!"

The commissioner bowed and Müller held the door open for Miss Graumann to pass out. There was silence in the room, as the two men looked after the quaint little figure slowly descending the stairs.

"A brave little woman," murmured the commissioner.

"It is not only the mother in the flesh who knows what a mother's love is," added Müller.

Next morning Joseph Müller stood in the cell of the prison in G—— confronting Albert Graumann, accused of the murder of John Siders.

The detective had just come from a rather difficult interview with Commissioner Lange. But the latter, though not a brilliant man, was at least good-natured. He acknowledged the right of the accused and his family to ask for outside assistance, and agreed with Müller that it was better to have some one in the official service brought in, rather than a private detective whose work, in its eventual results, might bring shame on the police. Müller explained that Miss Graumann did not want her nephew to know that it was she who had asked for aid in his behalf, and that it could only redound to his, Lange's, credit if it were understood that he had sent to Vienna for expert assistance in this case. It would be a proof of his conscientious attention to duty, and would insure praise for him, whichever way the case turned out. Commissioner Lange saw the force of this argument, and finally gave Müller permission to handle the case as he thought best, rather relieved than otherwise for his own part. The detective's next errand was to the prison, where he now stood looking up into the deep-set, dark eyes of a tall, broad-shouldered, black-bearded man, who had arisen from the cot at his entrance. Albert Graumann had a strong, self-reliant face and bearing. His natural expression was somewhat hard and stern, but it was the expression of a man of integrity and responsibility. Müller had already made some inquiries as to the prisoner's reputation and business standing in the community, and all that he had heard was favourable. A certain hardness and lack of amiability in Graumann's nature made it difficult for him to win the hearts of others, but although he was not generally loved, he was universally respected. Through the signs of nagging fear, sorrow, and ill-health, printed clearly on the face before him, Müller's keen eyes looked down into the soul of a man who might be overbearing, pitiless even, if occasion demanded, but who would not murder—at least not for the sake of gain. This last possibility Müller had dismissed from his mind, even before he saw the prisoner. The man's reputation was sufficient to make the thought ridiculous. But he had not made up his mind whether it might not be a case of a murder after a quarrel. Now he began to doubt even this when he looked into the intelligent, harsh-featured face of the man in the cell. But Müller had the gift of putting aside his own convictions, when he wanted his mind clear to consider evidence before him.

Graumann had risen from his sitting position when he saw a stranger. His heavy brows drew down over his, eyes, but he waited for the other to speak.

"I am Detective Joseph Müller, from Vienna," began the newcomer, when he had seen that the prisoner did not intend to start the conversation.

"Have you come to question me again?" asked Graumann wearily. "I can say no more than I have already said to the police Commissioner. And no amount of cross-examination can make me confess a crime of which I am not guilty—no matter what evidence there may be against me." The prisoner's voice was hard and determined in spite of its note of physical and mental weariness.

"I have not come to extort a confession from you, Mr. Graumann," Müller replied gently, "but to help you establish your innocence, if it be possible."

A wave of colour flooded the prisoner's cheek. He gasped, pressed his hand to his heart, and dropped down on his cot. "Pardon me," he said finally, hesitating like a man who is fighting for breath. "My heart is weak; any excitement upsets me. You mean that the authorities are not convinced of my guilt, in spite of the evidence? You mean that they will give me the benefit of the doubt—that they will give me a chance for life?"

"Yes, that is the reason for my coming here. I am to take this case in hand. If you will talk freely to me, Mr. Graumann, I may be able to help you. I have seen too many mistakes of justice because of circumstantial evidence to lay any too great stress upon it. I have waited to hear your side of the story from yourself. I did not want to hear it from others. Will you tell it to me now? No, do not move, I will get the stool myself."

Graumann sat back on the cot, his head resting against the wall. His eyes had closed while Müller was speaking, but his quieter breathing showed that he was mastering the physical attack which had so shaken him at the first glimpse of hope. He opened his eyes now and looked at Müller steadily for a moment. Then he said: "Yes, I will tell you: my life and my work have taught me to gauge men. I will tell you everything I know about this sad affair. I will tell you the absolute truth, and I think you will believe me."

"I will believe you," said Müller simply.

"You know the details of the murder, of course, and why I was arrested?"

"You were arrested because you were the last person seen in the company of the murdered man?"

"Exactly. Then I may go back and tell you something of my connection with John Siders?"

"It would be the very best thing to do."

"I live in Grunau, as you doubtless know, and am the engineering expert of large machine works there. My father before me held an important position in the factory, and my family have always lived in Grunau. I have travelled a great deal myself. I am forty-five years old, a childless widower, and live with my old aunt, Miss Babette Graumann, and my ward, Miss Eleonora Roemer, a young lady of twenty-two." Müller looked up with a slight start of surprise, but did not say anything. Graumann continued:

"A little over a year ago, John Siders, who signed himself as coming from Chicago, bought a piece of property in our town and came to live there. I made his acquaintance in the cafe and he seemed to take a fancy to me. I also had spent several years in Chicago, and we naturally came to speak of the place. We discovered that we had several mutual acquaintances there, and enjoyed talking over the old times. Otherwise I did not take particularly to the man, and as I came to know him better I noticed that he never mentioned that part of his life which lay back of the years in Chicago. I asked a casual question once or twice as to his home and family, but he evaded me every time, and would not give a direct answer. He was evidently a German by birth and education, a man with university training, and one who knew life thoroughly. He had delightful manners, and when he could forget his shyness for a while, he could be very agreeable. The ladies of my family came to like him, and encouraged him to call frequently. Then the thing happened that I should not have believed possible. My ward, Miss Roemer, a quiet, reserved girl, fell in love with this man about whom none of us knew anything, a man with a past of which he did not care to speak.

"I was not in any way satisfied with the match, and they seemed to realise it. For Siders managed to persuade the girl to a secret engagement. I discovered it a month or two ago, and it made me very angry. I did not let them see how badly I felt, but I warned Lora not to have too much to do with the boy, and I set about finding out something regarding his earlier life. It was my duty to do this, as I was the girl's guardian. She has no other relative living, and no one to turn to except my aunt and myself. I wrote to Mr. Richard Tressider in Chicago, the owner of the factory in which I had been employed while there. John had told me that Tressider had been his client during the four years in which he practiced law in Chicago. I received an answer about the middle of August. Mr. Tressider had been able to find out only that John was born in the town of Hartberg in a certain year. This was enough. I took leave of absence for a few days and went to Hartberg, which, as you know, is about 140 miles from here. Three days later I knew all that I wanted to know. John Siders was not the man's real name, or, rather, it was only part of his name. His full name was Theodor John Bellmann, and his mother was an Englishwoman whose maiden name was Siders. His father was a county official who died at an early age, leaving his widow and the boy in deepest poverty. Mrs. Bellmann moved to G—— to give music lessons. Theodor went to school there, then finally to college, and was an excellent pupil everywhere. But one day it was discovered that he had been stealing money from the banker in whose house he was serving as private tutor to the latter's sons. A large sum of money was missing, and every evidence pointed to young Bellmann as the thief. He denied strenuously that he was guilty, but the District Judge (it was the present Prosecuting Attorney Schmidt in G——) sentenced him. He spent eight months in prison, during which time his mother died of grief at the disgrace. There must have been something good in the boy, for he had never forgotten that it was his guilt that struck down his only relative, the mother who had worked so hard for him. He had atoned for this crime of his youth, and during the years that have passed since then, he had been an honest, upright man."

Graumann paused a moment and pressed his hand to his heart again. His voice had grown weaker, and he breathed hard. Finally he continued: "I commanded my ward to break off her engagement, as

I could not allow her to marry a man who was a freed convict. Siders sold his property some few weeks after that and moved to G——. Eleonora acquiesced in my commands, but she was very unhappy and allowed me to see very little of her. Then came the events of the evening of September 23rd, the events which have turned out so terribly. I will try to tell you the story just as it happened, so far as I am concerned. I had seen nothing of John since he left this town. He had made several attempts before his departure for G—— to change my opinion, and my decision as to his marriage to my ward. But I let him see plainly that it was impossible for him to enter our family with such a past behind him. He asserted his innocence of the charges against him, and declared that he had been unjustly accused and imprisoned. I am afraid that I was hard towards him. I begin to understand now, as I never thought I should, what it means to be accused of crime. I begin to realise that it is possible for every evidence to point to a man who is absolutely innocent of the deed in question. I begin to think now that John may have been right, that possibly he also may have been accused and sentenced on circumstantial evidence alone. I have thought much, and I have learned much in these terrible days."

The prisoner paused again and sat brooding, his eyes looking out into space. Müller respected his suffering and sat in equal silence, until Graumann raised his eyes to his again. "Then came the evening of the 23rd of September?"

"Yes, that evening—it's all like a dream to me." Graumann began again. "John wrote me a letter asking me to come to see him on that evening. I tore up the letter and threw it away—or perhaps, yes, I remember now, I did not wish Eleonora to see that he had written me. He asked me to come to see him, as he had something to say to me, something of the greatest importance for us both. He asked me not to mention to any one that I was to see him, as it would be wiser no one should know that we were still in communication with each other. There was a strain of nervous excitement visible in his letter. I thought it better to go and see him as he requested; I felt that I owed him some little reparation for having denied him the great wish of his heart. It was my duty to make up to him in other ways for what I had felt obliged to do. I knew him for a nervous, high-strung man, overwrought by brooding for years on what he called his wrongs, and I did not know what he might do if I refused his request. It was not of myself I thought in this connection, but of the girl at home who looked to me for protection.

"I had no fear for myself; it never occurred to me to think of taking a weapon with me. How my revolver—and it is undoubtedly my revolver, for there was a peculiar break in the silver ornamentation on the handle which is easily recognisable—how this revolver of mine got into his room, is more than I can say. Until the police Commissioner showed it to me two or three days ago, I had no idea that it was not in the box in my study where it is ordinarily kept." Graumann paused again and looked about him as if searching for something. He rose and poured himself out a glass of water. "Let me put some of this in it," said Müller. "It will do you good." From a flask in his pocket he poured a few drops of brandy into the water. Graumann drank it and nodded gratefully. Then he took up his story again.

"I never discovered why Siders had sent for me. When I arrived at the appointed time I found the door of the house closed. I was obliged to ring several times before an old servant opened the door. She seemed surprised that it had been locked. She said that the door was always unlatched, and that Mr. Siders himself must have closed it, contrary to all custom, for she had not done it, and there was no one else in the house but the two of them. Siders was waiting for me at the top of the stairs, calling down a noisy welcome.

"When I asked him finally what it was so important that he wanted to say to me, he evaded me and continued to chatter on about commonplace things. Finally I insisted upon knowing why he had wanted me to come, and he replied that the reason for it had already been fulfilled, that he had nothing more to say, and that I could go as soon as I wanted to. He appeared quite calm, but he must have been very nervous. For as I stood by the desk, telling him what I thought of his actions, he moved his hand hastily among the papers there and upset the ink stand. I jumped back, but not before I had received several large spots of ink on my trousers. He was profuse in his apologies for the accident, and tried to take out the spots with blotting paper. Then at last, when I insisted upon going, he looked out to see whether there was still a light on the stairs, and led me down to the door himself, standing there for some time looking after me.

"I was slightly alarmed as well as angry at his actions. I believe that he could not have been quite in his right mind, that the strain of nervousness which was apparent in his nature had really made him ill. For I remember several peculiar incidents of my visit to him. One of these was that he almost insisted upon my taking away with me, ostensibly to take care of them, several valuable pieces of jewellery which he possessed. He seemed almost offended when I refused to do anything of the kind. Then, as I parted from him at the door, not in a very good humour I will acknowledge, he said to me: 'You will think of me very often in the future—more often than you would believe now!'

"This is all the truth, and nothing but the truth, about my visit to John Siders on the evening of September 23rd. As it had been his wish I said nothing to the ladies at home, or to any one else about the occurrence. And as I have told you, I destroyed his letter asking me to come to him.

"The following day about noon, the Commissioner of police from G—— called at my office in the factory, and informed me bluntly that John Siders had been found shot dead in his lodgings that morning. I was naturally shocked, as one would be at such news, in spite of the fact that I had parted from the man in anger, and that I had no reason to be particularly fond of him. What shocked me most of all was the sudden thought that John had taken his own life. It was a perfectly natural thought when I considered his nervousness, and his peculiar actions of the evening before. I believe I exclaimed, 'It was a suicide!' almost without realising that I was doing so. The commissioner looked at me sharply and said that suicide was out of the question, that it was an evident case of murder. He questioned me as to Siders' affairs, of which I told only what every one here in the village knew. I did not consider it incumbent upon me to disclose to the police the disgrace of the man's early life. I had been obliged to hurt him cruelly enough because of that, and I saw no necessity for blackening his name, now that he was dead. Also, as according to what the commissioner said, it was a case of murder for robbery, I did not wish to go into any details of our connection with Siders that would cause the name of my ward to be mentioned. After a few more questions the commissioner left me. I was busy all the afternoon, and did not return to my home until later than usual. I found my aunt somewhat worried because Miss Roemer had left the house immediately after our early dinner, and had not yet returned. We both knew the girl to be still grieving over her broken engagement, and we dreaded the effect this last dreadful news might have on her. We supposed, however, that she had gone to spend the afternoon with a friend, and were rather glad to be spared the necessity of telling her at once what had happened. I had scarcely finished my supper, when the door bell rang, and to my astonishment the Mayor of Grunau was announced, accompanied by the same police Commissioner who had visited me in my office that morning. The Mayor was an old friend of mine and his deeply grave face showed me that something serious had occurred. It was indeed serious! and for some minutes I could not grasp the meaning of the commissioner's questions. Finally I realised with a tremendous shock that I—I myself was under suspicion of the murder of John Siders. The description given by the old servant of the man who had visited Siders the evening before, the very clothes that I wore, my hat and the trousers spotted by the purple ink, led to my identification as this mysterious visitor. The servant had let me in but she had not seen me go out.

"Then I discovered—when confronted suddenly with my own revolver which had been found on the floor of the room, some distance from the body of the dead man, that this same revolver had been identified as mine by my ward, Eleonora Roemer, who had been to the police station at G—— in the early afternoon hours. Some impulse of loyalty to her dead lover, some foolish feminine fear that I might have spoken against him in my earlier interviews with the commissioner had driven the girl to this step. A few questions sufficed to draw from her the story of her secret engagement, of its ending, and of my quarrel with John. I will say for her that I am certain she did not realise that all these things were calculated to cast suspicion on me. The poor girl is too unused to the ways of police courts, to the devious ways of the law, to realise what she was doing. The sight of my revolver broke her down completely and she acknowledged that it was mine. That is all. Except that I was arrested and brought here as you see. I told the commissioner the story of my visit to John Siders exactly as I told it to you, but it was plain to be seen that he did not believe me. It is plain to be seen also, that he is firmly convinced of my guilt and that he is greatly satisfied with himself at having traced the criminal so soon."

"And yet he was not quite satisfied," said Müller gently. "You see that he has sent to the Capital for assistance on the case." Müller felt this little untruth to be justified for the sake of the honour of the police force.

"Yes, I'm surprised at that," said Graumann in his former tone of weariness. "What do you think you will be able to do about it?"

"I must ask questions here and there before I can form a plan of campaign," replied Müller. "What do you think about it yourself? Who do you think killed Siders?"

"How can I know who it was? I only know it is not I," answered Graumann.

"Did he have any enemies?"

"No, none that I knew of, and he had few friends either."

"You knew there was a sum of money missing from his rooms?"

"Yes, the sum they named to me was just about the price that he had received for the sale of his property here. They did me the honour to believe that if I had taken the money at all, I had done so merely as a blind. At least they did not take me for a thief as well as a murderer. If the money is really missing, it was for its sake he was murdered I suppose."

"Yes, that would be natural," said Müller. "And you know nothing of any other relations or connections that the man may have had? Anything that might give us a clue to the truth?"

"No, nothing. He stood so alone here, as far as I knew. Of course, as I told you, his actions of the evening before having been so peculiar—and as I knew that he was not in the happiest frame of mind—I naturally thought of suicide at once, when they told me that he had been found shot dead. Then they told me that the appearance of the room and many other things, proved suicide to have been out of the question. I know nothing more about it. I cannot think any more about it. I know only that I am here in danger of being sentenced for the crime that I never committed—that is enough to keep any man's mind busy." He leaned back with an intense fatigue in every line of his face and figure.

Müller rose from his seat. "I am afraid I have tired you, Mr. Graumann," he said, "but it was necessary that I should know all that you had to tell me. Try and rest a little now and meanwhile be assured that I am doing all I can to find out the truth of this matter. As far as I can tell now I do not believe that you have killed John Siders. But I must find some further proofs that will convince others as well as myself. If it is of any comfort to you, I can tell you that during a long career as police detective I have been most astonishingly fortunate in the cases I have undertaken. I am hoping that my usual good luck will follow me here also. I am hoping it for your sake."

The man on the cot took the hand the detective offered him and pressed it firmly. "You will let me know as soon as you have found anything—anything that gives me hope?"

"I will indeed. And now save your strength and do not worry. I will help you if it is in my power."

After leaving the prison, Müller took the train for the village of Grunau, about half an hour distant from the city. He found his way easily to Graumann's home, an attractive old house set in a large garden amid groups of beautiful old trees. When he sent up his card to Miss Graumann, the old lady tripped down stairs in a flutter of excitement.

"Did you see him?" she asked. "You have been to the prison? What do you think? How does he seem?"

"He seems calm today," replied Müller, "although the confinement and the anxiety are evidently wearing on him."

"And you heard his story? And you believe him innocent?"

"I am inclined to do so. But there is more yet for me to investigate in this matter. It is certainly not as simple as the police here seem to believe. May I speak to your ward, Miss Roemer? She is at home now?"

"Yes, Lora is at home. If you will wait here a moment I will send her in."

Müller paced up and down the large sunny room, casting a glance over the handsome old pieces of furniture and the family portraits on the wall. It was evidently the home of generations of well-to-do, well-bred people, the narrow circle of whose life was made rich by congenial duties and a comfortable feeling of their standing in the community.

While he was studying one of the portraits more carefully, he became aware that there was some one in the room. He turned and saw a tall blond girl standing by the door. She had entered so softly that even Müller's quick ear had not heard the opening of the door.

"Do you wish to speak to me?" she said, coming down into the room. "I am Eleonora Roemer"

Her face, which could be called handsome in its even regularity of feature and delicate skin, was very pale now, and around her eyes were dark rings that spoke of sleepless nights. Grief and mental shock were preying upon this girl's mind. "She is not the one to make a confidant of those around her," thought Müller to himself. Then he added aloud: "If it does not distress you too much to talk about this sad affair, I will be very grateful if you will answer a few questions."

"I will tell you whatever I can," said the girl in the same low even tone in which she had first spoken. "Miss Graumann tells me that you have come from Vienna to take up this case. It is only natural that we should want to give you every assistance in our power."

"What is your opinion about it?" was Müller's next remark, made rather suddenly after a moment's pause.

The directness of the question seemed to shake the girl out of her enforced calm. A slow flush mounted into her pale cheeks and then died away, again leaving them whiter than before. "I do not know— oh, I do not know what to believe."

"But you do not think Mr. Graumann capable of such a crime, do you?"

"Not of the robbery, of course not; that would be absurd! But has it been clearly proven that there is a robbery? Might it not have been— might they not have—"

"You mean, might they not have quarrelled? Of course there is that possibility. And that is why I wanted to speak to you. You are the one person who could possibly throw light on this subject. Was there any other reason beyond the dead man's past that would render your guardian unwilling to have you marry him?"

Again the slow flush mounted to Eleonora Roemer's cheeks and her head drooped.

"I fear it may be painful for you to answer this," said Müller gently, "and yet I must insist on it in the interest of justice."

"He—my guardian—wished to marry me himself," the girl's words came slowly and painfully.

Müller drew in his breath so sharply that it was almost like a whistle. "He did not tell me that; it might make a difference."

"That... that is... what I fear," said the girl, her eyes looking keenly into those of the man who sat opposite. "And then, it was his revolver."

"Then you do believe him guilty?"

"It would be horrible, horrible—and yet I do not know what to think."

There was silence in the room for a moment. Miss Roemer's head drooped again and her hands twisted nervously in her lap. Müller's brain was very busy with this new phase of the problem. Finally he spoke.

"Let us dismiss this side of the question and talk of another phase of it, a phase of which it is necessary for me to know something. You would naturally be the person nearest the dead man, the one, the only one, perhaps, to whom he had given his confidence. Do you know of any enemies he might have had in the city?"

"No, I do not know of any enemies, or even of any friends he had there. When the terrible thing happened that clouded his past, when he had regained his freedom, after his term of imprisonment, there was no one left whom he cared to see again. He does not seem to have borne any malice towards the banker who accused him of the theft. The evidence was so strong against him that he felt the suspicion was justified. But there was hatred in his heart for one man, for the Justice who sentenced him, Justice Schmidt, who is now Attorney General in G——."

"The man who, in the name of the State, will conduct this case?" asked Müller quickly.

"Yes, I believe it is so. Is it not an irony that this man, the only one whom John really hated, should be the one to avenge him now?"

"*H'm!* yes. But did you know of any friends in G——?"

"No, none at all."

"No friends whom he might have made while he was in America and then met again in Germany?"

"No, he never spoke of any such to me. He told me that he made few friends. He did not seek them for he was afraid that they might find out what had happened and turn from him. He was morbidly sensitive and could not bear the disappointment."

"Why did he return to Germany?"

"He was lonely and wanted to come home again. He had made money in America—John was very clever and highly educated—but his heart longed for his own tongue and his own people."

Müller took a folded piece of paper from his pocket. "Do you know this handwriting?"

Miss Roemer read the few lines hastily and her voice trembled as she said: "This is John's handwriting. I know it well. This is the letter that was found on the table?"

"Yes, this letter appears to be the last he had written in life. Do you know to whom it could have been written? The envelope, as I suppose you know from the newspaper reports, was not addressed. Do you know of any friends with whom he could have been on terms of sufficient intimacy to write such a letter? Do you know what these plans for the future could have been? It would certainly be natural that he should have spoken to you first about them."

"No; I cannot understand this letter at all," replied the girl. "I have thought of it frequently these terrible days. I have wondered why it was that if he had friends in the city, he did not speak to me of them. He repeatedly told me that he had no friends there at all, that his life should begin anew after we were married."

"And did he have any particular plans, in a business way, perhaps?"

"No; he had a comfortable little income and need have no fear for the future. John was, of course, too young a man to settle down and do nothing. But the only definite plans he had made were that we should travel a little at first, and then he would look about him for a congenial occupation. I always thought it likely he would resume a law practice somewhere. I cannot understand in the slightest what the plans are to which the letter referred."

"And do you think, from what you know of his state of mind when you saw him last, that he would be likely so soon to be planning pleasures like this?"

"No, no indeed! John was terribly crushed when my guardian insisted on breaking off our engagement. Until my twenty-fourth birthday I am still bound to do as my guardian says, you know. John's life and early misfortune made him, as I have already said, morbidly sensitive and the thought that it would be a bar to anything we might plan in the future, had rendered him so depressed that—and it was not the least of my anxieties and my troubles—that I feared... I feared anything might happen."

"You feared he might take his own life, do you mean?"

"Yes, yes, that is what I feared. But is it not terrible to think that he should have died this way—by the hand of a murderer?"

"*H'm!* And you cannot remember any possible friend he may have found—some schoolboy friend of his youth, perhaps, with whom he had again struck up an acquaintance."

"Oh, no, no, I am positive of that. John could not bear to hear the names even of the people he had known before his misfortune. Still, I do remember his once having spoken of a man, a German he had met in Chicago and rather taken a fancy to, and who had also returned to Germany."

"Could this possibly have been the man to whom the letter is addressed?"

"No, no. This friend of John's was not married; I remember his saying that. And he lived in Germany somewhere—let me think—yes, in Frankfort-on-Main."

"And do you remember the man's name?"

"No, I cannot, I am sorry to say. John only mentioned it once. It was only by a great effort that I could remember the incident at all."

"And has it not struck you as rather peculiar that this friend, the one to whom the cordial letter was addressed, did not come forward and make his identity known? G—— is a city, it is true, but it is not a very large city, and any man being on terms of intimate acquaintance with one who was murdered would be apt to come forward in the hope of throwing some light on the mystery."

"Why, yes, I had not thought of that. It is peculiar, is it not? But some people are so foolishly afraid of having anything to do with the police, you know."

"That is very true, Miss Roemer. Still it is a queer incident and something that I must look into."

"What do you believe?" asked the girl tensely.

"I am not in a position to say as yet. When I am, I will come to you and tell you."

"Then you do not think that my guardian killed John—that there was a quarrel between the men?"

"There is, of course, a possibility that it may have been so. You know your guardian better than I do, naturally. Our knowledge of a man's character is often a far better guide than any circumstantial evidence."

"My guardian is a man of the greatest uprightness of character. But he can be very hard and pitiless sometimes. And he has a violent temper which his weak heart has forced him to keep in control of late years."

"All this speaks for the possibility that there may have been a quarrel ending in the fatal shot. But what I want to know from you is this— do you think it possible, that, this having happened, Albert Graumann would not have been the first to confess his unpremeditated crime? Is not this the most likely thing for a man of his character to do? Would he so stubbornly deny it, if it had happened?"

The girl started. "I had not thought of that! Why, why, of course, he might have killed John in a moment of temper, but he was never a man to conceal a fault. He is as pitiless towards his own weakness, as towards that of others. You are right, oh, you must be right. Oh, if you could take this awful fear from my heart! Even my grief for John would be easier to bear then."

Müller rose from his chair. "I think I can promise you that this load will be lifted from your heart, Miss Roemer."

"Then you believe—that it was just a case of murder for robbery? For the money? And John had some valuable jewellery, I know that."

"I do not know yet," replied Müller slowly, "but I will find out, I generally do."

"Oh, to think that I should have done that poor man such an injustice! It is terrible, terrible! This house has been ghastly these days.

His poor aunt knows that he is innocent—she could never believe otherwise—she has felt the hideous suspicion in my mind—it has made her suffering worse—will they ever forgive me?"

"Her joy, if I can free her nephew, will make her forget everything. Go to her now, Miss Roemer, comfort her with the assurance that you also believe him to be innocent. I must hasten back to G—— and go on with this quest."

The girl stood at the doorway shaded by the overhanging branches of two great trees, looking down the street after the slight figure of the detective. "Oh, it is all easier to hear, hard as it is, easier now that this horrible suspicion has gone from my mind—why did I not think of that before?"

Alone in the corner of the smoking compartment in the train to G——, Müller arranged in his mind the facts he had already gathered. He had questioned the servants of John Siders' former household, had found that the dead man received very few letters, only an occasional business communication from his bank. Of the few others, the servants knew nothing except that he had always thrown the envelopes carelessly in the waste paper basket and had never seemed to have any correspondence which he cared to conceal. No friend from elsewhere had ever visited him in Grunau, and he had made few friends there except the Graumann family.

The facts of the case, as he knew them now, were such as to make it extremely doubtful that Graumann was the murderer. Müller himself had been inclined to believe in the possibility of a quarrel between the two men, particularly when he had heard that Graumann himself was in love with his handsome ward. But the second thought that came to him then, impelled by the unerring instinct that so often guided him to the truth, was the assurance that in a case of this kind, in a case of a quarrel terminating fatally, a man like Albert Graumann would be the very first to give himself up to the police and to tell the facts of the case. Albert Graumann was a man of honour and unimpeachable integrity. Such a man would not persist in a foolish denial of the deed which he had committed in a moment of temper. There would be nothing to gain from it, and his own conscience would be his severest judge. "The disorder in the room?" thought Müller. "It'll be too late for that now. I suppose they have rearranged the place. I can only go by what the local detectives have seen, by the police reports. But I do not understand this extreme disorder. There is no reason why there should be a struggle when the robber was armed with a pistol. If Siders was supposed to have been interrupted when writing a letter, interrupted by a thief come with intent to steal, a thief armed with a revolver, the sight of this weapon alone would be sufficient to insure his not moving from his seat. I can understand the open drawers and cupboard; that is explained by the thief's hasty search for booty. But the torn window curtain and the overturned chairs are peculiar.

"Of course there is always a possibility that the thief might have entered one room while Siders was in the other; that the latter might have surprised the robber in his search for money or valuables, and that there might have been a hand-to-hand struggle before the intruder could pull out his revolver. Oh, if I could only have seen the body! This is working under terrific difficulties. The marks of a hand-to-hand struggle would have been very plain on the clothes and on the person of the murdered man. But this letter? I do not understand this letter at all. It is the dead man's handwriting, that we know, but why did not the friend to whom it was addressed come forward and make himself known? As far as I can learn from the police reports in G——, there was no personal interest shown, no personal inquiries made about the dead man. There was only the natural excitement that a murder would create. Now a family, expecting to make a pleasure excursion with a friend in a day or two and suddenly hearing that this friend had been found murdered in his lodgings, would be inclined to take some little personal interest in the matter. These people must have been in town and at home, for the excursion spoken of in the letter was to occur two days after the murder. Miss Roemer's remark about the dread that some people have as to any connection with the police, is true to a limited extent only. It is true only of the ignorant mind, not of a man presumably well-to-do and properly educated. I do not understand why the man to whom this letter was addressed has not made himself known. The only explanation is—that there was no such man!" A sudden sharp whistle broke from the detective's lips.

"I must examine the dead man's personal effects, his baggage, his papers; there may be something there. His queer letter to Graumann— his desire that the latter's visit should be kept secret—a visit which apparently had no cause at all, except to get Graumann to the house, to get him to the house in a way that he should be seen coming, but should not be seen going away. What does this mean?

"Graumann was the only person against whom Siders had an active cause of quarrel for the moment. There was one other man whom he hated, and this other man was the prosecuting attorney who would conduct any case of murder that came up in the town of G——.

"Now John Siders is found murdered—is found killed, in his lodgings, the morning after he has arranged things so that his antagonist, his rival in love, Albert Graumann, shall come under suspicion of having murdered him.

"What evidence have we that this man did not commit suicide? We have the evidence of the disorder in the room, a disorder that could have been made just as well by the man himself before he ended his own life. We have the evidence of a letter to some unknown, making plans for pleasure during the next days, and speaking of further plans, presumably concerning business, for the future. In a town the size of G——, where every one must have read of the murder, no one has come forward claiming to be the friend for whom this letter was written. Until this Unknown makes himself known, the letter as an evidence points rather to premeditated suicide than to the contrary. Oh, if I could only have seen the body! They tell me the pistol was found some little distance from the body. Is it at all likely that a murderer would go away leaving such evidence behind him? If Graumann had killed Siders in a hasty quarrel, he might possibly, in his excitement, have left his revolver. But I have already disposed of this possibility. A man of sufficient brains to so carefully plan his suicide as to conceal every trace of it and cast suspicion upon the man who had made him unhappy, such a one would be quite clever enough to throw the pistol far away from his body and to leave no traces of powder on his coat or any such other evidence.

"If I were to say now what I think, I would say that John Siders deliberately took his own life and planned it in such a way as to cast suspicion upon Albert Graumann. But that would indeed be a terrible revenge. And I must have some tangible proof of it before any court will accept my belief. This proof must be hidden somewhere. The thing for me to do is to find it."

The evidence gathered at the time of the death went to show that Siders had been paid a considerable sum in cash for the sale of his property at Grunau. And there was no trace of his having deposited this sum in any bank in G—— or in Grunau, in both of which places he had deposited other securities. Therefore the money had presumably been in his room at the time of his death. A search had been made for this money in every possible place of concealment among the dead man's belongings, and it had not been found. Müller asked the police Commissioner to give him the key to the rooms, which were still officially closed, and also the keys to the dead man's pieces of baggage. Commissioner Lange seemed to think all this extra search quite unnecessary, as it did not occur to him that anything else was to be looked for except the money.

It was quite late when Müller began his examination of the dead man's effects. He was struck by the fact that there was scarcely a bit of paper to be found anywhere, no letters, no business papers, except bank books showing the amount of his securities in the bank in G—— and in Grunau, and giving facts about some investments in Chicago. There was nothing of more recent date and no personal correspondence whatever. The same was true of the pockets of the suit Siders had been wearing at the time of his death. A man of any property or position at all in the world gathers about him so much of this kind of material that its absence shows premeditation. The suit Siders had been wearing when he was killed was lying on the table in the room. It was a plain grey business suit of good cut and material. The body had been prepared for burial in a beseeming suit of black. Müller made a careful examination of the clothes, and found only what the police reports showed him had already been found by the examination made by the local authorities. Upon a second careful examination, however, he found that in one of the vest pockets there was a little extra pocket, like a change pocket, and in it he found a crumpled piece of paper. He took it out, smoothed and read it. It was a post office receipt for a registered letter. The date was still clear, but the name of the person to whom the letter had been addressed was illegible. The creases of the paper and a certain dampness, as if it had been inadvertently touched by a wet finger, had smeared the writing. But the letter had been sent the day before the death of John Siders, and it had been registered from the main post office in G——. This was sufficient for Müller. Then he turned to the desk. Here also there was nothing that could help him. But a sudden thought, came to him, and he took up the blotting pad. This, to his delight, was in the form of a book with a handsome embroidered cover. It looked comparatively new and was, as Müller surmised, a gift from Miss Roemer to her betrothed. But few of the pages had been used, and on two of them a closely written letter had been blotted several times, showing that there had been several sheets of the letter. Müller held it up to the looking-glass, but the repeated blotting had blurred the writing to such an extent that it was impossible to decipher any but a few disconnected words, which gave no clue. On a page further along on the blotter, however, he saw what appeared to be the impression of an address. He held it up to the glass and gave a whistle of delight. The words could be plainly deciphered here:

Mr. Leo Pernburg
Frankfurt am Main
Mainzer Landstrasse

And above the name was a smear which, after a little study, could be deciphered as the written word "Registered."

With this page of the blotter carefully tucked away in his pocket-book, Müller hurried to the post office, arriving just at closing hour. He made himself known at once to the postmaster, and asked to be shown the records of registered letters sent on a certain date. Here he found scheduled a letter addressed to Mr. Leo Pernburg, Frankfurt am Main, sent by John Siders, G——, Josef Street 7.

Müller then hastened to the telegraph office and despatched a lengthy telegram to the postal authorities in Frankfurt am Main. When the answer came to him next morning, he packed his grip and took the first express train leaving G——. He first made a short visit, however, to Albert Graumann's cell in the prison. Müller was much too kind-hearted not to relieve the anxiety of this man, to whom such mental strain might easily prove fatal. He told Grau-mann that he was going in search of evidence which might throw light on the death of Siders, and comforted the prisoner with the assurance that he, Müller, believed Graumann innocent, and believed also that within a day or two he would return to G—— with proofs that his belief was the right one.

Three days later Müller returned to Grunau and went at once to the Graumann home. It was quite late when he arrived, but he had already notified Miss Roemer by telegram as to his coming, with a request that she should be ready to see him. He found her waiting for him, pale and anxious-eyed, when he arrived. "I have been to Frank-furt am Main," he said, "and I have seen Mr. Pernburg—"

"Yes, yes, that is the name; now I remember," interrupted the girl eagerly. "That is the name of John's friend there."

"I have seen Mr. Pernburg and he gave me this letter." Müller laid a thick envelope on the girl's lap.

She looked down at it, her eyes widening as if she had seen a ghost. "That—that is John's writing," she exclaimed in a hoarse whisper. "Where did it come from?"

"Pernburg gave it to me. The day before his death John Siders sent him this letter, requesting that Pernburg forward it to you before a certain date. When I explained the circumstances to Mr. Pernburg, he gave me the letter at once. I feel that this paper holds the clue to the mystery. Will you open it?"

With trembling hands the girl tore open the envelope. It enclosed still another sealed envelope, without an address. But there was a sheet of paper around this letter, on which was written the following:

My Beloved Eleonore,

Before you read what I have to say to you here I want you to promise me, in memory of our love and by your hope of future salvation, that you will do what I ask you to do.

I ask you to give the enclosed letter, although it is addressed to you, to the Judge who will preside in the trial against Graumann. The letter is written to you and will be given back to you. For you, the beloved of my soul, you are the only human being with whom I can still communicate, to whom I can still express my wishes. But you must not give the letter to the Judge until you have assured yourself that the prosecuting attorney insists upon Graumann's guilt. In case he is acquitted, which I do not think probable, then open this letter in the presence of Graumann himself and one or two witnesses. For I wish Graumann, who is innocent, to be able to prove his innocence.

You will know by this time that I have determined to end my life by my own hand. Forgive me, beloved. I cannot live on without you—without the honour of which I was robbed so unjustly.

God bless you.

One who will love you even beyond the grave. Remember your promise. It was given to the dead.

John

"Oh, what does it all mean?" asked Eleonora, dropping the letter in her lap.

"It is as I thought," replied Müller. "John Siders took his own life, but made every arrangement to have suspicion fall upon Graumann."

"But why? oh, why?"

"It was a terrible revenge. But perhaps—perhaps it was just retribution. Graumann would not understand that Siders could have been suspected of, and imprisoned for, a theft he had not committed. He must know now that it is quite possible for a man to be in danger of sentence of death even, for a crime of which he is innocent."

"Oh, my God! It is terrible." The girl's head fell across her folded arms on the table. Deep shuddering sobs shook her frame.

Müller waited quietly until the first shock had passed. Finally her sobs died away and she raised her head again. "What am I to do?" she asked.

"You must open this letter tomorrow in the presence of the police Commissioner and Graumann."

"But this promise? This promise that he asks of me—that I should wait until the trial?"

"You have not given this promise. Would you take it upon yourself to endanger your guardian's life still more? Every further day spent in his prison, in this anxiety, might be fatal."

"But this promise? The promise demanded of me by the man to whom I had given my love? Is it not my duty to keep it?"

Müller rose from his chair. His slight figure seemed to grow taller, and the gentleness in his voice gave way to a commanding tone of firm decision.

"Our duty is to the living, not to the dead. The dead have no right to drag down others after them. Believe me, Miss Roemer, the purpose that was in your betrothed's mind when he ended his own life, has been fulfilled. Albert Graumann knows now what are the feelings of a man who bears the prison stigma unjustly. He will never again judge his fellow-men as harshly as he has done until now. His soul has been purged in these terrible days; have you the right to endanger his life needlessly?"

"Oh, I do not know! I do not know what to do."

"I have no choice," said Müller firmly. "It is my duty to make known the fact to the police Commissioner that there is such a letter in existence. The police Commissioner will then have to follow his duty in demanding the letter from you. Mr. Pernburg, Sider's friend, saw this argument at once. Although he also had a letter from the dead man, asking him to send the enclosure to you, registered, on a certain date, he knew that it was his duty to give all the papers to the authorities. Would it not be better for you to give them up of your own free will?" Müller took a step nearer the girl and whispered: "And would it not be a noble revenge on your part? You would be indeed returning good for evil."

Eleonora clasped her hands and her lips moved as if in silent prayer. Then she rose slowly and held out the letters to Müller. "Do what you will with them," she said. "My strength is at an end."

The next day, in the presence of Commissioner Lange and of the accused Albert Graumann, Müller opened the letter which he had received from Miss Roemer and read it aloud. The girl herself, by her own request, was not present. Both Müller and Graumann understood that the strain of this message from the dead would be too much for her to bear. This was the letter:

G—— September 21st.

My Beloved,

When you put this letter in the hands of the Judge, I will have found in death the peace that I could never find on earth. There was no chance of happiness for me since I have realised that I love you, that you love me, and that I must give you up if I am to remain what I have always been—in spite of everything—a man of honour.

Albert Graumann would keep his word, this I know. Wherever you might follow me as my wife, there his will would have been before us, blasting my reputation, blackening the flame which you were to bear.

I could not have endured it. My soul was sick of all this secrecy, sick at the injustice of mankind. In spite of worldly success, my life was cold and barren in the strange land to which I had fled. My home called to me and I came back to it. I kissed the earth of my own country, and I wept at my mother's grave. I was happy again under the skies which had domed above my childhood. For I am an honest man, beloved, and I always have been.

One day I sat at table beside the man—the Judge who condemned me, here in G—— in those terrible days. He naturally did not know me again. I, myself, brought the conversation around to a professional subject. I asked him if it were not possible that circumstantial evidence could lie; if the entire past, the reputation of the accused would not be a factor in his favour. The Judge denied it. It was his opinion, beyond a doubt, that circumstantial evidence was sufficient to convict anyone.

My soul rose within me. This infallibility, this legal arrogance, aroused my blood. "That man should have a lesson!" I said to myself.

But I had forgotten it all—all my anger, all my hatred and bitterness, when I met you. I dare not trust myself to think of you too much, now that everything is arranged for the one last step. It takes all my control to keep my decision unwavering while I sit here and tell you how much your love, your great tenderness, your sweet trust in me, meant to me.

Let me talk rather of Albert Graumann. I will forgive him for believing in my guilt, but I cannot forgive him that he, the man of cultivation and mental grasp, could not believe it possible for a convicted thief to have repented and to have lived an honest life after the atonement of his crime. I still cannot believe that this was Graumann's opinion. I am forced to think that it was an excuse only on his part, an excuse to keep us apart, an excuse to keep you for himself.

You are lost to me now. There is nothing more in life for me. If the injustice of mankind has stained my honour beyond repair, has robbed me of every chance of happiness at any time and in any place, then I die easily, beloved, for there is little charm in such a life as would be mine after this.

But I do not wish to die quite in vain. There are two men who have touched my life, who need the lesson my death can teach them. These men are Albert Graumann and the prosecuting attorney Gustav Schmidt, the man who once condemned me so cruelly. His present position would make him the representative of the state in a murder trial, and I know his opinions too well not to foresee that he would declare Graumann guilty because of the circumstantial evidence which will be against him. My letter, given to the Presiding Judge after the Attorney has made his speech, will cause him humiliation, will ruin his brilliant arguments and cast ridicule upon him.

Do not think me hard or revengeful. I do not hate anyone now that death is so near. But is it inhuman that I should want to teach these two men a lesson? a lesson which they need, believe me, and it is such a slight compensation for the torture these last eight years have been to me!

And now I will explain in detail all the circumstances. I have arranged that Albert Graumann shall come to me on the evening of September 23rd between 7 and 8 o'clock. I asked him to do so by letter, asking him also to keep the fact of his visit to me a secret. Tonight, the 22nd of September, I received his answer promising that he would come. Therefore I can look upon everything that is to happen, as having already happened, for now there need be no further change in my plans. I will send this letter this evening to my friend Pernburg in Frankfurt am Main. In case anything should happen that would render impossible for me to carry out my plans, I will send Pernburg another letter asking him not to carry out the instructions of the first.

I can now proceed to tell you what will happen here tomorrow evening, the 23rd of September.

Albert Graumann will come to me, unknown to his family or friends, as I have asked him to come. I will so arrange it that the old servant will see him come in but will not see him go out. My landlady will not be in my way, for she has already told me that she will spend the night of the 23rd with her mother, in another part of the city. It is to be a birthday celebration I believe, so that I can be certain her plans will not be changed.

Graumann and I will be alone, therefore, with no reliable witnesses near. I will keep him there for a little while with commonplace conversation, for I have nothing to say to him. If he moves near the desk I will upset the inkbottle. The spots on his clothes will be another evidence against him. I will endeavour to get him to keep my jewellery which is, as you know, of considerable value. I will tell him that I am going away for a while and ask him to take charge of it for me. I, myself, will take him down to the door and let him out, when I have satisfied myself that the old servant is in bed or at least at the back of the house. The revolver which shall end my misery is Graumann's property. I took it from its place without his knowledge.

The 10,000 *gulden* which I told my landlady were still in the house, and which would therefore be thought missing after my death, I have deposited in a bank in Frankfort in your name. Here is the certificate of deposit.

I will endeavour not to hold the revolver sufficiently close to have the powder burn my clothes. And I will exert every effort of mind and body to throw it far from me after I have fired the fatal shot. I think that I will be able to do this, for I am a very good shot and I have no fear of death. One thing more I will do, to turn aside all suspicion of suicide. I will write a letter to some person who does not exist, a letter which will make it appear as if I were in excellent humour and planning for the future.

And now, goodbye to life. People have called me eccentric, they may be right. This last deed of mine at least, is out of the ordinary. No one will say now that ended my life in a moment of darkened mind, in a rush of despair. My brain is perfectly clear, my heart beats calmly, now that I have arranged everything for my departure from this world of falsehood and unreality. My last deed shall go to prove to the world how little actual, apparent facts can be trusted.

The one thing real, the one thing true in all this world of falsehood was your love and your trust. I thank you for it.

Theodor Bellmann
Known as John Siders

Joseph Müller refuses to take any particular credit for this case. The letter would have come in time to prevent Graumann's conviction without his assistance, he says. The only person whose gratitude he has a right to is Prosecuting Attorney Gustav Schmidt. He managed to have the police Commissioner in G—— read the letter in detail to the attorney. But Müller himself knows that it failed of its effect, so far as that dignitary was concerned. For nothing but open ridicule could ever convince a man of such decided opinions that he is not the one infallible person in the world.

But Albert Graumann had learned his lesson. And he told Müller himself that the few days of life which might remain to him were a gift to him from the detective. He felt that his weak heart would not have stood the strain and the disgrace of an open trial, even if that trial ended in acquittal. Two months later he was found dead in his bed, a calm smile on his lips.

Before he died he had learned that it was the undaunted courage of his timid little old aunt that had brought Müller to take charge of the case and to free her beloved nephew from the dreaded prison. And the last days that these two passed together were very happy.

But as aforesaid, Müller refuses to have this case included in the list of his successes. He did not change the ultimate result, he merely anticipated it, he says.

LEONAUR

ALSO FROM LEONAUR
AVAILABLE IN SOFTCOVER OR HARDCOVER WITH DUST JACKET

THE FIRST BOOK OF AYESHA by *H. Rider Haggard*—Contains *She & Ayesha: the Return of She.*

THE SECOND BOOK OF AYESHA by *H. Rider Haggard*—Contains *She and Allan & Wisdom's Daughter.*

QUATERMAIN: THE COMPLETE ADVENTURES—1 by *H. Rider Haggard*—Contains *King Solomon's Mines & Allan Quatermain.*

QUATERMAIN: THE COMPLETE ADVENTURES—2 by *H. Rider Haggard*—Contains *Allan's Wife, Maiwa's Revenge & Marie.*

QUATERMAIN: THE COMPLETE ADVENTURES—3 by *H. Rider Haggard*—Contains *Child of Storm & Allan and the Holy Flower.*

QUATERMAIN: THE COMPLETE ADVENTURES—4 by *H. Rider Haggard*—Contains *Finished & The Ivory Child.*

QUATERMAIN: THE COMPLETE ADVENTURES—5 by *H. Rider Haggard*—Contains *The Ancient Allan & She and Allan.*

QUATERMAIN: THE COMPLETE ADVENTURES—6 by *H. Rider Haggard*—Contains *Heu-Heu or, the Monster & The Treasure of the Lake.*

QUATERMAIN: THE COMPLETE ADVENTURES—7 by *H. Rider Haggard*—Contains *Allan and the Ice Gods, Four Short Adventures & Nada the Lily.*

TROS OF SAMOTHRACE 1: WOLVES OF THE TIBER by *Talbot Mundy*—55 B.C.--an adventurer set during the Roman invasion of Britain.

TROS OF SAMOTHRACE 2: DRAGONS OF THE NORTH by *Talbot Mundy*—55 B.C. —Caesar plots, Britons war among themselves and the Vikings are coming.

TROS OF SAMOTHRACE 3: SERPENT OF THE WAVES by *Talbot Mundy*—55 B.C.--Caesar is poised to invade Britain—only a grand strategy can foil him!.

TROS OF SAMOTHRACE 4: CITY OF THE EAGLES by *Talbot Mundy*—54 B.C.—Rome—Tros treads in the streets of his sworn enemies!.

TROS OF SAMOTHRACE 5: CLEOPATRA by *Talbot Mundy*—Tros and the Roman Empire turn to the Egypt of the Pharaohs.

TROS OF SAMOTHRACE 6: THE PURPLE PIRATE by *Talbot Mundy*—The epic saga of the ancient world—Tros of Samothrace—draws to a conclusion in this sixth—and final—volume.

LEONAUR

ALSO FROM LEONAUR
AVAILABLE IN SOFTCOVER OR HARDCOVER WITH DUST JACKET

THE COLLECTED SCIENCE FICTION AND FANTASY OF STANLEY G. WEINBAUM 1—INTERPLANETARY ODYSSEYS *by Stanley G. Weinbaum*—Classic Tales of Interplanetary Adventure Including: A Martian Odyssey, its Sequel Valley of Dreams, the Complete 'Ham' Hammond Stories and Others.

THE COLLECTED SCIENCE FICTION AND FANTASY OF STANLEY G. WEINBAUM 2—OTHER EARTHS *by Stanley G. Weinbaum*—Classic Futuristic Tales Including: *Dawn of Flame* & its Sequel The Black Flame, plus The Revolution of 1960 & Others.

THE COLLECTED SCIENCE FICTION AND FANTASY OF STANLEY G. WEINBAUM 3—STRANGE GENIUS *by Stanley G. Weinbaum*—Classic Tales of the Human Mind at Work Including the Complete Novel The New Adam, the 'van Manderpootz' Stories and Others.

THE COLLECTED SCIENCE FICTION AND FANTASY OF STANLEY G. WEINBAUM 4—THE BLACK HEART *by Stanley G. Weinbaum*—Classic Strange Tales Including: the Complete Novel The Dark Other, Plus Proteus Island and Others.

THE COLLECTED SCIENCE FICTION & FANTASY OF JACK LONDON 1—BEFORE ADAM & OTHER STORIES *by Jack London*—included in this Volume Before Adam The Scarlet Plague A Relic of the Pliocene When the World Was Young The Red One Planchette A Thousand Deaths Goliah A Curious Fragment The Rejuvenation of Major Rathbone.

THE COLLECTED SCIENCE FICTION & FANTASY OF JACK LONDON 2—THE IRON HEEL & OTHER STORIES *by Jack London*—included in this Volume The Iron Heel The Enemy of All the World The Shadow and the Flash The Strength of the Strong The Unparalleled Invasion The Dream of Debs.

THE COLLECTED SCIENCE FICTION & FANTASY OF JACK LONDON 3—THE STAR ROVER & OTHER STORIES *by Jack London*—included in this Volume The Star Rover The Minions of Midas The Eternity of Forms The Man With the Gash.

THE CRETAN TEAT *by Brian Aldiss*—The Cretan Teat is a wry and comic novel that interweaves its own fiction with an inner fiction about the discovery of a Byzantine painting of the Mother of the Blessed Virgin Mary suckling the infant Jesus and a fake ikon that becomes an instrument of Nemesis.

LEONAUR

ALSO FROM LEONAUR
AVAILABLE IN SOFTCOVER OR HARDCOVER WITH DUST JACKET

THE FIRST BOOK OF AYESHA *by H. Rider Haggard*—Contains *She & Ayesha: the Return of She.*

THE SECOND BOOK OF AYESHA *by H. Rider Haggard*—Contains *She and Allan & Wisdom's Daughter.*

QUATERMAIN: THE COMPLETE ADVENTURES—1 *by H. Rider Haggard*—Contains *King Solomon's Mines & Allan Quatermain.*

QUATERMAIN: THE COMPLETE ADVENTURES—2 *by H. Rider Haggard*—Contains *Allan's Wife, Maiwa's Revenge & Marie.*

QUATERMAIN: THE COMPLETE ADVENTURES—3 *by H. Rider Haggard*—Contains *Child of Storm & Allan and the Holy Flower.*

QUATERMAIN: THE COMPLETE ADVENTURES—4 *by H. Rider Haggard*—Contains *Finished & The Ivory Child.*

QUATERMAIN: THE COMPLETE ADVENTURES—5 *by H. Rider Haggard*—Contains *The Ancient Allan & She and Allan.*

QUATERMAIN: THE COMPLETE ADVENTURES—6 *by H. Rider Haggard*—Contains *Heu-Heu or, the Monster & The Treasure of the Lake.*

QUATERMAIN: THE COMPLETE ADVENTURES—7 *by H. Rider Haggard*—Contains *Allan and the Ice Gods, Four Short Adventures & Nada the Lily.*

TROS OF SAMOTHRACE 1: WOLVES OF THE TIBER *by Talbot Mundy*—55 B.C.--an adventurer set during the Roman invasion of Britain.

TROS OF SAMOTHRACE 2: DRAGONS OF THE NORTH *by Talbot Mundy*—55 B.C. —Caesar plots, Britons war among themselves and the Vikings are coming.

TROS OF SAMOTHRACE 3: SERPENT OF THE WAVES *by Talbot Mundy*—55 B.C.--Caesar is poised to invade Britain—only a grand strategy can foil him!.

TROS OF SAMOTHRACE 4: CITY OF THE EAGLES *by Talbot Mundy*—54 B.C.—Rome—Tros treads in the streets of his sworn enemies!.

TROS OF SAMOTHRACE 5: CLEOPATRA *by Talbot Mundy*—Tros and the Roman Empire turn to the Egypt of the Pharaohs.

TROS OF SAMOTHRACE 6: THE PURPLE PIRATE *by Talbot Mundy*—The epic saga of the ancient world—Tros of Samothrace—draws to a conclusion in this sixth—and final—volume.

LEONAUR

ALSO FROM LEONAUR
AVAILABLE IN SOFTCOVER OR HARDCOVER WITH DUST JACKET

THE PRISONER OF ZENDA & ITS SEQUEL RUPERT OF HENTZAU *by Anthony Hope*—Two famous novels of high adventure in one volume.

THE GLADIATORS *by G. J. Whyte Melville*—A Classic Novel of Ancient Rome—Three Volumes in One Special Edition.

THE COMPLETE CAPTAIN DANGEROUS *by George Augustus Sala*—The Adventures of a Soldier, Sailor, Merchant, Spy, Slave and Bashaw of the Grand Turk.

ORTHERIS, LEAROYD & MULVANEY *by Rudyard Kipling*—The Complete Soldiers Three stories.

SIR NIGEL & THE WHITE COMPANY *by Arthur Conan Doyle*—Two Classic Novels of the 100 Years' War.

THE ILLUSTRATED & COMPLETE BRIGADIER GERARD *by Arthur Conan Doyle*—All 18 Stories with the Original Strand Magazine Illustrations by Wollen and Paget.

THE OHIO RIVER TRILOGY 1: BETTY ZANE *by Zane Grey*—The land along the Ohio River is newly settled. Indomitable men and women—Col. Zane and his family, the McCollochs, Wetzel, the "Death Wind" Indian killer, among them—have hewn a life out of the frontier wilderness.

THE OHIO RIVER TRILOGY 2: THE SPIRIT OF THE BORDER *by Zane Grey*—Fort Henry still stands as a bastion for the settlers on the frontier along the Ohio River. More pioneers are now moving west to carve new lives out of the wilderness.

THE OHIO RIVER TRILOGY 3: THE LAST TRAIL *by Zane Grey*—This final volume of Zane Grey's Ohio River Trilogy is a gripping finale to a great series—another thrilling story of life and death on the early American frontier and a classic in the tradition of Drums Along the Mohawk.

THE NAPOLEONIC NOVELS: VOLUME 1 *by Erckmann-Chatrian*—This book comprises two linked novels—*The Conscript* & *Waterloo*—about the adventures a young conscript in the French Army. during the Napoleonic wars.

THE NAPOLEONIC NOVELS: VOLUME 2 *by Erckmann-Chatrian*—*The Blockade of Phalsburg* & *The Invasion of France in 1814*—the events portrayed in these two novels of the Napoleonic period properly fit in time between those of the first volume. They appear together here since each—unlike the other two in this series—is a stand alone work.

ALSO FROM LEONAUR
AVAILABLE IN SOFTCOVER OR HARDCOVER WITH DUST JACKET

THE CIVIL WAR NOVELS: 1 *by Joseph A. Altsheler*—*The Guns of Bull Run &
The Guns of Shiloh*—the first and second novels of a series of eight adventures which
follow the momentous events, campaigns and battles of the great American Civil War
between the Northern and Southern states.

THE CIVIL WAR NOVELS: 2 *by Joseph A. Altsheler*—*The Scouts of Stonewall
& The Sword of Antietam*—the third and fourth novels of a series of nine adventures
which follow the momentous events, campaigns and battles of the great American
Civil War between the Northern and Southern states.

THE CIVIL WAR NOVELS: 3 *by Joseph A. Altsheler*—*The Star of Gettysburg
& The Rock of Chickamauga*—the fifth and sixth novels of a series of nine adventures
which follow the momentous events, campaigns and battles of the great American
Civil War between the Northern and Southern states.

THE CIVIL WAR NOVELS: 4 *by Joseph A. Altsheler*—*The Shades of the Wilderness & The Tree of Appomattox*—the seventh and eighth novels of a series of nine
adventures which follow the momentous events, campaigns and battles of the great
American Civil War between the Northern and Southern states.

THE CIVIL WAR NOVELS: 5 *by Joseph A. Altsheler*—*Before the Dawn: a Story
of the Fall of Richmond*—the last of a series of nine adventures which follow the momentous events, campaigns and battles of the great American Civil War between the
Northern and Southern states.

THE FRENCH & INDIAN WAR NOVELS: 1 *by Joseph A. Altsheler*—*The
Hunters of the Hills & The Shadow of the North*—In this three volume, six novel set the
story of the war, with many of its real life characters, is told through the adventures
of its principal characters, Robert Lennox, the hunter Willet and his Indian companion Tayoga.

THE FRENCH & INDIAN WAR NOVELS: 2 *by Joseph A. Altsheler*—*The
Rulers of the Lakes & The Masters of the Peaks*—In this three volume, six novel set the
story of the war, with many of its real life characters, is told through the adventures
of its principal characters, Robert Lennox, the hunter Willet and his Indian companion Tayoga.

THE FRENCH & INDIAN WAR NOVELS: 1 *by Joseph A. Altsheler*—*The Lords
of the Wild & The Sun of Quebec*—In this three volume, six novel set the story of the
war, with many of its real life characters, is told through the adventures of its principal
characters, Robert Lennox, the hunter Willet and his Indian companion Tayoga.

ALSO FROM LEONAUR

AVAILABLE IN SOFTCOVER OR HARDCOVER WITH DUST JACKET

THE COMPLETE FOUR JUST MEN: VOLUME 2 *by Edgar Wallace*—*The Law of the Four Just Men & The Three Just Men*—disillusioned with a world where the wicked and the abusers of power perpetually go unpunished, the Just Men set about to rectify matters according to their own standards, and retribution is dispensed on swift and deadly wings.

THE COMPLETE RAFFLES: 1 *by E. W. Hornung*—*The Amateur Cracksman & The Black Mask*—By turns urbane gentleman about town and accomplished cricketer, life is just too ordinary for Raffles and that sets him on a series of adventures that have long been treasured as a real antidote to the 'white knights' who are the usual heroes of the crime fiction of this period.

THE COMPLETE RAFFLES: 2 *by E. W. Hornung*—*A Thief in the Night & Mr Justice Raffles*—By turns urbane gentleman about town and accomplished cricketer, life is just too ordinary for Raffles and that sets him on a series of adventures that have long been treasured as a real antidote to the 'white knights' who are the usual heroes of the crime fiction of this period.

THE COLLECTED SUPERNATURAL AND WEIRD FICTION OF WILKIE COLLINS: VOLUME 1 *by Wilkie Collins*—Contains one novel 'The Haunted Hotel', one novella 'Mad Monkton', three novelettes 'Mr Percy and the Prophet', 'The Biter Bit' and 'The Dead Alive' and eight short stories to chill the blood.

THE COLLECTED SUPERNATURAL AND WEIRD FICTION OF WILKIE COLLINS: VOLUME 2 *by Wilkie Collins*—Contains one novel 'The Two Destinies', three novellas 'The Frozen deep', 'Sister Rose' and 'The Yellow Mask' and two short stories to chill the blood.

THE COLLECTED SUPERNATURAL AND WEIRD FICTION OF WILKIE COLLINS: VOLUME 3 *by Wilkie Collins*—Contains one novel 'Dead Secret,' two novelettes 'Mrs Zant and the Ghost' and 'The Nun's Story of Gabriel's Marriage' and five short stories to chill the blood.

FUNNY BONES *selected by Dorothy Scarborough*—An Anthology of Humorous Ghost Stories.

MONTEZUMA'S CASTLE AND OTHER WEIRD TALES *by Charles B. Cory*—Cory has written a superb collection of eighteen ghostly and weird stories to chill and thrill the avid enthusiast of supernatural fiction.

SUPERNATURAL BUCHAN *by John Buchan*—Stories of Ancient Spirits, Uncanny Places & Strange Creatures.